CW01083130

A Kiss of Hammer and Flame

Amy de la Force is a bi writer of romantasy, and Lucy Cavendish Fiction Prize shortlistee. Drawing on her expertise as an ex-Apple copywriter and medieval sword fighter, *A Kiss of Hammer and Flame* is her debut novel in the Fated for Hael trilogy. Amy is an Aussie expat who lives in London. Connect on social media at @amydelaforce.

AMY DE LA FORCE

CANELO

First published in the United Kingdom in 2025 by

Canelo, an imprint of
Canelo Digital Publishing Limited,
20 Vauxhall Bridge Road,
London SW1V 2SA
United Kingdom

A Penguin Random House Company
The authorised representative in the EEA is Dorling Kindersley Verlag GmbH. Arnulfstr. 124, 80636 Munich, Germany

Copyright © Amy de la Force 2025

The moral right of Amy de la Force to be identified as the creator of this work has been asserted in accordance with the Copyright, Designs and Patents Act, 1988.
All rights reserved. No part of this publication may be reproduced or transmitted in any form or by any means, electronic or mechanical, including photocopy, recording, or any information storage and retrieval system, without permission in writing from the publisher.
No part of this book may be used or reproduced in any manner for the purpose of training artificial intelligence technologies or systems. In accordance with Article 4(3) of the DSM Directive 2019/790, Canelo expressly reserves this work from the text and data mining exception.

A CIP catalogue record for this book is available from the British Library.

Ebook ISBN 978 1 80436 995 1
Hardback ISBN 978 1 80436 996 8
Export Trade Paperback ISBN 978 1 83598 310 2

This book is a work of fiction. Names, characters, businesses, organizations, places and events are either the product of the author's imagination or are used fictitiously. Any resemblance to actual persons, living or dead, events or locales is entirely coincidental.

Cover design by JV Arts

Printed and bound in Great Britain by Clays Ltd, Elcograf S.p.A.

Look for more great books at
www.canelo.co | www.dk.com

For my husband Nick,

without whom, this book would not exist.

And to every woman living in this timeline,

who was told they weren't enough.

You contain multitudes, and

you are everything.

NG+XXV
LUMINAUX
KOLYATH
HAEL'STROMIA
N
OZUMBRE

PART ONE

'For when the Seers reappear'

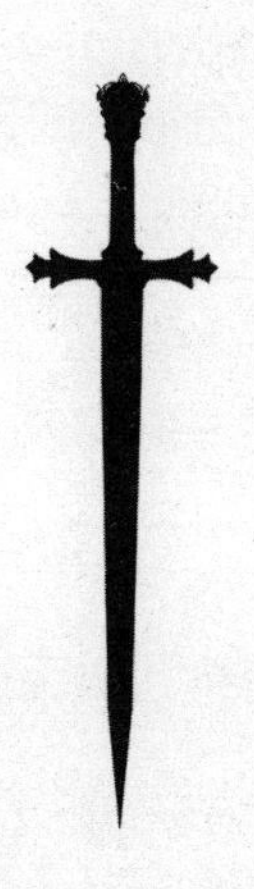

CHAPTER 1

It's just a sword.

But Cahra knew it wasn't. She knew it with every faltering step she fought to take, the star ruby-encrusted rapier winking in the firelight of the blacksmith's forge, taunting her as she balanced it across her outstretched palms. If she tripped, the blade would slice her open, a splash of red to complement its gems. Somehow that wasn't her concern.

Her fear was for the sword. Because a blade for the Steward of her kingdom of Kolyath was never just a weapon. It was a symbol of his power over others. Over her.

She should know. She'd forged it for the ruler she'd once tried to kill.

Cahra blew a wisp of pale copper hair from her face, battling the urge to drop the sword and run. Instead, she set the darkened blade on the counter and glanced at Lumsden. The master blacksmith smiled, his hair a chalky stripe around the crown of his balding head. But the old man's expression didn't meet his deep-set eyes, and his gaze didn't break from the figure dominating the smithy's metal counter.

Commander Jarett, the Steward's notorious head of the Kingdom Guards, bent to scrutinise Cahra's creation; a feat of form and function, or so Lumsden had proudly declared.

'Yes… His Excellency will be pleased,' Jarett told him, mesmerised by the Haellium blade. The Commander straightened, the sheer height of him looming like a Kolyath ice storm, scowling down at Cahra.

She froze, waiting for the storm to hit.

'I, however, would be pleased to be met with the decorum I am due. A bath and a comb of your girl's hair?' Jarett gestured to Cahra in distaste.

As the only female smith in Kolyath, her presence defied tradition, a fact that never failed to attract criticism. Mostly about how she looked.

The dread simmering inside Cahra boiled into a black fury. Would breaking Jarett's high-born hand be worth one final trip to the dungeons?

Before she could answer insult with injury, an unfamiliar voice spoke.

'Now, Commander, Master Lumsden's apprentice has surely laboured to perfect our esteemed Steward's sword, and what a sword it is! A weapon fit for a king.'

Cahra knew the manner of speaking well: smooth, enunciated. Definitely a high-born. A well-dressed young nobleman stepped from behind Jarett and smiled.

Great, another one. But the young high-born was right, she'd slaved over the Steward's rapier for weeks. Only the electric sting of fear and anger kept her on her feet now.

Yet his word choice made her smirk. 'King', the one thing Steward Atriposte wasn't. Her kingdom hadn't seen a royal in centuries. Not since the fall of their realm's empire and its capital of Hael'stromia – the jet-black city known as 'Hael'.

In spite of herself, Cahra felt a prick of curiosity as she eyed the young high-born.

Commander Jarett's eyes lit up, the storm cloud fading from his face, as if he'd realised the prestige such a blade would bring. 'I must present it to His Excellency at once. Lumsden, where is the sword's scabbard?'

Forgotten, Cahra made to slink back to the forge, the smoky scent and crackle of coals a balm against her ragged nerves and autumn's bitter forward march.

Until someone cleared their throat.

'My apologies,' the young high-born said, interrupting her thoughts.

Cahra just stared. A high-born apology? That was new.

'I do not wish to keep you from your work. I seek your services.'

'Of course,' Cahra said, bending to scrabble under the counter for a pencil and paper, and bumping a burn from crafting the Steward's sword. She hissed, the jolt sending pain searing down her forearm, troubling her more than she'd like to admit.

Gritting her teeth, Cahra forced a vaguely pleasant look to her face. 'And you are?'

'Terryl.'

'Terryl,' she said, scrawling his name. Despite the clamour of the Traders' Quadrant, she heard Lumsden shuffling back to the front counter. She'd always had a gift for senses, hearing in particular. It was a part of her, a necessity from growing up a beggar.

'*Lord* Terryl!' Lumsden corrected her, clapping and beaming at the high-born. 'Welcome.' She shot the old man a sideways glance.

Seers, what was so special about this one?

Apart from him sticking up for you against Jarett?

Grudgingly, Cahra looked up, right into the lord's eyes. Blue goldstone, she mused, an indigo gem that twinkled gold and silver like the starry night sky. She'd made a point of studying precious gemstones, as the Steward's court demanded them.

'Lumsden,' Lord Terryl greeted in return, dazzling eyes flashing back to Cahra. The lord's mouth curved up. 'And you are, Miss…?'

Chewing her lip, she realised she'd failed to introduce herself, and to a lord, no less. Anyone would think she'd never spoken to a noble before. Lumsden would be mortified. 'Cahra,' she told the young lord quickly.

'Cahra, of course.' He nodded. 'I spoke with Lumsden about you.'

She whipped her head up to the old man, who swiftly nudged her with his foot.

'The Steward's advisors speak highly of your artisanship at court,' Lord Terryl said. 'What might you craft, if I were to offer you a blank canvas?'

Cahra didn't know what confused her more, the question or the compliment. 'Sorry?' Mercifully, the damp coastal air swept the heat from her pinkening cheeks.

'A longsword that you could craft freely,' Lumsden explained. 'You would decide on the design, the materials, everything.' She caught the words the old man left unsaid: unlike with the Steward or his infuriating court, whose dictates choked her love of smithing.

'Speaking of materials,' Lord Terryl began, eyes sparkling. 'The Steward's sword. Was that a Haellium blade, the everlasting ore? And those rubies, like none that I have seen!' His full attention was on her, and she shifted under the intensity of his gaze.

'Star rubies,' Cahra said slowly. 'They're rare. Almost as rare as Hael'stromia's ore.' She gave the lord a pointed look.

Haellium, the metal forged from the ore of the realm's lost capital, was more precious than gold due to its pure indestructibility. But no one had mined it since Hael'stromia's fall, centuries ago. Commander Jarett hadn't said how he'd obtained some for the ruler's rapier.

The Steward's rapier was the only Haellium weapon in Kolyath, and with the man's vicious reputation, one was more than enough. Crafting a weapon like that for such a tyrant gnawed at her, and Cahra clenched her fists. Everything wrong with Kolyath – from its starving beggars, like she'd been as a kid, to its crushing taxes, all to aid a never-ending war – was the Steward's fault. She never should have forged that sword.

But what could she do, refuse? His guards wouldn't just drag her to the kingdom's Red Square for a spot of public torture, they'd take Lumsden too. To make examples of them, of all low-borns. Of what happens when you defy the Steward of Kolyath.

The ruler's punishments had moved beyond mere dungeon cells.

Cahra tensed at the memory, fear needling her. A weapon, Haellium ore, the capital; this conversation was skating dangerously close to forbidden territory for low-borns, like the ancient Seers and their prophecy. And its treasure, the real sword the Steward could never be allowed to get his hands on.

Hael'stromia's ultimate weapon, the reason for the realmwide war.

Cahra cleared her throat, changing the subject. 'Milord, a sword is a personal effect. I'd need to know your family's crest, or animal, plant, colour, anything to signify your kin…' On one hand, his request intrigued her. On the other, it seemed like a quick way to waste coin. Lord Terryl laughed, but not the haughty snigger of the wealthy high-borns who frequented the Traders' Quadrant. This was a soft chuckle, as if he saw her hesitance and found the situation amusing, and not her.

'You seek parameters for your artistry, which is fair. So, Miss Cahra, my favourite colour is blue.'

Her gaze flickered to the lord's face. He was handsome in that typical high-born way. Dark hair, chiselled jaw, sweeping brow and all the rest: unbroken nose, snow-white teeth. *Eyes the colour of blue goldstone.* He cocked his head. Cahra realised she was staring at him, and a hot blush finally crept to blot the freckles flung across her nose and cheeks. Knowing his favourite anything felt oddly intimate.

'Blue,' she said, doing her best to think, speak, like a person. 'Blue can be, erm, plain. Royal blue, for example, is overused. How about a brighter blue, like cobalt? It has a vibrancy, a resonance. There's life in it—'

What in Hael was the matter with her? Besides living on little sleep for weeks, and the Steward, the rapier, the Commander. High-borns in general.

Lord Terryl studied her again, for so long she thought she'd said something wrong, then smiled. 'That, Miss Cahra, is why I sought you.'

She tried to take the praise and failed. 'Just Cahra, please, milord. However, it will be days before I can start on your longsword.'

'Then it shall certainly be worth the wait.' He handed her a cream-coloured envelope, his gloved hand grasping hers, warmth radiating from the supple leather as he held her gaze. 'Measurements, for the sword,' the young lord told her, inclining his head as he smiled. Swallowing, surprise rendered her speechless as he said, 'A pleasure to meet you, Cahra.'

He was bowing to her!

'And you, Lord Terryl,' she said, attempting her best curtsey and still managing to fumble it completely.

The young noble smiled and lifted his hand in farewell, nodding at Lumsden, then slipped into the noonday sea of people.

'What do you make of it?' Lumsden surveyed her over his steaming cup of tea, his brown eyes ringed with lavender. Smoky quartz and amethyst, she'd decided long ago.

Cahra slid a cool glance at the old man, lifting her hammer and giving it an airy swing. 'The job, or him?' She shrugged, watching the lord go. 'Just another high-born,' she said, returning to the safety of the forge at last.

Or so Cahra told herself.

-

That night, Cahra sat in her homespun hammock in the rear corner of the smithy and sketched, her scratchy blanket half falling off from leaping out of bed that morning. A candle's tiny flame straining her eyes, she squinted in the dark at the firelight bouncing between the chunks of ore, workshop tools and coal that littered the path to the front counter. And felt… excited, she realised in surprise.

Balancing her scrawled notes on her lap, Cahra overlaid them with a fresh piece of paper and began. An outline, rough at first: the sword's geometry, based on a scale of the young lord's height, and arm and hand length. Then the sword's handle, the hilt ending in a round pommel with a metal disc insert. Forget the Steward's new rapier or any other sword, Cahra wanted this to be her masterwork. Lost in her thoughts, she continued to draw as she glanced at the smoking flame and absently sketched a few lines, the candle flaring wildly. Then looking back, she inhaled. She'd drawn an oval, in a triangle, tip down, in a circle – and while the design was simple, it triggered a cascade of ideas: gems in a multitude of blues, maybe even a few sapphires, etching paint with a metallic cobalt to match—

Cahra kept going, not stopping until she'd refined the pommel motif, which would be simple yet stunning and set the aesthetic for the longsword's handle and its extravagant blade. It was midnight by the time she finished and she knew she'd feel her exhaustion the next day, but she had it, she undeniably had it. This would be her best weapon yet!

With a satisfied smile, she stuffed the pile of sketches under her hammock, blew out the stumpy candle and snuggled into her blanket.

–

In minutes, Cahra was asleep, oblivious to the magicks stirring in the symbol she'd unknowingly drawn – the Eye of the All-Seeing – as it flared with brilliant light beneath her bed, and the first omen of the realm's ancient prophecy manifested:

'For when the Seers reappear…'

In the lost capital of Hael'stromia, the weapon awakened.

CHAPTER 2

At the heart of the realm's fallen empire, the capital of Hael'stromia lay dormant. From afar, the obsidian pyramid loomed so high above its pike-mounted barriers that they felt quaint. But up close, the fortress city was a monster, rooted like petrified wood in ancient sands, its pyramid's three corners pointing with ominous, skeletal fingers towards the warring sister kingdoms of Kolyath, Luminaux and Ozumbre.

The pyramid – the capital's palace and temple – stood as a monument to past glory. But it was not Hael'stromia's keeper. Within the pyramid's colossal structure, swathed in the silence of unrelenting years, of death, stirred a weapon fuelled by magicks older than the capital's jet sands. A weapon that the tri-kingdoms of Kolyath, Luminaux and Ozumbre had each battled to control for generations.

A weapon; not an inanimate tool of force, but an immortal, born of the Netherworld beyond the earthly plane. A being with the powers to shape or shatter worlds.

Not merely 'a' weapon.

The weapon.

Hael.

-

The flaming eye sockets of Hael'stromia's weapon flickered open, guttering as if his fires starved of air. A mortal concern that Hael found almost laughable, for the Netherworld's infernal bonfires fed him still. As had the suffering ripped from the skeletons around him.

Hael's imposing form arose from the black sandstone of his altar. Arcane power rippled within him, and like an asp perceiving the faintest tremors in the air, he extended his mystical senses beyond the room, his shrine and its stone columns etched with the tales of his death and rebirth. Bound to the Netherworld, his magicks enabled him to feel the slightest whispers of dark energy in this, his sacred domain, and the passages of the capital's pyramid. But there was nothing; no Oracles, no scrying Seers of any kind. Hael frowned, pondering. Hael'stromia was a necropolis yet. Why had he awoken?

Not a soul had dared to goad the capital's walls in several years, leaving him the warden of long-departed memories, now faded into myths. He had not sensed the warmth of another life form's presence for so long that it aroused in him a near-forgotten ache for the world beyond his confines, beyond the solitude and roaring silence.

Springing soundlessly to his feet, Hael blinked, the sensation in his eye sockets akin to the stinging of crushed glass. Despite the pain and crypt-like darkness, his vision was perfect. Hael beheld his pallid skin, delicate as moonlit paperbark, a labyrinth of inky veins pulsing beneath the surface. His fragility laughed in the face of the centuries that had tried and failed to end him, ravaging his immortal form. Hael stilled himself, seeking a remnant in the ashes, an ember of his unspeakable powers. His destruction.

But, again, there was nothing.

A thread of frustration unspooled within him. He was a blade in its sheath without a call to arms, locked in this, his chamber, until the prophecy transpired.

The prophecy. A phrase deeply entwined with his existence, for the last High Oracles had foretold the rise of both a new Scion and the pyramid that served as palatial temple. And, of course, Hael – the dark weapon of the tri-kingdom empire, bound to the destiny of its capital of Hael'stromia. The prophecy's fulfilment promised change, an end to civil war. Without it, the realm's divisions would persist.

But not forever.

'For when the Seers reappear,
When the Key has been bestowed,
When the mark walks the path to enter the Nether in life,
Then shall Hael rise again.'

Hael had been awaiting the first omen of the prophecy, '*For when the Seers reappear*', as long as he had been sealed inside this room. When the following two omens were enacted, he would be liberated, free to defend his empire's city seat, this pyramid, the capital restored.

But in four centuries, nothing had come to pass. Certainly no Scion.

Nothing but war between the three kingdoms it was his duty to protect.

His core burned with anticipation. How much longer must he endure?

Retreating to his resting place, he settled into the comforting embrace of cool stone in the blackness of his cage. Awaiting the first omen of the prophecy, Hael was at time's mercy, as he had been for the past 400 years. His undying watch had been one of isolation.

Fortuitously, as the weapon, he was well acquainted with isolation. Perhaps too well.

All of a sudden, a slender beam of radiant white light cleaved the shadows, emanating from beyond the sealed doors of his shrine, vibrant and alive.

Could it be—

The light dissipated and Hael's stomach lurched as his supernatural eyes saw a vision: not a man, as was customary, but a woman, her eyes as fierce as a battle-hardened warrior's. She held a drawing of an olden sigil that he recognised immediately. Hael's desiccated heart, bound as it was to service, stirred with a profound curiosity.

And, strangely, the longing for earthly company. The feeling took him by surprise, anticipation igniting in his chest.

Who was she?

Was this mystery human female the one, his future Scion master? How – and why?

Had the Oracles foretold this young woman, a divergence to shatter centuries of convention? Could she be the harbinger of revolution he had awaited for so long?

With a sizzle and a spark, the fires of Hael's eyes roared into a soaring onyx inferno. Power blazed through him, the room's air crackling, his thousand-year-old body erupting as an occult flame wreathed his form. *This is it.* Hael could not see the woman's face, and he did not know her name. But he would, he vowed. He would solve the riddle of the human woman who had roused him from his slumber. He parted his lips and a word rumbled through the void, sacred and resonant. A promise whispered to the enveloping darkness.

A promise that the foul regimes of the past, the present, were drawing to a close.

'*Scion...*'

The new era, a new Scion, beckoned. And as destiny whispered throughout the veil, Hael knew, with a surge of escalating darkness, that it would soon be time to rise.

The prophecy had finally begun.

CHAPTER 3

Smithing is like magick, Cahra thought, hoisting her hammer above the fire-forged blade – creation, something from nothing, from base materials. The way she'd forged herself.

She swung her hammer in the sweltering heat, the rhythmic clang of metal ringing among the motley assortment of chisels, tongs and punches, each practised strike a pounding heartbeat in the Traders' Quadrant. Cahra leaned her elbows on the anvil, inspecting the blade of Lord Terryl's longsword in the forge's light. She'd shaped the metal with care, drawing out every bump and imperfection. It would be easy to sharpen, heat-treat and finish off by hand. With a satisfied smile, she called to Lumsden.

'I'm off!' Cahra dumped her leather apron on the workbench that edged the path to the rear of the smithy, wiping the sweat from her forehead and surveying herself, sighing. Her trousers were ripped at both knees, her boots holed, the evidence of her fireside labouring. This was the reality of life as a blacksmith, toiling from sunrise to sunset with no time or coin to waste on clothes. She adjusted her leather vest, the only woman's garment she owned, and rubbed the soot from her face. As far as decorum went, her appearance would have to do.

–

The sun dipped behind a row of squat grey shacks, barnacles that clung together, as Cahra returned from the jeweller's, the gemstones for Lord Terryl's longsword sagging in her pocket. The precious gems, bartered for by Lumsden, would form the centrepiece of the sword's hilt, the insert for the pommel – the shapes she'd sketched and hadn't been able to stop thinking about. She exhaled softly, eyes drifting over the opalescent orange sky fading into dusk, the coming winter a raw whisper against her skin.

Past the markets, pockets of slums marked the Traders' Quadrant, their narrow alleys snaking like saltwater through Kolyath's crevices. A mismatched cluster of eroded granite and ratty tents, the dwellings always looked set to buckle under the weight of the harsh climate. Yet they endured, pinched, packed, but persevering. And once a year, their people celebrated.

Cahra gazed at the decorations for the annual Festival of Shadows and its highlight, Veil's Eve, dotting windows on the dim streets with paper cut-outs depicting eerie silhouettes. Absently, she wondered what Lord Terryl might be doing for Veil's Eve, if high-borns even mingled with the masses in the streets. As she would, after finishing his blade.

Lost in thoughts of the lord and his sword, Cahra barely noticed the candles flickering behind window decorations as she passed.

Nor did she notice the weapon at her back, until it was upon her.

'Gimme the coin,' a male voice growled from behind. Stilling, Cahra scolded herself. She should have known better, traipsing the backstreets at night with a pocketful of jewels. What in Hael was she thinking? All she'd wanted was to get back to Lord Terryl's sword. But the time for daydreaming was done. She inhaled, restraining the breath in her chest before letting it out, slowly. Deliberately. It was funny how it always felt so close, the side of her she hid like a crude relic, beastly and buried. Her old life, her old instincts.

Her old self.

Cahra pushed ever so slightly against the weapon at her back and felt no pain. Her lips quirked to one side as she spun and elbowed a blade from her attacker, her opposite fist hooking a clean punch to the jaw, arms snapping up beside her head again. A brutal dance she'd learned on Kolyath's cutthroat streets, where survival depended on raw instinct.

'No one in this part of the Quadrant can afford to sharpen their knives,' she snapped. 'Now what—' Then Cahra saw.

The dirt-encrusted face. The fear-steeped gaze. The rags and no shoes, just worn soles against the freezing cobblestones.

A tiny, scowling cauldron of resentment. It was like looking at who she used to be.

She watched the boy, younger than her, itching to fight but knowing he'd been bested. Just a few years older than she was when Lumsden saved her from the kingdom's dungeons. This kid hadn't been so lucky. Cahra stood over him, silent, then lowered her arms.

And whispered something she hadn't said in a very long time.

'*Hael won't help us.*' The words tumbled out of her mouth before she could think. The beggar's credo: the words of those without a home, a family, a place in the Steward's rotten high-born kingdom. Kids like him. Kids like her.

The boy stared at her with sky-blue eyes like aquamarines.

Cahra shot a wary glance around them. She knew the risks. The Steward's stance against helping Kolyath's beggars was well-known, as were his Red Square retributions. But they were alone. And this kingdom, this life...

'It wasn't coin,' she told the startled boy. Pulling a hand from her pocket, Cahra dropped a tiny sapphire into the kid's palm, marking his gaunt face, his vivid blue eyes and the pitted scar through his left eyebrow. She would recognise him again now.

Cahra jerked her chin to the laneway. 'Go.'

The boy waited, unsure if her goodwill was some kind of trick.

She nodded at him again. '*Go*. You know these streets don't stay empty for long.'

He watched her, his eyes brighter somehow, tightening his little hand around the gem. The boy nodded, once. Then he ran.

Cahra stared at the empty space where he'd been and breathed deeply, the cold, moist air of nightfall in her lungs. She swallowed against the lump that was hardening in her throat. For one moment, she allowed herself to experience a bittersweet feeling of pride. Not for her, but for the boy. For every kid out here, just trying to survive.

Hael won't help us.

But someone had to, surely? Like Lumsden had helped her.

The lonely life Cahra now led sharpened into focus. She'd been vigilant ever since the old man had helped her escape the Steward's wrath, the scars and wishes she harboured living only in her head, unvoiced. So far, it had been the safest way.

But would it always be like this? Would she always feel so alone?

Pulling her coat tight against the coming frost, she weaved through the drab greys of Kolyath's austere streets. It was quiet, and the solitude was a familiar comfort, and a curse, as the image of the boy and the sapphire ruminated in her mind. A reluctant admission that maybe, even in Cahra's guarded world, there might be glimmers of something more.

Something like hope.

–

Days bled into nights as Cahra poured herself into crafting Lord Terryl's longsword, her world shrinking to the smithy and its forge's fiery breath, warming her after sundown.

She painstakingly weaved the lord's cobalt theme and its complementary shades of blue, from the gem-encrusted pommel to hand-painted flourishes dancing from the handle to the blade, every detail reflecting her dedication to crafting a sword the lord might like.

And every night, she dreamt, the dark hours filled with night terrors that seemed to soak like ale straight through her, causing her to wake bolt upright in a cold, stark sweat. Shivering, she'd pull her blanket to her chin and try to remember the details of her dreams, but never quite could. All she could recall were icy wisps, a slumbering smoke upon her skin and the suffocating smell, the hiss and deadly snap, of fire. Burning.

Dawn was barely a smidge on the horizon when Cahra dragged herself from bed on the last day of working on Lord Terryl's longsword, eyes gritty from another restless night.

But her mission was clear: complete the sword. So she shrugged off the bone-deep fatigue like an old coat, working from first light until first candle and beyond, and buffed the blade with her aching hands until the job was done.

When she finished, triumphant, Cahra held the weapon to the forge's dying flames. The pommel was majestic, with a rich array of sapphires ringing a glittering blue goldstone, the gems twinkling like distant stars trapped in a sea of polished silver. The handle, wound with cocoa-coloured leather so soft and supple it moulded to even Cahra's calloused palms, led the eye to the guard dividing the hilt from the engraved blade. Her fingers traced the flamboyant brushwork that danced along the fuller, flushing the longsword's length. She'd spent hours polishing the sword until it shone like dew in sun-kissed light.

Suddenly, her task was complete.

Holding her breath in anticipation, Cahra lifted Lord Terryl's sword to test its weight, slicing the blade through the air. The heft was exactly balanced, offering no resistance despite the extravagant handle. It was like the sword caressed the wind itself.

From his seat at the smithy's workbench, Lumsden's eyes widened as he followed the longsword's arc with a reverential gaze, lingering on the blade's metallic paint. The old man gave Cahra a slow nod, all the approval she'd ever need, confirming what she already knew. Lord Terryl's sword was absolute perfection.

Cahra stepped back to admire the weapon in all its glory, delight and accomplishment swelling in her chest. Each sparkling stone, each vibrant brushstroke, every inch of its flawlessness was the result of her hard work. She had finally begun to master her craft, just as Lumsden had promised years ago.

Her thumb brushed the tattoo encircling her wrist: a bold, black hammer, with red ink depicting a fiery forge burning behind it. It was the crest of the Blacksmith's Guild and her chosen profession, the symbol more than just ink. It was a sign of her place in the world, a symbol of her skills and dedication.

This longsword, her craftsmanship – it was her ticket to a better life, a life as a respected journeyman blacksmith. The status was more figurative than anything these days, with the realm's three kingdoms at war with one another. But it was a start, she thought. Maybe one day, she could even become a master blacksmith like Lumsden.

Yet as she stood there, staring at the spellbinding weapon she'd created, a sobering thought snuck in among the joy. A voice inside her, a hard voice, that laughed at her fantasies, speaking the truths she'd rather forget: that her life in Kolyath, whether she had a trade or not, could be snuffed out in a heartbeat. That no matter what she did, how she changed, it would never be enough. A part of her would always be afraid.

She would always be in danger.

All it would take was the Steward learning that Cahra was the girl who'd tried to kill him.

CHAPTER 4

Cahra rubbed her arms as she wandered the Traders' Quadrant, grateful for the chance to clear her restless mind. She needed a distraction. But with Lord Terryl's longsword complete and no hammering left to occupy her, she'd gone out in search of ale.

Cahra dragged herself down the dark cobblestone road towards the Quadrant's tavern. Her muscles ached, and she wondered how she'd go lifting a tankard. But after the last week, she sorely needed one. Despite her happiness at helping the boy with the aquamarine eyes, what she'd done was incredibly dangerous. Not because of the attempted theft, as mugging was common in Kolyath. It was her goodwill; if the boy told anyone she'd helped a beggar, she'd be arrested by the Commander's Kingdom Guards and promptly hanged. The Steward didn't believe in alms for the poor. All he believed in was tyranny and taxing people to the bone over the stupid, pointless realmwide war.

But there was nothing to be done for it now. Nothing but ale.

Cahra breathed in the sickly-sweet air, dense sprigs of pale flowers creeping like a tomcat here and there, their scent undercut by the stink of filth on the streets as she walked. Some alleys were subdued, people huddling in meagre homes, firewood and candles lit if they could afford them. Others were busier than ever, as both the slums and opulent establishments came alive with drink, dancing and rampant debauchery. She watched a group of friends slip into an underground pleasure den, their laughter echoing into the night.

But the boy's face swam back into mind, and she faltered mid-step. Yes, she was here for celebration, for solace. Yet was that the only reason?

Or had she wondered, when she'd given the boy that sapphire, if he'd tried to rob her because he had friends who depended on him? Which begged the question: what friends did Cahra have?

She spied the swinging green signage of the Pedlar's Pouch tavern and willed herself to shake off her strange mood. She'd been here before, delivering a knife, a lock, a pan, whatever the tavern's owner Jon had bartered Lumsden for, and she eyed the weather-beaten stone of its single-storey frontage, a ramshackle affair. Behind it, the cramped, tacked-on rooms wound in a horseshoe shape around a courtyard, already alive with a bonfire and the strains of fiddlers' music. Reaching the door, she spotted the baker's and tailor's apprentices at a table with several other traders from the Quadrant, clinking tankards and laughing raucously.

But as she stood, hand on the door latch, Cahra suddenly felt out of place despite her Guild tattoo granting her entry. Her shirt collar scratched at her throat, too tight, and the peppery smell of bodies permeating the room, layered with the yeasty reek of old, stale ale, made her want to gag. She froze as she stared into the darkened tavern.

Breathe. Don't think about the dungeons.

Cahra threw a hand out for the doorframe before her rising panic could overtake her, catching it and swinging herself about-face to lurch into the street. But her ears were ringing, head swimming and her heart pounded so violently she feared it might explode. She plonked down at the base of the steps, burying her head in her lap, waiting.

It would fade, it would all fade, she knew. She just needed to *breathe*.

Think about gemstones: garnet, onyx, sapphire. Just like she did when she relived Kolyath's dungeons in her nightmares.

Her lips moving silently, Cahra started listing gems, holding her breath to slow the manic drumbeat of her heart, the terror skulking beneath her skin. Slowly, she began forcing breath after jagged breath, over and over, until the air began to feel less leaden in her lungs and her legs stopped shaking, her fear ebbing like rainwater to the sea.

Eyes still shut, she felt a strong hand at her shoulder. Expecting to see Jon, or maybe a fellow apprentice, she peeled her eyes open. Instead, two blue goldstone orbs stared back at her, and she recoiled in horror as she realised it wasn't some low-born perched beside her but Lord Terryl, his graceful brow furrowed.

'What ails you?' The lord's gaze was incisive. Thank the Seers for the black of night, because the heat in her cheeks knew no bounds.

'N-nothing,' Cahra stammered. 'I, erm, I… I was so busy today that I forgot to eat.' Flashing Lord Terryl a smile, she leapt to her feet. Too fast; she nearly fell on her arse again, light-headed as she was. He caught her by the elbow.

'Allow me to remedy that,' the young lord said, his concern persisting.

'Oh no, milord, you have people to attend to. I'm fine,' she babbled.

'Cahra,' Lord Terryl said, apparently noting her disorientation and setting her gently on her feet. Her embarrassment grew, as her smith's body made her heavy as a cart, and now he knew it. 'Were you working on my sword today?'

She hesitated.

His lips twitched. 'If you forging my sword is why you're fainting in the street, it would be ungentlemanly of me to send you on your way.'

She opened her mouth to protest, but finally saw Jon. He had indeed spotted her and was carrying two ludicrously full tankards.

'Lord Terryl,' the giant, burly man hailed him, flashing Cahra a sidelong grin. She managed a weak nod.

'Jon,' the lord greeted in return. They knew each other? 'What fortuitous timing. Miss Cahra needs a meal. What might you tempt us with, this evening?'

Jon, beaming ear to ear, presented the young lord with a tankard, before turning to Cahra with a roguish look. 'Half-pint for you, missy? A full mug might knock you right out; I'll be running for my life from Lumsden and his hammer if you end up on the floor!'

You mean my hammer, she thought, scowling. 'Just give me the damn ale,' she said, before recalling the company she kept and fighting the urge to shrink beneath the floorboards.

Jon chuckled heartily and led them to a table in the back, setting her tankard on it.

Cahra exhaled, taking a sip of the cloudy, malt-rich ale, and turned to Lord Terryl. Who was now sitting not across from her…

…but supportively by her side.

Ignoring the hammer of her heart against her ribcage, Cahra forced herself to study her surroundings. The doorway she'd entered was one of two, the other's crooked frame anchored to the opposite corner of the crowded room. She watched a group of ruddy-faced men exit, sloshing ale all over the tacky floorboards. A candelabra's tapers flickered near them and she noted the low ceilings smudged with smoke from years of men's pipes and scorched meat. Scanning the room, she flinched as a loud *crash*, then voices, echoed from the kitchen. She released the breath straining in her chest, hands balled into fists, her knuckles white.

Breathe. Her panicked turn still had her feeling anxious. But these were her people, in her Quadrant. She was safe here, Cahra told herself.

If only she believed it.

Lord Terryl looked at her, the hearth's flames catching his dark hair and lighting it to match the gold flecks in his starry eyes. 'What would you like to eat?'

Inhale. Exhale. 'I appreciate it, but you don't have to. I can pay my own way.'

'I am sure that you can.' He looked amused. 'You do require sustenance, though, and I know just the dish. Tell me, do you like pork?'

'Yes,' Cahra heard herself reply. She supposed a full stomach would do her good. While it was true she'd hardly eaten, it was also normal. Lumsden tired so easily these days that she tried to save their modest food for him.

'Excellent.' Lord Terryl turned to Jon again, his words lost to the din of the tavern. The conversation ended with the two men belly-laughing.

Who *was* this young lord?

He settled back into his seat, face flushed. 'I ordered a specialty Jon makes for me, after I have travelled and require a hearty meal,' Lord Terryl said warmly.

'Travelled?' She frowned. He no doubt lived in the Nobles' Quadrant of Kolyath near the Steward's castle, but it was hardly a day-long hike from where they were.

He lowered his voice. 'The Wilds,' he said. 'There are villages outside Kolyath that need wares but cannot enter the kingdom. I offer them trade.'

'The Wilds?' She gaped at him. 'But the people of the Wilds are nomads, exiles.' Nature worshippers, who had little but the clothes upon their backs, or so the rumours went. 'And Lord Terryl, leaving the kingdom is banned!' As was such worship – a death sentence, if it was discovered. Only the prophecy's magick existed for the Steward.

The thought of this young lord being discovered by their ruler...

It's what made the Steward, and everything about Hael'stromia, so dread-inducing. The entire kingdom knew Kolyath's ruler would do whatever it took to get the prophecy's weapon, and obliterate any and all obstacles in his way. Those who'd vanished from the Quadrant because of whispers of the weapon were never seen again.

Not alive, anyway. Cahra gulped her ale.

'It is, but some merchants incur exceptions,' Lord Terryl said.

'Oh?' She'd just assumed he was an everyday noble. A merchant lord was strange, but what did she know about high-borns? Lord Terryl having met Jon at least made sense now.

'I supply ore and minerals to Kolyath,' he explained. 'However, outside the kingdom, I also trade in everyday items with the people of the Wilds, depending on what they request.' The lord gauged her reaction. 'You are wondering why I aid them.'

Cahra couldn't help herself, shrugging. 'Maybe.'

Hael won't help us.

'The people of the Wilds are just that – people. They need things, things that the Wilds cannot provide. Tools. Medicines stronger than herbs of the forest floor. Weapons for hunting. The alternative is venturing beyond these lands and, as you know, the other sister kingdoms are not exactly welcoming alternatives.'

Cahra watched him and the way he moved, sounded, as he spoke. She was practised at pinpointing verbal sleights of hand, but he didn't seem to be lying to her. So she didn't either. 'In Kolyath, it's rare to be so kind,' she said slowly.

'Especially for someone in my position,' he said, voicing the words she hadn't. 'There was a time when I, too, was like my peers. But as I came of age, I learned something.' Lord Terryl returned her gaze. 'There is value in helping others.'

Cahra didn't know what to say, firstly to the idea of a helpful high-born, and secondly to the fact that one was apparently sitting next to her. So she said, 'Right,' and peered at him. 'Why would you tell me any of this?'

'I believe that you might understand,' the lord said simply. Again, she found herself scanning his posture, his chest and shoulders open and relaxed. What did those words mean? Her life had taught her to be cynical, but unnervingly, something in her felt he was sincere.

Before she could decide how to reply, he moved on.

'May I ask, how did you become a blacksmith?' Lord Terryl asked, a welcome segue. 'Your weaponry is much desired at court.'

At the mention of the Steward's castle, Cahra pressed the tankard to her lower lip. Where to start?

Maybe not with the dungeons.

'I met Lumsden when I was small. He helped me escape… a difficult situation, then offered to train me as his apprentice. So I said yes. Ever since, I've learned as much as I possibly can about blacksmithing: steel-making, forging, grinding, heat-treating, engraving, gemstones, scabbards, the lot. The harder I work, the more I repay Lumsden for his kindness.' She hadn't thought about it before, but it was the truth.

Nothing she did could ever match Lumsden saving her from the Steward and that cell. But that's why she was here. Hers was a life debt, and for him, she would pay the cost.

'Honourable,' Lord Terryl replied, his fine shirt rustling as he leaned in. 'Was it difficult, learning the various skills?' He looked at her intently.

For an instant, Cahra felt the familiar sting of shame. Men were always surprised, confronted, by her physical strength. Only, when she met his gaze, he didn't seem to be judging her physique or making fun of her.

Gripping her ale between both hands, she said, 'Practice, I guess. It's been nearly ten years now.' She thought about all the things she'd pushed herself to learn. 'But I suppose it is unusual,' she admitted. 'The Military Quadrant's smithy is ten times our size as it arms Kolyath's soldiers. At ours, it's just me and Lumsden. But we only make weapons for court, not war.' Cahra squirmed, drinking deep from her ale. She'd never talked so much about herself before.

'Ah, yes.' A shadow flitted across Lord Terryl's face, and she surprised herself by wondering what he was thinking.

'Have you seen it? The war,' she said softly. Here was someone who'd been outside the kingdom's walls, and though she knew she shouldn't ask, she had to know.

Their eyes met. 'You might say that,' Lord Terryl said, voice low, then stopped again. 'However, such talk is not for…'

'Ladies?' Cahra finished, giving him a pointed look. 'I'm not exactly one of those.' She gestured at her mug for emphasis, tapping a finger on the time-worn table, as she asked, 'What about Hael, then? Surely if you've travelled, you've seen Hael'stromia.'

'Such questions.' A hint of amusement softened his features.

'It's the metal of Kolyath's gate,' Cahra mused. 'It drives me mad. What *is* it? All we know is that it's the capital's Haellium, but I've never seen anything like it, anywhere.'

She recalled the first time she'd spied the gate, where the Farming and Military Quadrants met at their southernmost tip. The 'gate to Hael' that led into the Wilds was black and brutal, so dark it seemed to swallow all the sunlight, with spikes and thorns sharp enough to lop a leg clean off. Every kingdom had a gate, it was said, and Hael'stromia had several.

The lord gazed at her for a long moment, Cahra realising the ale was loosening her up too fast on an empty stomach. She hastily replaced her mug. *Where is that food?*

Then Lord Terryl spoke. 'I have seen Hael'stromia.'

Cahra sat up, her eyes wide. 'Really?'

'Yes,' he admitted. 'The first thing you see is the black tri-cornered pyramid, its summit piercing the murky clouds. Then the capital, girded by its soaring defences, with bars thrice as high as Kolyath's gate. Catch a glimpse between them, and the city, entombed by its own shattered walls and crumbling buildings, lies bare. It is quite a sight.'

Cahra lifted her eyes to Lord Terryl's and asked the one question burning in her mind. 'Did you go in?'

He smiled, brief and brittle. 'No. The rumours are correct, the capital is impenetrable. I was simply passing on my western travels.'

There were tales, of those who reached one of its gates, only to meet some tragic end. Her eyes slid to the young lord's. 'Probably for the best.'

Talk of Hael'stromia dwindled as their dishes arrived. She inspected the white meat in soup with potatoes, carrots and a splash of something green.

Meanwhile, Lord Terryl was transformed as he inhaled the fragrant steam wafting from the table, a hum of contentment on his lips. 'The pork is seared and boiled in water, then the succulent meat is served with it as broth. Exquisite!'

His pleasant air caught her off guard after his sober words about Hael'stromia. Cahra raised a spoonful to her lips, then another, and had to agree with him as she demolished her bowl. When was the last time she'd eaten so well? She honestly didn't know.

Satiated, Cahra rested her head against the wall, thoughts drifting, untethered, as she gazed at her unexpected dining companion. Her bout outside the tavern was all but forgotten as the heady buzz of alcohol teased away the last of her nerves.

Lord Terryl caught her looking at him. 'Do you feel much improved?'

'I do.' As much as she disliked expressing gratitude to high-borns, she made herself say the words and meet his eyes. 'Thank you, Lord Terryl.'

'My pleasure,' he said, face bright. 'And please, call me Terryl.'

Cahra blinked, stunned. He wanted her to dispense with titles? Bewilderment rippled through her, and she could only nod, speechless.

A comfortable hush settled between them, although she still had so many questions. His face shone with a curious warmth, and she wondered: did he have questions for her too? She'd never spent so much time with a high-born, especially a man who seemed so earnest. Cahra opened her mouth to speak, only to hear the Quadrant clock's deep chimes strike ten. She groaned inwardly. Where had the time gone?

'I have to go,' she said, pushing back her chair, wood screeching on the floor as if equally reluctant to leave the pleasure of his company. She forced herself to stand.

Terryl's expression faltered, yet his tone was light. 'So soon?'

A half-smile flickered across her lips. 'The morning may start late for you, milord, but mine begins before the sun rises.' She lingered. 'Oh, and your sword is ready to collect.'

'So, I shall see you tomorrow, then?' Again, Terryl's voice was casual, but his eyes held hers in his thrall, as if searching for an answer to something left unsaid.

His was a simple question, but the flutter in her stomach said otherwise. 'I – yes,' Cahra said, stumbling over the word, then over her chair as she stepped away. 'I'd better go,' she repeated, backing through the teeming tavern, eventually tearing her gaze from his face. Then, spinning on her heel, she hurtled for the door.

At the threshold, she glanced over her shoulder one more time. Her mind raced as she replayed the night's events: Terryl's stories of the Wilds, his own kindness and the way his eyes lit up when he spoke of helping others, those outside the kingdom. Ordinary high-borns didn't care about such things; they only cared for money, power and the Steward's favour.

But one thing was becoming abundantly clear, Cahra thought, as she turned to leave.

There was nothing – *nothing* – ordinary about Lord Terryl at all.

CHAPTER 5

The next morning, Lumsden, head bent over his ledgers at the smithy's metal front counter, murmured into his tea, 'Apparently, Lord Terryl is on his way.' Behind the old man, the young lord's longsword hung proudly on display for passers-by to envy. Lumsden always said showing buyers Cahra's work helped start fruitful conversations.

'Mm-hmm,' Cahra said absently, pacing. She'd awoken that morning feeling – strange, unsettled. Nervous. She dismissed the word her mind dared to suggest. *Nervous? Ha!* With a frown, she shoved the thought all the way down into her boots, scuffing them every now and then to channel her edginess. Her, nervous about a noble's opinion? *Never!*

Lumsden cast her a sideways look, his eyebrows knitting as he noted her agitation. 'You've outdone yourself,' he assured her.

'Thanks.' She raked a hand through her hair, sighing at her sooty palm. She'd washed, but no amount of soap erased the signs of smithing.

'Except?' The old man probed in a patient voice.

She met his gaze, positive the tension seething in her gut was reflected on her face. She'd poured everything into that sword and it was her best work. But what if it didn't meet Lord Terryl's high-born expectations? A pang of apprehension struck her, an unexpected guest at what should have felt like a triumph. *Seers, what if he hates it?*

More to the point, why did she care what he thought, or felt?

Lumsden watched Cahra with an impenetrable expression, in that way he had that felt like she was hiding behind a pane of glass. 'You're afraid that he won't like it.'

She blew out a breath. 'He's a *lord* – who commissioned a weapon he's never seen. It's madness!' She groaned, cradling her head in her hands. 'Why did you let me do this?'

The old man chuckled, telling her, 'Because you deserved the opportunity, Cahra. What's madness is you doubting your craft.'

Lumsden took a slow sip from his mug of tea. 'The weapons you create are masterworks. And the more the court talks of them...'

The more the Steward's court talked of her work, the more commissions they'd see. Lord Terryl's sword could prove quite lucrative for her and Lumsden.

She rolled her eyes, hiding a smile as she resumed pacing, the drag of her boots against the sand filling the silence.

Breaking the tension, Lumsden spoke. 'Cahra, you're scratching around like a hen. Why don't you go and fetch our bread? It seems the bakehouse has forgotten again...' The old man began grumbling to himself.

Cahra glanced outside. A walk might do her good, help her shake her frustration. 'Okay, I'll be back,' she announced, snatching her overshirt against the brisk Kolyath breeze and hopping over the counter to hit the street's stones with a thud.

–

It was close to midday and the Traders' Quadrant was awash with the bustle of bodies, Cahra's every sense heightened and assailing her. She'd lived on these streets her whole life, but her learned vigilance was overwhelming, a relentless undercurrent to everything she did. Drawing a fortifying breath, she slowed her steps, grasped the fresh loaf of bread and remembered what she'd taught herself to do when she was younger: tackle one sense at a time.

Focusing, she listened. Back in the direction of the bakehouse, a woodworker's saw heaved and rasped in a steady chant, a metronome she gratefully latched onto.

At the road's other end, she sniffed out the distinct tang of the tannery and the pungent odour of animal pelts steeped in vats of salt and acid.

Now, sight. Cahra raised her eyes to Kolyath's uncharacteristically glass-blue sky, a rare reprieve from the kingdom's usual overcast gloom. She turned her face to the sun's rays, letting their warmth ground her, then lowered her gaze to the black Festival of Shadows ribbons that wound among the eaves and between the shops of the Quadrant's main road.

She'd always loved Veil's Eve, when Kolyath gathered during autumn's blood moon to embrace the dark in a night-long vigil as people did in the time of old Hael'stromia, with no lanterns, no fires, just the night and stars, the sky and moon. All as Kolyath's weak summers waned into a new season, the cold wending from the rocky coastline up and over the kingdom's walls. It was also one of the more dangerous times, where history morphed into whispers of the fallen capital, the Seers, the prophecy and the weapon. Veil's Eve wasn't just a celebration, it was a subtle show of defiance against the Steward by the many, the low-borns of his kingdom. Savage demonstrations by the Kingdom Guards in the Red Square always followed.

For now, Cahra concentrated on the decorations, the black sheen of a ribbon's tail flapping farewell over her shoulder. Anchored to her senses and flowing with the crowd, she cradled her loaf of bread and navigated back to the smithy.

Until Commander Jarett's furious bellow rent the Traders' Quadrant, the man's words tolling like an ominous bell:

'Who is the owner of this sword?'

–

Cahra tucked her hair beneath her vest, popping a chunk of bread into her mouth and strolling past the smithy, her old life and the instincts it had borne already surging back. Turning a corner, she passed the shops trailing like straggling children from the main street.

As soon as she'd vanished from view, she broke into a sprint.

Racing along the first backstreet parallel to the main road, she leapt over a tumble of weeds and flung herself headlong into the gap between a wall and canvas sheet – her wall – landing on the hammock in her corner of the smithy. Glued to the shadows, Cahra dropped and slunk behind the sleeping forge, barely drawing breath as she listened.

'Lumsden.' Commander Jarett had lowered his voice but the result was chilling, a bloodhound about to strike and make its kill. 'I will not ask again.' She watched him lean towards the old man on the other side of the curtain that hung for privacy when brokering, between the counter and the workshop. It was the only thing separating them from her. 'Where is she?'

Lumsden said, 'And what if I crafted the longsword?' Cahra's eyes flew to where Lord Terryl's blade had hung, awaiting the young noble. The only complete work in the smithy.

'That ostentatious hilt? I think not. This is *her* work,' Jarett spat. 'And if you do not hand over that brat, I will make short work of *you*.' Cahra's heart thundered in her chest. 'Who was this weapon commissioned for?'

Lumsden was silent. 'Of course, he could have instructed her in such a symbol…' Symbol? What was the old man talking about? He knew Lord Terryl had done no such thing.

What is happening?

'He?' Jarett thumped the counter, his meaty fist a boulder.

Lumsden didn't spook easily, but then, he already knew the horror of the dungeons. 'Terryl, the merchant lord,' Lumsden told the Commander. 'It's his sword.'

'And your apprentice? Where, pray, is she?'

'At the fishmonger's, picking up our supper.'

Cahra saw Jarett's silhouette whirl from the counter and bark, 'To the fishmonger's! And send guards to apprehend Lord Terryl!' Jarett returned to Lumsden. 'I will find one, then the other. We will get to the bottom of this odd phenomenon. *Do not* hinder me, old man.' Jarett's profile faded in full, leaving six guards in his wake.

Cahra was shaking. *What in Hael have I done?*

Lumsden appeared from behind the curtain, Lord Terryl's longsword in hand. Rounding the forge, he caught sight of Cahra, his eyes flickering towards the back. She ducked into the safety of the smithy's rear. No one on the street would see them now.

'Cahra. Lord Terryl's sword, the sigil on the pommel. Where did you get it?' Lumsden whispered, his face ashen.

'What do you mean? I made it up, like I always do. It's just geometry,' she said.

The old man shook his head. 'No. The pattern you created…' His voice was hoarse. In that moment, Lumsden looked so frail. 'It's the Sigil of the Seers, Hael'stromia's Oracles. According to the Commander, it's the first time it's been seen outside the castle in centuries.' He took a steadying breath. 'Jarett thinks your sword is the first omen of the prophecy.'

'What?!' Cahra choked, staring at Lumsden in dizzy disbelief. 'He can't be serious.'

Jarett speaking of the prophecy and its omens to a low-born only meant one thing: he thought they knew something about the weapon. An ingrained fear burned in Cahra's chest at every macabre Red Square death she'd seen, victims whimpering, screaming, for their lives—

She clenched her fists, trying to shut the grisly memories out. The blood…

Lumsden closed his eyes. 'Cahra, he's on his way to the fishmonger's, and when he doesn't find you there, he'll come straight back.' The old man clasped her hands. 'For *you*.' His eyes shone. 'My girl, you need to run.'

'*No*.' The vehemence in her word came out a snarl. 'I won't leave you.'

Lumsden looked into her fearful eyes. All she saw was smoky quartz and amethyst, and all she wanted to do was sob. 'I won't have you in the dungeons, never to be seen again. You don't know what you're facing. It's the prophecy, the *weapon*. They'll never let you go. And if Atriposte learns that it was you all those years ago…'

'I won't leave you,' she told him again, her voice trembling.

'My dear girl, I fear that if you don't, we're both as good as dead.'

NO.

Breathe, Cahra told herself, sucking in air and trying to deaden her rush of panic. She could make it on the streets, she'd done it before. She could outrun this, scrape together some kind of life in the alleys of Kolyath again. But when her gaze fell to the old man, defeat hit her like a sledgehammer to the ribcage. Lumsden wouldn't last one winter, let alone survive the gnawing hunger, the biting cold, the never-ending cruelty of life as a homeless beggar. She seized the edge of the workbench, her knuckles white. She needed to think, find a way out that kept them both safe, alive. *Think. THINK!*

'Cahra.' Lumsden's words were soft. 'Please don't fight me. We haven't much time, and you know that I'm too old to flee.' His words, but they were confirmation. And it hurt.

There was only one thing for it, if Lumsden was to live. If she was going to save him. It was her turn, after all, Cahra thought numbly.

He couldn't lose everything, his life, because of her.

'Tell Jarett and the Kingdom Guards I did it,' she said, inhaling as she straightened. 'And that I acted alone.' Cahra's eyes caught a glimpse of Lord Terryl's longsword, her seemingly perfect blade. 'Why didn't he take the sword?'

Lumsden's gaze fell to the weapon he was holding. 'Because he underestimates me.' He lifted his eyes to Cahra. 'And because what they really want is the omen-bringer.'

She nodded, swallowing, then ran back to her corner, throwing on her coat. This was the only way, she thought, to keep Lumsden safe. She yanked her pouch of off-cut gemstones and what little coin she had from her hiding spot. The old man grasped a satchel, tears welling.

'You have to harden yourself against them all, you hear me?' She gripped Lumsden. 'You know the Commander and his guards, what they do to people. Give them nothing at all, nothing but me. Your allegiance to the Steward, his favour, will keep you alive. Okay?'

The old man's voice shook as he asked, 'What will keep you alive?'

Cahra smiled fleetingly at him, knowing the expression would never meet her eyes. 'Experience.' She slung the satchel over her shoulder. Jarett would be on his way back now.

Then she noted the bag's weight, frowning.

'The bread,' Lumsden told her.

'No, you need it—' She opened the bag. The old man stayed her hand.

'And a few essentials.' He smiled, his words hanging in the air.

Realisation struck Cahra in the chest, piercing the walls she'd built around her heart. This was it. This was goodbye. When would she see the old man again? This kind soul who'd plucked her from the dungeon's brink of death?

With a shaking hand, she extended her small fortune, the collection of gems and coins she'd scrimped and saved, placing them in Lumsden's wrinkled palms. 'Take it,' she urged.

But he shook his head. Instead, he gave her Lord Terryl's sword, squeezing her hands as he set them on the weapon's hilt. 'In case the Commander does have want of it, after all,' he explained, eyes trailing across the corner of the smithy that was no longer hers.

It crushed her, all the things she'd never said to him. She'd never get the chance now. Without another thought, Cahra wrapped her arms around the little master blacksmith and held on tight, her tears threatening to spill. She didn't want to let him go.

But Commander Jarett was coming for her.

'Thank you,' Cahra whispered to Lumsden. 'For finding me that night. For giving me a second chance at life. I'll never, ever forget you.' She hugged him, crying in earnest now.

Lumsden's response was a soft laugh, Cahra committing the familiar gravelly timbre of his voice to memory.

'It was an honour to serve,' he told her, dabbing his moist eyes. 'Now be safe. Don't waste your chance worrying about one as old as me.' He looked down. 'Go now, my girl,' he murmured, as Cahra released him, clutching the longsword.

Before the old man could look up again, she had.

–

With nimble, dexterous movements, Cahra shifted the bulging satchel, concealing Lord Terryl's sword under an oily rag. As she pressed the weapon against her leg, a wave of self-loathing crashed into her. Leaving Lumsden, relying on his sacrifice yet again… She swallowed her disgust like the bitter herb it was. But she clung to the knowledge it was the best way to keep him safe. He could say she'd overpowered him, stolen the blade and ran.

Ran where?

She dashed between the rotting piles of refuse on the maze-like backstreets, shaking her head at the angst and fear splintering her focus, as her heart pummelled her heaving chest.

Down the street, turn at the next alley and then what?

Seers, help me!

That was when Cahra spotted Terryl.

CHAPTER 6

Cahra snaked across the main road thronging with people to Lord Terryl, head down, a smile caked on her face. She took his elbow and moved him off the street into an alleyway.

Terryl looked pleased to see her, if not puzzled. 'Cahra—'

She fixed the smile but lowered her voice. 'I'm sorry.' Her eyes flickered to his. 'Look like nothing's wrong,' she said, and to his credit, he did so.

When Terryl spoke, his voice was humourless. 'What is this?'

They were standing in the alley behind the road, in front of someone's ramshackle garden.

Cahra gazed at the vines strangling a wilting spray of ugly yellow buds, pretending they were the subject of her and Terryl's conversation. The alley was secluded, but she knew all too well nowhere was safe from the Kingdom Guards.

She wanted to crawl inside herself and wish this moment away, but there was no time for anything but the truth.

'Terryl, your sword, the pommel I designed – the Commander thinks it's something it's not. I'm sorry, but I think I've gotten you into trouble…'

She looked at the messy garden, then noticed the yellow buds were mugwort, said to be used for warding off evil – and for divination, the practice the Steward's ancestors had banned for its association with the Seers. Seers who, he claimed, were responsible for the death of the last King of Kolyath centuries ago. The irony of the situation wasn't lost on her: the Steward's belief in the prophecy yet his hatred for scrying magick, existing side by side. She quickly ground the mugwort herb under her boot. The last thing she needed was to get arrested for anything else to do with Seers. Low-borns weren't permitted to speak of them, and the punishment… Well, it wouldn't bode well for her situation.

'My longsword? What does the Commander think it is?' The lord asked, eyebrows furrowed in confusion. She unwrapped the blade, the young lord's eyes flashing to the handle. Terryl stared from Cahra to the pommel and back, his face an impasse, betraying nothing.

Out of nowhere, he began to murmur in his smooth, melodious voice, words strung together in an odd rhythm, like a poem Cahra didn't know:

'For when the Seers reappear,
When the Key has been bestowed,
When the mark walks the path to enter the Nether in life,
Then shall Hael rise again.'

It was her turn to stare at the lord now.

Terryl shook his head, searching her face. 'Where did you get this sigil,' he asked her. It didn't seem to be a question.

Cahra threw up her hands. 'I don't know! It just came to me when I was sketching. Every weapon is geometry, shapes and angles. I used a circle for the pommel, a triangle, then added an oval...' She took a shaky breath.

Terryl's voice softened. 'It is the Sigil of the Seers,' he said, pointing to the oval. 'And this is the Eye of the All-seeing.' The young lord paused, and she followed his finger as it traced a triangle. 'The tri-kingdoms of Luminaux, Kolyath and Ozumbre. They are all here, bound by the Hael'stromian realm and the ring of endless time.'

Cahra's head flew up.

'And this.' He touched the lone blue goldstone. 'This jewel signifies the capital, the birthplace of the ultimate weapon.' The young lord looked up, meeting Cahra's anxious gaze. 'The first omen of the prophecy is that the Seers reappear, and the pommel you created bears their sigil – in Kolyath, a sigil only ever seen in the throne room of the castle's keep. The Seers, it seems, have indeed reappeared.'

It was all there: the eye, the kingdoms, the capital.

'I didn't know,' she said miserably, as trepidation crawled inside her, burrowing deeply at what she'd apparently unleashed.

Suddenly, Terryl jolted back to life, as if awakening. His eyes flickered to her. 'Commander Jarett knows the sword is mine.'

Guilt skewered her at the gravity of his words.

She nodded. 'Lumsden told me to run.' She shifted her satchel to her other shoulder. 'The Kingdom Guards are after us. Lumsden said I was at the fishmonger's, to give me time. But they'll return to the smithy again soon.' Cahra was deathly afraid for the old man, but she couldn't think about that now. She'd fled to save him. Now she had to save herself.

And the lord she'd dragged into this mess.

'I see.' Terryl watched her. 'You are risking your life by warning me.'

She fidgeted under his astute gaze, scanning left to right for Jarett, the guards, any sign of danger. But the young lord was right. She hadn't hesitated to warn him. Why?

'I saw you across the street. You would've walked into a trap.'

A trap that's all my fault. Her self-reproach bubbled up, a scream of frustration threatening to burst out from inside her.

Terryl studied Cahra before placing a hand on her shoulder. 'Then we run. And leave the kingdom of Kolyath far behind us.' He glanced about, the alleyway around them empty. 'The fastest way to the gate is through the city.'

Cahra gasped at the young lord. 'You'll help me? How? *Why?*'

'My trade in the Wilds,' he said. 'I have authorisation to leave Kolyath.'

She fought to understand. 'But milord…'

He shook his head at her. 'Please, Cahra, you and I are beyond such formalities, now. We must get to my residence,' Terryl told her with conviction. 'My people will need to be assured that I am safe. Then, we shall need their help to withdraw safely from the kingdom.' He paused, meeting her eyes with grave concern. 'It is not without risk.'

Cahra, still in shock, nodded. 'All right.' What other option was there?

Terryl gave her an assuring nod. 'Then let us be off.'

–

Cahra hid her face behind her upturned collar, her length of hair still tucked away, the sword and satchel tight against her body. Terryl had ditched his fancy coat, ruffled his shirt and dirtied his face, trousers and boots; she admitted, she was impressed by his swift thinking.

They walked jauntily along, looking like a merry pair late for an appointment. Meanwhile, Cahra was moving on instinct, alert for any peak of noise or flash of motion – anything that might signal the Kingdom Guards. Then she realised where she was, her breath catching as they neared the place every low-born feared. The Red Square.

While the guards were nowhere to be seen, their presence was everywhere as Cahra and Terryl approached the execution centre. In the shadow of the Steward's castle dwelled Kolyath's open-air theatre of pain, the timbers of its platform stained a violent rust-red from countless slaughters. It dominated the expanse of public space, vacant nooses swaying in the frigid wind, and she shivered as the guillotine's blade glinted at her with deadly promise. Nearby, iron cages displayed the gruesome bodies of those tortured for scrying magick, their remains left out to rot. Despite the horror clinging to the leaden air, the other low-borns she passed still cast fearful glances at the square, unable to look away. As Cahra hurried away, every plea for mercy she'd heard over the years haunted her, as if buried in the bedrock. Terryl gently urged her on, the square a spectre on the fringe of her awareness.

Relief washed over Cahra as the kingdom's Red Square faded into the background, only to be replaced by a very different scene: the stately mansion Terryl called his home. She stared at the three-storey building, its facade adorned with hand-carved wooden shutters and plant pots brimming with blooms in vibrant marmalade hues. She'd never been close to anywhere so obviously for high-borns before, let alone permitted inside. It may as well have been the Steward's keep. She couldn't believe Terryl had come home to this every night, then gone to collect his longsword at the smithy where she'd slept in the corner of a giant shed.

But as the young lord confidently strode through his grand front door, any remaining doubts about her presence had to be cast aside. With a hesitant step, Cahra followed.

Walking inside Lord Terryl's home, it was like someone flipped a lever. One moment, there was silence. The next, it was absolute chaos.

Three people descended on them: a man, clothed in finery like Terryl's but simpler, with a face as hard as the marble bust she swerved to avoid knocking over. He was then joined by another man, taller than the first and dressed in hardy leathers, and a woman. The woman's skin was dark as midnight with a glow that Cahra envied, her hair tied back in long, black braids, while the second man's complexion was pale, with ash-blond hair that was paler still. Cahra peered at their jerkins, not dissimilar to her vest, except… *There. Stitching for pockets.* Or rather, for concealed weapons. Terryl employed his own personal guards?

'Sir—' The first man said, halting as Cahra stepped from behind Terryl. The young man's hair was a lighter brown than the lord's and short, his angular jaw tensing as he spoke. 'We've been looking for you.' He couldn't have been much older than Terryl, she thought.

'I see.' He exhaled. 'Am I correct in assuming that the time has come?'

The man nodded sharply, his eyes – grey like iron, and just as uncompromising – scrutinising Cahra. 'The blacksmith?'

'Cahra, this is Raiden,' Terryl said, by way of introduction. He went on before she could ask how this man knew who she was. 'Cahra will be accompanying us.'

'Moving you is going to be mission enough,' Raiden warned him, 'without adding Commander Jarett's next-most-wanted to the list.' The man tossed Cahra a cool glance.

She swallowed her fear, eyes hardening in defiance. *Who is this jerk of a high-born?*

'Cahra is with me.' There was an edge to Terryl's voice that made her look at him. 'The time has come, and it is against us.' The lord's eyes flashed to the man and woman. 'Piet, Siarl, evacuate the house and ready the transport.' Terryl's guards bowed and departed as he swept on down the hall. 'The chest in my quarters and the papers on my desk?'

A woman on Raiden's heels curtseyed. 'It is done, H—'

'Good, good,' he said, cutting her off with a brief smile, then turned to Raiden. 'No one in this house shall be left behind,' the lord told him.

Raiden's face was grim. 'I'm working on it.'

Terryl took point, leading the way as they pressed down the hall, Raiden at his side, Cahra following closely. The rooms blurred into a rich tapestry of mahogany and dark velvet, with fleeting glimpses of elaborate oil paintings framed in ornate gold, as she passed.

'My lord, Queran's arrow just arrived,' Raiden said. 'We don't have long.'

Terryl nodded. 'Then Cahra and I shall depart.'

'I'm with you,' Raiden said, hand on the hilt of his sword.

'No. I need you to finalise things here, ensure people's safety.'

'Respectfully, I need to ensure your safety.' The hard look to Raiden's face returned.

Cahra watched as the two men stared at each other. Terryl's expression was resolute, and he wasn't backing down. *Wow, so he can act like a noble.* She almost laughed out loud.

Raiden let out a resigned sigh, his chin lowering in defeat. 'Do you think you can make it to the carriage?'

'We got this far,' Cahra said, folding her arms.

Raiden turned, as if remembering she was there. 'Is that the sword?' She stilled, then handed it to him. Raiden lifted it gingerly, inspecting the pommel. He looked first at Cahra, then at Terryl. 'You'd better hurry,' Raiden said; to her or Terryl, she wasn't entirely sure. 'You can't be seen with this.' But as Terryl turned to leave, a skulking figure prowled in from the doorway to their left.

Cahra threw her fists up before Raiden's sword was half out of its sheath. But the man just exhaled and nodded to the figure. 'Queran! Thank the Seers, you're here.'

'Did you get my arrow? They're minutes behind me,' the tall man told them from the shadowed cowl of his cloak.

'Go,' Raiden said to Cahra and Terryl. 'We'll follow.' He flicked his head to Queran. 'You're up top. Move fast.'

Queran nodded. 'Understood.'

Terryl exited the mansion into his immaculate rear garden, overflowing with topiaries and white snowdrops that wafted nectar. Already planning their next move, Cahra noted the service lane for the other wealthy houses on Terryl's street at the far end of the large garden, a better escape route than going out the front door.

He paused at the arched gate to the lane. 'My caravan has been relocated, now that Commander Jarett's Kingdom Guards are searching for us, to mere streets from the stables.'

Cahra didn't ask how Terryl or his people knew to do that; she was too busy trying to visualise the path to get there and the streets they'd be forced to tread by foot to even make it near the stables. She watched as the cloaked man, Queran, eased himself from the mansion's top-floor window and swung, flipping spryly onto the grey tiles of the building's roof. A moment later, a sleek bow was taut within his grasp.

Private guards, an acrobatic archer… Terryl was definitely full of surprises.

Clearing her throat, Cahra asked, 'We need to get back on the main street, don't we?'

'It is the only way,' Terryl confirmed. She glanced to the left, where the abandoned temple to Kolyath's ancient Seers bordered the nobles' neighbourhood. Meanwhile, the Steward's grounds stretched right, fortified by imposing stone walls that marched to the ever-watchful castle towering on its high hill. Cahra repressed a shiver, the tension in her body returning as she thought about the dungeons awaiting her in its depths.

And started to remember.

–

Cahra pressed her scrawny body, huddled and shivering, into the rear corner of the dungeon cell. She could feel the bricks through the rips in her shirt and the chill of snowflakes whispering from a far-off grate, dusting her hair as they seeped into her skin and little bones. She shifted the weight of her crouch from one foot to the other, trying to fight the bitter cold. Behind her, the wall felt like the safest spot. No one could cut her from behind now. That scar, like so many from living in the kingdom of Kolyath, had taught her so.

Hugging her scraped knees, she squinted in the darkness. All she could see was torchlight flickering from the steep, snaking steps onto a locked gate at the dungeon entrance. At least she'd know if anyone was coming. But what would she do when they did? She traced her hand along the wall, picking for loose mortar. If she could just break off a stony shiv, maybe she'd be the one doing the cutting.

–

'The goods wagon attached to the carriage is your hiding place,' Terryl was saying.

She nodded absently.

It had been so long…

–

She froze, tilting her head towards a creak, followed by a louder bang, then hushed footfalls on slick stone. The kind men made when they thought they were being quiet.

The steps continued downwards. She watched as a silhouette reached through the barred gate like a ghost, then flinched as the figure emerged from the shadows, snapping a key into the lock and turning it with a screech. The dungeon gate swung open.

Cahra bit her lip, digging her fingernails into the wall, faster now.

–

'We will make it to Kolyath's gatehouse, Cahra,' Terryl told her softly.

So long, but she'd never forgotten…

–

The first thing Cahra saw were shoes. Shining in the gloom, like someone had polished them until their hands bled, her nostrils filling with the sooty beeswax used to blacken boots. She peered at the pressed trousers, looking for the familiar red stripe of the Kingdom Guards. But the flash of blood-red she spied in the dim light wasn't a uniform. It was a velvet cloak.

Her hand stilled against the bricks.

A large figure halted outside her cell. 'Come forward,' he ordered.

She couldn't see the man's face, but she could tell from the bite in his command that he was a high-born used to getting his own way. His wasn't the grunt of the stupid guards that had arrested her for stealing. This was someone important.

She hesitated, feeling the hot prick of fear at last.

'Finally, I meet the urchin who has given my Kingdom Guards such trouble,' he said, as she took step after cautious step, stopping several feet away from the cell's locked door. 'You are smaller than I imagined,' the man mused.

That's what they all thought. Just a little girl. How much trouble could she be? Until she was scampering off to peddle their high-born trinkets.

But the man was still speaking, apparently also used to people paying attention. 'Listen to me, you miserable little guttersnipe,' he hissed, a gloved hand shooting through the bars of her dank cell to seize her chin. 'I am Atriposte, Ruler of the Kingdom of Kolyath, and you will heed me!' The man shook her – hard.

–

Terryl drew her gaze, his eyes alert but gentle. 'Cahra.'

Everything her life had taught her. She would need those lessons now.

–

Steward Atriposte, the ruler of Kolyath. His eyes were filled with hatred and rage.

She knew what he saw when the Steward's bulging amber eyes glared into hers: the layers of dirt so caked they were a second skin, the hair that hadn't been washed in months, the muddy-coloured eyes to match. She wasn't pretty. But gulping back the bitter acid in her throat, she didn't need to be. She only needed to do what every beggar in Kolyath did.

Survive.

'I bet you're smaller than every girl imagines,' Cahra said, clenching her fists and spitting a gob of saliva right in the Steward's face.

He recoiled, dropping her, his face inflaming to a tomato shade of red as he wiped furiously at his cheek. With a snarl, he fumbled to unlock her cell. She inched back.

Then he charged, as she'd guessed, hands reaching for her. Bad men liked to hit. Before he could, Cahra leapt to headbutt the Steward's chin with the top of her small skull, slipped the mortar shiv between her fingers…

…and stabbed Steward Atriposte, Ruler of the Kingdom of Kolyath, in his thick neck.

–

She'd never return to the dungeons, never let the Steward's guards capture her alive. She'd made a vow, and Cahra knew she'd face any peril, even death, before she'd yield to Atriposte, the ravager of Kolyath.

'Terryl.' She closed her eyes. 'There are things about me, things that you don't know—'

But their conversation came too late. The sounds she'd been dreading since she'd said goodbye to Lumsden had finally found them: raised voices, the stampede of boots on stones and the harrowed peal of an alarm bell in a high tower. The Kingdom Guards were coming.

Cahra turned to Terryl. He was a noble; surely he'd trained in fighting and endurance. 'I know what we need to do,' she said, gazing in the direction of the rising uproar.

And the chase began.

CHAPTER 7

It was like the gates to Hael had opened. Cahra sprinted down the kingdom's main street, Kolyath now a living maze as she tore past manicured hedges and shot over flower beds in the wealthy district closest to the Steward's castle. The Kingdom Guards were a bend behind, armour clanking as they stormed towards her. Terryl was somewhere behind her too, but Cahra didn't dare to slow and check on him.

Terryl's carriage was their destination, near the stables and Kolyath's gatehouse. Access to the gate was strictly controlled by the Steward.

But as Cahra neared the stretch of road leading to the Haellium gate and their freedom, her stomach churned at the sight of the Kingdom Guards amassing. So she changed course, her legs burning, lungs screaming for air, barely noticing Queran's arrows flying from above.

Suddenly, Terryl was beside her as she veered left. The guards struggled to mobilise, their hulking chainmail a hindrance for pursuits in Kolyath's twisting, cobbled lanes.

'The markets,' Terryl puffed, his breathing surprisingly steady. He might be a lord, and more used to the Steward's court than streaking through the kingdom's streets, but he was keeping pace better than Cahra had expected.

She nodded, running for the marketplace. The swarm of traders hawking wares, noisy haggling and the jostling, unruly crowd would always be a labyrinth, no matter the hour. This route wouldn't lead directly to the stables, but if they could weave their way through the thrumming market, using it as cover, they may have a chance to lose the guards.

Cahra skidded to a stop. The markets were just beyond a small alley intersection ahead, the perfect place to blend in, to disappear. But stationed outside were four of Jarett's guards blocking the narrow entrance, their capes the colour of the blood they'd spill if she and Terryl got too close.

'Damn it!' Cahra swore.

Right before feeling a prod in the middle of her back. She whirled, grabbing a small arm belonging to a familiar face. The boy with the aquamarine eyes.

'You!'

The boy pulled her and Terryl into the safety of a darkened doorway, flashing Cahra a lopsided smile. 'You in trouble?'

'You could say that.' Cahra peered around the door frame at the four guards, weathered paint flaking onto her shoulder. 'We need to get into the markets. Got a distraction?'

'Maybe,' the boy said. 'How big?'

She pulled a gold coin from her satchel. 'This big.'

'Oughta do it,' he said matter-of-factly, closing his fist around the coin.

Terryl eyed them both warily. 'Do what?'

The boy picked up a rock, poked his head around the corner, then hurled it at a window diagonally opposite them. Glass shattered and people shrieked. Passers-by moved for the commotion, as did the guards.

'Buy my help,' the boy said, grinning. He turned to Cahra. 'I would've helped you anyway.'

'I know.' She smiled. 'What's your name?'

'Ellian,' he said shyly.

'Well, Ellian, I'm Cahra.' She crouched next to the boy. 'And you've done your job. Now I need you to stay low for a few days, okay?' His little fist looked like a rock itself as she gazed into his soulful blue eyes. 'Be careful.' He turned to go. 'Hey, one more thing… In a week's time, go to the Traders' Quadrant and find the master blacksmith named Lumsden. Tell him a friend said he'd have some work for you.' Lumsden would need a new apprentice, someone he could trust. Cahra swallowed.

He nodded, then stilled, casting her a final glance. 'Bye,' he said softly.

Then Ellian was gone again, flitting from doorway to doorway away from them, yelling at the guards, 'I see them! Two grown-ups, running away. Hurry!'

Cahra watched the guards charge to Ellian. She took a steadying breath as the boy held the men's attention, pointing away and down the street, before beaming back at her.

With any luck, Lumsden would be able to give the kid a home, a trade, a future. A life. Like the old man had done for her so long ago. Before she'd gone and screwed everything up.

Shakily, she exhaled. 'Let's go,' she said to Terryl.

Cahra could feel the lord's eyes on her as they entered the marketplace, the guards still searching the alley with the broken window. Once Cahra and Terryl reached the trail of stalls and carts brimming with smoked meats, hard cheeses and root vegetables, old parts of her clicked into place like oiled keys amid the shouts of vendors. Snaking her arm to brush against a sheet of brown linen, the flick of her wrist was nearly imperceptible. She swung to Terryl's far side a few strides later and wrapped the sheet around her head and neck as a scarf. A similar trick and she'd swiped a hat for him.

From beneath the safety of her disguise, she slowed a little, gazing at the market's Festival of Shadows decorations and the small, dark stalls selling rough chunks of tenebrite, a crimson substance mined from the craggy, snow-capped mountains north of Kolyath's walls. Tenebrite, known as the fire-keeper's stone, radiated cosy warmth for an extremely long time, and was central to Veil's Eve as it kept the fires in people's homes burning during the vigil. The mineral was a symbol of resilience in the kingdom and used for various things other than just warmth; the ink of Cahra's Guild tattoo, for one. Her thumb found the flame behind the hammer on her wrist, the red dotted with crushed tenebrite.

As they neared the end of the marketplace, Terryl whisked Cahra to one side and pressed her sidelong to his shoulder, their heads together. She swallowed, waiting for a gaggle of washerwomen to pass.

'We are close,' Terryl said. 'This is where it becomes perilous.'

Like it hadn't been already, she thought, holding back a snort.

Terryl continued, 'Two carriages await. One plain, the other – mine – adorned with blue. I must board it as if nothing is the matter.' Cahra tried to ignore the warmth of Terryl's breath on her neck as he surveilled the road. 'The goods wagon coupled to my carriage is your goal – enter via the rear doors, keep moving and you'll come to a false back with space to hide where the wagon and carriage meet. Once you are inside, you will be safe.'

Despite the danger, Cahra raised a brow. 'Do this often, do you?'

Terryl chuckled in response. 'There are many things that you do not know about me.' He grew serious. 'We have but a few streets left.' He turned from the women that had passed, pausing to look at her. 'That boy could have turned us in, you know.'

Cahra shook her head. 'He won't.'

'How do you know?'

She met his gaze. 'I just do.'

Terryl's eyes searched hers, the young lord nodding eventually. 'All right. I trust you.' Something in the way he said it stirred a soothing warmth in her.

They resumed their previous ruse, trying to look as unlike themselves as possible. Terryl laughed, as if Cahra had just said something incredibly funny, before murmuring to her, 'The next street.' He drew her to a farmer's horse-drawn cart stacked with bales of hay, a few shops from what was clearly Terryl's carriage. Evidently, his favourite colour really was blue, large swirls and tinier flourishes skittering over the cab's polished hardwood. *High-borns.*

Cahra's eyes darted from Terryl to the simple goods wagon, wondering if the lack of decoration was deliberate and a ploy to draw attention from the wagon to the stylish carriage. The goods wagon looked like a big wooden box, with doors at the rear that faced the frontage of a shut shop, and it was right out in the open. Cahra peered up at the surrounding buildings, eyeing the narrow gaps between the shop and those nestled on either side of it. Maybe there was a less direct, less obvious approach.

Turning back, a slow smile spread across her face. 'I've got an idea.'

'I shall stay here, until I am certain that you are safe,' Terryl told her.

Cahra shook her head, gaze flashing to the wagon. 'No, I need those doors open. Could you pretend to inspect your cargo?'

Understanding shone in Terryl's eyes. He nodded, leaving to step onto the busy street. A twist of her head and she watched the lord signal to Queran, then approach his carriage. The second, plainer coach, hitched to a wagon of its own, stood dutifully alongside the first with a handful of saddled horses, shifting as they awaited their riders.

With Terryl in play, Cahra focused her attention on the problem of the goods wagon. The scarf she'd stolen covered most of her face, so she comfortably slipped between the two buildings closest to the wagon, where the light was weakest, and began her gruelling ascent.

It was a delicate balance of agility and strength, and she paused to catch her breath, hovering ten feet off the ground as she waited for a break in the crowd. Counting the seconds, Cahra inhaled. It was now or not at all.

From her spot between buildings, the toes of each boot digging into a different wall, Cahra shimmied from her vertical split and leapt for the beams under the shop's awning, clinging tightly to its wooden frame. Then she crept rung by rung along the roof's underside. Looking down, she spotted Terryl, circling his goods wagon and scanning the street for her. She smiled, knowing he'd never think to look up. No one ever did.

The wagon doors were open. Hanging directly above them, she breathed deeply and released her grip, dropping between the doors, hands catching the lip of the roof to swing herself inside and out of view.

It was dark in Terryl's wagon, but somehow Cahra managed to sneak between the overflowing baskets and boxes of goods to the enclosure's end. In the rush of their escape, Terryl hadn't told her anything about how to get inside the wagon's secret compartment. Now, engulfed in darkness, she had to figure it out herself. She ran her hands across the wooden surface, feeling left and right for a smooth hollow, a loose board, a hidden handle, anything to suggest an access point. Sighing, she finally leaned against the wagon's wall. Wood clicked and sprang, pressing back against her shoulder blade and she gratefully leapt to pry free a narrow panel – a door in front of her – and slipped inside.

Silently shutting the door behind her, Cahra waited for her eyes to adjust to the dark, then looked around. The compartment was lighter than the rest of the wagon, with daylight cracking in places above her head. She could just make out the outline of a seat affixed to the wagon's end like a bookcase with one low shelf in the small, oblong room. She quickly sat, rapping her hand against the wall and listening. The cracks in the wood aided her hearing, and she caught what sounded like Raiden's voice, before doors banging and horses' hooves. With a jolt, the wagon began moving. The hardest part was over.

But deep down, she knew it wasn't.

It was the beginning of a fight Cahra couldn't afford to lose.

CHAPTER 8

Cahra perched inside Terryl's cramped wagon, her back straight against the aged hardwood.

She tried to chase away the quiet and ease her racing mind, counting each inhale and exhale of musty air. Cahra couldn't see much in the dimness of the hidden compartment, but listening for trouble was second nature to her, the grating creak of the wagon's wheels the only sound. Unfortunately, the noise just intensified the familiar unease tightening inside her.

She didn't know how Terryl's people were going to get through Kolyath's gatehouse, she realised. The realmwide war made every kingdom, including hers, a stronghold against spies and insurgents, so breaching its security should be impossible. And yet here she was, drawing ever-shallower breaths in the secret compartment of some high-born's wagon of wares, a man she'd met three times, trying to flee the only home she'd ever known and its evil ruler. All because she'd unwittingly set a few gems into some kind of ancient sigil.

How had she done it? Cahra sighed, folding her arms. The whole thing made no sense. She was a low-born, she knew so little of the prophecy or the omens that foretold the rise of Hael'stromia. She hadn't even known what those omens were. Which was exactly the point – she didn't know anything! Now things were so crazed she was running from the Steward, a feat she'd never in her wildest dreams considered, let alone attempted.

If Terryl's carriages even made it to the kingdom's gate.

Doing her best to calm down, she tried to inhale the illusion of security the little compartment gave her, stashed away inside. But Cahra was in more trouble than ever before, and she had no idea what came next for her whether Terryl's people escaped Kolyath or not. What if by some miracle, she really did break free?

Then what?

She'd be surviving day to day, moment to moment, always on the lookout for someone ready to stab her in the back. Her old life as a beggar, all over again.

Cahra peeled the damp strands of hair from the nape of her neck, fanning her face with both hands as she sat and waited in the dark. She felt too hot, and sweat-slick from running, though she should have been cooling down by now. Pulling at her itching collar, she stripped her shirt and coat off down to her smithing vest, then leaned forward and pressed her clammy palms against the holed knees of her trousers.

She felt strange again, like she had outside the tavern. Like she had when she'd awoken this morning. Only, it was worse.

Cahra swallowed, her tongue odd, prickly in her mouth. The wagon's compartment loomed before her, small and dark. A wooden cell she couldn't escape. Her vision skewed, the sweat from her brow painting hot slashes, and she threw her hands out to the wagon's sides. Gulping stale air, she squeezed her eyes shut, and from behind her eyelids, white dots danced as she battled to get breath into her lungs, her old self's instinct to hold her breath and hide barrelling through her. Cahra clenched her teeth, biting down on a strangled sob that clawed its way from the back of her throat. She would not give herself away.

Her eyes snapped open, spying splinters of light seeping in near the ceiling, and she stared and stared at those cracks, willing the rays to fill her vision and ease the dizziness, the high-pitched ringing invading her ears, her mind.

Breathe. Don't think about the dungeons. Think about gems. The survivor's voice inside her head appeared at last. Kolyath's gate wouldn't be far now.

But it wasn't working. She shook her head in frustration, dropping her hands to the bench, gripping it. No matter how she tried to wrench control of her anxiety, it wasn't enough. Cahra slid from the seat to the ground, curling into a ball.

She grimaced, hugging her knees as she lay on the floor of Terryl's darkened wagon, bile pooling in her stomach and inching up her windpipe. The panic was dragging her under, drowning her, and all she could do was ride the ebb and flow of weakness that wracked her, trapped in this coffin. The dots of light circled like wolves in her periphery.

Then she froze, her vision whirling, nausea crashing, as the dots behind her eyelids… vanished. The specks swaying in her vision had faded, into what? Squinting in the haze, the air now stagnant, she hacked a cough into her clenched fists.

The rusty tang of blood spilled from her mouth into her hand.

Cahra sat up as her eyes made out a tall crack of vertical white light, large as a spire. She leaned her arms back, palms to the floor, and recoiled at the sting of freezing stone. Yelping and leaping to her feet, she braced herself against the impending wave of dizziness, but none came.

Frowning and peering again at the feeble light source, Cahra realised – they were doors, climbing like zealous ivy to reach a ceiling she couldn't see. How tall was this room, that ceiling?

Wait. Where *was* she?

Staring into the darkness enveloping her, it felt immense, a senseless void of space. She backed away, stumbling, spinning when her boots hit something that skittered with a hollow thud behind her. She angled her face towards the floor…

A skull. She'd kicked a skull. And beyond it, bones, bones everywhere, littering the ground in monstrous, mountainous piles. She turned back to those unfathomable doors, and then it was there, stealing into her nostrils and stabbing her with its scent. The sickly odour of molten ore, and scorching meat, and coals so hot they glowed bright white—

Just like in her dreams. Of *burning*.

She had no breath left to gasp. The pressure in her chest, the sickness in her gut; it was like her every nerve was on fire, and all were spearing for her heart.

In the darkness, twin flames ignited, bathing her vicinity in a sea of blood-red fire.

Cahra opened her mouth to scream – and her eyes flew wide open. Instinct kicked in and she clamped her mouth shut with both hands before making a sound. She was bolt upright in Terryl's goods wagon, safely stowed, its wheels creaking to a halt.

Slumped against a wall, Cahra peered at where she knew Terryl's coach sat latched to her wagon's end, heart pounding with every moment. And thought:

What in Hael was THAT?!

But before she could brood on her hallucination, it hit her. The wagon had stopped. They must be at the kingdom's gatehouse. Cahra turned an ear towards a crack in the ceiling and a newly familiar voice, now dripping with high-born affectation. *Raiden?*

'My good sir, Lord Theudoric is travelling to the far reaches of the Wilds, in order to inspect his north-eastern operations. He shall return with spoils for our esteemed Steward.' She couldn't make out the response, but the disdain hedging Raiden's next words was clear. 'Sir, as you should know, and you plainly do not, my lord's reserves fund Kolyath's armoury. Shall we call for the Steward, so you can explain why you are delaying his express wishes?' He was definitely sneering. 'Then I suggest that you not waste any more time.'

Gutsy move. Also, Terryl had a fake name? And a fake story too, Cahra hoped. Because if the lord was arming the Steward in the war...

She shuddered, praying she wasn't hiding in another tyrant's wagon. She knew so little about Terryl, but her desperation had left her with no options but to trust him, balancing that fear against their new alliance.

Cahra pulled back and spied a hole in the wagon's side large enough to see through. Proceeding with caution, she pressed her eye to the peephole.

Her vision was consumed by one of the round grey towers of the gatehouse and the Kolyath guards and soldiers on watch in its shadow, thoroughly unfazed by Raiden and his haughtiness. An official gripping paperwork looked more ruffled. Cahra knew the arch of the gatehouse loomed above them, and the archers' battlements above that. She swallowed, stealing a step backwards. Being wartime, the Steward had decreed all passage to and from the kingdom required his court's executive approval, but Terryl had been adamant his people could deliver them to safety. Would it work?

The horses jerked into a slow walk.

Cahra held her breath as she peered into the peephole again. There, standing stark against the daylight, was the dark gate of Kolyath – the kingdom's infamous 'gate to Hael'.

She stared at the metal, transfixed. The gate was thirty feet tall, the matte black metal of its Haellium bars thick as stonemasons' arms, each bar edged with barbs and topped with lances. She'd never seen the gate this close-up before. Apparently, Hael'stromia had three: one entrance for Kolyath, Luminaux and Ozumbre, the kingdoms that hated each other so much they'd gone to war over the capital itself.

The wagon was moving through Kolyath's gate now.

Cahra kept a wise distance from the peephole, but she couldn't resist a peek beyond the kingdom's gate. What she saw were lush, straw-coloured hills of sweeping grasses, met by winding trunks and dense green foliage where Kolyath ended and the Wilds seemed to begin, shadows gathering at its edges.

A slender trunk with serrated leaves caught her attention and she fixated on the tree, the realisation sneaking up on her. A horse chestnut, the emblem of her blacksmith's trade. She'd always loved the complexity of it, with its short base but bright, broad branches that utterly refused to accept it was a smaller tree, making its foliage conspicuously top-heavy. Thick and strong, she supposed. Like a blacksmith.

A hard lump rose in her throat as she thought of Lumsden and the smithy. How could she have just left him and her home, and all that she was, behind?

Blinking back tears she refused to let fall, Cahra kept watch at the tiny peephole as Kolyath slipped from view and, with it, everything she'd ever known. Her heart burned with the guilt of abandoning Lumsden and fear surrounding her next steps.

No home, no way to make coin, no prospects. Seers, what am I going to do now?

Her past was in Kolyath, her future out here somewhere. Meanwhile, she was caged in the now with nothing but her thoughts and feelings for company.

The way she felt about herself, she didn't want either of them.

The time-worn wheels of the wagon rocked as Terryl's carriage pulled it along. *Thud*. A bump, then another, bigger this time. The wagon jolted, flinging Cahra to one side, her head cracking against the low wooden ceiling. She instantly sat, a dull pain spreading at the top of her skull, and threw her hands out to steady herself. A loud thwack sounded that didn't come from the wheels rolling beneath her.

She glanced nervously towards the peephole, confusion swirling with her thoughts – as an arrow buried itself above the tiny hole.

Cahra leapt back, gaping at the razor-sharp head. Had she been looking into that peephole, she'd now be the proud owner of an arrow to the brain. Shouting was coming from behind her, where Terryl's carriage connected to the wagon, and she strained to snatch any words but the speakers were too muffled. She knew she'd be safest with her back to Terryl if archers were firing from the walls, but a few scant panels separated her from them and it fed her panic as the wagon raced with the gait of Terryl's horses.

He was making a break for the Wilds.

More and more arrows came raining down. With each bone-rattling impact, Cahra gripped anything stable as she slouched, ducking to keep her head clear of the wagon's roof. Arrowheads burst through its wood with cacophonous cracks, lashing like the whips of the guards in Kolyath's Red Square. She shook the thought away and focused on her enclosure, sighting six arrows in the hidden compartment alone, never mind the rest of Terryl's wagon. Cahra lowered herself to the ground and wedged her body under the seat, knees whacking the floor as the coach and its cargo thundered urgently along.

With the war raging, would Kolyath dare follow them into the Wilds?

Gurgling cries pierced the air. She knew the sound of awful, human death throes. More cracks; wood splintering. Cahra's heart railed against her ribs. Was Terryl's carriage faring under the attack? Her stomach turned at what it might mean for their escape.

Listening intently, she found herself closing her eyes, concentrating even harder to hear, to sense. The thuds of arrows were slowing, Cahra noting the terrain was getting less rocky beneath the wagon's thin wheels. When she hadn't heard the sound of an arrow hitting its mark for a full few minutes, she stood gingerly, pausing near the peephole.

Another ten seconds, and it was like something swallowed up the light.

She felt the horses pulling Terryl's transport slow to their previous walk. The ground seemed even again. Cahra dared to place her eye upon the peephole.

Outside, it was as dark as twilight, the Wilds' majestic trees blocking the sun's rays, though she could see fleeting specks of blue as she angled her gaze to the foliage's ceiling. Yet shadows clung to every dark leaf, an unfathomably heavy air in the earthy-scented woodlands. Nature whispered between towering trunks, and she could almost feel it beckoning to her, this wild place untouched by ugly, selfish kingdoms. A place where maybe even she could survive.

Cahra continued gazing out the peephole until, finally, the wagon's wheels stopped. The carriage doors slammed, and she threw on her shirt and coat, hurrying through the false panel to the wagon's exit, anxious to learn her fate.

Had they made it? Were they safe?

The sparkle in Terryl's blue goldstone eyes and the bright smile on his face reassured her as he opened the wagon's double doors, and with a deep breath, she took her first step into a free but unknown future.

'Welcome to the Wilds, Cahra.'

CHAPTER 9

Leaping from Terryl's goods wagon, Cahra's well-worn boots hit the ground with a jolt. She winced as pain erupted along her aching soles. It had been years since she'd bolted through Kolyath's streets like that, let alone in her battered smith's boots. Her feet would hurt for the rest of the day now, maybe longer. But it was a small fee to pay for freedom, she told herself, even if it hurt like Hael. She toed a few steps forward, gingerly, then shouldered her satchel.

Then she froze, her eyes meeting something even more shocking than escaping the Steward of Kolyath: men and women vanishing into the trees in droves, their weapons lowered, faces hidden and as mysterious as the land itself. Some stopped to talk to Raiden as he shared out thanks in the form of Terryl's goods, and Cahra's mouth fell wide open. The Wildspeople, who notoriously cared as little for the realm's three kingdoms as the kingdoms did for them, had defended Terryl and his people? Why?

Before she could unravel the idea, Terryl broke in. 'We made it,' the lord breathed, gazing at the greenwood grove. He peered at her with concern. 'Are you injured?'

Cahra shook her head, not wanting him to fuss. Instead, she drank in the raw, dark beauty of the Wilds, thick with shadow and the inexplicable hush of night. The sun's rays seemed unable to penetrate the abundant canopy, yet greenery ran riot across vast swathes of the forest floor. It wasn't grass but bracken, net-like vines and a furry array of mosses, which blanketed fallen branches and climbed the trunks of ancient elms that reached as if with arms to touch the sky. Cahra bent down, the moss damp and velvety beneath her fingertips, and something loosened just a little in her chest.

Terryl watched her, curiosity lighting his fine features.

'Where are we?' She inhaled, the fresh air sweet and lovely in her lungs.

'A safe place to rest, for a time,' he said softly.

Cahra straightened, stifling a yawn and leaning back against the wagon's sturdy wood. The surge of energy from sprinting through Kolyath was dwindling fast.

'They found us out,' she mused aloud, eyes flickering to Terryl. 'After the gate, I mean.'

'It was always a possibility at the gatehouse, but it does not matter, now.' He smiled. 'We are under the cover of the Wilds.'

'And no one's following?' She suppressed a shudder at the thought of the Steward's guards, or the soldiers of his army, rounding a copse of trees and discovering them. Terryl's own guards were noticeably absent.

'Not that we can ascertain.' Terryl glanced to Raiden, who was inspecting the arrows sticking out from the lord's carriage and the wagon hitched to it, the one Cahra had been hiding in. She spotted the second coach and wagon, along with the horses belonging to Terryl's guards and wondered who else made up this travelling caravan – but was quickly distracted by the sound of Raiden unsheathing a blade from his belt to sever the offending arrows with gusto.

'Fear not,' Terryl said, following her eyeline. 'Kolyath would be crazed to follow us. They have a kingdom to defend.' He gave her a wry look, then gestured to the Wildspeople.

The tightness in her chest loosened even further, and she stretched.

'So now what?' They'd never talked about what came after the escape, as there hadn't been time. And while Terryl had kept his word and gotten her out of Kolyath, well, she didn't like surprises.

'First,' he said, 'Raiden's people will examine the carriages and conduct any repairs. After which, I should like for you to join me. You and I have much to discuss.'

An invitation to a lord's personal carriage. If they weren't under the threat of capture, would she be flattered? She nodded, suddenly very interested in her boots.

When she looked up, Raiden was watching her. Watching them both.

She knew the look on the man's face. It was a staple in her own arsenal.

Raiden doesn't trust me.

Terryl excused himself to speak to the man then, so Cahra made straight for the trees. Who knew how long they'd be travelling, and in the wake of madcap running, the usual sensations were at play: hunger, exhaustion and the increasingly urgent need to relieve herself. But before she'd taken two steps into the trees, one of Raiden's men blocked her path.

'Nature is calling,' she said. The guard didn't budge. Bristling, she added, 'Lord Terryl invited me to his coach. I guess you'll be explaining why I was made to soil his seat, then?'

The harshness to his face persisted, but he grudgingly stepped aside.

Cahra stalked off, shaking her head in disbelief. She might be free of Kolyath's grip, but had she swapped one dungeon for another?

Am I their prisoner?

Raiden's fake name and the story about Terryl flashed into her mind. They couldn't possibly be working for the Steward, not after all this...

Trying to ignore her worry, she wandered into the woods. She'd appeal to reason, to Terryl himself. It was all she could do. Because while she was free of the Hael that was her kingdom, as she squatted in the dark forest, reality hit her like a wintry gale.

She was completely alone. No Lumsden, just her, a speck in the sunless expanse of the realm's unbroken Wilds. The enormity of her situation sank into her.

Alone.

Cahra could feel her shoulders shaking, and she braced her fists either side of her on the ground. *No*. However frightened she might feel now, she'd faced worse before and lived. She had to believe she'd face whatever came next. As long as she kept moving.

Inhaling slowly, Cahra rose and returned to the caravan, eyes open. Should things take a turn and force her to run again, even from Terryl, or more to the point, Raiden...

...she'd be ready.

The young lord approached, his usual polish restored: fresh trousers, and a shirt and tailed coat that rested trimly on his shoulders. Cahra knew how she must look and smell after making their escape. She pulled her coat tight and smoothed her hair self-consciously.

'Shall we?' Terryl asked her.

She nodded. The lord's people had cleaved the arrows from his coach and wagons, the swirling blue paintwork still gleaming in the low light of the Wilds. She climbed into the coach to sit facing the goods wagon she'd stowed away in, still attached at the rear. Terryl sat facing the front, across from her, and smiled.

She looked at him, and a flicker of hope sparked within her, that things might be okay.

Then Raiden entered, sitting down next to Terryl.

Cahra glanced at Raiden as outside, Terryl's carriage driver urged the horses forward and they restarted their journey. She was beginning to think the hard look to Raiden's face was, well, just his face.

Meanwhile, Raiden set the longsword she'd forged for Terryl across his knees, the glittering pommel angled at her accusingly. *At least it's not the tip of the blade.*

Raiden eyed her coolly, and she thought back to her earlier question…

Now what?

Sighing, Cahra had a feeling she knew.

-

Despite the overt luxury of Lord Terryl's coach, Cahra felt anything but comfortable. The seat's plush fabric caressed her palms, downy as fleece, and the plump cushions at her back were trimmed with gold stitching, buttons and the finest lace she'd ever seen. But there was no comfort in the face of Raiden's gaze, his grey eyes of iron, keen as a fighter's blade. Luckily, Cahra knew how to make iron yield.

Raiden spoke first. 'Tell us about the sword.'

Here we go. She resisted the urge to sigh. 'What do you want to know?'

'Who instructed the creation of this sigil?' Raiden stabbed his finger at the sword's pommel.

'No one.' She glanced at Terryl. 'As I told Terryl—'

'*Lord* Terryl,' corrected Raiden, flashing teeth.

'Raiden,' Terryl said gently.

Cahra exhaled outright this time, managing not to roll her eyes. 'As I told Lord Terryl, I designed it. Every weapon is simple geometry, so I drew a pattern for the pommel's insert.' She gestured to the longsword's handle.

'You're telling us that no one told you how to create this sigil?' Raiden scoffed at her.

She supposed it did seem unlikely.

'Well, unfortunately, it's the truth. I wish I had some kind of explanation, but I don't. I'm sure you know, but Lord Terryl proposed the commission to me as a "blank canvas". He knew nothing of the longsword's design. It's why I warned him when I saw him in the street.' The unfamiliar urge to help a high-born still confused her. Cahra's eyes glided to Terryl.

Why *had* she warned him?

Raiden went on. 'And nothing else out of the ordinary happened?'

'No,' she said, rubbing her face as she realised everything had only happened today, and the day wasn't even done yet. She raked her fingers through her hair and took a breath, recounting her morning. 'I went to get bread. The sword was on display behind the counter, waiting to be collected. I came back and saw Commander Jarett interrogating Lumsden, so I snuck into the smithy to find out why. Then I learned about the Sigil of the Seers, and the Commander knowing I'd forged the sword. Lumsden sent him north so I could run south with Lord Terryl's longsword. That's when I found you.' She nodded at Terryl. 'Thankfully, before the Kingdom Guards did.'

Even now, just the thought of him being captured by the guards sent her pulse tearing along inside her. Seers, she thought, had she saved the lord's life? Surely, that had to count for something…

Raiden's next words were less harsh. 'What else do you know?'

'Only what Lumsden told me. That the Commander said it was the first time the sigil had been seen outside the castle in centuries.' At Lumsden's name, a guilt-ridden pang hit her in the depths of her chest. 'That, and something about the prophecy.'

Cahra never wished to the Seers like others did. But for Lumsden, she prayed that he was safe, that he'd done what she'd told him to and renounced his ties to her. And that Jarett and his guards had bought every single word.

'What, exactly?' Terryl leaned forward.

'That this was the prophecy's first omen.'

'And what do you know of the prophecy?' Raiden crossed his arms.

Cahra scoffed. 'Apart from Jarett thinking the longsword is related to it? Not much. Before today, the same folk stories as everybody else.' She counted them off on her hands. 'Hael'stromia fell centuries ago. The ultimate weapon, the sword or whatever it is, is housed within the capital's walls. Kolyath supposedly keeps getting closer to beating Luminaux and Ozumbre at getting Hael'stromia's weapon every year. And these omens, that no one has ever seen, mind you, will announce the capital's rebirth.'

Before today, she hadn't known what the omens were. And she hadn't cared. In fact, she still didn't. The loss of Lumsden, the smithy – her life, as depressing as it had been – the loss of all she'd known, was like a dead weight driving her, crushing her into the ground. What would she do now? Where would she go?

Raiden looked her right in the eye. 'That no one has seen outside Kolyath's keep, until today.'

She shook her head, turning to Terryl. The lord was quiet. 'You can never go back to Kolyath now, can you?' she asked him softly.

Cahra had worried running would make her look guilty, but Lumsden had been right. If she'd stayed, there was no telling what the Steward would have done, and no hope of the old man saving her this time.

Maybe no hope of living through the night. She swallowed.

But she hadn't thought of what running would do to Terryl. How guilty he'd look too.

'No,' Terryl conceded. 'I think not.'

She slumped in her seat. The whole thing was twisted, some kind of mad coincidence. But her fault or not, she was responsible for Terryl losing his home. 'I'm sorry.'

'It is for the best.' Terryl smiled. How was he always smiling? 'Truthfully, Cahra, there are things that I would like you to know, about me.' Terryl went on, as Raiden blanched. 'For example, I have multiple homes. Kolyath… Well, there are other options.'

Cahra fell silent. 'Oh.' But his tentative honesty thawed her enough to say, 'Like?'

Raiden interjected before Terryl could reply. 'One final question. Did the Commander mention the name "Thierre" to Lumsden?'

'No. Who?' Cahra asked, puzzled, noting the look that exchanged between the two men, as she pretended to study the sword again while saying the name over and over in her head. *Thierre.* If it was important to them, then she'd better remember it.

Meanwhile, Terryl was staring at the sword. He lifted his palms in silent request, Raiden handing it to him. The lord inspected the pommel then the blade, its steely surface etched with a metallic paint of cobalt blue. The pommel's blue goldstone reflected in his eyes as Terryl raised them to her.

'It really is a work of art, Cahra.'

After what she'd been through getting to him and getting the sword out of harm's way, she almost cried.

'Thank you,' she told him, then swallowed, his brief pleasantry giving her the confidence she needed to finally ask, 'Where are we going?'

Terryl's reply was swift. 'To Luminaux.'

'What?' Cahra recoiled. Luminaux was an enemy of Kolyath. The thought of her arrest on arrival didn't exactly appeal. 'Seers, why?'

Terryl stared out the window, the piney conifers giving way to old, unyielding oaks, before returning her gaze. 'It is my homeland.'

She studied him: his eye contact, his tone, all the way to how he arranged his limbs as he spoke the words to her. It was the truth. And suddenly, it all made sense. Why he wasn't like other high-borns in Kolyath, and how being a merchant lord factored in.

Cahra hummed. 'You weren't joking when you said you had other options.'

'Kolyath is one kingdom that I have resided in. Luminaux is my home.'

Cahra weighed Terryl's words, saving the unexpected sting of being misled for later. 'So you're not arming the Steward in the war, like Raiden said at Kolyath's gate?'

'Certainly not,' Terryl said, laughing. Raiden snorted.

Cahra pressed on. 'And what about me? Am I your prisoner?'

Terryl looked horrified. 'Absolutely not! While I wish to return home, your safety is still my concern. Further, I should like to request something of you: an audience with my kingdom's King and Queen. They must hear of your story, and of Kolyath more generally.'

She considered. 'And then?'

Terryl spread his hands. 'That is yours to decide. You will have permission to remain in Luminaux, should you wish it. However, if you desire otherwise, you shall be free to go.'

Another honest answer. Cahra rolled her shoulders and leaned back, exhaustion from the day's ordeal taking hold. It was clear Terryl seemed to need her, at least for the time being.

'Fine. But if I'm no prisoner, and assumedly under protection until we get to Luminaux, someone needs to tell your people.' She glared at Raiden.

'Of course,' Terryl replied, Raiden's eyes burning in indignation.

With a smug smile, Cahra asked, 'Any more questions?'

'No. For now,' Raiden added, shooting Terryl a look.

She nodded, her eyelids sagging with drowsiness that crashed in great waves. The downy gold pillow curved at her back, the coach's rocking to the horses' rhythmic hooves – everything served to soothe her aching body. She tuned out Terryl and Raiden's talk of those travelling with them, unable to hide a yawn.

Then Cahra slept. For a while, at least, her body pushing to permit her a short period of actual rest. Eventually, all was quiet.

But so cold, an unshakeable chill descending…

CHAPTER 10

Terryl found himself watching Cahra sleep, her earthy hazel eyes, usually so vibrant, now shuttered and slumbering peacefully. She had wedged her body into the seat's far corner, as if seeking safety even now in his private carriage. It was a glimpse of vulnerability that he had not yet seen from her, and it stirred an intense protectiveness in him.

Terryl stared outside at the thick, gnarled trunks and aerial roots of the ancient Wilds. The blackened cavity of a hollow tree seemed to gaze right back at him. Yet they had escaped, his disguise had worked and their mission, though precarious, was intact. Now, all they had to do was reach the safety of Luminaux's lands.

Exhaling, Terryl recalled his first uncertain steps into Cahra's kingdom of Kolyath. After Luminaux, things were so different: the snow-laced chill of the craggy coastline; the gloomy grey-green vegetation with its feral petals splayed in burnt yellows and oranges; the sombre palette of black, grey and mottled brown birds and their dreadful, bleating cries. All had been a portent of things to come.

Raiden, seemingly satisfied that Cahra was actually dozing and not privy to their conversation, leaned back. 'What do you make of her story?'

'I believe that she is telling the truth, insofar as she knows,' Terryl replied softly.

Raiden frowned. 'Which is less than I imagined.'

'We knew that Steward Atriposte shared precious little with those of Cahra's social class. Information is power in Kolyath.' Terryl couldn't keep the disdain from edging his voice, again thankful for the benign workings of his own kingdom. 'We were fortunate to learn what we could from Atriposte's court, while we were able.'

'Before they outed us as foreign spies, tortured us and hanged us in the Red Square, you mean?' Raiden jerked his head at Cahra's sleeping form, scowl deepening. 'She nearly cost us everything. Including your life.'

'She also saved it,' Terryl reminded Raiden quietly. The sharp edge to Raiden's voice, his clenched jaw, the brief, uneasy glances – Raiden might mask his consternation as anger, but Terryl knew fear when he saw it, especially when it pertained to him. Raiden felt it keenly, not only as the Captain of Terryl's detail, but also as his oldest friend. 'Besides, our time in Kolyath was always temporary,' Terryl went on. 'At long last, we may go home and I, for one, am delighted. It has been too long.'

Raiden didn't miss a beat. 'So long,' he said, 'that Tyne's latest correspondence was a raft of reports, which you'll be expected to have memorised.'

Terryl groaned as his Captain reached for the stack of documents beside their napping guest. He was still contemplating Cahra, who was making tiny snuffles as she snored.

'What if she truly is the bearer of the prophecy, and of the first omen?' Her hair was tousled, serving as a pillow beneath her rosy cheek. Terryl sat, curious as to how this young woman, so different from anyone he had ever met, fit into the Oracles' designs.

Raiden exhaled, glancing at the girl. 'If she is, it's one Hael of a feat. Who would have guessed a humble blacksmith from Kolyath?'

'Who, indeed,' Terryl murmured, as Raiden handed him the first document.

–

Terryl leaned back in his seat, twiddling a silver quill between his fingers, trying to focus. There was much news from Luminaux and Commander Tyne's accounts were brief, which typically meant that things were worse than the man let on. Terryl had also spotted a letter from his sister in the sundry papers and he yearned to tear it open for Sylvie's candid account. However, Raiden had made him promise to finish the Commander's reports before Terryl partook in anything else, knowing that he would be expected to be up-to-the-moment on everything concerning the kingdom. Even if he had not set foot in it in years.

It was two years, to be exact, since Terryl and Raiden had arrived in Kolyath following a series of painstaking negotiations with Steward Atriposte's court. Admittance from outside the kingdom was not entirely banned, as the Steward led his subjects to believe, simply scrutinised given the ongoing war. Yet Terryl's diplomacy and lucrative offerings from his northern mining operations piqued the interest of the Steward's court advisors, and over time such calculated overtures led them to permit him entry for a meeting. When things went smoothly, it was not long before Terryl received an official request to supply Kolyath with materials. And so, his people's subterfuge began.

A tiny shaft of daylight flickered through the window then, catching Cahra's hair and lighting its strawberry blonde with auburn fire. Terryl studied her, a welcome distraction, surprised to note the soft curves of her face in lieu of her waking vigilance.

He smiled, the thought of Cahra free gladdening him. At least her trade had skimmed good coin from Steward Atriposte's foul nobility. Her profession, her artistry with weapons, was a defiance in itself, and the thought moved him as he glanced from her to the exceptional longsword that she had bestowed upon him. How had such a talent bloomed in as wretched a kingdom as Kolyath? The question had him flummoxed. But then, the most genuine souls he encountered in the castle city had dwelled far from Atriposte's mercurial court. Among them, Cahra held a unique place. He found himself ruminating on that. On her.

Such thoughts swiftly prised the tightness from his chest.

Terryl blew out a breath, shuffling his papers, and tried to focus as he retrieved the next report. According to Commander Tyne, the kingdom of Ozumbre had been testing Luminaux's defences, poking and prodding and gauging reactions, unquestionably sending intelligence back to Ozumbre's King Decimus. Meanwhile, Luminaux had prospered, but morale was always a fine line in wartime. And his father and sister had endured another colossal clash of egos, this time not about marriage suitors, but Sylvie's abject refusal to entertain their parents' matchmaking at all, citing it an 'idiotic distraction' from her duties as General of Luminaux's Royal Army and Commander Tyne's deputy in charge. Terryl could practically hear Tyne grumbling about being dragged into another family quarrel as he finished reading the Commander's update.

Terryl pinched the bridge of his nose. 'Honestly,' he muttered, tossing Tyne's latest communication to Raiden.

His Captain just chuckled, casting his eyes across it. 'Welcome home.'

Yet Terryl knew he would not be the only one subject to a scene upon arrival in his native kingdom. Raiden was undoubtedly going to have a punishing time explaining what had transpired today to Commander Tyne. But if Terryl thought that Raiden was overprotective, the Oracles help them once his father got wind of their exploits.

Terryl ploughed his way through the rest of Tyne's reports, knowing that the faster he digested the information, the faster he would get to Sylvie's letter. Handing Raiden the last of the documents, Terryl's fingers clasped the envelope, his sister's swirling script a comfort given his distance from home still. Raiden handed Terryl a dagger to open it.

As Terryl's fingers grazed the edge of the envelope, a sudden motion caught his eye. Cahra, still fast asleep, had started twitching.

CHAPTER 11

No, no, no, not again!

Cahra was back, in that place, with the blackness and its chink of light, and the biting stone beneath her fingertips, icy raw, and that *smell*, that reminded her of the tannery in Kolyath, with its acrid reek of curing skin—

She crammed her eyes shut and forced one ravaged breath after another. She was here, in the echoing emptiness of this room that confined her with the terror seeping into her soul at being trapped in the dark forever. Then she remembered the bone piles, trembling. This was no room, or vault, or even dungeon.

It was a tomb.

And she was not alone. Cahra was on her feet now, her muscles tensed to fight, to run, but unlike when fleeing the Steward and Kolyath, there was no escape. She stood, listening but hearing nothing at all. Yet she sensed silent feet padding towards her. Something was coming.

The whisker of light between the doors may as well have been a horizon away in the pitch distance, offering no answers as she begged her eyes to adjust to the dark. She assumed it to be a torch's flame, and she searched for another, only to glimpse the harrowing bones. Her breath snagged in her chest as Cahra really noticed for the first time how dank, how stale, how positively *ancient* everything felt here.

Then she saw it. A silhouette. She could just make out its tattered garments, swaying as it advanced upon her step by step. Like a cat, with grace, intention, an animal's gait. Only with the height, the contours of a man. But this was no man, no soldier, no Kolyath guard.

No. This was a predator.

A predator… With fire for eyes.

Fists raised, Cahra leapt back over the dusty, crusty bones that crunched and clattered, and snatched a leg bone from the floor. Those eyes – by the Seers, those *eyes* – they were *burning*! And she was going to die here, in this Hael-forsaken place—

The flaming eyes narrowed, followed by a gleaming flash of white teeth, and fangs, fangs like a beast too. Was the creature smiling?

It opened its mouth, licking its lower lip before uttering in a low, unearthly voice like the crackle of crashing thunder and lightning combined: '*Scion…*'

Cahra felt the urge to shriek then, but she shoved the impulse down, down into the ball of her back foot – then pitched herself forward and into the path of the creature, wielding the bone and swinging it like a blacksmith's hammer.

The creature shifted so fast it locked her arm in place before she'd taken a full step, and she gasped at how quickly it moved. Not to mention those eyes, like smouldering rubies, the flames pointing downwards like the Sigil of the Seers' inverted triangle, straight to Hael. The creature effortlessly levered the bone from her grasp, hurling it into a pillar beside them, dust flaking from the unseen ceiling as the tomb trembled in reply.

'*I do not wish to harm you, Scion.*'

It was not of this world! Cahra refused to drop her fists. 'What do you want then?' Apparently, not to kill her… Yet. 'And what do you mean, "Scion"? Where in Hael am I, and *what* is going on?'

Curiously, the creature tilted its head at her. Then it froze.

'*They are coming,*' it snarled, its timbre thawing with each sentence, despite the rancour of its words.

'Who's coming?' Cahra spun, eyes flashing around them.

The creature shook its head, vexed, the flash of skin so white and bright she blinked. Then, teeth gnashing, its eyes exploded into black flames as it dissolved into smoke. Cahra raised her arm in defence, the air around her lashing with savage power, as a petrifying shriek, a real-life scream in the actual world, finally awoke her.

It was coming from her mouth.

CHAPTER 12

Cahra's heart-stopping scream halted the coach so fast she saw Terryl go flying forward – Raiden throwing a protective arm out, a dagger instantly in his other hand. Wide awake now, she kicked the blade from Raiden's grasp and gaped. Terryl stared in shock between them.

'What in Hael is wrong with you?' Cahra spat at Raiden.

'You're the one shrieking like a wraith,' Raiden snapped back, throwing open a door and leaping from the coach.

Cahra glowered, watching from the window as the man circled the travelling caravan, weapons out.

'Forgive him,' Terryl said quietly. 'Raiden is forever concerned with attracting unwanted attention. I, however, am more concerned for your well-being. Are you all right?' Lips pursed, Terryl's savvy gaze swept her.

'Bad dream,' Cahra said, the anger dulling inside her just a little. She squirmed, fidgeting with her coat's hem. The burning place in her dreams stole the air from her lungs, yet it was so familiar. The memory of her panicked turn in Terryl's wagon flooded back and she fought the urge to shiver as she realised she hadn't been asleep to dream of that place.

That *tomb*.

What was happening to her?

'Well, you are awake now,' Terryl stated, his voice soft. 'And it is as you said earlier, you are under my protection. Perhaps they shall set your mind at ease.' He nodded outside.

Cahra's eyes flashed from Terryl to the glass, where she could see Raiden's people finalising their security checks. She grunted, but watched as the man named Queran dropped from the nearest tree, bow slack, shaking his head at Raiden. The black-haired woman fighter from Terryl's mansion emerged from the underbrush with stealthy precision to join them, casually tossing a dagger in one hand. Cahra didn't want to admit it, but Raiden's people did help to calm her. Moments later, however, as he climbed back in and slammed the door, she forgot all about it the second Raiden settled his iron eyes on Cahra.

Face drawn, Raiden fired at her, 'Want to tell me what that was about?'

'No.' Cahra glared back. 'Want to tell me why your blade was pointed at my head?'

Raiden opened his mouth but Terryl silenced them both with a question.

'Report?' The edge to the lord's tone was plain.

Raiden straightened. 'The perimeter is clear,' he replied. The horses hitched, the coach jostling back into motion.

Terryl nodded. 'How long until we stop?'

'Approximately one hour,' Raiden told him, his eyes scanning the trees outside. 'We're approaching the first secure location.'

'Secure location?' Cahra tried not to mimic Raiden, but it was tough.

'A pre-determined spot, known to our group and those we trust,' Terryl explained. 'We have them scattered along this route to offer us places to rest, replenish supplies and regroup if need be. Each has been vetted for security, so as to avoid any potential threats.'

Like Kolyath's army, Cahra thought with a shudder.

Terryl looked pointedly between her and Raiden. 'Now, must I enforce a rule of no sword-play in the carriage?'

'No,' she and Raiden begrudgingly replied, Cahra narrowing her eyes at the man.

'Excellent,' Terryl told them. She watched as he slipped a little cream envelope into his jacket pocket, then squirmed at her nosy urge to ask about it, looking away.

As promised, the coach pulled to a stop an hour or so later. Raiden leapt out again.

'Wait here,' he said, shutting the door.

Cahra peered into the near-endless trees. Were the woodlands so different from when they'd first entered the Wilds? It was hard to tell. Each shadow seemed to twist and morph, playing tricks on her vision, her frayed nerves. The vastness of the land was overwhelming and yet there was a dark and haunting beauty in it, a rugged allure to the verdant shadows that tugged at something deep within her.

Alone with Terryl, her eyes found his. The young lord's smile came effortlessly.

Then a minute later, Raiden banged on the door. 'We're ready for you,' he told Terryl, holding the door open for the lord. Raiden watched Cahra through wary eyes.

She ignored him, hopping from the coach step to the spongy forest floor. The fresh scents of tree sap and damp earth wafted to greet her. 'Refreshments,' Raiden said gruffly, jerking his chin at a table of delicious-looking food and drink to one side of the small clearing.

She nodded. The nausea from her hunger pains was getting harder to shut out, but she cleared her throat as Terryl made to leave, asking, 'Erm, can we talk?'

Terryl turned back, his features soft. 'Of course. First, I must check on my people. There is bread, meat, cheese and fruits to be had. Avail yourself, and I shall be with you.'

He raised an arm to her as he strode away, reminding Cahra of the first day they met. Which reminded her of the smithy. Of Lumsden.

Please, just let the old man be alive.

Cahra swallowed, bracing herself against the thought, and made a beeline for the table. She plucked a pastry with dark blue jam baked into it from a shiny dish, also taking a hunk of bread, a little soft cheese and a big green apple, straying from the others to sit alone on a fallen log. Sighing, she bit into the flaky pastry, jam bursting onto her tongue.

No tasty treats would dull the pain of never seeing Lumsden again.

She hadn't really thought they'd make it out. That she'd escape. But if she'd known... if she'd known, she would've taken Lumsden, the boy Ellian and any and everyone she could, as many as she could fit in that wagon with her.

Instead, she'd left them to their fates. To the Steward and his ruthless Kingdom Guards.

She shut her eyes on the guilt, the revulsion she felt, the tears welling against her will, and focused on the scene before her: Terryl striding from the coach to the table via everybody else, talking and laughing and looking every bit the kindly lord from Luminaux.

Terryl looked after his people. She was a coward who'd left Lumsden behind. Shame flooded her as she thought of the old man stuck in Kolyath.

All of a sudden, she didn't feel so hungry.

Pausing to look for her, Terryl made his way over, seating himself beside Cahra with that languid elegance all high-borns seemed to have. Except Raiden, she thought, eyeing him from across the glade. That man saw the world through shrewd eyes, his actions calculated. Like he lived for a fight. Or maybe for starting one, she thought with a smirk.

Yes, Raiden was an arse, but he was ever-vigilant for danger. It wasn't unlike her, always looking and listening and ready to move. But it was an exhausting way to live.

And now I'm right back here again.

Before her mind could grab hold of that thought and torment her with it, Terryl handed her a cup of water. She marvelled in silence as she took it, the liquid clear as spring dew.

Cahra whispered to him, 'Where did you get this?'

'There is a stream nearby,' Terryl replied. Her expression must have been something, because he chuckled. 'I take it that you have never drunk such water?'

'It's so clear,' she breathed, taking a sip. The water tasted pure, cool and pristine, no dirty sediment or metallic taste.

'Hmm,' Terryl said. 'The well in the Traders' Quadrant was of a lower quality than in the Nobles' own. Perhaps, that is it?'

Cahra looked at him in dismay. 'Why am I not surprised?' she said angrily. 'Seers, how did you stand it? Living there, I mean.'

Terryl looked up, viewing Raiden and his people with admiration. 'I had help.'

'Right,' she said, feeling unexpectedly envious. 'So Raiden is your…'

Terryl's eyes crinkled, fondness in his gaze. 'Raiden is many things,' the lord said. 'My advisor, my confidant. My friend. And he is my second in charge, not to mention an incredibly accomplished swordsman. We trained together, though he outpaced me swiftly. Thanks to your longsword, I may have motivation to catch up.' Something crossed his face, Terryl's good humour slipping ever so slightly. She wondered if it was talk of the longsword, a reminder of the prophecy. Or maybe his home of Luminaux. There was still so much she didn't know about the lord. But there was something she'd figured out.

'Raiden's got quite a command over the caravan.' Cahra paused, guessing the rest. 'He's head of your private guards, isn't he?'

Terryl slid his eyes towards her. 'Correct. He is Captain of the detail of elite guards travelling with us.' He loosened and leaned back, as if not bothered by Cahra knowing, and admiring her powers of deduction instead. 'As you might imagine, entering Kolyath from Luminaux necessitated planning. That included enlisting a few choice professionals.'

She sat back too, taking a bite from her floury hunk of bread. 'And the others?' She spied Queran keeping to the shadows, the red-haired man's bow strung across his back, brown cloak tossed over a rangy shoulder.

'The quiet one over there,' Terryl said, following her gaze, 'is Queran, our top archer. He may appear reserved, but his watchful eye misses nothing. Also, he can split an arrow lodged in a bullseye from over three hundred yards.'

'Has bow, likes heights. Got it,' Cahra said around a mouthful of food, then pointed to the woman she'd seen at Terryl's mansion earlier. 'What about her?'

'That is Siarl,' he told her, nodding at the dark-skinned woman with twin blades hanging from her belt. Siarl's braids were immaculately woven and trailing down her back, her laughter rippling through the glade. 'Siarl is a master of dual weaponry and yet to be defeated, with the singularly best reflexes that I have ever seen.' The lord glanced sideways at her as he said, laughing, 'Be warned. Her intellect is as quick as her blades.'

Cahra brightened, squinting at the woman's knives; longer than a quillon dagger, judging from the length, and fashioned a bit like a rapier. Light and lean for speed, no doubt. Plus, Cahra always respected women with upper arms to rival her own.

She wondered if Siarl would let her look at those daggers. Maybe they forged things differently in Luminaux? It'd be great to learn a few more smithing tricks.

Assuming there's a future for you in it. The thought hung heavy in Cahra's mind.

Finally, Terryl gestured to the brawny man with hair and skin as pale as winter snow, whose physique towered above the others as the man good-naturedly twirled a great-hammer.

'Piet is our wall,' Terryl explained to her. 'Fighting him is like striving to topple a mountain.' The lord laughed heartily. 'Don't let his brawn fool you, though. Piet is a gentle soul at heart, and there is not a single person in Luminaux that he would not defend with his life. He and the others have proven invaluable on our travels.'

'Is everyone here a fighter?' Cahra arched a brow.

Terryl chuckled. 'No.' He drew her attention to a woman, older than herself. 'Langera, from our Kolyath residence, is behind the culinary delights that you see here.'

Cahra rushed to ask, 'She's from Kolyath?'

'Ah,' Terryl said sadly, understanding. 'I am afraid not. She accompanied us when we set out from Luminaux.'

She ignored the pang of loneliness that followed, guessing she'd better get used to it. 'And you? What talents are you master of, exactly?'

Terryl seemed caught off guard. 'Well,' he said, thinking.

Moments passed. 'Nothing?' Cahra laughed, enjoying the sight of him flustered.

'Now, now,' he tutted gently. 'If I must, I would say that my talent is people. While I know my way around a sword, I prefer not to need one.'

'Oh, so I shouldn't have gone to all that trouble then?' Cahra joked.

Running a hand through his perfect hair, Terryl's laughter was a warm, melodious sound that echoed merrily through the trees. 'I thank you, and I am very pleased that you did craft mine. I believe my talent is connecting with people. My f—' He stopped abruptly.

They sat in the Wilds' simmering silence. Should she ask?

'What is it?'

He hesitated. 'I was going to say, it is something that my family, my parents, seem to have trouble with. Myself, not so much,' Terryl admitted.

Cahra blinked, eyes wide. It was like the man had just shared something with her that he might have preferred not to. So she gifted him her next words.

'I never knew my family,' she said, watching Terryl's people make light-hearted banter. There was a community to them, she thought. They'd faced danger as a group. 'Lumsden was the closest I had to any of it.' Cahra popped the last piece of bread into her mouth.

Terryl studied her. 'I was not aware.'

She sipped her water and shrugged. 'Why would you be?'

He was silent for a moment. 'You said that you knew little of the capital and its prophecy. Would you like to learn more?'

Cahra nodded, grateful for the reprieve. Terryl really did have a knack with people.

The Wilds were still as Terryl began, the hush comforting despite the darkness. 'Hael'stromia,' he started, his voice barely above a whisper in the quiet, 'isn't simply the city at the centre of the kingdoms of Kolyath, Luminaux and Ozumbre. Four hundred years ago, our realm's capital housed great Oracles blessed with the magick of foresight and the ability to thwart any faction who endangered peace across the lands with their ultimate weapon. When Hael'stromia fell and the Seers, blamed for its loss, were run from the capital, such divination was forbidden in the kingdom of Kolyath, with Ozumbre joining them in solidarity. But before the Seers disappeared, they beheld a vision: the realm's prophecy, as related to its chief weapon.' He paused in his story. 'You really do not know of the three omens?'

'No,' Cahra said. 'I'm not high-born enough to know much of this.'

The lord's face darkened. 'Another example of Atriposte strong-arming power by withholding information.'

Cahra wasn't surprised at Terryl's disdain. After all, he did come from a rival kingdom. 'Is the King of Luminaux any different?'

The sour expression left his face, blue goldstone eyes shimmering. 'You will find that there is much that is different, indeed.' He continued, 'Unfortunately, one topic all three sister kingdoms agree on is the war to control Hael'stromia. Kolyath and Ozumbre desire it, and do not wish Luminaux to have it. It has been this way for centuries.'

She mulled over Terryl's words, her thoughts churning. She'd never experienced war, outside of Kolyath's harsh austerity. The closest she could imagine was the Red Square in the aftermath of the kingdom's torture or executions, the cobbles stained blood-red.

She traced a pattern on the log she was sitting on and said, 'But Hael'stromia has been abandoned for ages. If the capital is in such a woeful state, then why does every kingdom want it?'

'They covet Hael'stromia's fabled ultimate weapon.'

'I'm aware,' Cahra muttered. It was the only thing Kolyath's Steward cared about.

'Well, once in control of the weapon, a kingdom could lay claim to the empire's old seat of power and rule over the other kingdoms, their lands and resources,' Terryl explained. 'Of course, to do so, their possession of the weapon is required. That is where the prophecy and its three omens come in:

'For when the Seers reappear,
When the Key has been bestowed,
When the mark walks the path to enter the Nether in life,
Then shall Hael rise again.'

'That's the prophecy? Well, that's vague,' Cahra said flatly.

'Perhaps. The first line, the first omen, is what Jarett seized upon.'

'You said the first line after I found you,' she remembered.

Terryl nodded. 'I know it all by heart.'

'But why?' She frowned.

He rubbed his temples, saying, 'This morning, you told me that there were things that I did not know about you. I have revealed the same.' He studied her. 'Have I your trust?'

Cahra deliberated. Her instincts told her yes, but she'd been thrust into the unknown. 'It's not that I don't trust you. I've just known you for such a short time, by my standards. This morning, I was excited for you to collect your sword. Since then, I've fled my kingdom, I currently have no idea where I am, and my future is in the hands of a foreign lord and his, what, private army? And I have no idea what'll happen to me once we reach Luminaux…' She broke off, her voice quavering on the last point.

Terryl was aghast. He'd clearly not realised any of what she'd been thinking. 'Cahra, you are *safe*. I know that may seem hard to comprehend, given what we have been through, but you have my word. No harm will come to you, not from myself or anyone in Luminaux.'

'You swear it?' She couldn't stand how fearful she sounded.

His eyes grew wide. 'On my honour! I believe you when you say that none of what has befallen you and I was intentional. As does Raiden,' Terryl said, before she could argue. 'If my longsword truly does herald the first omen, then you are the catalyst for the prophecy's first development in centuries. Surely, you know what that means?' His expression softened. 'My kingdom will be delighted to host you.'

She breathed out, feeling the tension in her neck and shoulders ease. 'If you say so.'

'Oh, I do.' His voice brimmed with playful assurance. 'In fact, I believe there is much that you might like in Luminaux.'

'Really?' Cahra asked, her doubt caving to his enthusiasm. 'Like what?'

Terryl looked thoughtful. 'Well,' he began, gesturing around them, 'you seem to like the greenery of the Wilds, thus far. Luminaux rests at the foot of mountainous meadows, and the kingdom's parks are just as lovely, if not perhaps more charmingly cultivated.'

Cahra paused, not wanting to look foolish. Then she asked, 'Erm, what's a park?'

Terryl's eyebrows shot up, then he nodded, comprehending. 'Of course. Kolyath's primary green space was the Steward's grounds.' His face tensed at the mention of the ruler. 'A park is a large, public garden where anyone can walk or sit. Luminaux's parks are tranquil, and often contain statues or fountains,' he explained.

'Right,' she said slowly, unable to picture anything but Kolyath's weedy flowers.

Terryl was watching her intently, fingers tapping the clean line of his jaw as he searched for something else to snare her interest. 'Ah!' he exclaimed. 'There is a tavern in the Artisanal Emporium, our sister to your Traders' Quadrant, serving rich, robust cuisine that will astonish your tastebuds: fowl that is pan-cooked then stewed in wine, accompanied by onion and mushrooms. There are sweets like meringue with a crisp, sugary texture that melts on your tongue – and pastries, so many pastries, with creams, nuts, even honeyed cacao. Such decadent confections!'

Cahra's mouth watered. Mock-reluctantly, she murmured, 'Go on.'

Terryl beamed, her words emboldening him as he proceeded with great enthusiasm, and for the first time, Cahra noticed the near-invisible dimples indenting his flushed cheeks. 'Another highlight that we have in common is Luminaux's own master blacksmith…'

It was then that she stopped hearing him, Terryl's words about smithing fading to a hum as her mind returned to Kolyath – to Lumsden – and the only person who'd ever made her feel cared for, like a parent. Terryl was lucky. He was going home to his family, Cahra thought, a harsh lump rising in her throat.

She was arriving in Luminaux to nothing and no one, a Kolyath outcast.

'Cahra?' Terryl's voice pulled her back to the present.

She forced an apologetic look. 'I think I'm getting tired,' she said, then glanced away. His suggestions for where to go were nice, but she knew she'd be exploring them by herself. 'I guess I could go adventuring – once we arrive, and you go back to your old life, that is.' She toyed with a stick, poking a mound of dirt and ignoring the growing pressure in her chest.

Terryl's voice was soft and clear as he said, 'Perhaps I could offer you a guided tour of the kingdom? If you desired it,' he added, a hopeful look crossing his face.

'What would Raiden say? A lord keeping company with a low-born smith?' She found herself unable to look away as she awaited his response.

At this, Terryl beheld her, his gaze tender and sincere. 'A title does not matter, Cahra. It is the mind, the heart behind it, that is of import.'

For a moment, Cahra forgot how to breathe. Then she nodded. 'Okay. I'd like that.'

The sudden intensity of their conversation left her with the abrupt urge to move, so she stood, stretching her arms above her head, the movement forcing several slow, deep breaths. The Wilds *were* different from before, she realised. Brighter, finer slants of light rent the woods, sporadically criss-crossing to fling large, jagged shapes onto the mossy carpet. It was like a god had shattered a glass sky.

'So… How long are we stopping for?'

'We need to rest, however briefly. It will make the remainder of the journey less taxing.'

'Oh?' She noted the caution in his voice.

'We are not yet out of danger,' Terryl said slowly. 'The Wilds are not Kolyath, that much is true. Yet threats outside the sister kingdoms do exist, and laws do not. The Wilds can be a desperate place for some.' She must have looked worried, for the lord's next words were, 'I do not wish to alarm you unduly, and we are taking the safest route between the kingdoms. I simply wish to be candid with you about the circumstances we now find ourselves in.'

Cahra nudged a small stone with her boot. She was with Terryl and seasoned fighters. There was nothing to fear, nothing more than normal.

She kicked the stone into the glade, turning to Terryl. 'What about the Wildspeople? They saved us from Kolyath.'

At this, he shook his head. 'That was their choice. I do not feel comfortable asking the people of the Wilds to support a fight not theirs, not against trained soldiers in deadly warfare. It would not be ethical to ask them to risk their lives.'

It was the right answer, one she never would have heard from a Kolyath high-born. Admiration kindled, flaring in her chest.

She finished the last of her pastry, crumbs tumbling to her lap, then realised she hadn't seen him eat. 'Terryl, aren't you hungry?' She thrust her apple into his palm. 'Seers, take it! I'm not the only one who has sprinted for miles.'

'Perhaps I am,' he admitted. 'Though I have been sitting, doing little in my carriage. Everyone else…' He gestured to his people.

There was something about the way he said the words, the fondness he conveyed, the respect for the company he kept, that made Cahra feel warm, if only for a few brief moments.

Finally, Raiden signalled to Terryl. 'Excuse me.' The lord smiled. 'Do enjoy the interlude. Traversing the Wilds can be arduous, so I advise relaxing while you can.'

As Terryl moved away, Raiden strode briskly to join him. The woods stirred, a rise of rustling leaves whispering secrets to the wind, as they were followed by Piet, towering over everything and lumbering to them with a grin. Siarl, her braids shimmering in the low light, and Queran, silent as a spectre, arrived together. Raiden spoke a few words then slipped away, disappearing fast behind the treeline.

Cahra smirked. She supposed even the likes of Raiden had to answer nature's call. Shaking her empty cup, she looked for Langera to ask about more water.

CHAPTER 13

Returning from the stream, Cahra's conversation with Terryl lingered in her mind. She found herself replaying his words, his smile, the intensity of his blue goldstone eyes; like solitaires, so dazzling. And he supported her, making her feel warm despite the briskness of the Wilds. She did worry about Raiden though. Terryl's Captain didn't seem to like her.

She sighed and pressed on, then froze. Something echoed from behind, in the trees to her left. She hesitated, doubting her ears, but then it came again: the unmistakable clash of metal on metal. Of an armed skirmish.

Raiden.

Without a second thought, Cahra took off in his direction.

Her senses, honed from years of living with fear at one shoulder, death at the other, pinpointed the fight easily. She crouched and stole towards it, boots muted on the springy moss, looking from behind a shrub to see Raiden battling three soldiers. Despite years of smithing, Cahra had seen few sword fights in her life. But she understood the truth of Terryl's words, the courage and control in Raiden's powerful strikes. He was skilled, twisting and slashing to deliver cuts with speed. But the Captain still fought three foes, each unwilling to go quietly. Cahra shifted her weight, an unseen twig cracking underfoot – then, cursing, she grabbed the nearest bough and swung to climb into the tree.

One of the soldiers Raiden was battling turned, but before the man could investigate, Raiden took advantage, forcing his attention. Peering down at them, Cahra released a breath, then realised an archer was concealed in the undergrowth, a crossbow trained on Raiden. She heard a grunt, glimpsing the Captain. He was hurt. She watched in horror as he faltered, pulling a slip of a knife from his side and hurling it, hitting his opponent in the throat with a dull thack. The dark ripple of red followed.

But the move cost Raiden. The crossbow now had a straight shot. As he fought to dispose of the two soldiers still standing, the man below Cahra stilled for his attempt. Then she was running, sprinting the last few steps to the branch's narrow end – and jumped, plummeting from the lofty tree, her weight the brawn of a blacksmith.

Right onto the soldier with the crossbow.

The force of the impact reverberated through Cahra's legs and she gritted her teeth, hunching like a beast as she bit down on the shooting pain that rocked her knees and ankles. Feeling movement, she sprung from the man's back, gripped a fallen branch, then whirled and swung with all her might. The wood dropped him like a stone.

Raiden stared, recovering quickly to dispatch first one then the other combatant, a spray of blood signifying the final felling. He approached her.

'I take it they're…' Cahra trailed off.

He gave a curt nod, studying the man unconscious at her feet. 'That was unexpected.' Raiden stared at her.

'I'll say,' she told him. 'Who are they? Why did they attack you?' Cahra gave him a look. 'Or did you attack them?'

'Of course not.' He scowled, then paused. 'Look at their insignias.'

Cahra gazed at the only kingdom crest she knew. 'They're Kolyath,' she whispered. Her eyes flew to Raiden. 'Surely—'

'We took a risk, stopping this early. One we won't be taking again.' His eyes flashed to their lone captive. 'But we may extract some answers yet.' Raiden's jaw tightened as he yanked the dagger he'd thrown from his victim's neck, sliding a glance to Cahra. 'Please. Get the lord to his guards,' he said quietly.

'I will,' she promised, glancing down at the unconscious soldier as she turned to go.

Raiden's iron eyes narrowed. 'I won't be long.'

A shiver slithered down her spine at the menace in his voice.

Leaving the dead behind, Cahra staggered as fast as she could back to the little glade. Hearing Terryl's people, she sighed with relief as she broke through the low-lying shrubs and into the open. Terryl looked up from his plate and, seeing her – dishevelled and limping – dropped his crockery and hastened to cover the distance, Siarl and Piet at his side, his people falling into formation. Queran and a second archer broke from them, darting towards her.

'Raiden,' she called, puffing and pointing, Queran nodding as he ran.

'What happened? You're hurt,' Terryl said, brow creased as he signalled for aid.

Cahra shook her head. 'It's nothing,' she told him. 'But Raiden was attacked. He's dealing with the survivor.' Siarl flicked a glance to Piet before peeling away from him, unsheathing one of her long daggers. She trailed Queran into the woods.

Piet moved closer to Terryl. 'We must leave,' Piet said, watching the clearing's edges. Everyone was primed for threats now.

'Not until Raiden returns,' Terryl instructed. The look on the lord's face was enough to silence whatever argument was brewing.

Cahra stepped towards him, forcing her breaths to slow. 'Piet is right. We need to go.' As Terryl turned on her, she said, 'There was a soldier with a crossbow, from Kolyath.'

At that, Piet looked ready to knock Terryl on the head and toss him over one shoulder, anything to get him back to the coach.

'Very well,' Terryl said, face darkening.

Piet nodded to her. She smiled, then quickened her pace, following.

Terryl climbed into the coach, his horsemen ready to launch into a gallop. Cahra stood, Piet taking point on the side closest to the clearing.

'What are you doing, Cahra? Get in,' Terryl said.

'In a minute.' She narrowed her eyes, listening, sensing, for anything, any kind of sound or change in the air around them.

Annoyance flickered in Terryl's gaze as he said to her, 'Cahra, you're not a warrior.' The lord took a measured breath, trying again. 'I understand your wish to contribute, I do. However, if you are truly the prophecy's omen-bringer, then your protection is important.' Terryl let his words hang in the silence. 'Please,' he urged, 'get in the carriage.'

The concern for Raiden was all over Terryl's face, so she'd forgive his tone, this once. Climbing into the coach, she positioned herself by the other window, sitting Terryl back and out of sight as she kept watch.

'I told Raiden I'd find you,' she murmured, reaching out with every sense she had, scanning for danger.

'Well, you did,' Terryl conceded, his stern expression relaxing as it lingered on her, Cahra rubbing her injured knee. 'I am as safe as I am going to get.'

She just nodded.

'You're hurt,' he said again, his tone of gentle concern.

She turned and looked down at her knee through the rips in her trouser leg. 'I'm fine,' she said. 'I fell is all. Nothing broken, it'll just swell a bit.'

'Here.' Terryl patted his seat. 'I am told that elevation is required for such injuries.' She went to argue, unable to consider plunking one of her muddy boots onto Terryl's unspoiled cushions, when he reached for one. She shook her head. 'Cahra,' he pressed.

Finally, tentatively, she lowered her foot onto the gold-striped pillow.

Minutes later, facing the clearing, Cahra straightened as Raiden and the others emerged from the Wilds, her eyes flashing between them. Terryl's second in charge limped, looking as guarded as ever as he returned, a tall woman with a tan leather satchel in tow. Queran and Siarl were fanned behind him, weapons out.

As Raiden approached, Cahra called out to him, 'Should we be expecting trouble?' Meanwhile, Piet gave Raiden a nod at the door.

Raiden shrugged off his jacket as he and the woman – a healer, Cahra realised, noting the hat, robes and bag of the Physicians' Guild – climbed into the coach. Raiden sat heavily.

'No. But we'd best not linger,' he said, motioning out the window.

'What happened?' Terryl asked as the coach began to move.

Raiden removed his bloodied shirt and Cahra tried not to gawk as she saw stab wounds near the man's lungs, but seemingly not in them. He was lucky it hadn't been far worse. He gritted his teeth as the physician next to Cahra pulled a strip of cloth from her satchel and sprinkled it with a pungent-smelling liquid, before pressing it to Raiden's side.

'Do it, Merali,' he ground out. The woman leaned forward, needle and twine breaking skin as she made several tight stitches to staunch the flow of blood. 'What happened,' Raiden said, gripping the armrest, 'is that Cahra jumped out of a damn tree and disabled a soldier about to loose a crossbow at me.'

Terryl's eyebrows shot up. 'That is not what you told me,' he said slowly.

Her cheeks felt hot. 'You would have fussed, and there wasn't time,' she replied. Raiden snorted but nodded in recognition.

'Well, Cahra, I take it back. Clearly, you are a warrior.' Terryl's brow furrowed. 'Yet what of this attack? Was it related to our escape, or was it simply a happy coincidence?' Despite his humour, worry crept through his usual mask of pleasantry.

'Both. They were Kolyath scouts, and when interrogated, one revealed they'd stumbled across us while on duty. But they also knew that a group had escaped the gatehouse, a party with a caravan of wagons. When they found us…' Raiden spread his palms.

'Which means that more may follow.' Terryl leaned forward, hands steepled.

'Once their scouts fail to report in, at least. So we return to original measures. Minimal stops, the securest camps and the shortest time possible between here and home.' Raiden hissed softly as Merali applied a swab doused in spirits to his stitches.

Terryl didn't argue. 'Agreed, we must get our people to safety.'

Raiden twisted, testing the stitches, before nodding to Merali and rebuttoning his shirt. 'To Hael with that, I've half a mind to escort you back now.' She'd never heard Raiden curse. She wondered if this was what he was really like with Terryl, or if it was just down to the blood loss.

The lord straightened. 'No. Everyone here is at risk.'

Raiden looked ready to launch into an impassioned argument, then he noted Cahra. His face was drawn as he said to Terryl, 'This is reckless. You know what Commander Tyne will say once he learns of this day's events.'

Terryl exhaled through his nose. 'Raiden, I cannot keep letting you put my life above all others. I shall not, *will* not, do it – I cannot be responsible for any more d—' Terryl raised his own eyes to her then, as if also remembering she was there. 'We can make it back as one, if we exercise caution, correct? We have done so before.'

She looked to Merali, who was cleverly focused on packing her satchel.

'Yes. My lord,' Raiden said, shoulders stiffening as the veins of his neck bulged. Cahra looked between Terryl and Raiden.

Was this normal? She couldn't imagine a Kolyath lord stomaching dissension in his ranks. She'd seen Commander Jarett backhand his guards and leave them bleeding in the street for less.

Terryl did say Luminaux was different.

'Merali, would you tend to Cahra's leg? She was injured when she fell.'

Cahra began to protest, but the healer was already peering at Cahra's knee through her ripped trousers and reaching into a satchel. Merali unscrewed a little, round tin, saying, 'Now, this may hurt,' as she smoothed a balm into Cahra's purpling knee. Cahra ground her teeth, silent.

Raiden watched her bite back the pain, a new light of respect dawning in his eyes. 'That was quite the leap you made, back there.'

Cahra looked up from her leg, her eyes meeting Raiden's. She couldn't help but grin at his acknowledgement. 'Oh, I know,' she said with pride.

CHAPTER 14

When the coach pulled off the road again – Raiden's people clearing a screen of brambles, only to carefully replace them once the caravan had passed through – it was close to sunset. In the Wilds, Cahra felt the same edge, the same crispness to the air, as Kolyath at twilight, the sun's beams cooling as they cascaded from the sky that faded to a cornflower blue.

Cahra tumbled out of the coach with her satchel. Would she ever get used to travelling like this, squished into a tiny movable box? Oh well, she thought drily, it wasn't like she'd get the chance again once they arrived in Luminaux. This journey was funded by Terryl's coin, and a lordly high-born she was not.

She turned, and two hills rose like horns behind her, the coaches, wagons and horses of the caravan tucked into the valley they formed. The air was a song of mist and soil with the evening's arrival, and Cahra inhaled it deeply, her eyes on the lord's people as they lugged items from the wagons to the mouth of a cave.

Terryl joined her, graceful hands clasped neatly at his back. 'My apologies,' he said. 'I had every intention of delivering us to an inn, but after this afternoon, Raiden believed it safer to make camp at a secure location than chance being seen.'

Cahra stretched, her muscles aching. 'It's okay,' she told Terryl. 'I've had worse.' Her stomach dropped. It was getting harder to hide her past, and it didn't help that she was painfully aware of being the only low-born. No one else here was ex-beggar material.

Raiden arrived before she could dwell on it. 'Supper is on the way,' he told them as she watched Queran, Siarl and a few others scale the steep hills above the cave.

She turned to Terryl. 'What can I do to help?' Hours of sitting had left her eager to move.

'Nothing,' he cut in, the lord's gaze falling to her knee. 'Simply rest.'

Giving him a flat look, she pointed to Raiden. 'What about him?'

'Excellent point.' Terryl called out, 'Raiden!' The Captain looked up, handing off a stack of plates to Piet. 'Mind your stitches. Leave the setting up for us tonight.' He smiled. 'My orders,' he added, strolling off before the man could argue.

Raiden exhaled, eyeing Cahra. 'I suppose I have you to thank for that?'

'I didn't expect him to actually do it,' she said, surprised.

Raiden turned to her, saying slowly, 'Indeed,' then moved for the cave.

Cahra scanned their surroundings. 'How safe are we here?'

Despite Raiden's injuries, his attention was on his lord. 'As safe as we can be in the Wilds. This is one of our securest camps, regularly checked by locals, people we can trust. If there was trouble, they would leave a signal for us.' Cahra and Raiden passed the threshold, the entrance smaller than a door and edged in porous-looking rock that scraped her knuckles.

Cahra was relieved at the idea of resting properly. Her body had been on high alert since they'd fled, and she could feel the bone-tiredness starting to creep in. She'd sleep soundly knowing Raiden's people were on watch. If she'd been in Kolyath, on its cobbled streets, well, any rest would've been fitful, one ear cocked for danger, a sharp rock or stick cradled to her chest as a weapon—

She could feel her shoulders tensing at the thought so she cut it off, asking Raiden, 'Since Terryl's deemed us the lame horses, now what?'

Raiden's mouth twitched, amusement in his eyes. She'd nearly made him laugh. 'Assuming I'm fit to start a fire, perhaps that?' The others were heaping wood and kindling by the entrance, so Raiden went to fetch some.

Cahra didn't know what to do next. She wondered if anyone had a pencil and paper, in case she was struck by the urge to sketch.

Would a Luminaux smithy even take a Kolyath apprentice?

She watched in amusement as Raiden crouched over the firewood, striking rocks and growing increasingly frustrated. Finally, he sat back, brow furrowed, and scratched his head.

'What?' he muttered, glancing at her sharply.

Kneeling, Cahra laughed. 'You have all these camps but you can't start a fire?'

'I'm not usually the one to do this,' he groused.

She reached into her satchel. 'Try quartz.' Grinning, she pulled a rough stone from her bag and held out her other hand. Raiden looked at it, confused. 'Your knife,' she told him, then sighed and rolled her eyes at him. 'Afraid I'm going to stick you in your other side?' Raiden's face darkened, but he handed it to her. Cahra whittled a stick into little shavings, arranging the tinder in a small circle on the pile of wood. She selected a piece, pressed it to the quartz and tilted Raiden's knife, winking.

And remembered something, rummaging through her pack.

'Oh! I almost forgot.' Cahra withdrew a lump of tenebrite for Veil's Eve, the final night of the Festival of Shadows. She pushed it deep within the wood pile. 'To keep the fire burning,' she told him.

She hit the quartz with the knife. It sparked for her on the first go.

'How did you do that?' Raiden asked as he uncrossed his arms to warm his hands.

'Blacksmith, remember? Fire is my friend.' Even before she'd been one, she thought, when she'd lived on Kolyath's streets.

Her and Terryl's eyes met, and the story of her past, her growing up a homeless, kinless urchin, was on her tongue again. She swallowed, ridding herself of the words.

Despite all he'd said and done, she couldn't tell him. He was a lord, and she was—

A beggar. Always a lowly beggar, no matter the esteem she earned.

She stood and ambled farther into the cave. Someone had lit torches and placed them around its edges, which was wise as she could feel a cool breeze gliding past to the entrance. Cahra raised her palms to a flaming torch, the heat radiating like it would thaw her soul.

'You never told me,' Terryl said quietly from behind her.

She'd barely heard his footsteps, she'd been so deep in thought. 'Told you what?'

'The things about you that I do not yet know.' He echoed her words from his garden, right before they'd fled Kolyath in his coach.

Cahra's chest hurt the more she looked at him. But it wasn't Terryl's fault, it wasn't anyone's. Life just happened, like it always did to her. Her childhood, the dungeons.

But unlike then, now she was free. So why did she feel so lost?

Cahra tried to smile. But her sadness was so close to the surface, too close, and all it would take was to think of something dreadful happening to Lumsden—

She took a shuddering breath. Then Terryl's hand was on her shoulder, his warmth permeating her skin, melting her numbness in a way the fire couldn't. The cave was dim where they now stood, Terryl's dark hair gleaming beneath the torch, but she could still make out his blue goldstone eyes. He didn't say a word, he just stood by her. And saw her pain.

In the darkness of the cave, Cahra found the courage to let go, and finally wept.

-

When she was done, Cahra and Terryl sat by the soft light of the torch under a blanket, hot mugs of cider in their hands as they waited for Langera to roast the wild pheasants Queran and the others had caught.

'I feel like a child,' Cahra said, wiping away the last of her tears. 'I *never* cry.'

'Perhaps you needed to. You are grieving, in a way. Your life will not be the same.' Terryl gazed into her eyes. 'It will be better.'

Will it? Taking a sip of the mulled alcohol, she said, 'If you say so.'

Terryl flashed a playful smile, saying, 'The Oracles best heed my will.'

'I never believed,' Cahra said after a moment, staring into the torch's flames. The carefree flicker of its fire was comforting, the way the orange light whipped and twirled, dancing towards the ceiling. He gave her a questioning look. 'The Seers. The prophecy.'

'Ah.' Terryl raised his mug and drank, then lowered it to his lap again. 'Cahra… Regardless of what Jarett, Atriposte or any one person thinks – prophecy or no prophecy – I must thank you. For stopping me and warning me. For giving my people a chance to escape. We are all here tonight because of you. I am deeply grateful.'

Cahra opened her mouth, but she didn't know what to say. Eventually she managed, 'No, thank *you*. For getting me out of the kingdom. I didn't dare to hope for an answer, and then you stepped in. I'm thankful too,' she told him. She really was grateful for him.

Her cheeks felt hot. It wasn't just the cider warming her insides.

Cahra downed the revelation with a gulp of her drink, grimacing as she straightened her legs to cross them at the ankles.

Terryl asked her, 'How is your knee?'

'It's fine. Better than last time.' She lifted the rogue joint, testing it.

Terryl cocked his head. 'What do you mean?'

It would never end, these conversations circling back to her past. It would never stop. Until she made it.

She took a deep breath, locking it in her lungs until they ached, then slowly let it out. 'When I was younger, in Kolyath,' Cahra began, 'I was homeless. Lumsden took me in when I was a child. Before that, I lived on the streets. It's what I wanted to tell you in the garden.'

Well… One of the things.

She thumbed the handle of the mug, waiting for the judgement, the rejection.

But it never came. Terryl just watched her with those thoughtful gemstone eyes of his. 'I suspected that it was perhaps something like that.'

Her mouth fell open. This time, she really *didn't* know what to say.

She sat in silence as Terryl went on. 'Everyone has a beginning. Sometimes it looks quite different to what we end up doing, being. For example, my own beginning is rather divergent to what I am doing these days.' He almost sounded like he'd laugh, but didn't. 'What I am trying to say, somewhat dismally, is this: it shall not matter, if you do not let it. You are so much more than your station. Take what you will from your beginnings, but if you do not wish them to define you, do not let them.' He held her gaze.

Cahra sat frozen, her heart pounding, his words echoing inside her. Never in her life had anyone gifted her such kindness. Not even Lumsden, who had loved her, in his way.

With searching eyes, Cahra raised her gaze to Terryl's and found him staring back, an earnest smile on his lips. Terryl put down his mug of cider. Then he delicately took her hand, his soft skin brushing the callouses on her palm before gliding to the tattoo on her wrist, and the crimson of the fire-keeper's stone that coloured her Guild ink.

'They say that ground tenebrite gives these markings their vibrancy,' he murmured, the feel of his touch making her heart skip. 'Is that true?'

'Yes,' she whispered, struggling to speak. 'For smiths, it symbolises the forge's fire, its ever-burning heat. It's why Veil's Eve is so important to us… It's tonight, you know.'

'Ah, of course,' he replied, tracing languid circles around the tattoo with his fingers. 'Veil's Eve, when the space between the veil and void is at its thinnest.'

'And when people lift the veil on hidden truths and bear witness to those of others,' Cahra breathed, the words all rushing out at once.

'Oh?' Terryl arched an eyebrow. 'Do you have anything else that you wish to share?' The lord's voice was low and teasing.

Seers, yes… She felt heady, bewildered yet exhilarated. But suddenly, he withdrew, Cahra also catching the telltale footfalls that now approached.

From the shadows, Raiden's voice broke in. 'Supper is served.' He turned to her. 'How's your leg?' The Captain's words were gruff, but at least they were sincere.

Meanwhile, Cahra's head was still spinning from what he'd interrupted. Eventually, she flashed Raiden a smile. 'I'm okay.' She went to stand, Terryl at her side as she levered herself to her feet.

Raiden watched Cahra's careful movements as they returned to Langera, who was doling out servings of pheasant, gravy and a selection of vegetables, the succulent scent of cooked meat and rosemary and thyme wafting ever closer. He cleared his throat.

'So,' Raiden said to Cahra, 'I was thinking. As a way of rewarding you for your help, how would you like to learn a weapon?'

Cahra, mere steps from mouth-watering food, hobbled to a stop. 'Are you serious?'

'Don't worry, I've already sought his permission,' Raiden told her, nodding to Terryl. 'Look, you saved me today. You saved *him* today,' Raiden continued, as the lord smiled. 'And you have my thanks. So if, somehow, we needed your help again in future, knowing you can hold your own against a soldier wouldn't hurt.'

'I held my own just fine today,' Cahra retorted.

'Against a weapon-wielding soldier focused on *you*. What do you say?'

She considered. Terryl had dismissed her as a fighter, which normally she wouldn't give a fig about, but she had been trying to help him. It wouldn't hurt to learn a weapon, especially from someone like Raiden. Hael, it might even help her smithing.

'I say yes.' She grinned. 'When do we start?'

'Not tonight,' Raiden chuckled, then winced, cupping his stitches.

She snickered and took a step towards the table, and was then gritting her own teeth as she slid on a stray rock, sore knee barking. 'Fair,' she admitted, Terryl at her arm. 'I'm fine,' she said, catching Raiden's look.

Raiden's eyes flitted between her and Terryl. Maybe it should have made her nervous. It was almost like he knew something had shifted, however slight.

But she didn't care. For once, she felt happy. She didn't want it to end.

The food was delicious, the pheasant tender with a crisp exterior, and the vegetables shimmered in a sweet honey glaze. Cahra talked and laughed with the people of Luminaux for the rest of the night, Terryl keeping her company. As the evening progressed, others peeled away to sleep or guard the cave, leaving her and Terryl alone. Even as her body craved sleep, the memory of Terryl's hand on hers buzzed in the corner of her brain. But eventually, she couldn't resist the lull of the fire's warmth.

Terryl chuckled. 'You need rest,' he said, his voice hushed as people hunkered in the cave's corners, with Raiden's sentries by its entrance.

'Mmmm,' Cahra mumbled, her eyes fluttering shut again. She heard Terryl chuckle as he stood to leave. She was on the verge of nodding off when he returned.

'Come along,' Terryl said, gently tugging Cahra to her feet with surprising strength. He led her to a dying torch, half-way down the cave's length, then sat her on clean bedding as he eased off her boots. She was too tired to be embarrassed about her holey socks as he held the bed covers open for her and she fell in. Pulling the blankets to her chin, Terryl paused. And though her eyes were closed, she could feel him watching her.

Just as she was on the precipice of sleep, Terryl ventured to stroke her hair, and she smiled at his intoxicating touch, at the warm luxury of the strange bed. She rubbed her eyes, struggling for words to keep the moment from slipping away.

But her consciousness was pulling her, dragging her into its peaceful depths, and it was all Cahra could do not to surrender.

All thoughts faded as she let the darkness come, a smile on her face.

CHAPTER 15

Terryl left Cahra to her slumber, his coverlet hugging her form, the steady rise and fall of her chest a sign of hard-won peace. He was not sure where he would sleep, but it mattered not. Cahra was finally resting, a temporary recess in their turbulent journey. After the day's trials, she had unquestionably earned that. They all had.

Just as he had earned reading his sister's letter.

In the torchlight, he pulled Sylvie's envelope from his breast pocket and tore it open, deciphering the coded words as he rushed to read:

T,

Darling brother. Ignore what the Commander has told you so far. You know where his loyalty lies, and regrettably, it is with Father. I have been battling Father and Mother since you left us, not only about my duties (Mother implored me to relinquish my post and get a hobby – needlework! Could you imagine? I should rather stab myself with one, which is precisely what I have been trained for. Ridiculous!), but also about talk of suitors. Of course, they were all men. Yet, brother, these matters are not the reason for my letter. For having finally given up on matchmaking for me, our parents have refocused their attentions on you. This is what Tyne has neglected to tell you.

Father has decreed it. He and Mother have named you a bride.

And it is Lady Delicia.

I know that this will disturb you greatly. Yet I do believe that you can fight it, as I have fought their pairings all these years. However, I will say this: the longer you stray from home, the harder it will be to undo what has been done. You know their will. I pray that you and the others are safe, and that you return to us soon.

Love,

S

Upon finishing, Terryl held on to the letter for a time before folding it carefully away into his pocket again. Ire surged through him, its epicentre his closed fists. He wanted to roar. Howl. Pound his fists against the cave floor. All three at once. Not only at Delicia for her duplicitous manoeuvring, but also at his parents. The raw offence of it seared into his chest like a red-hot poker. For she had done it, Delicia had finally done it.

She had exacted her revenge, as she had vowed the day that he left her.

Though he was loath to depart from Cahra, he sorely needed Raiden's counsel. Yet as he looked for his Captain, he found Raiden already watching him, a mug in hand beside the fire, its mound of smouldering coals sustained by Cahra's little lump of tenebrite.

'Where's Cahra?' Raiden asked, a nonchalant question that would have fooled most. The Captain's eyes told him the man already knew.

He could tell exactly what Raiden was doing. 'She is injured and alone in this place. And she was allocated a straw bedroll,' he said, crinkling his nose at the thought.

'How do you know she didn't have one in Kolyath? I'll bet all your classy wine that bedroll would've been an upgrade,' Raiden said.

He dismissed Raiden's words. 'Cahra has proven herself as a member of our company. She deserved to heal comfortably. Besides, was her usefulness not the rationale behind your offer to instruct her earlier this evening?'

Raiden paused, his expression serious. 'Sir, when did you meet Cahra?'

'What?' he asked, caught off guard by both the tone and the 'sir'.

'You seem – as if you two were socially acquainted, before today,' Raiden said. And he realised: this had nothing to do with Cahra.

'You know!' he accused Raiden, stunned. 'When did Tyne reveal my parents' plans?' He could barely control the anger in his voice. 'And why did you not tell me?'

Raiden's face fell, guilt glinting in his eyes. 'Today, at the house. A letter arrived, coded and messengered through our network. Commander Tyne never bothers writing to me, he leaves my reports to Sylvie's aides,' said Raiden. 'And as for telling you, how could I? When you returned to the house, Cahra was in tow. And has been ever since,' Raiden argued. 'Then we fled. But she cannot distract you. Not only because we're approaching Luminaux, but because you have a bride now.'

He bristled at the word 'bride', and at the intrusion of his parents into his personal affairs before he had even set foot in the kingdom. Yet exhaustion tugged at him and arguing with Raiden achieved nothing. 'So my sister says. Do you know of her, this "bride"?'

'I do,' Raiden said.

He glared into the fire's glowing coals. 'As I wish that I did not.'

'You don't mean that.'

He kept staring at the embers. 'Delicia is truly naive to think that I will stand for this. After so long and at such distance, has she found no other?' He gazed in the direction of Cahra's sleeping form, his distemper rising with his thoughts of home.

Raiden asked, 'Why chance another, when she has you?'

'She does not have me! She never did,' he muttered, his fingers knit below his chin as he tried to strategise a way out of his predicament. For he would end this travesty.

'Well,' Raiden said, then stopped at the look on his face.

'Yes, we courted, once, for a few months, years ago,' he ground out. 'And it ended when I chose to leave Luminaux.' To serve it, in Kolyath. The simplest decision of his life.

'Exactly,' Raiden told him. 'It seems Lady Delicia is picking up where you left things.'

'Like Hael,' he snapped.

Raiden gagged on his drink. 'Thierre—'

'I will not do it. I will *not!*' He was on his feet now, all noble bearing tossed aside. 'She cannot compel me into such a union!'

Raiden stood, placing a hand on his shoulder. 'She has no right. Unfortunately, however, your parents do.' Raiden's grey eyes were frank. 'This isn't Sylvie and her suitors. This is the Crown Prince of Luminaux, the future of the throne. Your kingdom.'

The words of his oldest, dearest friend fell heavy as Raiden said, 'I am sorry, Thierre. But I don't think you can win this fight.'

CHAPTER 16

The Scion. Hael could scent her in the darkness: the sweet musk of humans, the tart crispness of something like apple mead, and her essence – rich and treacly with a hint of spice, like the wildflower agrimony. Oh, the irony of the blossom and its tall yellow petals. In his time, agrimony had been a medicinal herb for the eyes.

His fires rippled in response, the flames in his sockets simmering as he waited for her. Hael remained cowled, knowing the sight of his gaunt face would terrify, more so than the fires that served as his first and second sight. Fortuitously, his tattered robes bared little flesh, barring his ashen, corpse-like hands. He let the cuffs of his sleeves fall, shrouding them.

Regardless, he had succeeded. He had called to her, and she had come.

He watched as she slept, rousing to roll from her back to her side on the dark slate. The tiles were cut to triangles that swept from the bone rubble girding him and the Scion, to the moat edging the room and up to its metal doors; his metal, Haellium, upon which the carved inscriptions had been spelled to contain him. Feeling for the ground, the Scion finally awakened and sat up, staring at him.

Hael had learned from their bygone encounters that despite her natural defiance, the inborn battle instincts and raised fists, she feared him. And so he stood, a tangible presence that she could see, hear and calmly converse with. For they would speak.

'*Please accept my apology. I did not wish to affright you when last we met,*' Hael appealed, attempting to explain himself. '*I predicted peril.*' His eyes narrowed, perceiving the stiffness in one of her legs. '*Was I correct?*'

She continued to stare with two-toned eyes, brown and green, reminding him of trees. Not the trees of his city, their ebony bark and fronds and buds. The trees of the greenwoods, the realm's 'Wylds'. Of its roots and leaves, and browns and greens. Of life, the natural order. The one that he had supplanted as the weaponised Reliquus.

Even trees met their earthly ends.

'Yes,' she said finally, as if weighing his words. She looked up at him, a stretch as Hael towered above mere mortals. Or he had, centuries ago.

Hael pondered her upon the cold ground, then, as it had seemed to bother her before. He searched her with his occult eyes for an injury so ruinous that it could defeat her senses. But his flames only licked an aura of pain, acute pain, half-way up her leg. The tendon below her right kneecap; it was damaged.

'*You require healing.*' He knelt before her, faster than her human eyes could track, and she jumped. Centuries to prepare for the next Scion and Hael was fumbling before her. He felt foolish. Yet this was so different to Scions past. They had been initiated and knew what to expect when they were called upon by the Oracles. But her, she knew nothing of him, of Hael'stromia, and certainly nothing of the old ones, the old rites.

She knew nothing, and he was as a monster to her.

Slowing, Hael persisted, ensuring his movements were drawn out, non-threatening. '*Your knee. You have aggravated an old injury, that I sense. I can heal it, if you wish.*' Imbuing his features with what little softness he possessed, he raised his flickering gaze.

For the first time, her shoulders slackened somewhat. 'How? How did you know I'd be in peril?'

He could almost smile. '*It is the nature of my gifts, to know when you are in danger. Your enemies will continue to strike.*'

'And why is that?' She looked at him, hazel eyes fierce and full of light.

'*You are the Scion,*' Hael said simply.

'Seers, not this again,' she snorted, rolling her bright eyes. She was spirited, this one. 'What does that *mean?*'

'*You are the omen-bringer.*' A second fit of pique looked ready to erupt, if her features were any indication. How could he calm her? What did this Scion not yet know? '*You are why I have awakened,*' he decided upon. '*I call upon you now so as to serve.*'

Like the warrior he was, his statement had struck true. She whispered, 'What?'

'*There will be time for us to speak with each new vision. Fear not, Scion. You are learning to pass between the veil and void.*' Perhaps it was too much to speak of such things, for she looked at him as though she might cast her reason to the wind. He digressed, asking, '*Would you have me heal your leg?*' Although he spoke calmly, quietly, he knew his voice and the way the air vibrated when he spoke with his Netherworldly cords, the infernal tones that made each word sound like a god's. Or daemon's.

Curiosity illuminated her face, though her eyes were distrustful as she asked him, 'What would I owe you in return?' A shrewd question.

'*Nought. I am strong enough to heal you.*' Hael paused. '*A second time, however, would entail assistance.*' Four hundred years of his affliction. But he could do this, for her.

Of course, she knew nothing of his powers. The skeletons were amassed in piles from corner to corner. Prisoners of the realm, consigned to the safest place in the capital: the palatial temple where the weapon himself dwelled. A boon when the city's defences had activated and his bone-crunching Nether-hounds were confined inside. The prisoners had met their ends during the first months of captivity. The hounds he had summoned, however, had only fallen as Hael's dark magicks had weakened.

He banished his thoughts as the Scion nodded, toiling to straighten her damaged leg. Hael's eyes drifted to her bare feet. No sigil, yet.

To the matter at hand. With time and strength, he could heal her from afar. But now, weakened, her injury had to be within reach. And so he placed his fingertip atop her kneecap, a tear in the fabric of her trousers permitting him to see the bruised, distended joint. Whether she flinched from the pain of his touch, or from the touch at all, he was uncertain. But when his pale skin radiated with what he hoped would form a comfortable cold against the swelling, he gently pressed his thumb, then his third, fourth and fifth fingers to her knee. The fire of Hael's being, the Nether that had rebirthed him, ebbed, the ice of death rising in its place, infused with the source of his powers: destruction and creation.

The Scion watched as her inflammation faded away, as though it had never been.

She gazed up at him, the green of her eyes luminous this time, as she drew her knee to her chest, then chanced to stand.

'How did you do that?' she breathed, 'Who are you? *What* are you?'

He smiled at last. '*Reliquus of the Order of Descry, sempiternal of this realm and Vassal Champion to the Scion. To you.*' Still kneeling at her feet, Hael bowed to press his head upon the floor's dark tiles, before raising his gaze to hers.

'*It is my honour to serve you, Scion. I am Hael.*'

CHAPTER 17

Cahra awoke, the remnants of a dream clinging to her consciousness, which was new. She usually forgot her dreams the moment she woke up. But this time, the image of Hael's ruby-red fires for eyes remained. The being haunting her visions was a mystery. She took a deep, steadying breath and stretched.

The memory of Hael faded, the blackness of his hood replaced by the dimness of the cave she'd slept in, a lone torch still burning. She sat up, expecting her shoulders to feel stiff, like every day she awoke in Kolyath, but noted with surprise that she was fine.

Then she remembered Hael's miraculous healing and her heartbeat quickened. Throwing off the covers, she peered at the hole in the knee of her trousers. The swelling had completely disappeared. And not just disappeared, Cahra thought, as she bent and straightened her knee, over and over again. It was like the injury had never happened to her. She grinned, unable to help a little shriek of glee. Until, that is, the next thought struck her.

This bed. There was no way it was hers.

She could feel the lavish fabric beneath her fingers, the plushness of the mattress, which was no doubt why her body didn't ache. That was because there were not one, but *two* thick mattresses, a topper of feathers placed above the wool-filled base, where even straw would have been a luxury after her hammock in the smithy. The pillow was also full of down, but what really unnerved her was the showy sheet and blanket, silk and fur-lined respectively. All a vibrant blue, embroidered with gold. Just like Terryl's coach. Cahra nearly choked.

She had slept in *Terryl's* bed. A *lord's* bed!

Then came the next thought.

SEERS! Surely she, he, they hadn't… The evening's memories crashed into her, more from sheer panic than any cider-fuelled forgetfulness. She'd only drunk one mug of the stuff, however large it was.

No, she thought at last, she hadn't bedded him on his lordly mattresses, prompting a sigh of unadulterated relief. The last thing she wanted was to spoil whatever was between them by slipping back into old ways. She'd relieved her maidenly honour of its duties years ago, another rebellion against, well, anything. The idea of a low-born being pure or chaste had felt like a good place to start. It wasn't as if she'd had a dowry for a husband.

Cahra ran a hand through her hair, then cringed at the oil and dirt that greased it, resolving to wash immediately. She leapt from the bed, willing the most casual air possible, and hurried for the fire. Her knee didn't twinge one bit. At that, she hid a smile.

Langera looked up and beamed, apron dusted with flour as she cradled a large wooden bowl in one arm. 'Breakfast shan't be long,' she said.

'Great,' Cahra said quickly. 'I was actually looking for where to bathe?'

Merali glanced up from a wooden chopping board, helping with the morning's fare. The willowy physician looked her up and down, and said, 'I can lend you a shirt and trousers, if you would like to wash your own.'

Normally, Cahra would have snapped a retort at such a comment, but there was no malice in the woman's words. Only a kind offer.

Had it really been so long since she'd had a female friend?

'Thank you,' she said slowly, 'though yours may be a bit long on me.'

'True,' Langera laughed. 'Come on,' she said, Merali taking the mixing bowl from her as Cahra followed her into the cave, stopping at the chef's bed. A wool mattress, but with no featherbed top or any other indulgences.

Cahra had *definitely* slept in Terryl's bed.

Ignoring her embarrassment for the second time that morning, Cahra accepted the dress Langera handed her. Her outstretched arms sunk under its weight, the lacy white frills gushing out of her grip as she eyed the poufy skirt in horror. The woman couldn't be serious.

'Don't you have anything like that?' She gestured to Langera's own dress, a simple blue shift, nipped at the waist and tied with a bow at the back. Cahra could do without the bow, but the rest was plain, clean and nice enough.

'I, too, need to wash my things,' Langera chuckled. 'Now, there are pools for bathing farther into the cave. You've good timing, as the Captain and his squads are outside training, so the pools will be empty.' She handed Cahra a fresh bar of soap and a towelling cloth. 'Borrow the sundress as long as you like,' the woman said, smiling.

'A day will be long enough,' Cahra said. Then blinked, adding, 'Erm, it's pretty.'

Langera laughed, seemingly not offended. 'Not your style?'

Cahra raised a brow. 'I hit things with a hammer for a living.'

Langera angled her own in return. 'You can't do so in a dress?'

Cahra opened her mouth to speak, shutting it as Langera twirled with a flourish, sauntering back to Merali and the fire, humming as she went.

Once Cahra was clean and had scoured her clothing, she stepped from the pool and dried herself. Then eyed the flouncy dress, sighing.

She had absolutely no doubt she was going to regret this.

It was the first and only time Cahra wished she had a mirror. She peered down at the sleeves, too tight around her upper arms and under them, the seams biting into her skin. This dress would not take kindly to sweating. But then, Cahra supposed, it wasn't made for women who actually did things. She wondered how Langera worked all day in such get-up.

Having retrieved her satchel on the way over, Cahra upturned it, dumping the bag's contents onto the ground. She didn't think she'd find anything to make the sundress less girly, but she still pulled a face when she came up short. Then found something, two somethings, that she wasn't familiar with: a small dagger, and a diamond the size of Cahra's fist.

A few essentials. Lumsden's words before he'd given her the satchel.

The old man had kept a precious gem like this in the smithy? If Jarett had found it… Cahra shook her head, stunned at his boldness. She picked up the gold dagger; for throwing, she thought, touching the intricate handle. But it was when she pulled the knife from its sheath that her breath quickened. This bladework, this artisanship—

It was one of Lumsden's.

She thought she was done with crying after last night, but she soon found her eyes dampening again. Blinking back tears, she clutched

Lumsden's dagger, the only physical thing she had to remember the old man by. Resheathing the blade, she tucked it safely away.

Cahra didn't own a brush, so she combed her fingers through her hair, then repacked her satchel, gathered her clothes and the soap and towel, and returned to the cooking fire. Langera squealed in delight, unable to hide her excitement over Cahra's transformation.

Cahra exhaled through her nose, the humiliation piling on this morning. She thanked the chef with a quick smile and turned to go.

'Are you hungry? Take some fruit,' Langera insisted.

Cahra shook her head, only wanting to find Terryl, though she was still mortified at the prospect of kicking him out of his own bed. She spotted the blanket they'd sat on the evening prior and remembered everything.

It was oddly light outside, given the early hour and the dimness of the Wilds. Cahra spotted Raiden easily, pacing between groups and shouting drills, correcting angles and demonstrating attacks. She still couldn't see Terryl, until the crick of stones under a boot sent her spinning to find him by the cave's entrance. Staring at her.

Feeling the hot creep of a blush, Cahra turned to Raiden. 'He's good.'

'The finest,' Terryl agreed. 'I see you have colour in your cheeks again. Are you well?'

'Yes,' she said quickly, stepping to him. 'Except… *Thank you*. I feel so embarrassed – it was your bed I woke up in, wasn't it? Did you sleep?'

Terryl smiled, eyes bright. 'Cahra. You were exhausted and hurt. I put you where it would do you the most good.' His gaze lingered on her knee, hidden beneath layers of ruffles. She flushed again, the frills of the dress making her feel like a giant doll.

Minutes later, Raiden turned towards them, then took one look and fell about laughing. 'Training?' He grinned at her, sword in hand.

'You think I can't?' Cahra folded her arms.

Raiden belly laughed. 'Not in that thing!'

It was at that moment that she decided to keep the secret of Hael healing her knee, because she was going to kick his arse when he least expected it. 'Oh, you're wrong.'

Raiden, clearly not one to shy from a challenge, just laughed and tossed his blade, unfastening the decorated buttons of his jacket. 'Let's see how you go with your fists, then.' He dismissed his men for breakfast, half heading inside, half lingering by the cave to watch the early morning show.

Oh, boy. Well, at least she knew a thing or two about brawling. She glanced to Terryl, then locked eyes with Raiden and raised her fists. The Captain circled, assessing her position, before returning to face Cahra again, still grinning.

'Okay, blacksmith,' Raiden said. 'Show me a punch.'

CHAPTER 18

The next few days were uneventful as the caravan travelled, rested and travelled some more. They camped in a deserted farm, a tree-shielded elevation and even slept in the coach and wagons of Terryl's caravan. And Cahra trained, as Raiden promised, Piet stepping up as weapons master. She adored it. She supposed she'd always wanted to learn a weapon, but just never had the chance in Kolyath. By the time she was grown, Cahra was already one of the lucky ones. She had a trade, a livelihood. Asking for more was tempting fate to take what little she had. But Terryl seemed determined to fulfil her unspoken wish to wield one of her own creations, whenever and whatever that might be. He often watched her as she trained.

Terryl. Cahra snuck a glance at him in the coach, in profile as he observed the Wilds, so lovely with his blue goldstone eyes, dark chestnut hair and honeyed skin. She felt his eyes on her all the time now, even when she wasn't looking. As if he was piecing her together and the picture was getting clearer. She didn't quite understand it. Yet there was a part of her that liked Terryl's attention, a part of her that wanted him to, what, fancy her? Cahra had never kissed someone in a romantic way; it had always been so raw, so rushed. But now, sometimes she found herself wondering what it would be like to kiss Terryl. Not the desire of it, but the tenderness of it, of his warm lips on hers. The idea both excited and terrified her.

Except…

She looked down, at the borrowed dress she still wore, and at her newly brushed hair. A rarity, free of the usual soot and oil that darkened it from her pale copper to a mousy brown. Cahra imagined herself in her smithing leathers, with her ripped trousers, socks with holes, ragged boots and dirty, calloused hands. Not to mention her scars, pink and ugly from the countless times she'd burned herself at the forge, or snagged herself on a blade, or—

Inwardly, she shrunk. Yes, she craved Terryl's desire, even for a moment. Because once she was out of this dress and back in her old things, her unshapely men's clothes… Would he even see her? Would it be so obvious again, the space between them?

Him, a lord, and she—

A beggar. Always a lowly beggar, she thought, sighing.

Once again, Cahra found herself gazing out the window at the darkly beautiful Wilds. No matter how long they travelled, the lush, green woodlands never failed to captivate her. Even in the dimness of the silent, shaded trees, there was something comforting about the unbroken Wilds and those who dwelled there.

Until, that is, she heard noises outside the carriage and away from the road. Raiden, also alert to the commotion, signalled out the window.

Moments later, Siarl and Piet were flanking the coach on horseback.

'What's happening?' Raiden asked.

Siarl answered, her voice strong and steady. 'A skirmish between a Wildswoman and what looks to be a Kolyath patrol.'

'This close to Luminaux?' Terryl said, startled.

Cahra watched Terryl's Captain in silence. 'Raiden,' she said, his grey eyes flickering to hers. 'A Wildswoman under attack…'

'How many?' He finally ground out the words to Siarl, his eyes on Terryl.

'Around a dozen.'

Cahra was appalled. 'A dozen? Against one woman?' Why was Raiden hesitating? There was a rigidness to the man's face. Maybe she'd overstepped, but to Hael with it. She didn't answer to him, and threw open the carriage door. One Wildswoman against that many soldiers was despicable.

'Cahra!' Terryl called, staring at her in astonishment.

'Damn it!' She heard Raiden swear as she leapt out, the coach still in motion. Cahra dropped and rolled onto a patch of grass, Queran abandoning his horse to leap for the door she'd just vacated, doing one of his fancy flips onto the coach roof, bow in hand. The other coach door slammed, a pair of boots hitting the dirt with full force.

'Squad one!' Raiden bellowed from the ground. 'Stay with your lord! Squad two, you're with me!' He nodded to Queran atop the coach as it rounded a tight corner. Then Raiden spotted Cahra. 'What in Hael are you doing?' he hissed at her, eyes flashing. 'Training's not over yet. You're not ready for this.'

'Exactly!' she shot back. 'The perfect opportunity to hone my skills.' Anything to get him off his arse to help the woman in trouble.

'If anything happens to my lord…' he growled, marching to Queran's abandoned steed.

'He'll be fine. If you'd just—'

Raiden swung onto the horse, extending an arm towards her as he grabbed the reins. His famous hard look returned, but it was different this time, for there was actual urgency.

'Cahra, there's no time to argue.' Frowning at his words, Cahra took his hand as he hauled her up behind him on the saddle. 'Hold fast,' he said as they leapt into a gallop.

Arriving by a shallow stream, Cahra and Raiden hit the ground running. Eight of his people were already fighting, but Raiden still charged in, not one to stand around and watch.

Cahra followed him, treading lightly and wondering how to help. Given her love of hammers, Raiden had handed Cahra's training to Piet and his great-hammer, who had suggested starting with longer-handled weapons like staves.

Somehow she didn't think a stick would help her in this fight.

One of the Kolyath patrolmen fled, Cahra stepping from behind a tree to trip the man. He recovered, whirling to throw a wayward punch. She dodged it and grabbed the nape of his neck to slam the soldier into the tree's trunk. Cahra grinned, but her elation was short-lived as somebody grabbed her from behind, pinning an arm around her throat. Struggling to breathe, she grappled with her assailant, who then flung them into the same tree. It wasn't the worst hit she'd ever taken, but too-familiar white stars exploded across her vision. At least she now had air. Gulping down a hot breath, Cahra hurled her fist back and into the man's groin, spinning and flinging her elbow to connect with what she knew would be a skull. Her next punch landed with the entirety of her smith's bodyweight behind it, ending in a satisfying thud. The soldier crumpled.

Looking up to scan the battle, she saw they'd won. Raiden sought her out, their eyes meeting after he surveyed the men unconscious on the ground around her.

He asked, 'Are you injured?'

'Fine,' she said, dabbing her bloodied forehead with the back of her hand. 'You know head wounds. Where's the Wildswoman?'

He nodded to a small hill near the water. 'Recovering.'

She looked at Raiden then, knowing how hard it must have been for him to relinquish his post by Terryl's side. 'You did the right thing,' she told him. 'Coming to her rescue.'

Cahra found the Wildswoman sitting by the babbling stream. The woman's hair was lush and dark like treacle, cascading down her back and shimmering in the morning sun. When she turned, her skin had a dusky warmth to it and she stared with eyes of peridot, a gem the colour of freshly cut grass, ringed in amethyst. Pretty, Cahra thought.

And the woman was young, older than Cahra but nowhere near the matronly image she'd conjured in her mind at hearing 'Wildswoman'. She scolded herself for judging anyone based on just a word. She hated these stupid titles, labels, all of it.

Why couldn't everyone be the same? Then maybe she and Terryl…

Cahra's heart fluttered at the thought, but she quickly smothered it. She forced a smile and knelt by the Wildswoman, asking, 'Are you okay?' She saw the woman was still staring into the distance. Maybe she was in shock. Cahra looked for injuries, noting the woman's faded black robes. They were old, but they looked to be made of good cloth.

The woman shuddered then, as if only just hearing Cahra speak. 'Yes… yes, I am.' She peered into Cahra's eyes, focusing this time. 'You… saved me.' She held her forehead, as if it pained her, then stared at Cahra. 'Who are you?'

'My name is Cahra,' she said. Those faded robes, and the patrol they'd just fought… Where was this woman from? What was she doing here?

'I am Wyldaern,' the woman replied, still looking a little ill.

'Are you sure you're all right?' Cahra said, sweeping her with keener eyes this time. That's when she saw it.

The Sigil of the Seers.

Maybe the neck of the woman's robe had fallen open as she sat, or in the fight, or—

It didn't matter. Now it was Cahra's turn to stare. The Seers' symbol gazed at her from an amulet around Wyldaern's neck.

'The sigil,' Cahra whispered aloud, sitting heavily.

If she thought Wyldaern was staring at her before…

'I've seen it,' she said weakly. 'I fled the kingdom of Kolyath because of it.' Memories of her and Terryl's fraught escape came flooding back.

Wyldaern stood with effort then, swaying. Cahra raised a forearm to steady her, the woman gripping Cahra's blood-stained hand.

She couldn't explain what happened next. Cahra felt a jolt, as if struck by lightning, that made her mind spark with blistering light. From the left and right sides of her sight, a stretch of brilliant, incandescent white closed in, meeting at a single thread in the very centre. She opened her eyes as Wyldaern did the same.

They gazed at one another.

'You.' Wyldaern stumbled backwards and it was only Cahra clutching her that stopped her landing in the stream. 'By the All-seeing, do you know? Who you are?'

Cahra frowned. 'I told you, I'm Cahra. I'm a blacksmith from—'

Wyldaern's peridot eyes were large as lakes. She shook her head vehemently. 'No.' She paused, grasping Cahra's arm. Footsteps approached. 'Tell none of our conversation,' Wyldaern said. 'Not these people, not a soul. You do not yet know who you can trust. Do you understand? *Tell none*. Give me your word!'

'What? These people saved my life…'

'Your word! You are not safe here!' Wyldaern shook her.

'Okay! You have my word,' Cahra said hastily. *What in Hael?*

'I am an acolyte, not the conduit. The next will come from She,' Wyldaern murmured.

'*Who?*' Cahra whispered back.

Wyldaern readjusted her robe, covering the amulet, and cupped her hands in the stream's clear waters. When she spoke, the woman's voice was calm and collected as she dabbed water onto Cahra's bleeding head.

'Thank you for coming to my aid.' She smiled. 'I am a disciple of the Wilds, travelling to my teacher. Though I confess, I fear for the rest of my journey, now. And perhaps yours, too,' she said, looking behind Cahra.

Raiden approached. 'We may be able to assist with that journey, if you travel east. Those were Kolyath soldiers, far from their walled kingdom. Why did they attack you?'

'Nature magick is forbidden under the Steward Atriposte. I believe they took umbrage on behalf of their kingdom's aide.' An odd turn of phrase, Cahra thought.

Raiden gave a terse nod. 'Not the most tolerant of folk, are they?'

'No, they are not,' was Wyldaern's swift reply.

'So she can travel with us?' Cahra shot Raiden a hopeful look. She could see him sizing up Wyldaern, assessing whether she was a threat. 'I can help her back,' she offered. She'd only just met the young woman, but something told Cahra she was safe. Besides, she wanted to know what Wyldaern had been talking about. How was she in danger with Terryl and those who'd helped her escape Kolyath?

Raiden nodded finally, turning to Cahra and asking, 'Can you ride?'

'Actually, yes.' She knew how to start and stop, sort of. She may have stolen a horse for a joyride in Kolyath once, twice. A few times.

'Take the horse you and I arrived on,' Raiden told Cahra. 'We ride for the caravan.' Raiden took one last look at Wyldaern then turned to the others, seemingly dismissing the woman as a nomad living on the lands.

Cahra asked her, 'Can you walk?' Receiving a nod, she helped Wyldaern to her feet, whispering, 'You're a Seer, aren't you?'

'I am not the conduit,' Wyldaern said. 'You seek the Oracle to speak of the prophecy. I am not She,' the woman panted as they hobbled along.

'Slowly,' Cahra told her. She needed to get Wyldaern back to Terryl and Merali. 'Look, I don't so much seek the prophecy as what in Hael it has to do with me. I've been on the run with these people for a week now.' Cahra shifted to shoulder Wyldaern's weight.

'Who are they?' Wyldaern asked, straining.

'That was Raiden, Captain to Lord Terryl and his people, who are awaiting our return. Like you, we've already been attacked once, so we're all eager to reach our destination.' Cahra didn't feel it was her place to disclose the journey's end, even if Wyldaern did fill her with an uncanny sense of calm.

'Stop,' Wyldaern said, as they passed a dead soldier on the ground.

'What? Why?'

'Here…' Wyldaern shuffled from Cahra's grasp to sink beside the uniformed man. She leaned forward, plucking a small pin from his crinkled collar. 'We must hurry. Things are more dire than I thought,' the woman said under her breath.

'What do you mean?' Cahra frowned, moving towards her.

But Wyldaern was already on her feet, staggering over to another dead patrolman. Bending, the woman picked another pin from another collar. And again and again as she found more soldiers. Cahra supposed training with Piet should prepare her for corpses like these, she thought.

When Wyldaern returned, her soft features solemn, she held up a silver pin and asked, 'Do you recognise this crest?'

Cahra squinted at it. 'Should I?'

'This one, then?' Wyldaern asked, holding up another.

'Kolyath,' Cahra said. The air in her lungs abruptly chilled.

'And Ozumbre,' Wyldaern said gently, holding up the first pin.

'What?' Cahra said, breath rattling in her chest. If Kolyath had joined forces with the kingdom of Ozumbre... *Seers help them all.*

'We need to leave,' Wyldaern told her.

Cahra nodded, heaving Wyldaern's arm over her shoulder again and half-carrying the woman the rest of the way back to the horse.

'You're strong,' the Seer noted. No surprise, just observation.

'Like I told you, I'm a blacksmith,' Cahra replied, focusing on her breathing. 'Lugging heavy metal around is all I do.'

'Is it?' A suspiciously knowing look shone on Wyldaern's face.

Cahra didn't understand. But she could see the horse.

She unwound Wyldaern from her shoulders and climbed onto the steed, then hauled the woman up, pulling on the reins to turn them back towards the road.

Cahra set her jaw as she echoed Raiden's earlier words. 'Hold fast.'

CHAPTER 19

Cahra arrived with the Wildswoman – the *Seer* – Wyldaern at her back, rejoining Terryl, Raiden and their people as the caravan wound towards Luminaux. Cahra slowed the horse, pulling alongside Raiden next to Terryl's window.

'Any trouble?'

At the sound of Cahra's voice, Terryl peered out. 'Thank the Oracles,' he breathed. Seeing his relief, warmth spread through her and she smiled.

'All's quiet,' Raiden answered from upon another horse, scouring their surroundings.

She hated to bear him bad news. 'Raiden.' Cahra lifted her arm to hand him the pins Wyldaern had found on the dead patrolmen.

He took them, raising stony eyes to meet hers. 'Where did you get these?' That tone. It was alarm, pure and simple.

'We found them on the soldiers as we left. Some with one pin, some with the other.' She watched as the dread on his face solidified.

Raiden's eyes flickered to Terryl. The Captain raised his arm, two riders with him in an instant as he watched Wyldaern, telling Cahra, 'We ride hard. Cahra, get in the carriage.' Then he ordered, 'Squad two, escort our guest to the goods wagon.' His people made to move.

'Wait, Wyldaern needs Merali's aid! And you don't give *me* orders,' Cahra retorted. 'I'm not one of your guards.'

Raiden turned on Cahra, eyes blazing. 'Do you have any idea of the danger we face? Are you so sure she's not involved?' Raiden jerked a thumb at Wyldaern.

Cahra just murmured over her shoulder to Wyldaern, 'Still "tell none"?'

The Seer remained silent.

'To the kingdom,' Raiden commanded his people. Then to Cahra, the Captain said, 'This is the least safe we've been since we left Kolyath.

I can't protect my lord, or you, if our enemies have united and we have no knowledge of their plans. We're going,' he growled.

Cahra was about to cut in that she didn't need protection, when Wyldaern beat her to it, sliding from the horse.

'Protect or imprison her?' the Seer interjected, fervour in her voice. 'What, exactly, are your plans for Cahra once you reach Luminaux? Atriposte would have clapped her in chains, then tortured and slaughtered her with relish. Will your King Royce be so different?'

Cahra recognised the pain blazing in Wyldaern's peridot eyes, remembering Terryl's words about the ancient Oracles. What hardships had Wyldaern endured as a Seer, blamed by the entire realm for Hael'stromia's downfall?

'Yes.' Terryl's voice rang out like a bell from a high tower. He opened his coach door and everyone stopped as he stepped from it. 'It is not Luminaux's King, but we, as a people, who are different.'

Raiden, incredulous, flashed his iron eyes between the lot of them. 'For the love of…' He leapt from his horse and unsheathed his broadsword, his people doing the same as they formed a defensive ring around Terryl – Piet hefting his great-hammer over a pale shoulder, Siarl springing from behind them, daggers out, Queran nocking arrows from the coach's roof, hood shrouding his red mane – all twenty-plus eyes on some invisible perimeter.

Cahra dismounted, following suit. 'Te—'

'Prince Thierre,' Wyldaern stated, standing tall as every weapon in the vicinity now trained on Cahra and the Seer.

Cahra raised her hands slowly, stepping between Wyldaern, and Raiden and Terryl. 'Who is Prince Thierre?'

'King Royce of Luminaux's son, and the heir apparent, their Crown Prince,' Wyldaern replied, not taking her eyes off Terryl.

'That is one Hael of an accusation,' Raiden spat. But he had positioned himself between Cahra and Wyldaern, and his lord. Just as Cahra stood between Wyldaern and them.

She stared at Raiden, then at the noble she'd met weeks ago in Kolyath.

And remembered.

The woman at Terryl's house. *'It is done, H—'*

Highness?

And in his private coach. *'Did the Commander mention the name "Thierre" to Lumsden?'*

Prince Thierre.

And Terryl, talking to Raiden. *'I cannot keep letting you put my life above all others... I cannot be responsible for any more d—'*

Cahra's mouth went dry. Any more deaths?

Thinking about it, she'd only heard Raiden call him 'Terryl' once.

In fact, no one touched him. Because they revered him, like a god. Because he was *royalty*.

Cahra wavered, knees weak, and it was Wyldaern's turn to lend an arm to steady her.

'Cahra,' Thierre said – Prince Thierre, such sadness in his blue goldstone eyes.

Not once, *not once,* had she asked herself what could be wrong with him, or why he seemed so perfect. Now she knew. Because he was a Prince of the realm!

Cahra closed her eyes, feeling the prick of tears she was too hurt and angry to shed. These people – *his* people, from a rival kingdom – were just using her and Wyldaern to further their agenda—

No. She shook her head. They had been kind, had rescued her and saved Wyldaern. But was it selfless? It had to be. They didn't know Wyldaern was a Seer.

She breathed in the sting of betrayal, each fragment of it cutting her like shards of a shattered mirror. She pushed her feelings down, down, crushing them, burying them under the low-born heels of her blacksmith's boots.

And it worked, for a moment. But she could feel it. The hurt and fury, no matter how she tried to ram it into the ground. Cahra didn't trust anyone. She'd spent the last decade avoiding crossing paths with people: other apprentices, potential friends, all because she didn't know who she could trust after her dungeon escape. It'd taken years for her to open up to Lumsden after everything she'd been through. And this lord – this *Prince* – shows up, and weeks later, her home, her safety, all hope is *gone*—

Raiden cautioned, 'We need to get off this road.'

'Cahra,' Thierre pleaded with her.

She couldn't even look at him. 'Wyldaern, please show them.'

'Can you be so sure that you can trust these people, after what you just witnessed?'

'They came to your aid without knowledge of you,' Cahra said quietly.

Raiden's eyebrows furrowed as Cahra approached. 'Hold fire,' he told his fighters.

Cahra's eyes were daggers as she said, 'Mull all you like, Raiden, but you'll want to hear what Wyldaern has to say.' She turned to beckon to Wyldaern, but the young woman was already shadowing her as if more worried about Cahra's safety than her own.

'I will reveal my faith,' Wyldaern vowed under her breath to Cahra, 'but *tell none* about our earlier conversation. Not until your trust is earned.'

Trust. Cahra laughed mirthlessly. She reached Raiden, and they faced each other. He regarded her, lowering his sword. His guards withdrew their weapons.

She refused to look at Ter—

Thierre, Thierre, Thierre. The Crown Prince of Luminaux.

Thierre watched, forlorn, as Cahra opened the coach door for Wyldaern, who took her seat opposite his. In Cahra's place.

Raiden halted Cahra before she climbed in. 'If that woman in any way threatens him, I'll have Queran put an arrow in her.'

'You mean, "His Royal Highness"?' she shot back, sneering as she jerked from him. 'Save your threats. In a minute's time, you're going to feel like complete idiots. Like *I* do,' she seethed. She climbed in, folding her arms and facing Raiden's vacant seat.

'Make haste,' she heard him command, entering with Thierre. They all sat staring at one another, Raiden demanding, 'Care to tell us why we're here, then?'

Cahra flicked a glance to Wyldaern and nodded. Cahra would 'tell none', although she wasn't exactly sure what that meant, given she and the Seer had hardly spoken. The only thing of note was that eerie white light.

Slowly, Wyldaern pulled the Sigil of the Seers from her robe.

For a moment, no one breathed.

Then Raiden and Thierre both sunk back into their seats, staring. At one another, then at Wyldaern and Cahra.

Cahra shot them a spiteful glare.

Raiden had the sense to look remorseful. 'I had no idea.'

'Of course you didn't,' Cahra erupted. 'You barely let me talk!'

'Kolyath is in league with Ozumbre! If those soldiers had learned of the Prince…' Raiden's face went pale.

Cahra threw up her hands, turning on Thierre. 'Seers, why in Hael are you here then? If it's so damn dangerous, then why?'

'Someone has to,' Thierre stated. 'Certainly, it could be one of my father's spymen, or any manner of soldier. But as I told you, I connect with people. I am learned in other royal courts, history, geography, culture, warfare. And I am not like my family. I cannot live in a kingdom and not know anything of other lands in turmoil.'

'Oh, so you wanted an *adventure*,' Cahra retorted. 'Royal life a royal bore, was it?' Poor form, directed at a lord, she knew, worse still at a Prince of the realm's tri-kingdoms. Raiden looked ready to throttle her. She didn't care.

'It matters not why you are here,' Wyldaern said. 'Cahra's safety is what matters.'

'As does yours,' Raiden told the Seer.

'Oh? A minute ago, you were ready to shoot her,' Cahra snapped.

'The sister kingdoms believe the Oracles to be a people now extinct,' Thierre said, apologetic then curious as he watched Wyldaern. 'Was it a vision that led you here to us? How you knew of my true name?'

'Yes,' Wyldaern replied, glancing at Cahra. 'So I must ask the question. What are your intentions for Cahra and myself?'

'As Cahra has been, you are now our honoured guest,' Thierre said to Wyldaern. Cahra looked away. 'And we, your humble hosts, and with hope, allies.'

'That remains to be seen,' the Seer answered. 'What if I had not shown you the sigil? What would I have been to you, then?'

'An unknown,' Raiden replied, crossing his arms.

'Enough.' Thierre waved his hand with a fraction of the command he could employ. Cahra's jaw tightened, as did her chest; the ribs encasing her heart. 'Enough,' he said, softer. 'There is no need to be at odds, now that all is revealed.' Wyldaern was silent. So was Cahra.

'Fine,' Cahra said finally. 'So now what? Wyldaern must continue on her journey.' She thought aloud. 'Maybe I'll join her.'

Thierre looked wounded. What did he want from her? He was Luminaux's Prince, he could befriend anyone he liked. He didn't need her.

And he had *lied* to her, even if it was lying by omission, not once, but twice. What else had he not told her? Was anything between them real?

Cahra knew she wasn't being fair. Deep down, she understood the need for secrecy.

'Prince Thierre' would have been killed on sight in Kolyath. But that didn't make his secret any less hurtful, or any less a betrayal of her trust.

Because as Terryl, as a lord, it had felt like the two of them weren't so different.

But as a Prince…

There was no hope. And she felt stupid and naive and totally, utterly *humiliated* that she, a beggar, had feelings for a *Prince*, had even thought he might have feelings for—

'Cahra.' She was yanked from her thoughts by the sound of her own name as Thierre called to her, his throat bobbing as he swallowed.

'What?' She instantly regretted her disrespectful tone.

'If you wish to go, that is your choice.' Why was he so upset? It had been her fantasy, not his. She and Thierre would never be anything and she just needed to forget her idiotic, childish feelings, forget him and get away. Far, far away, from him. From all of them.

'But first, we must ride for Luminaux.' Thierre was still speaking. 'If Kolyath and Ozumbre have aligned, we are at risk every second that I am not behind our walls.'

'On the condition that Cahra and I can leave at any time,' Wyldaern declared.

'Of course. As I have said, you are our guests,' Thierre told her.

'Your word, that we may leave,' Wyldaern said. 'On the throne of your King Royce.'

Cahra looked between the two of them, first at Wyldaern for her brazenness, then at Thierre, so taken aback the whites of his eyes showed.

'I give you my word,' Thierre vowed. Wyldaern seemed satisfied. He surveyed her, asking the Seer then, 'Are you in need of healing?'

Wyldaern gave him a thin smile. 'I shall manage.'

'So,' Raiden said, raising his head. 'A question.' He eyed Wyldaern. 'By the stream, you said you were going to see your teacher.'

'That is not a question,' Wyldaern told him. 'What of it?'

'An Oracle, then,' Raiden continued.

'Shall I repeat myself?' Wyldaern smiled, but her gaze was unyielding.

'And you want to go, too.' Raiden cocked his head at Cahra. Another non-question. Cahra didn't like where this was heading.

'So what?' Cahra countered, 'If I'm free to leave?'

'A Seer, and the messenger of the prophecy's first omen. *Your* people's prophecy,' Raiden said, turning to Wyldaern. 'What are you not telling us?'

'Raiden.' Thierre sighed. He sat slumped, clearly dispirited after their exchange. Cahra ground her teeth against feeling sorry for him. 'They are not telling us whatever they are not telling us because we must regain their trust. Despite events, that is prudent. At least, until they meet the King and Queen, and can decide of their own volition.'

Raiden, who looked like he wanted to argue, said nothing.

'Avail yourself of our hospitality,' Thierre went on. 'Experience Luminaux, then judge us, leave us, if that is your will. We are not the sister kingdoms of Kolyath or Ozumbre. See our kingdom with your own eyes and decide.'

Wyldaern asked, 'And if this is a ploy? To keep us in Luminaux?'

Thierre locked eyes with the Seer as he said, 'I gave you my word.'

Cahra spoke. 'We will give you one night. *One*. Then we're gone.'

Then I'm gone.

Wyldaern gave a supportive nod.

Thierre inclined his head in return, his indigo eyes flickering to Cahra for a moment, then away. As if hesitating. 'Cahra, there is something else.'

Cahra stared at him. 'No,' she said, her voice hollow, even to her.

No. No more lies.

Thierre opened his mouth, then shut it. Before looking blankly out the window, his lips a taut line as the coach rode for Luminaux.

Cahra just stared into the Wilds, wondering how she'd managed to care so much for someone she didn't even know.

–

Everyone was silent for the rest of the journey, as the horses rode hard to get Thierre behind Luminaux's walled defences. Any excitement Cahra had felt about the kingdom was long gone and, in its place, there was only anguish. It must have showed, because she could feel Thierre watching her, casting her pained glances, but she refused to acknowledge them. There was no point. Even if somehow, impossibly, he felt an inkling of what she did, he was a Prince. Whatever she'd stupidly imagined may have been between them, whatever they'd shared when he touched her hand—

It had no hope.

Cahra kept her face angled to the outside world, away from Thierre, and started to notice subtle changes in the Wilds along the cobbled road to Luminaux. Little things, at first: the dimness easing, more daylight breaking through the speckled foliage of the forest ceiling. Dainty red, white and pink flowers lined the roadside, green undulating grasses at their backs. The houses they passed were neater, lovelier, with curving stone paths and tended gardens. And the sound of animals had returned, the melodious songs of robins and sparrows warbling through the windows of the coach. She studied the homes, the white wood, clean glass and boldly painted doors – all the hues of the rainbow – greeting them at every turn. Cahra could hear the splish-splash of a brook nearby. Life was returning.

And with it, enough misery for her to drown in.

She watched Wyldaern, the Seer unmoved by the vistas outside. At least Cahra wouldn't be alone to face Luminaux's royals.

Cahra closed her eyes as the realisation hit. Seers, she thought, then glanced at Wyldaern and committed to less cursing. But arriving in Luminaux would require meeting the kingdom's King and Queen, Thierre's parents.

She'd never be with him, but she'd have to meet, greet, *curtsey* to his royal parents. See his castle, like the Steward's in Kolyath.

It was too much, Cahra thought, inhaling a shaky breath.

Wyldaern noticed, shifting closer to her. Cahra wanted to smile at the Seer's kindness, but she couldn't force the expression to her face. All she felt, all that consumed her was a grim churning in the pit of her stomach with the knowledge that Thierre had lied. He had seen her

– Cahra had shown him who she really was – and he had broken that fledgling trust.

Had held her hand. Laid her in his bed.

She shook her head, as if she could wrench the memories from it. It didn't matter, none of it mattered! It didn't matter what she thought or how she felt about him, he was *Crown Prince Thierre of Luminaux*.

No matter what he'd said about titles, a low-born would never matter to Thierre.

Cahra looked up from her clasped hands, knuckles white, as if gripping something, anything, would stop her falling to pieces. Silver birches swayed in the sun, the trees glowing like happy apparitions, and she scented sweet jasmine on the breeze that tousled her hair. Then a familiar metal caught her eye – bars, wrought and thorned and jet-black as night, that were set into the nearing kingdom's dry-stone fortifications.

She watched as Thierre's smile lit up his blue goldstone eyes. Without a word, he and Raiden raised an arm out each window, signalling their arrival to their home kingdom.

Wyldaern glanced at Cahra, who took a single, sinking breath.

They'd arrived in Luminaux.

CHAPTER 20

Atriposte, ruler of Kolyath, lounged atop his gilded throne, perusing the battle report that had arrived via rock dove. Kolyath had triumphed against Luminaux's armed forces, moving his kingdom toward the area's strategic goal: the enemy's most active, lucrative mine. Atriposte bared his teeth in a self-satisfied smile. Their last encounter with Luminaux had scattered his army during its retreat. This time, his men returned the courtesy with blood. It was progress, warranting a celebration.

He slid the scroll into his throne's left secret compartment, the compartment on the right concealing his favourite throwing dagger. Then Atriposte snapped his fleshy fingers, a mute servant appearing a moment later. Frowning at the delay, Atriposte twisted to unleash a torrent at the sluggish wench, but the drudgling was already pouring his wine. He snatched it, swirling the rich red in its goblet and eyeing the servant through narrowed amber eyes, his hand drifting towards his hidden dagger. He was recalling the thrill of its swirling steel when a figure in gold armour burst in.

Impatient, he watched Sullian, Commander of the Kingdom Army, traverse the vast expanse of the great hall. Above them, hammers forming the heraldry of Kolyath adorned the vaulted ceiling, a relic from the bygone era of Kings and an enduring symbol of the reign of Stewards. Sullian's gait, paired with the perturbed look to his face, could only mean bad tidings. But then, Atriposte already knew why Sullian was here.

Standing to one side at the foot of his throne was Jarett, Sullian's brother and Commander of the Kingdom Guards. Jarett's face was draped in a smirk, his own armour less battle-worn yet still capable of crushing a man's ribcage with a punch from his plate gauntlet. Jarett's large, jutting brown eyes basked in Sullian's penance to come.

'Your Excellency,' Sullian rasped, chest heaving. 'I have word.'

'And is that word "failure"?' Jarett arched an eyebrow.

Sullian's face reddened with the intensity of his anger.

Jarett laughed, a harsh sound that echoed through the hall. 'Do not be too hard on him, Your Excellency. My dear sibling merely lacks the finesse required for this line of work.' His rivalry with Sullian for Atriposte's favour was well-known. Less so, Atriposte's practice of baiting one with blatant disregard for the other, a winning tactic since the brothers had joined his kingdom ranks.

'Well, Commander Sullian? I am waiting.' Atriposte drummed his fingers on the armrest.

'The girl blacksmith and Lord Terryl eluded my men,' Sullian managed to grate out.

Atriposte's face didn't betray his thoughts racing inside.

Of course they did, Atriposte, you irredeemable fool. Your own brother would have seized them before they reached the gatehouse. He earned his position as Father's successor. He would have known. But Markus cannot, can he? And why is that?

Atriposte's jaw clenched against the errant question, knowing the answer.

Because you killed him.

Atriposte made a show of examining an invisible speck of dust on the polished floors, the white marble patterned with cracks instead of swirls, as if lightning was trapped within it. He paused to eye Sullian's dishevelled state, the sheen of sweat lining the man's face.

Curling his upper lip in sour distaste, Atriposte exhaled sadly. 'Ah, Sullian, my once-mighty Commander. You disappoint me.'

Sullian flinched, before pulling himself up to his full height, features tight with the burden of failure.

Because you killed him. Atriposte indeed had, and the words echoed through his mind. But there was no time for guilt now when the room was fraught with such stupidity.

And that girl blacksmith… He recalled her filthy face, vaguely. There was something so familiar to it…

'You have failed me,' Atriposte told Sullian, his voice exuding a most deadly calm. He dared to slip his fingers into the slit of the armrest's compartment, yearning for his blade. Clutching the handle, he drew it free of its sheath. The red diamond of his signet ring flashed in the rake of sunlight burning from the high windows. So did the glittering blade.

Sullian's face twisted with unease, his stance wavering at the sight of that dagger. 'Your Excellency,' he said, 'I bear ultimate responsibility for the failings of my men.'

Before Sullian could go on, his brother cut in, a sardonic smirk playing on his lips. 'Yes, you do,' Jarett chimed, crossing his arms. 'You had one job, and it seems capturing a girl was too much for you.'

Sullian's eyes flashed dangerously. 'And you?' he snapped, words dripping with contempt. 'You let her and the lord escape in the first place!'

'At least when I erred, it wasn't a second time.' Jarett's eyes taunted.

As the brothers broke into a cacophony of accusations and counter-criticisms, Atriposte struggled to decide which he would rather hurl his blade at.

'And what of my prized army, Commander? Did it not occur to you to give chase at the gate?'

Sullian began, 'It is the Wilds, and as Jarett himself experienced, the Wildspeople—'

At this, Atriposte's head snapped up. 'The Wildspeople what? Slay trained soldiers with their pointy sticks?' He pinched the bridge of his nose, hissing an exhale. 'One of these days, Commander, I shall tire of your tenantless intellect. *Both* of you,' he muttered.

The brothers flinched, then glared at one another.

Yet despite the scores Atriposte had put to death for minor deeds, he stayed his hand with Sullian and Jarett. Not due to favour, and certainly not any loyalty, but a likeness between the three of them.

Yes, they were alike. In their ire, in their desire to prove themselves. In their resultant ache for violence.

Because you were always Father's second-best son, until you culled the competition. And just in time, too.

'I don't want excuses,' Atriposte ordered, leaning forward. 'I want her. And him.'

Sullian stood tall, defiance in his eyes. 'It is only a matter of time,' he said firmly. 'These people do not travel inconspicuously and we have narrowed their likely routes.'

Atriposte's mind wandered as Sullian droned on, anger ebbing into icy determination. He would have this Cahra girl, and the merchant Lord Terryl, and he would have them alive. No mistake from Sullian or anyone else would stand in his way.

Do not give him too long a leash. You saw what happened with Father. One minute, they are on your side. The next, their knife is in *your side.*

Atriposte had seen his father execute Commander after Commander in this very room. Not only did it fail to solve incompetencies, it eroded loyalty. Not to mention that it had prompted his father's own untimely death. For Atriposte, it was a lesson of import: no ruler is invulnerable. Unless they possessed a large enough deterrent. Thinking of the weapon, Atriposte smiled.

So, he had begun his reign by purging his father's council. This had been followed by Atriposte reigniting the kingdom's war rhetoric – and his subjects' unity and loyalty – by raising low-born taxes to support his new advisors in their courtly patronage, blamed on the lofty expenditures of war and leaving Kolyath's base residents too starved to mount an uprising. Then, his favourite: practitioners of scrying magick hung by their ankles, disembowelled and left to putrefy in his kingdom's execution square.

He had learned from his father's mistakes. Terror and violence were not enough, nor were bullying, torturing and killing, like his father had, with the tormenting of his own sons. Atriposte's strength had to prevail for a reason, one that people would condone. Hael'stromia and the weapon were that reason, the war the vehicle; the outcome, prosperity and stability.

And Atriposte would take it through force. Neither Luminaux's weakling King Royce nor Ozumbre's barbarous King Decimus would take the capital's ultimate weapon from him. Kolyath was the perfect fit, as it had been the last time it controlled the weapon and Hael'stromia. The last time any of the tri-kingdoms had done so, before the city's loss.

We shall see. Whether your unregal blood dooms you to life as a sitting imposter, or whether the prophecy has something to offer you, Steward.

At the foot of his throne, Jarett spoke. 'Please, Your Excellency, do not coddle him. Let him attempt to remedy this most egregious of mistakes. If he can.'

'I *will* find them and cut down any and all who stand in my path,' Sullian growled.

A sly smile forming, Jarett mused, 'Perhaps start with that old mule blacksmith.'

There it was, the thirst for violence. Atriposte could see it in their faces, eyebrows carving a murderous line. It was precisely what the Commanders were good for, and why he kept Sullian and Jarett all these long years: the rabble feared him, feared Kolyath. Atriposte's soldiers and guards were the plate-fisted enforcers of his grand cause.

Realising the Commanders had fallen silent before him, awaiting his next orders, Atriposte waved a hand at Sullian. 'If you must.'

Shooting a glare at Jarett, the army Commander bowed, turning to go.

'Halt,' Atriposte ordered. 'I was to send for you, and you have saved me the trouble. Your presence is required to greet a valuable guest. It seems an accord has now been struck,' Atriposte continued, as Sullian eyed him warily, 'and I am to receive a gesture of goodwill from our new sister kingdom comrades.' He reluctantly sheathed his dagger at his side, then rang a shrill bell to signal the attendants in reception, booming, 'Come!'

He watched as first Jarett then Sullian spun, drawing their swords in unison when they beheld who, or more precisely, what, entered the room.

The Commanders' blades gleamed as a breathy laugh rasped and rumbled like nothing Atriposte had ever heard. Certainly nothing human.

'You'll not end me with that, young one,' the figure taunted, garbed in an off-white hooded robe, ripped and tattered at the hem. A shiver of sheer delight fluttered from the nape of Atriposte's neck down the length of his spine. This…

This was worth partnering with Ozumbre for.

The nefarious figure, every line and curve of its silhouette radiating danger, turned. 'Atriposte, blood of Stewards. We meet at last,' the figure said, his voice chillingly casual.

The sound made Atriposte's hairs stand on end, his every instinct screaming.

Instead, Atriposte managed to grant a seemly smile in return. 'And you, Grauwynn, Oracularus of Hael'stromia.' His tone was almost respectful. Almost.

The elderly Seer reciprocated, amused. 'You shall warm to our gifts, my good Steward, that we promise, especially when you hear of the All-seeing's latest revelation.' Grauwynn withdrew his ghostly cowl, revealing drab beige skin pulled taut over his bones, wrinkling like crepe in the hollows of his face. The wiry man's eyes shone a disconcerting shade of violet as he beheld the Commanders.

'Yes?' Atriposte eyed his fingernails, looking bored. Theatrics were of the utmost importance.

To one side, Jarett, who had silently observed the exchange, began to laugh. Sullian's face tightened, but he remained silent, his grip on his sword easing.

Yet nothing in Atriposte's life, tallying middle years, had prepared him for the boon laid before him as Grauwynn said, 'Your fugitives.' The Oracle gazed into Atriposte's eyes. 'I know where they are going.'

PART TWO

'When the Key has been bestowed'

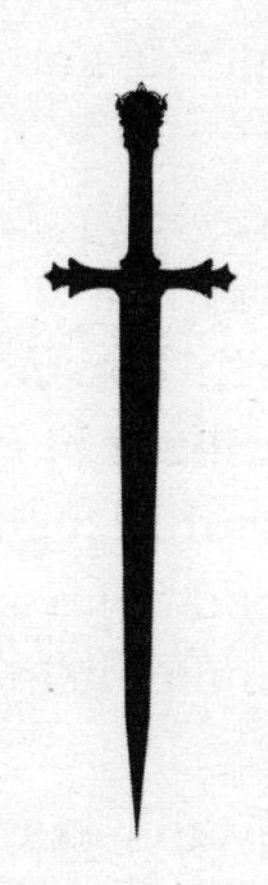

CHAPTER 21

Trumpets blared as Luminaux's Haellium gate opened, slowly enough for a swarm of soldiers in blue tabards to rush through – their archers lining the parapets, Cahra realised, not focused on Thierre's caravan, but on the surrounding Wilds.

She sat back from the window as the coach's wheels creaked forward, Luminaux's Royal Guards swarming it like birds of prey: swiftly and strategically, footmen first, then bowmen on the ground and finally a mixed cavalry carrying all manner of shining weapons. She watched their units fall into formation as the lengthy caravan inched through the gate, guards closing ranks behind them as she stared out the window at the passing gatehouse. She couldn't help but feel like game caught in a hunter's trap.

Cahra had barely seen Kolyath's exit through the tiny peephole in Thierre's wagon, but Luminaux's entrance was grand. The stone walls weren't her kingdom's dull grey but a soft, pearly white, and she noted the undented armour and oiled weapons of the Royal Guards. They were well-equipped, unlike Kolyath's. There, she'd been lucky to escape with a scratch and not a maiming slash to her limbs often enough as a child, thanks to the Steward's failure to properly arm his own Kingdom Guards.

Luminaux's Royal Guards, however, were well-provisioned and methodical, not to mention endless, their helmed faces lining the street as Terryl's coach proceeded through it. Alongside them, more and more everyday folk began appearing, staring, smiling, even cheering loudly.

Why is everybody gawking at us? Cahra frowned, wondering what in Hael was going on, the clamour of trumpets eating away at her nerves.

Then she realised. It was Thierre.

This was his homecoming, for Luminaux's dashing Prince, who'd been away on a foreign mission and returned to his kingdom at last.

She was in a royal parade. 'I think I'm going to be sick,' she mumbled to Wyldaern. The Seer squeezed her hand.

It was a night terror made real. She, a low-born, was seated in the royal carriage for a procession that would lead her to the palace doors.

Her vision blurred as they ambled through the kingdom, Cahra only seeing the same perfect rows of ivory houses with their pitched slate roofs and wrought-iron balconies and windowsills overflowing with boxes of plump red and pink blossoms, the imagery stifling, the coach moving past the markets, the bread and pastry houses, the blacksmith's—

She realised what she'd spotted, her eyes on the large, lovely workspace that was Luminaux's smithy. Just seeing the forge smouldering in the back like a tame volcano made her miss the heat, the sunset glow of flames, the awe of smelting ore into sublime creations… She sniffed, longing to catch the faintest scent of coal, and felt almost hopeful, buoyed for the briefest of moments, before they rounded a corner and the smithy disappeared out of sight. Cahra leaned back heavily, saying nothing.

When she finally lifted her head again, Thierre was watching her.

She'd guessed Luminaux and Kolyath would have similarities, being sister kingdoms, but their only likeness was different quadrants for trading, the military and farming, and a hilltop keep. Only here, it wasn't so much a hill as a soaring elevation backed by a fertile mountain range. As they neared it, Cahra could see the palace wasn't walled off from its kingdom's subjects; that in itself was a difference to Kolyath. Luminaux had nothing to fear from its own.

Despite the glee of the crowd and the fragrant jasmine wafting through the window, whisked along on a balmy breeze, a knot of tension was hardening in Cahra's stomach as they began the ascent up the paved road to the palace. By now, people were clapping and shouting praise for their Prince, Thierre leaning out the window, waving to all.

It was madness, or maybe that was just the pins and needles in Cahra's arms and legs, as if her body was readying itself to jump right out of Thierre's coach and run all the way back to Kolyath. Instead, Cahra sat on her hands, willing the roiling inside her to subside as she forced her body to stay the course, this course, that would lead her to Thierre's real life.

The royal life that she was in no way prepared for.

To distract herself, Cahra stared at the fine buildings, all the way from the wealthy residences that trumped even Thierre's mansion in Kolyath, to little shops such as a florist's, a sweet-maker's, a perfumer's and more. All with hand-lettered signage of blue and gold, like the banners that lined the kingdom's streets, a circle with a gold star in its upper right, an ominous black pyramid at the insignia's centre.

She gazed at those flags and their black triangles all the way to the palace's summit, past the impeccable gardens and into the courtyard of the royal keep.

And couldn't help but think of Hael, alone, in darkness.

-

Once the caravan stopped, Cahra had no idea what to do. Thierre exited first, the guards and kingdom onlookers erupting into jubilant applause, Raiden a step behind him. The Captain turned, telling Cahra and Wyldaern, 'You're guests here. Act like it.'

Cahra wanted to scowl but forced a grim smile to her face, Wyldaern's own features arranging into something of a placid simper.

Raiden stepped back, offering the Seer his hand. She took it, nodding primly, the trim of her robe spilling around her simple sandals.

Cahra breathed in, slowly and deeply. Then exhaled as she too left the coach, shielding her eyes from the sun.

As soon as her boots hit the ground, she realised she was the last to appear. Thierre strode forward with Raiden, Piet, Siarl, Queran and the rest of his apparent Royal Guards, Cahra seeing Langera and Merali at the rear.

Straightening, Cahra faced Luminaux's court members gathered by the palace doors. Though built from the pearly stones she'd seen earlier and ice-blue glass with gold accents, the palace wasn't a stern ivory castle. Unlike the Steward's keep in Kolyath, Luminaux's perched elegantly on its rise, sprawling and championing less, not more, to its majesty.

Cahra's gaze traced a reluctant path from the building's upper levels to the royals on the steps, dwarfed by doors emblazoned with a fleur-de-lis crest, her apprehension threatening to spill from her like a gushing torrent. There were two men, and three women – one middle-aged and two younger like herself.

Cahra picked out the King and Queen with ease, the formal regalia an obvious giveaway. Between the King's cloak and the Queen's gown, their matching royal blue and gold tailoring was exquisite, the brocade fabric sewn in tiny interlocking shapes with circles, triangles, ovals and stars interspersed with crescent moons. The second, older man had a longsword and a warrior's look to him, like Raiden, with the hard-baked scowl to match. Then Cahra turned to the young women. Sisters? The first was a rare beauty, with Thierre's blue goldstone eyes and raven-coloured hair pinned in a tight braid flipped over one of her silver shoulder guards, a sword and the small, round shield of a buckler at the woman's belt. Her fine-boned face bore a polished detachment that failed to negate her looks. But the second woman… No, not related. This woman was blonde, with glossy tresses far paler than Cahra's own drab hair and eyes the lemony colour of waterworn jade, in such deep contrast with the emerald lace bodice and silken skirts that clung to her hourglass figure.

Their eyes met then, and there was something in the young woman's gaze that made Cahra defy the urge to shrink beneath it.

She turned from the blonde woman as the Queen dashed to meet Thierre, sweeping her son into her arms. His mother was no doubt where he got his blue goldstone eyes from, only hers were a lighter, brighter shade of blue. Thierre's father just stood, arms folded at his back as she'd seen Thierre himself do. The warm sun deepened the King's rich brown skin, a smile finding its way to his crinkly navy eyes.

'Hail, Crown Prince Thierre of Luminaux!' A herald stood at the top of the stairs and announced Thierre, blowing on a trumpet. He chuckled and waved the sound away as his mother laughed, the two of them approaching the four left standing on the steps.

Before Cahra could shift on her feet, the horn sounded again and Raiden beckoned to her and Wyldaern, the Seer going first.

'His Majesty, King Royce of Luminaux,' a footman proclaimed as Thierre greeted his father, the two clasping arms before the King folded his son into an embrace. Raiden and Wyldaern followed to approach the ruler.

'Her Royal Highness, Queen Avenais of Luminaux,' the footman continued. Thierre's mother took his arm with a laugh.

'Her Royal Highness, Princess Sylvanir, General of the Royal Army of Luminaux.'

'Sylvie,' Thierre greeted. 'Congratulations are in order!' Then he smiled, teasing, 'So, do I salute you, now?'

His sister smirked, arching a dark brow. 'On the battlefield,' she said, grinning.

He winked and raised his fist to his chest. It was only Cahra's gifted hearing that allowed her to catch the words under his breath, 'It may yet be today, sister.'

What did that mean? Fighting the urge to unravel Thierre's words, she dimly noticed Sylvanir sneaking a glance at Wyldaern.

Thierre moved to the next man in line. 'Commander Tyne.' He inclined his head. 'Each of your reports was simply riveting, a literary delight.'

Raiden choked, a step behind Thierre, stifling his laughter.

Not taking the bait, the Commander just retorted, 'You're back early.'

'Yes,' Raiden murmured, clearing his throat.

There was only one person left. Thierre seemed to collect himself, standing opposite the woman with the lemon-jade eyes. Cahra felt Wyldaern's on her.

The Queen, her own eyes sparkling, squeezed Thierre. 'We have wonderful news, darling. You and Lady Delicia are to be—'

'I know.' Thierre's voice was downright cold. All affection, even the playful mocking for his kingdom's Commander-in-chief, was now gone.

Cahra stared at him. Thierre had always been so courteous, so unruffled, a true nobleman. She'd never seen him act like this before.

For a moment, Thierre didn't say anything more. But when he did, it was one word. 'Delicia.' As if not in greeting, but in warning.

'Come, Thierre, is that any way to receive your betrothed?' Disapproval fluttered briefly across his mother's face.

Her words faded, replaced by a ringing in Cahra's ears, a high-pitched wailing she was half-convinced was coming from her mouth, though no one else seemed to hear it.

'My Queen, please, there is no need. My beloved is simply weary after a long and arduous journey,' the young woman said in a soothing, saccharine voice. 'Thierre...'

Thierre, who'd been gazing at Cahra, now twisted to face Delicia.

Cahra shivered, unexpectedly cold, as if she'd just showered in a hailstorm. Yet all her muscles were tingling. Burning. She stood, a statue, but felt as if she couldn't get enough air into her chest, couldn't keep it in her lungs. Her heart pounded in her ears.

Did Thierre's mother just say 'betrothed'?

Wyldaern was facing Cahra now, her face pinched with concern.

Betrothed.

To a girl that was the embodiment of nobility, of light, from her flaxen hair and creamy skin, all the way to her svelte physique. Even her voice, the way 'beloved' lilted from her tongue, with such high-born affectation.

All in cutting contrast to Cahra and her messy hair, face marred from fighting, her muddy eyes and nasal voice and too-strong body and wrong-size dress, everything about her common, unremarkable, beggarly—

I can't do this.

Cahra wanted to melt into the marble of the lustrous courtyard, unable to look away as Thierre stared darkly at the woman, Delicia – *Lady* Delicia, Thierre's noble fiancée – before he turned and moved for Cahra.

She instinctively flinched backwards, pain etching Thierre's face as she did so. Stopping a respectful distance away, his eyes were pleading. What that was supposed to mean, Cahra didn't know. She didn't know anything any more.

And then Wyldaern was there, propping Cahra up as she sagged against the Seer.

'Cahra,' Wyldaern whispered, rallying her, 'You will endure. We both will. We shall speak to Luminaux's King and Queen, and we will rest. Then we will travel to the Oracle, where you shall learn your fate.' She glared at Thierre. 'And be free of this one's falsehoods.'

Wyldaern stepped in front of Cahra, staring coldly at Thierre, and said quietly, 'One more deception, Prince, and we depart. I do not care for your heedless reasons, nor your kingdom's hospitality.' Her tone was scathing. 'Let us speak and be done with this.'

Then Wyldaern strode for the palace steps, head high.

Cahra didn't know how to move her legs. But moment by moment, her limbs thawed, as she focused on each of Wyldaern's footsteps. Eventually, Cahra managed to follow her, Thierre looking on.

Betrothed. Beloved. Thierre is to be married.

Cahra shut her eyes, letting the soothing numbness be her guide, her footsteps leaden.

Delicia's jade-tinged gaze marked every one.

CHAPTER 22

All eyes were on Cahra as she stilled to speak, perched on a leather chair that dwarfed her – a feat given her solid blacksmith's frame – in a room of Luminaux's palace that could only be described as a den of war. Its walls were hunter's green and adorned with an armoury of weapons carrying the scent of oil and steel: pairs of poleaxes, morningstars, halberds, even great-hammers, all with handles crossed like 'X's marking danger. A sprawling map of the realm was unfurled in the centre of a mahogany table, Hael'stromia's black pyramid flanked by blue, red and grey hand-carved pieces for Luminaux, Kolyath and Ozumbre's armies, doing battle on the table as they were in life. But Cahra's gaze was on that map, eyes drawn to the painted black pyramid at its heart depicting Hael'stromia. *Hael.*

The memory of his fiery eyes that burned with their own light filled her.

Eventually, Cahra glanced up from the map to the Luminaux royals awaiting her tale. Thierre's longsword lay on the table, tormenting her. As did everything about this place.

At least Lady Delicia had been dismissed, potential talk of the war too much for her high-born sensibilities.

Looking anywhere but at Thierre, Cahra caught Wyldaern's peridot eyes, the Seer nodding in encouragement. Cahra could almost hear the words inside her head, the words that had roused her outside the palace.

You will endure.

One night. She could endure one night. Then she'd be free of Thierre forever.

Longing for nightfall, Cahra began.

Luminaux's royals were in differing degrees of shock by the end of Cahra's story. King Royce moved to peer at the longsword she'd forged for his son, glancing quizzically between Cahra and the sigil on the pommel. Commander Tyne, arms braced on the table, glowered at the red and grey pieces on the map, the furrow etched between his eyebrows clearly a product of fierce and frequent thought. When Cahra spoke about Lumsden revealing 'Lord Terryl' as the sword's owner and her finding Thierre before the Kingdom Guards did, Queen Avenais gasped. And Thierre himself stressed that not only had Cahra saved Raiden during the first attack, but she and Wyldaern had found Kolyath and Ozumbre's pins on the soldiers in the second one. Gracious of him, to assert she wasn't a foreign foe.

But that didn't make Thierre a friend.

All the while, Princess Sylvanir, Thierre's sister and General under the Commander, leaned against a floor-to-ceiling bookcase. A booted ankle crooked behind her armoured leg, she stared from Thierre to Cahra and back again.

As with Delicia, Cahra didn't flinch under the young woman's piercing gaze, but not from resentment or defensiveness. There was something Cahra respected about her and the idea of a woman leading a kingdom's army. Cahra wasn't a soldier, but she'd known the looks and comments that went along with existing in a man's field. She wondered if Luminaux's General had experienced them too.

Wyldaern spoke next, her Sigil of the Seers on display, to the delight of the Queen, which surprised Cahra. All she'd ever heard of the Seers from the Steward's proclamations was 'heretic this, heathen that', despite the prophecy providing for his precious war. Wyldaern explained she'd been travelling to her teacher, stopping to forage for food when the allied patrol had attacked. As with Cahra's, the Seer's tale ended with the pins.

And it was those enemy pins, that new piece of information – that Luminaux's rival kingdoms had conspired – that was the royals' cause for concern, and debate.

Cahra didn't have concerns or strength for debating left. Not after hours of questions about Kolyath, Steward Atriposte, Commander Jarett and the Kingdom Army, when all she wanted to do was sleep. Instead she listened to the royals brood and plan, and tried not to think.

Of Thierre, sneaking her glances from the opposite end of the room.

Of Delicia, the perfect bride for Luminaux's Crown Prince.

And of herself, leaving them to their pre-wedded bliss in the morning.

Cahra sat up from slouching in her chair as Wyldaern handed her a turquoise teacup. Upon the Queen discovering Thierre hadn't eaten since breakfast, food and drink were swiftly laid out on a serving table at the room's rear, a huge honey-roasted ham on a silver platter with a rainbow medley of baked vegetables, and enough wine to tipple then topple an army. Cahra had eaten her fill, but had no wish to drink, so Wyldaern had fetched her a cup of the tea the Seer had been sipping. Cahra took it, the steaming cup a comfort.

Meanwhile, the mood in the room had shifted, now abuzz with the implications of Cahra and Wyldaern's revelation about the pins. King Royce and Commander Tyne were poring over the realm's tabletop terrain, General Sylvanir pacing and frowning at random pieces, shaking her head.

'Anything?' The Commander didn't look up, also scowling at the map.

'Nothing, except that all campaigns are now compromised,' the General said through gritted teeth, indicating several points on the table: their blue pieces outside Luminaux's gate; more to the north, half-way to Kolyath, at the bottom of what looked like caves; more still flanking Kolyath and Ozumbre's kingdom gates. 'Based on the latest reports, each location is, at most, a day from not one but both forces. If this alliance has occurred at a kingdom level, they outnumber us everywhere. They could strike at any time.' Sylvanir turned to Tyne, the indigo of her arresting eyes – hers and Thierre's – flashing. 'We must retreat.'

Silence. The Commander's forehead buckled.

'No. We cannot forfeit the northern mines.' It was King Royce, his voice of hoarfrost. 'Or the surrounding Wilds.'

'And if it comes to the mines or our men?' Tyne countered.

Sylvanir remained unmoved. 'Pull them back. We strike once we have a clear strategy.'

The King replied, 'Is that not why you are here?'

'It is,' she fired back, 'unless you'd rather I flounce about in pretty dresses so that I might snare one of the landed gentry, instead of defending our kingdom?'

Thierre bristled at the reference.

Raiden glanced between them, then to Cahra and Wyldaern. 'Is there anything else? Anything that could help us fight them?' His gaze lingered on Wyldaern.

'I wasn't exactly privy to the workings of Kolyath's court,' Cahra said.

Why don't you consult the Prince, isn't that why you were there?

The King and his advisors kept arguing. Exhaling, Cahra lifted the teacup to her lips. And sniffed, her eyes flashing to Wyldaern.

Queen Avenais smiled at Cahra and the Seer in turn. 'Chamomile,' she said. 'Exquisite, is it not? Steeping it extracts such a soft, sweet flavour.'

'Quite.' Wyldaern nodded, eyeing the Queen then murmuring to Cahra from behind her cup, 'It is also a herb used for purification and protection.'

Cahra was too tired to question why Luminaux permitted herbs when Kolyath didn't. That said, their royals had welcomed Wyldaern as a Seer. In Kolyath, well, she would've been hauled off to the Red Square. Cahra never understood why the Steward hated the Seers and scrying magick when he was so obviously in favour of the prophecy's weapon.

Wyldaern softened. 'It heals, too. The tea will aid your sleep,' she said.

Cahra grunted. *Good.*

'We keep more than chamomile,' the Queen mused, her silver speech polished with practiced high-born persuasion. 'Eyebright, sage, meadowsweet... Our kingdom did not forbid worshipping nature, or scrying magick. The ways of old,' she said pleasantly.

Cahra frowned. What was the woman getting at?

'There must be a way.' Thierre's voice broke through the din, Cahra's upper body tensing at the sound. She gripped her teacup, the piping heat biting into her skin.

'There is.' Sylvanir was steadfast. 'We cut our losses and regroup. Unless you're so willing to face our adversaries united, whose forces amount to double our own now.'

'How do we combat an enemy of that size?' The familiar hardness to Raiden's face was a mirror of Commander Tyne's.

It was Tyne who spoke next, the Commander turning to Cahra. 'What do you know of the second omen of the prophecy, girl?'

Wyldaern narrowed her eyes, as Thierre interjected coolly, 'Her name is Cahra.'

Beside the table, Sylvanir straightened, eyes on her brother.

The Commander just laughed. 'Well, *Cah-ra*,' he said, drawing out both syllables, 'the Seers have indeed reappeared.' Tyne gestured to the longsword and then to Wyldaern. 'That's the first omen. Now, the Key needs to be bestowed.' He turned his gaze on the Seer. 'I don't suppose you'd know anything about that?'

'Perhaps a tincture?' The Queen's blue eyes lit up as she clapped excitedly, telling Wyldaern, 'You are welcome to pick from my personal garden, should you need the divination herbs.' So that's it, Cahra thought. The woman wanted a demonstration.

But Wyldaern's eyes were on Cahra. Fatigue weighed on Cahra's bones, her very soul. The nervous exhaustion was wringing her skin, making it feel too tight for her body, and all she wanted was to lie down on the ground and sleep, shove her consciousness into tomorrow. So she could forget today.

'May we rest first?' Wyldaern demurred sweetly. 'I am weary and there was not time to stop for healing after our attack. I must confess, my head is paining me.'

'Of course,' Queen Avenais soothed, summoning one of her attendants with a wave. 'Fetch my physician,' she instructed, 'and show our guests to their rooms.' The Queen smiled. 'We shall call upon you for supper at eight o'clock.'

'Thank you, Your Royal Highness,' Wyldaern said, curtseying deeply. Cahra gave it her best attempt, struggling to right herself. Finally, they were dismissed.

As she and Wyldaern were leaving, Cahra heard the Queen ask after Lady Delicia, one of her attendants replying the woman was in her quarters in the palace.

In Thierre's room?

Stop. Cahra bit the inside of her cheek, then ground her teeth against the pain. *Don't think of her, or him. Just get through tonight.*

Endure.

Sleep's oblivion was looking good.

–

Cahra retreated to her guest room, shutting the arched door behind her as Wyldaern bid her good rest. She slumped against the wood, sinking to the cool alabaster tiles. Vision blurring, she could just make out the patchwork of her smithing leathers next to her, the last remnants of her old life in Kolyath with Lumsden, before lords and swords and prophecies and princes. And bitter, utter heartbreak.

Thierre.

Hot tears arrived before she could blink them away, the hurt, the anger, swelling. Before she knew it, Cahra was stripping off her dress, dumping it on the floor and, with it, every piece of her defences. When she finally stood in her underclothes, she had no energy left to bathe. To eat. To do anything. Except not be awake.

Cahra staggered to the bed, threw back the blankets and buried herself in its centre.

Silently, she let the tears fall.

CHAPTER 23

Thierre counted soundlessly after Cahra and Wyldaern departed, knowing exactly how long to wait before he could raise his voice. He had overheard enough quarrels from the hall as a child to know, straining to listen through the passage's far door while his father and Tyne scrutinised campaign after campaign.

The room's grandfather clock struck then.

So did Thierre.

'You should have dismissed them hours ago,' he fumed. 'Did you not notice their fatigue? Raiden's men only rescued the Seer this morning, and C—'

'You did not heal her?' His mother arched a sculpted brow. 'Luminaux has not welcomed a Seer in decades. This is how you honour them?'

'I take responsibility.' Raiden cleared his throat. 'After the attack, my priority was the Prince. We rode hard for Luminaux.'

Thierre's father nodded sharply.

Commander Tyne's frown, however, deepened. Tyne had always seen their missions as a liability, regardless of his seals of approval.

'And why were you vulnerable? I'll tell you. You lost your focus, and your operation was compromised, in an enemy kingdom. You were damned lucky to escape with your lives!'

'Compromised because of the prophecy,' Thierre corrected, his jaw tightening. 'You cannot be looking to blame me for the Oracles' will?'

'And how exactly was buying a foreign kingdom's weapon part of your mission?' Tyne crossed his arms, armour clanking to punctuate his point.

'Would you rather I had paraded my princely rapier?' Thierre threw up his hands, turning to face his father. 'This is preposterous.'

Meanwhile, Sylvie was studying Cahra's longsword. She lifted it from the table, the sword's weight no bother, and swept the two-handed blade from her shoulder into a cut.

Her gaze locked onto Thierre's, eyes big and bright. 'Oh, she *is* good. Perhaps your blacksmith could fashion something for me?'

'She is not my blacksmith,' Thierre retorted, earning one of Sylvie's classic looks. 'Besides, you have weapons by Luminaux's finest masters.'

'I do,' she replied, stooping to peer at Cahra's pommel and the little blue stones that formed the Sigil of the Seers. She traced the symbol with her fingertip, eyes on her brother, her own glittering as she said, 'But none of them have ever made me anything like *this*.'

'Indeed,' Tyne conceded gruffly. 'She is skilled, for such youth.'

'She was nearing the end of her apprenticeship.' Thierre recalled Lumsden proudly telling him when he had first come to enquire about one of Cahra's pieces.

Thierre should have brought Lumsden and everyone he and Raiden had befriended. Had he doomed all who had known him in Kolyath to their deaths? He swallowed. But now was not the time for sentimentality.

Anger flaring, he turned to his parents. 'Regardless. Kolyath believes this sword, this sigil, to be the first omen of the prophecy. Cahra risked her life to warn me, so I brought her back with us. Finding the Seer, Wyldaern, was simply serendipitous.'

Sylvie's eyes flickered to Thierre. 'Can I ask—' she began in an oddly muted voice, but their father cut her off.

'You have my thanks.' The King's words were too perfunctory for Thierre's liking, and not nearly thankful enough. 'The omen-bearer and a Seer. It is the edge we need against the scourge of Kolyath and Ozumbre.'

'I have not yet finished,' Thierre interrupted. 'I brought them, however, they shall not remain here. Wyldaern travels to meet her teacher and Cahra wishes to accompany her. As do I.'

The King's stare was unyielding. 'No.' It was a decree.

Thierre flinched. 'What?'

'Hael'stromia's black sands shall pale before I permit you to go gadding about again. It is too dangerous. It was too dangerous before, yet I allowed this folly. It was a mistake.'

He stared at his father. 'You have welcomed a Seer and the bearer of the prophecy's first omen into your kingdom. Tell me, what was the mistake?'

Tyne answered for him. 'Your near-death at Atriposte's hand.'

The Commander's reply set Thierre's ire ablaze and he was ready to retaliate when Sylvie murmured, 'Thi, he's not wrong.'

'I cannot believe you are defending them! You are the one who warned me about Delicia—' No sooner had the words left Thierre's mouth than they sank to the ground like dead weights. Sylvie's eyes flashed at his breach of trust.

I either disclose too little, or too much. I cannot win. Thierre exhaled, attempting an apologetic smile.

His mother sighed, eyelashes fluttering, and signalled for one of her handmaids. 'Thierre, what precisely is it that you find so distasteful about Delicia? She is the daughter of a lord and decorated veteran. Her family has the requisite wealth and standing. Truly, it is an inspired pairing.'

'She is insufferable,' Thierre said heatedly. 'A self-seeking opportunist who would happily trade her father for a sack of jewels.'

Sylvie burst out laughing. The Queen stared at her children haughtily, as Sylvie said, 'What? I did tell you as much, Mother.'

'I think that she is delightful,' Thierre's mother sniffed.

'Of course you do. Except that she is not, and you are not being forced to marry her.' The room's eyes on Thierre, he did not hesitate. 'Call it off.'

For the first time since Cahra and Wyldaern had left, the room fell silent. Tyne wisely retreated to an armchair near the exit, giving them the privacy for yet another family row. Raiden flashed Thierre a remorseful look, joining the Commander.

'Please,' Thierre begged his parents.

'Thierre.' The Queen rose, her face a mask of motherly concern. 'I wish we could heed your request, but it has been decided, darling. You are to wed Delicia come the spring.'

Thierre's heart pounded. 'That is but months away!'

'And we have been preparing for far longer.' His mother batted his distress away with a flick of her manicured hand, her attendant arriving.

'You cannot be serious,' he said, stunned. *There must be some recourse.* The Queen tasked the maid with another pot of chamomile. 'Mother, this is my life we are talking about. It is more important than your blasted tea!'

She tutted at him, frowning. 'Thierre, if you cannot be gracious, retire to your rooms, and take that churlish language with you.'

After hours of diplomatically playing his family's game, Thierre was out of patience. 'I shall tell you what I take with me: the knowledge that my own parents are forcing me into a lifelong commitment with a woman I despise!' He warned, 'If you think for one moment that I am yielding to this mockery of a marriage, *you are sorely mistaken*!' And with that, Thierre stormed from the war room, slamming the heavy door behind him.

–

Thierre stalked down the stairs and into the empty hallway. A moment later, the door banged shut, a second set of footsteps following.

'Thi,' Sylvie called. He didn't stop. 'Thierre!' His sister grabbed his arm as he reached the hall's far end. He turned, glowering at the cream columns juxtaposed against the forest green of the marbled floor.

'Cahra. She's the reason you are spurning Delicia, isn't she?'

Thierre sighed. His sister had always been too good at reading people.

Sylvie watched him as she asked, 'Just what is going on between you?'

'I spurn Delicia because she has twisted a past dalliance into something that I am now beholden to, without my consent – and she knows it.' Thierre hesitated, his hand on the bronze doorknob. 'Cahra…' He sighed. 'I am not sure what is between us.'

'But Thierre, she's a *Kolyath commoner*. Surely, you knew that Father and Mother would never agree?'

'Of course I knew,' he hissed. 'That is not the point.'

Sylvie yielded a small nod. 'I suppose.'

'How did you do it? How did you deter our parents' meddling, when it was you?'

'It was different for me,' his sister told him slowly. 'I'm not the heir to the throne. And I've done my duty, within the bounds of what is "appropriate",' she snorted, gesturing to the sword and buckler at her side, the plates of armour strapped to her body for protection. 'But I didn't let them dictate my choices.'

Thierre nodded. 'Then nor shall I.' All too suddenly, he felt so incredibly tired.

'You should rest. You've had an eventful week,' she said, and he felt the sharpness of her dark blue eyes scrutinising him. Before he could say anything, Sylvie threw her arms around him in a bear hug, strong limbs crushing his aching shoulders. Withholding a grimace, he let the smile behind it arise instead.

'I missed you, Syl,' Thierre said, and it was true.

His sister flashed him a roguish grin. 'Me too,' she said, and squeezed his arm again. Then she paused, fidgeting with the armour strapped to her forearm, her eyes darting away as a tiny crease dented the space between her eyebrows. 'I do have one question for you—'

Thierre stifled a laugh. Two years apart, but he'd know that flustered look anywhere. 'Out with it,' he said, the warmth in his voice giving him away. 'Who?'

Sylvie's hesitation hardened into a filthy scowl. 'How is this amusing?'

'Because it is the only time I see you flummoxed,' he told her, allowing a grin to surface from the depths of his infuriation at their parents.

'Indeed,' Sylvie said crossly, plated arms folding across her breastplate. Anyone else would have the good sense not to anger the lynx of a soldier that was his sister. Thierre, however, had been living dangerously for quite some time.

In a small voice, Sylvie asked him, 'What do you know of Wyldaern?'

'Little, but what I do, I will gladly share,' he offered. 'May we speak about it later? For now, I should like to take your advice and retire to my rooms.' The longer he stood still, the more Thierre feared his limbs may refuse to move again.

Sylvie nodded, face eager at the prospect of learning more about the Seer. Then she glanced down the hall. 'I should get back to Tyne. I'll come find you before supper.' She squeezed his shoulder, then returned to her Commander and their parents.

He watched her go, the way Sylvie moved with swift, unwavering purpose, her warrior's boots silent against the polished floor, the only noise the faint jangle of weapons against her armour. He *had* missed his sister. She was the only one who understood what it was like to be a child of their parents, and her support meant everything to him.

Thierre left the hall and was met by a guard of Raiden's. He greeted the man, saying, 'I need your help. Can you ensure our guests' clothing is laundered and ready for them again as soon as possible? Then, I need you to convey an urgent request to Sabean for me.' Thierre gave his instructions and the guard bowed, leaving.

Rounding a corner, Thierre glimpsed the entry leading to his private quarters and exhaled in relief at the familiar sight. Reaching his door, he stilled, touching the rosewood and savouring his first moment of safety and solitude in two long years, without the need for Raiden or his guards watching his every move. He stood at his door like that for a minute then, smiling despite the state of his personal affairs, Thierre entered his rooms.

Within an instant, the smile vanished from his face.

'Get out,' Thierre said flatly, the words close to a snarl.

'Thierre,' Delicia crooned with a toss of her blonde curls, as she reclined upon the cherry-coloured chaise in his spacious reception room. 'Your mother is correct, is that any way to greet your fiancée?'

'Get out before I throw you out.'

The tinkle of her teasing laughter cut the air. 'You would not dare.'

Thierre strode for Delicia.

'Oh!' She giggled outright, leaping quickly to her feet in a flurry of skirts. 'Kolyath and its brutes have changed you! Or your new peasant friends.' So, she had noticed Cahra. Thierre clamped his mouth shut. 'My darling heart, the charity I might comprehend,' Delicia mused, then looked him up and down. 'Your ensemble, however... By the Oracles, what *are* you wearing?'

'You wish to speak of my attire? I am garbed in clothing appropriate to my duties: something restrained. The precise opposite of whatever that is,' he retorted, waving his hand in the direction of her corseted gown, tailored purposefully, he knew, to accentuate her figure. The same ploys as years before. She had not changed.

'I will have you know that Lord Kenley was most appreciative—'

'Go marry him, then,' Thierre muttered, cutting her off.

Delicia narrowed her green eyes. 'Careful, beloved. I would not wish for your mother to hear of your callous disdain for your betrothed.'

Thierre smiled. 'Oh, she knows.'

Delicia's eyes widened. Clearly, she had not anticipated that. She took a step forward, her ballet slipper scuffing his hardwood floor. Thierre bridled at the sound, at the audacity of her commandeering him, when all he wished for was to be alone.

'Thierre.' Simply the sound of his name on her lips was infuriating. 'Are you really so unhappy to see me?'

Thierre turned on her. 'You forget to whom you speak,' he snapped. 'I am not one of your puerile ladies-in-waiting. I am the one who romanced you, the only other in this room who knows exactly why our courtship failed – and it was not of my doing. Speaking of the upstanding lords of Luminaux, please do me the favour of seeking them for private "counsel", as you did the *last* time we were together, and the *last* time I was away serving my kingdom. Then I can put an end to this farce of a marriage.'

Delicia turned from him and he was unsure whether she would cry or scream, both of which he had endured after learning of her infidelity prior to Kolyath. It was the last time that they had spoken.

'No pithy riposte?' Moments passed. 'Then it is as I said.' Thierre pushed past her, through his reception and to his private bedchambers, throwing over his shoulder as he went, 'Get. Out.'

A pause. '*Can*,' Delicia repeated, tilting her heart-shaped face to him, 'not *have*. Put an end to things, you said.' A smile formed on her peachy lips. 'Oh, my dearest love. Your parents have not broken our engagement, have they?'

Thierre froze, his anger churning. When he spoke, his voice was dark as he replied, 'They will. In time.'

But Delicia had already left the room.

And time was Thierre's scarcest resource.

CHAPTER 24

As soon as Cahra raised her head, she knew. She was no longer in her Luminaux guest bed. She knew this place by now, this place of darkness, and of death.

She was in Hael's tomb.

Cahra cracked a puffy eye open and there he was, like a sentinel in the darkness. The fires of Hael's eyes were slits, as if he were peering at her, thinking. She squinted back, hardly able to see him and not just from her recent tears. Then she registered everything at once.

Her warm skin on the icy tiles of the floor. Hael eyeing her from behind a column.

By the Seers! Yelping, Cahra sprang to her feet, yanking a threadbare robe that had been draped across her round her shoulders like a shawl. Once she knew she wouldn't drop the fistful of fabric, she spun on Hael. 'Where are my clothes?!'

One of his flames flared, as though he'd raised an eyebrow. '*Where is your body?*'

She scowled. 'In bed.' The flame rose higher. She rolled her eyes. 'I was asleep!'

'*You remain so.*' There was a pause. '*Is it customary, to sleep disrobed?*'

Cahra felt her cheeks burn hot. 'Not for me, no.' Pulling the shroud tighter, she found sleeves and fumbled to dress herself, tying it at the waist. Then she folded her arms. 'Why am I here?' She squinted. 'And why are you hiding from me?'

'*You are pained, Scion.*' Hael's fires narrowed again. '*However, I sense no injury.*'

'Cahra,' she corrected. She couldn't stand titles now. 'And I'm not hurt,' she said. *Not physically*. 'My… my trust was broken.'

Hael's simmering red flames burst into a nightmarish black, his silhouette descending into smoke and shadow. The air around them crackled as he snarled, '*By whom?*'

'The Prince of Luminaux.' It hurt, but Cahra found relief in saying it out loud. The crack in her chest began to ease with every word.

'*A mandrake playing at monarchy,*' Hael ground out. Then his anger seemed to relent. '*Yet, unexpected. Given the centuries that I have been interred here, the game may have changed. And the tri-kingdoms are seasoned players.*'

Centuries? She frowned, her mind whirling with questions. Like why Hael remained a disembodied black cloud when he'd never been before.

She was clothed, but he hadn't moved or answered her question. Then she processed what he'd said. 'Oh? What do you mean "unexpected"?'

'*In my time, Luminaux was the most loyal kingdom to Hael'stromia and the realm. They were peaceful, unlike Ozumbre, or Kolyath, in the end. I would not have believed the fruits of Luminaux to be deceivers.*'

She hadn't either, but here they were.

Cahra supposed it spoke to Thierre's claims of Luminaux not being like the other kingdoms. Maybe he was right. But did it really matter? Tomorrow, she and Wyldaern would be leaving to meet the Seer's teacher, the one Wyldaern called the 'conduit'. The Oracle.

Cahra glanced back at Hael's smoky form. She was here, and this was her chance to ask her questions about the Oracles, the prophecy, why Hael was here and where here was.

'Hael, what is this place?'

'*Last we met, you were also dreaming,*' he said, as if comprehending something she didn't. '*You do not remember?*' Then, softer, Hael said, '*Yet, you remembered me. My name.*'

'What?' Cahra was remembering something, all right. She vaguely recalled he had said these dreams were visions. Of what?

His unearthly voice soothed her. '*You know where we are, who – what – I am.*' Hael's smoke and shadow glided to the sandstone slab, then stilled. '*This is Hael'stromia, the capital's palatial temple. And I am the Reliquus.*'

The Reliquus. The word was familiar, but it was like wading through syrup to place it in her mind. As for Hael'stromia, that one, she knew.

They were here somehow, she and Hael, in the capital's tri-cornered pyramid. Cahra turned in a slow circle, registering the bones, the pillars, the slab and the faraway light. And, finally, Hael's black cloud before her.

'Why are you hiding from me?' She repeated her question, surprising him, by the look of his cloud shifting. Something was off. Hael had appeared to her as man-like before, a full head taller than her, but a physical being in his worn robe—

She looked down, at the cuffs of the robe she was wearing. Hael's robe. And looked up to where his body should have been.

'*Do not fear,*' he said. '*You required a garment and I obliged. But my confinement has left me... weak. Malnourished. I cannot appear before you as I did.*' It was then she found his flames, near-concealed by smoke. The fires in his eyes were like dying candles.

Shame and fear; she knew them well, remembering her own fear, the vulnerability of letting Thierre in, of being seen. And the pain of betrayal when he shattered that trust.

Believing in the Prince had been a mistake.

But now, this wasn't about her. It was about Hael. How long had it been since he'd seen another soul, if he'd been trapped in here for centuries? Trapped, just like she'd been trapped in Kolyath's dungeons. No food, no water, no companionship. Solitary confinement, that's what this was, and he'd been here longer than anyone had ever lived.

All because of the stupid prophecy.

She couldn't stand it. She refused to be afraid, not of Hael. And she refused to let him suffer alone in darkness.

Cahra stared into the core of his dark cloud, her own eyes soft. 'Show me,' she whispered, her voice firm but warm.

Hael's ghostly form heaved. '*I cannot.*'

'I'm not afraid,' she said, raising her hand to his wispy smoke.

'*I* cannot,' Hael repeated, angst in his voice.

'You healed my leg,' she reminded him. 'How can I help you?'

Eventually, a sigh rippled through him. '*It will cost you, Scion.*'

'Cahra,' she reminded, smiling. 'This may be the last chance I have to talk to you before I meet Wyldaern's Oracle. I have questions, and I can't sit here talking to a cloud for however long we have. So, Reliquus,' she said gently, 'name your price.'

Hael's eyes flared at the mention of the Oracle, but he stayed silent.

She didn't break his gaze. 'What do you need?'

He shuddered, as if dreading his own next words. '*Your suffering.*'

'My – what?' Cahra blinked.

'*Your negative emotions. Anger, sadness, fear.*' His flames seemed to shimmer with remorse. '*It is how I survive in such a state, the curse that binds me to this form. My powers, while fed by negativity, can serve to alleviate it. For a time.*'

Cahra laughed bitterly. 'You can take my feelings away? Have at them,' she said, hearing the hostile edge to her voice, glad to be rid of anything related to Thierre. She looked at Hael's hovering black cloud. Of course, it was a perfectly nonsensical request. But then, what part of any of this was normal? 'Will it last?'

Hael's smoky form shifted. '*No. That which I consume will be returned to your conscious form.*' He hesitated, as if to say more.

Cahra sighed, knowing it was too good to be true. But it was better than nothing at all. Besides, she couldn't stand looking into his eyes, those flagging flames, that managed to convey such hurt. She would help him however she could.

'What do I need to do?'

'*Sit, and be at peace. A partial draw should restore me*,' he murmured.

How partial? 'This won't, you know, kill me in my sleep?'

'*You will be safe. However, if you do not feel comfortable, you do not have to—*'

'No,' Cahra said, shaking her head. 'You helped me, I'll help you.'

'*That is different. It is my duty, as your shield.*'

'Stop changing the subject and let me do my part.' She sat as instructed and focused on the feeling of her breath in her chest, holding it to slow her heartbeat. An old trick she'd learned as a child to calm her fears.

Hael hovered next to her, his smoke like satin upon her skin as it encircled her wrist, her outstretched hand. '*This… abreption… can be painful. You will feel a pull as the energy, your suffering, is drawn from you. Take heart, the sensation will not last.*'

Cahra frowned. *How painful?* But even as she thought the words, they didn't trouble her enough to stop her. Despite his current guise as a cloud, this was the closest Hael had ever been to her. It felt… funny.

'And this will fix you?'

'*It will be enough for a time, yes.*'

It was strange. As her agitation increased, Hael's appeared to fall away. She could sense it, his focus, the fixation as he stilled, his smoke and shadow subdued beside her.

'*Close your eyes,*' he murmured, his voice a coarse purr against her earlobe, so close that she shivered. She could have sworn he huffed a low, amused rumble. '*Inhale, slowly, deeply... then exhale.*' His grip on her grew firmer.

There was a flurry of air, like when he turned to smoke. Cahra wanted to peek, but didn't dare. Hael uttered his final words to her.

'*Shall we begin?*'

She nodded, eyes squeezed shut. She had no idea this whole thing would be so... *suggestive*. Cahra inhaled, trying to steady herself, and shook her hands out to relax her.

Then the abreption struck.

She writhed against the urge to scream as a jagged, blinding pain ripped into her palm, invading her body and abruptly shattering every thought. She felt it, just as Hael had warned: an agony like serrated barbs, shooting and snapping to hook her insides and wrench them out, inch by excruciating inch. The sensation was unbearable, as though her very soul was being siphoned into oblivion. Hissing as the pain surged deeper, she sucked in desperate gasps of air between her gritted teeth and counted to ten. When she got to nine, the torment stopped.

Gone.

It was all *gone*. Her rage, sorrow, pain. Gone, exactly as he'd said. And in its place, something Cahra had never known.

Peace.

She inhaled the simple stillness, the silence, her emotions no longer rioting at volume in her head. And with her relief, she sensed growth, an orange flame in her core, radiating through her skin and into the dark around them both. Here, now, she felt different, content for the first time in her life. It was a void, she realised, of everything that had ever sought to drown her. It was a void, and it was bliss.

Cahra exhaled, her breath of sunlit warmth, safety and security. She couldn't help it. She opened her eyes, smiling, forgetting all about Hael. Then stifled her sharp intake of breath as the being before her transformed from a monster to something else entirely.

Hael's withered skin brightened to a dewy ivory, pale and smooth as moon-kissed silk, plumping with his muscles to fill his thewy arms and chest, the robust bulk of a warrior's body that rivalled even Piet's. Black hair fell in sharp swathes to his shoulders, Cahra taking in the gracefully arched ears, the dignified forehead, the hewn nose and angular cheekbones. Hael's abundant mouth peeled back to reveal gleaming fangs as his lips curved into a smile, watching her watching him.

Hael gazed at Cahra, eyeballs glowing so fiercely with their ever-burning flames, the flickers dancing down his body. His voice was wraithlike, of gravel and howling wind, yet dulcet, honeyed even, as he said, '*Thank you, Cahra.*'

Hael was beautiful – hauntingly so. Cahra's voice was full of wonder as she asked, 'What *are* you?'

Hael knelt before her, clasping her fingers, then lowered his lips to her hand, kissing it with a tenderness she hadn't imagined a being like him capable of.

His lips on her skin were sweet *fire*, leaving Cahra breathless and light-headed, the heat shimmering down her spine and rendering her speechless.

'*You asked this of me, last we spoke. I am Hael, the Reliquus, "that which remains". Sempiternal of this realm, and Vassal Champion to the Scion.*' Hael stood, bowing deeply. '*Or in your parlance "the weapon".*'

Cahra blurted out, 'The weapon is a man?' *A man called Hael, just like the capital.* There was no way that was a coincidence.

'*Once. Now, it is inconsequential.*' Hael raised an eyebrow, chuckling. '*And the Scion is a woman.*'

'Inconsequential?' Her head spun. Not a sword, or a shield, or any manner of weapon she could forge. The weapon – it was *alive*!

'*It has never occurred prior.*'

'Well, maybe the Scion has never been a blacksmith, either.' Cahra braced one arm behind her, still in shock.

Hael quirked his chin at her, then at the tattoo on her wrist, as if she'd just answered some unknown question. He sat cross-legged in front of Cahra, reminding her of meeting Wyldaern beside that pebbly stream.

'*You have questions.*'

She rallied her wits. He'd worn breeches underneath his robe, thank the Seers, but it hadn't saved her from Hael shirtless, his hulking, marble chest fully on display, the rippling muscles of his stomach tapering down to...

'Yes,' she said, clearing her throat. 'All I know is what Luminaux's royals have said, and Wyldaern – the Seer – and I have barely had a chance to talk. I need to know that what the Prince told me is actually true and that I'm not going mad! Who are the Oracles and what happened to them? How does the prophecy work? Why are you trapped here in Hael'stromia? How are you trapped here – how are you possible at all? How are we here, in these dreams, these visions? And why did I craft the Sigil of the Seers? *Why me?*'

The silence was long after Cahra had rattled off her questions.

When he spoke, Hael's voice was gentle. '*Much, I wish to tell you. And much, I may. But some of your questions are for the Oracle. It is not my place to reveal that which is Hers. This is the way of the second omen.*'

'So the second omen does involve me?' Cahra's voice was small.

Hael bent to her eye level and smiled. '*You shall find that everything involves you.*'

'But *WHY?*'

Cahra looked up into the fire-lit rubies of Hael's eyes, so much lovelier up close. When she'd first seen his flames, she'd felt as if her bones were trying to leap from her body. But looking into them now, all she felt was awe and the same feeling in her core as when she'd met Wyldaern. Cahra didn't need to note eye contact, tone of voice or body language; none of it mattered, because in her heart, she knew that she was safe. With Hael.

'Did you call to me tonight, like you did in our last vision? Is that why I'm here?' The question seemed to come to Cahra from far away.

'*No,*' Hael said, surprised. '*I felt your pain, and I wished to intervene, but I did not summon you.*' He thought for a moment. '*Perhaps, it was you who summoned me?*'

But that's impossible, Cahra thought.

I was asleep.

This time when Hael smiled, twin sets of fangs delicately brushed his lilac lips. '*Now, to your questions.*'

CHAPTER 25

Cahra awoke to silence; no clamour of weapons as Raiden's people trained and laughed, and no morning light or gemstone eyes. Nothing but her body tangled in silk sheets, chest tight, in one of Luminaux's ample guest bedrooms. The candle beside her was a smoking stump.

As if Hael himself had been there, watching over her.

Hael was right. Her negative feelings *had* returned to her. She sighed.

Cahra sat up, peering across the moonlit room. It was past midnight so she fell back against the impossibly soft mattress and lay there. No more caves, or camps, or anything else to experience travelling with Thierre. He was home now, he and his high-born bride.

Cahra's future was her own again. It should have made her happy.

But all she felt was a yawning emptiness, a void.

Not 'the veil and void' – where they'd met in her visions – as Hael had called it with his resonant, otherworldly voice that could span time and space to find her, to call to her and know she was safe. Which was how she felt with him: safe. And flustered. The memory of Hael towering over her, so darkly handsome, with his body that made her teeth, her tongue, so unwieldy in her mouth she fumbled for her words... She didn't know what to make of it, of him and their 'abreption'. Except that he had offered her the truth. And the answers he had given to her questions – she needed to talk to Wyldaern. But it was the dead of night.

Cahra looked about the space. Drawing the sheet around her, she moved for the sunroom and gazed out over the sleeping city, firelights in its homesteads faint and few. The night sky reminded her of Thierre's eyes and she shut her own to the painful thought. At least the palace was quiet.

She sighed, grappling with her own void, the one Thierre's actions had caused in her. She didn't want to think about the Prince, but he was everywhere she looked: the enormous four-poster bed she'd slept in, even the walls, the floor, the gilded ceiling of this grand room. Everything in it was gold and mirrored glass and great, gaudy colours; and suddenly, how she longed for Kolyath's depressing greys. At least she knew what to expect there, how to survive. Life in her kingdom hadn't been good, but it was familiar.

Stop. Endure.

Cahra hurried from the sunroom, the night air nipping at her skin as she searched for her clothes, which were nowhere to be seen. Frowning, she yanked open a wardrobe and found replacements in the form of a linen shirt and trousers, not giving the extravagant dresses a glance as she pushed past them to a shelf with a pair of plain, leather slip-on shoes. She dressed quickly and moved for the door.

A note sat atop a silver dome, as she neared the parlour table.

> *You were still sleeping, so I brought you something to eat. Please, ensure that you do. We shall need the energy in the morrow.*
> *Wyldaern*

It was a kindness, and tears pricked at Cahra's eyes. She scrubbed them from her face. No, she wouldn't cry again. Not until she was free of this kingdom and its Prince. She turned for the door, leaving the food untouched.

–

Cahra needed air, space, to escape the hollow excess of the guest room and go… where? She was out in the hallway now, white columns seemingly endless in either direction. Frustrated, she turned, following the lanterns. She knew the view she'd seen from her room was along here somewhere. If she could just find an empty room with a balcony to sit on. And not fling herself from it, she thought drily.

Charging blindly down the hall, Cahra stopped short, whirling to stare at a dark arch to her left, a short tunnel that opened into—

'The night sky,' she breathed.

Cahra didn't know why she felt such relief. All she knew was she'd awoken and felt like she was suffocating; those too-soft sheets, that too-big bed, the absurdly large space for just one guest. The impulse to upend every single thing in Thierre's audacious guest room. Instead, she'd run for the fresh night air.

She set foot on the airy disc-shaped podium that jutted boldly from the palace's side like an outstretched palm. The gleaming gold and glass of the building was a stellar object in the sky, a beacon far above the winding city below. When she looked up again, she noticed a faint blot against the darkness, blacker than the pitch of midnight and, squinting, realised it was the peak of Hael'stromia's pyramid. The sight of the structure in real life sent a thrum of excitement through her as she remembered the feel of Hael's warm breath on her earlobe and his wraithlike voice that gave her goosebumps.

Cahra took a deep, loosening breath and exhaled slowly, gently, watching the stars go on and on, past Hael'stromia and far beyond the limits of her sight. She wondered if Hael could see past the stars to other celestial objects. If he was asleep somewhere in that pyramid. Or if he was awake right now, like her.

Her gaze snagged on a silhouette in the corner, eyes twinkling as they turned from a spyglass angled to the skies above.

She whirled to leave.

'Cahra, *please*.' She gritted her teeth at the pain in Thierre's voice, the only thing that made her hesitate. He rushed to reach her.

She cursed her feelings and, before she could stop herself, lashed out against her hurt. 'What more could you possibly have to say to me? Better yet, what *should* you have told me? Let me start you off. "Hi, my name's Terryl, I mean Thierre, well actually, it's Prince Thierre of your enemy kingdom, Luminaux, and by the way, I'm to be *married*—"'

Thierre opened his mouth. Then shut it.

'Exactly,' she mumbled, turning to go.

'Cahra,' Thierre repeated, and it took everything in her not to run, down the hall and to the guest room, or Wyldaern's room next door, anywhere she could pretend he didn't exist. 'Do you truly see me as your enemy?'

She raised her eyes to him. To his dark hair, swept to one side as he raked his fingers through it, chewing on his lower lip. Those lips she'd wondered what it would be like to kiss. To the refined angles of his face. And to his blue goldstone eyes, multi-faceted and sparkling like the midnight stars around them.

His eyes, which were gazing at her with such sorrow.

'No, Terryl, Thierre – whoever you are. You don't get to say my name and act like you have the right to ask me anything at all.' She took a breath and the sweep of her own pain came out in one agonising sentence. 'You *lied* to me! About who you really were, and you knew. That I didn't trust anyone, ever. But you deceived me anyway.'

It wasn't just that he'd lied. He'd made her feel seen, like she was more than a low-born smith. Like she was someone who mattered. Now, standing before him, all she felt was just how wrong she'd been.

Thierre's lips twisted with guilt. 'Please, forgive me,' he whispered. 'I am sorry, for not being who, or what, you wished me to be. But after everything, do you not understand? Prince Thierre, the first in line to the throne of Luminaux, cannot exist outside this kingdom. There can only be Terryl, or else I am a liability to my father, my mother, my sister – to my kingdom, our forces and everything that Luminaux is and stands for and shall ever be, the moment I leave the safety of these walls. To anyone and anything that I have cared for, and to those who care for me. And it is not for nothing. I risk everything for the safety of my people, by gathering intelligence and knowing our enemies' plans, their strengths and weaknesses, under their noses. Terryl does more for Luminaux than Thierre ever could. *To keep the people I care for safe.*'

'And who are they?' Then she blurted out, 'How could you not tell me you were engaged?'

Thierre erupted. 'Because I did not know! Not until this last week, that my parents had plotted this *farce* of an arrangement, and with someone that I would sooner tear my eyes from my own head than wed—' He stopped.

So did Cahra's heart. *He doesn't want to marry her!*

'And me?' Cahra whispered, the events of the past week, of his hand touching hers, burning in the back of her mind. 'What am I to you?'

Thierre – Prince Thierre – stared with such heat that Cahra feared for her own restraint.

'You,' he began, moving for her, 'are who I wish to the *Oracles* that I never had to lie to, never pained, never caused for you to look upon me with such regret.' He took another step. 'You, Cahra...' They were barely inches away from one another now, and for the life of her, she could not will her feet to move. Thierre lifted his hand, stopping a finger's breadth from her face, his own uncertain.

Cahra hesitated. But before he could lower his palm, and before she could stop herself, she stepped into his touch, the surprising gentleness of his fingers cupping her cheekbone.

What am I doing?

Astonishment flooded his features, then he exhaled, cradling her face in both hands.

'You, Cahra,' he breathed, closing his eyes and resting his forehead against hers. 'You are the one for whom my heart yearns.'

When he opened his star-flecked eyes, Thierre leaned in, pressed his lips to Cahra's, and kissed her.

–

And she ran.

Cahra cringed, tossing and turning in the palace guest room bed, as she had for hours.

She'd fled all the way back to the safety of that room, locking the door behind her.

Thierre – *Prince Thierre* – kissed her, and she'd run. But not before basking in the lazy lust of his lips on hers. A dreamy, dizzying kiss. The best she'd had.

Yes, she'd been furious with him. Shocked, hurt, saddened and everything in between. All the reasons she was leaving with Wyldaern.

But she'd also wanted to kiss Thierre too. And she'd let it happen, let him talk to her, let him touch her face...

Maybe his royal status had finally spooked her. Or the fact that whatever was between them, it could never go anywhere. Not while he was engaged, and even if he wasn't. But in that moment, when Thierre had kissed her, she'd forgotten who and what he was.

So why had she fled?

Burrowing out of the covers to squint at the clock, Cahra groaned. It was half-past five in the morning. She'd hardly slept. Rubbing her face, she sat up, looking around the lavish room. Its shadows were receding as dawn broke, the furniture lit with glorious gold. Like the grand wardrobe, dressing table and console weren't extravagant enough, she grumbled.

Cahra sighed. There was no point idling if she couldn't sleep. And having learned from the sheer embarrassment of Hael seeing her in her underthings, this time she'd left her clothes on before going to bed. She flushed at the idea of his red-hot flames roving over her bare skin. *Seers, will he ever forget?*

Crossing the room, Cahra shoved her feet into a pair of shoes and then stopped. Where did she think she was going? It was barely sunrise. She unlocked the door and strained to listen, one ear angled down the hall. Nothing. Everyone was asleep. She stood by the door, wondering whether she should stay or go. Glancing at the tapestries and vases, the outrageous chandelier that hung, as big as she was, before the mirrored walls and boundless bed, she shook herself into action and shut the door behind her.

Fumbling her way through the palace on hushed feet, Cahra somehow managed to locate the entrance, nodding to the guards as she slipped through the gilt doors and out into the glittering royal courtyard. It was a cool dawn and she wished she'd grabbed her jacket. But the scent of Luminaux's jasmine sat heavy in the humid air and the sky was brightening to an optimistic shade of blue. She'd warm as she walked.

Cahra didn't know where she was going, but as she watched Luminaux's banners rippling overhead, she realised she had some quiet time to think now.

Hael. His name was there, on her tongue, before she'd taken her next breath. And the thought of him… Not just the mad thing she'd done by letting him steal away her sadness, or even the mad things he'd told her of the Seers, but the sheer shock of watching him go from a nightmare made flesh to – to what he truly was, an enthralling, powerfully built warrior… And that grin! As if he'd known how her body heated when he'd kissed her hand—

Cahra sucked in a breath. The sister kingdoms didn't worship gods. But if they did? She had the feeling they would've looked a lot like Hael.

And this time, she remembered their conversation clearly. Was it the abreption? Had Hael's new-found vigour helped her memory? She didn't know, but he'd given her answers. Of course, all they'd done was raise more questions.

She ducked beneath a tree dripping with clusters of magenta flowers, the abundant blooms like feathery fingers reaching for her as she passed.

She'd been surprised to learn the Seers were Hael'stromian, like him. When Cahra asked Hael what had happened to them, his face had darkened, saying the scrying order had fled the city when its defences activated, locking him inside. The Seers had promised to free him, only the High Oracles had received a vision as Hael'stromia fell and shared it. The last they would see until the new era.

Hael had seen the vision, and its truths: the age of the Oracles would end and Hael'stromia would fall, until the rise of a new leader, a new Emperor, who would usher the kingdoms into the future. One of peace.

She'd laughed at Hael's words. None of the rulers seemed up to the task, not even Thierre's father, King Royce. She didn't know of Ozumbre's King, but she'd heard things. Things that made the Steward seem merciful.

Cahra blew out a breath, frustrated at Hael for not answering all of her questions, apparently best left for Wyldaern's Oracle. She didn't know what to expect from the visit, or the Oracle herself. Another disciple of Hael'stromia's Seers, like Wyldaern, she supposed. Even Hael had been cagey about it, saying Cahra would see him again soon, in another vision.

One where she was actually dressed, she thought with a blush.

Cahra glanced up, finding she'd made it down the hill into the city's flat streets, and the pearl-white of tall, tidy shops, and ornate chairs and tables under blue striped awnings. Then it came to her, subtly at first, a hint of a mouthwatering scent on the gentle breeze. *Bread!* Bread, sweet and sour and heady with yeast, the aroma so strong she could almost taste the crunch of its outer crust, the fluffy warmth of dough inside. Cahra searched for the source of the irresistible smell, surely the kingdom's bread or pastry house. But then a sound snatched her attention away.

A hammer on metal.

She was in Luminaux's Artisanal Emporium! All thoughts of food emptied from her head as she bolted for the blacksmith's, following the telltale clangs. Cahra rounded a corner and there it was: big and dark and lit by fire, the sun's rays yet to bless the shop with daylight. She could see not one but two forges in the back, two anvils in the middle and a counter just like the smithy in Kolyath, only it extended half-way across the shop, the rest an open door. She gazed at the miraculous find, squinting to see what the city's master blacksmith was making as pure happiness flooded her chest.

The blacksmith glanced up, seeing Cahra. He looked a hardy man, as most smiths did, younger than Lumsden but older than her. His whiskers were greying, unlike his hair, cut close to the scalp as was typical. One less thing for sparks to set alight.

He dipped his head to her. 'Morning! You're up and about early, woken by the smell of Fabiel's rye, were you?'

Cahra smiled. 'I like this time of day.'

'As do I.' The man smiled back. 'I am Quillon. What can I do for you this morn?'

'I'm Cahra,' she told him, then nodded to the forge. 'What are you smithing? A blade?'

Quillon laughed, a deep, warm sound. 'Nothing so grand, just a few nails. But my boy's fetching water and won't be back for a half hour.' As he leaned heavily on the counter, she noticed his left leg ended in a metal prosthetic. Smithing was physically demanding work, yet here was another who knew its joy and wouldn't give it up. She grinned.

'Nails are a two-person job,' she said. 'Want a hand?' Quillon noted her own build, and her clean shirt and trousers. She looked at herself and laughed, rolling up her sleeves, the shirt tight around her biceps as she told him, 'Honestly, these could do with a little soot.'

'Suit yourself,' he chuckled again, gesturing in welcome as she entered the workshop, the joy hitting her like a hammer as she drank in the sharp, smoky scent of coals burning in the fiery forge-light. She wanted to stand in Luminaux's smithy and stay like that forever. But there was work to do.

'Right, the nails,' Cahra said.

Quillon pulled a rod from the forge's coals, its tapered tip glowing yellow, and placed it on the anvil. 'Hold the rod steady,' he said, then picked up a chisel and struck the metal. Once the nail was quickly cleaved off, Quillon set to work splitting the next.

After they'd worked through a handful of nails, Cahra gathered the courage to ask, 'Can I try?'

He smiled. 'Don't be disheartened if it takes more than one go.'

Cahra sunk onto her thighs, feeling the familiar weight of a hammer in her hand as her palm hooked around the handle, an extension of her arm, the chisel light in her opposite fist. She watched Quillon move the rod closer, and the moment it was motionless on the anvil, Cahra began.

One strike, and the nail was split clean from the rod.

Quillon's eyebrows flew up, as Cahra said, 'Quick, the header.' He scooped the nail and dropped it onto the header tool, hammering the nail's head flat.

He tipped the finished nail onto the anvil, peering first at it, then at Cahra with respect. 'So, you're not only a striker, you're a trained smith. Where did you learn to do that? How have I not seen you around before?'

'I'm not from Luminaux,' she told him.

Quillon scratched his chin thoughtfully. 'Well, if you decide the Wilds aren't for you, we could use your skills.' He offered Cahra a broad smile. 'Think it over, will you?'

She nodded, the lump in her throat wishing she could, as she wished that him thinking she was a Wildswoman were true.

Quillon's apprentice returned then, humming and carrying two wooden pails. The boy leaned over the nail to see what all the fuss was about.

'Seers, that's a clean break!' He whistled, looking at Cahra as Quillon frowned at the boy's cursing. Cahra hid her smile, the scene reminding her of Lumsden. 'I'm Leon.' The boy grinned. 'Who are you?'

Cahra introduced herself, then stayed and chatted with them as they started their morning's work. They moved around the smithy, and her eyes were drawn to the intricate designs etched onto various pieces of metalwork, including Quillon's polished foot.

'You've got such a talent for detail,' she said, her tone appreciative.

Quillon patted the metal of his leg lightly, a proud smile on his face. 'Designed, forged and engraved. Some of my proudest work.'

'I'll say! It's impressive,' she told him.

For a brief moment, Cahra found herself transported back to the smithy in Kolyath, seeing Lumsden, his balding head bent over his ledger full of notes. But the image faded into the memory of a high-born with blue goldstone eyes clearing his throat, opening his mouth and upending her whole world. She exhaled.

Cahra knew, though. Where she was, and where she wasn't. What had happened after that lord, that Prince, had entered her life. It was time to accept the way things were.

Lumsden was gone. And she could never return to Kolyath.

She was alone, again.

Only here, in *this* smithy, there was no lord to clear his throat behind her. Cahra opened her eyes, squared her shoulders and turned to the hill that would take her back to Luminaux's palace, and the next fateful leg of her journey.

And found a young woman with dark, gleaming hair and peridot eyes smiling at her. 'I thought you might be here,' Wyldaern said.

CHAPTER 26

'How did you find me?' Cahra asked. The sun was breaking over the jettied buildings on the quiet streets of Luminaux. Moving from the main road, the kingdom's pearly shops gave way to small timber-framed homes with cream walls and royal blue criss-crossing beams.

Even the slums were nice here, Cahra thought.

'I heard you leave,' Wyldaern said, strolling beneath the low awnings with her hands clasped neatly at her waist. She tilted her face to Cahra, her soft, dark curls falling to one side, the hem of her black robe sweeping forward with each step, brushing against her ankles. 'I remembered the way you looked at the blacksmith's from the carriage. It was as though you had spotted a lost love.'

Luminaux and love. Two things Cahra didn't want to think about.

Wyldaern caught the look on her face. 'He hurt you,' she murmured.

Cahra knew who she meant. 'He did,' she said slowly, sighing. 'Thierre misled me, and not for the first time. Learning he was a Prince, not a lord, and that he was engaged…' She shook her head. 'I just feel so stupid.'

But then, Kolyath didn't have royals. How was she to know what to look out for? Cahra could feel her anger rising at the thought. 'Anyway, it doesn't matter any more. We're leaving soon. I never have to see him again, if I don't want to.'

'And do you? Want to?'

Cahra flashed back to Thierre's lips on hers. As good as the kiss was, and as much as she had wanted it, wanted him… 'I don't know.'

Wyldaern nodded. 'I think I understand.'

Surprise filled Cahra's face. 'You do?'

But Wyldaern had a faraway look in her eyes and longing in her voice as she said, 'The thought of what could be, if only fate had other plans for you.'

She nodded back, wondering if Wyldaern meant her life as a disciple of the Seers. Had the woman had other plans for herself, a love of her own?

They'd arrived at a small garden square where dainty flowers sprung from the earth, their peach and rose-coloured petals frolicking on the ebbing breeze. Around its edges, the garden was dotted with a variety of scrying herbs. One of the parks Thierre had mentioned, Cahra supposed.

She took a deep breath. 'Wyldaern, there are things I need to ask you.'

The woman's eyes cleared as she looked at Cahra. 'I can imagine. Shall we?' Wyldaern gestured towards the park's bench, and they sat.

Cahra leaned her elbows on her knees, sorting through her many questions. She almost didn't know where to start. 'Do you know what I'm going to say?'

'Because I am a Seer?' Wyldaern looked amused. 'Sadly, no, although I can probably guess.'

Cahra nodded, gathering her thoughts. 'In Thierre's carriage, he asked you if a vision led you to us, and you said yes, that it was how you knew his identity. What did you see?'

Wyldaern turned to face her. 'Cahra, I must be clear. I am not Thierre. I cannot and will not lie or keep secrets from you. But some questions you shall ask of me are best left for She. It is our – the prophecy's – way of things. Within such bounds, I will answer what I can. So, to your question. A vision did lead me to you, but the Oracle will tell you why.'

Cahra snorted. 'That's what Hael said when I had questions.'

Wyldaern straightened. 'You have spoken with the Reliquus?'

She glanced up, at both Hael's title and her tone. 'Since Thierre and I left Kolyath. Why am I having visions of Hael? How are they possible, if he's trapped inside the capital? And what does this have to do with the longsword I forged for Thierre?'

Wyldaern's lips were pressed together in a tight line.

'And you can't tell me, because the Oracle has to, right?' She sighed in frustration, rocking back against the park bench. 'Okay, what can you tell me?' She thought of Hael. Hael, the unfairly attractive warrior. Hael, the—

Cahra whirled to Wyldaern, forcibly lowering her voice. 'And Hael is the *weapon!* How does no one know the weapon is a man?! The way everyone talks about the prophecy and the war to control Hael'stromia, I thought the weapon was a magickal sword that shoots lightning or devours souls or something, not an actual, physical *man!*'

'The Reliquus isn't a man,' Wyldaern said slowly.

Cahra slid her a glance, the image of Hael's muscular torso threatening to burn her cheeks again. 'He's *definitely* a man.'

'What I mean is,' Wyldaern cleared her throat, 'the Reliquus is not a human male. Hael is... a Netherworldly being.'

Cahra thought of Hael's fires, of him healing her knee. 'I guess that's true,' she said. 'But how? How come no one knows about him?'

'Much has been lost since the fall and the Reliquus simply faded from public view, replaced by the concept of an "ultimate weapon",' Wyldaern explained. 'Less dangerous, particularly when the kingdoms declared war.'

'How do you figure?' Cahra said, frowning. 'Look at what the idea of the weapon has done, the way the Steward reigns over Kolyath. It's all *because* of the weapon. The Steward wants to crush the other kingdoms with its power.'

Wyldaern fixed her gaze on Cahra. 'Because a weapon, conventionally defined, depends on physicality; reach, contact and the like, to strike. Whereas the Reliquus, Hael...' She trailed off. 'Let us say, the stakes are different. The Oracle did not correct such thinking, that the weapon was merely a tool. It would only have served to galvanise the tri-kingdoms if they knew the Reliquus could single-handedly fell a military force.'

He can what?! Despite the sun's warmth, a chill sunk into her bones.

Wyldaern smiled, a token that somehow didn't meet her eyes. 'He was granted dark powers that we cannot comprehend. Magicks from the Nether, from between—'

'The veil and void,' Cahra finished, the Seer nodding. 'But Hael's not evil?'

This time, when the Seer smiled, it was in earnest. 'No, that he is not. There is no light without darkness, no creation without destruction. Despite Hael's origins, he is part of the great balance.'

So Cahra's instincts had been right about him. That was a relief, after Thierre.

Wyldaern was watching her. 'The two of you are in contact early.'

'Hael said he'd tried to contact me before, when I was in danger. Maybe the other Scions were less reckless,' Cahra said, only half-joking.

The Seer was still studying her.

Cahra's fingers grazed the bench. 'And you know about him. Because you're a Seer?'

'Because of the Oracle. So, yes, I suppose.'

'Have you met him?'

'No.' Wyldaern laughed softly. 'It would squander the precious magicks he has left. He needs those to communicate with you.'

The Seer's answer caught Cahra off guard. She had seen with her own eyes just how weakened Hael had been. It never occurred to her she might be the cause.

Or, as it turned out, the solution. Well, her suffering. 'But why?'

Again, Wyldaern gave her that look, the one that said she'd have to wait.

Cahra groaned. 'Fine, but you have to answer this one. When you said "tell none" about our first conversation, which part? The white light, or something else?'

Wyldaern sagged in relief. So she *could* answer. 'I knew then, of Luminaux's Prince masquerading as Lord Terryl. As I said, you did not know who you could trust.' She went on, 'Though it appears that he was right, about this kingdom. It is not Kolyath or Ozumbre.'

Cahra had to agree. Regardless of what she thought about any one individual, Thierre's family was doing something right. Quillon and Leon at the smithy seemed happy.

Another reason she'd never fit in here.

'You couldn't, you know, *see* that before?'

Wyldaern smiled ruefully. 'No. The Oracle, She has far greater powers than I. My visions are more discriminating as to when, or even if, they appear.'

'Can I ask you,' Cahra found herself whispering, 'how does it work?'

Wyldaern's hand intuitively went to her necklace, thumbing the Sigil of the Seers. 'Sometimes, as I said, I am gifted visions. I am also learning to scry for answers.'

Thinking of how little she knew, about everything, Cahra mumbled, 'Sounds handy.'

Wyldaern held her gaze. 'You will get answers. That, I can promise.'

Cahra stretched her legs, thinking about how Wyldaern had helped her, so far: marshalling her strength before Delicia, chastising Thierre – a royal – for deceiving her, even getting her away from Thierre's parents when she couldn't cope.

Only to find her at the smithy and aid her, yet again.

Cahra looked at Wyldaern. 'Why are you helping me?'

The Seer paused, eventually saying, 'I follow the teachings of the Oracle, and She has much to impart to you. It is my duty to deliver you to her.'

Duty. Hael had said something similar. The word stung more than Cahra expected.

It was strange. Ever since she'd fled Kolyath, she'd felt like things were changing, like maybe *she* was changing. Running to keep Lumsden safe, warning Thierre and his people, saving Raiden, training in a weapon, Hael, even wearing a dress. But after it all, after she kept trying just to get through each day, and not give in to hopelessness...

Maybe she wasn't changing at all, maybe she wasn't ready to trust. Maybe everything since Kolyath had been a mistake.

Cahra didn't notice the silence that had descended until Wyldaern spoke.

'And yet, it is not only my duty, Cahra. I am here with you because I wish to be.' Wyldaern turned to her, expression fierce. 'You are the reason Raiden and Thierre came to my aid in the Wilds. You are a good-hearted person, and Kolyath was lucky to have you. I am lucky to know you. For that, and reasons that I cannot yet explain, you have my support on your journey.'

Slowly, Cahra let Wyldaern's words sink in. She'd never been good at compliments. She raised her eyes to the Seer's smiling face.

'You were tough in your terms with Thierre for our safety, our freedom. Thank you.' Cahra exhaled. 'For fighting for someone you'd just met.'

Wyldaern gave her a gentle nod. 'You are welcome. Besides, you did the same for me when you and Thierre's Royal Guards rescued me.'

Cahra grinned back at her. 'Okay, last question, for now. When I meet the Oracle, what happens then? About the Key, and the rest of what Commander Tyne said?'

'Much that I cannot speak to, but She will. And you will learn of your fate, your involvement in all of this. But first...' Wyldaern paused.

Cahra waited. 'Mmm?'

With a laugh, Wyldaern asked, 'Can we please return to the palace for breakfast? I am famished!'

–

Before eating, Cahra entered her room, catching herself in the full-length mirror. She was coal-streaked and sweaty from smithing. Something told her walking into the royal dining room looking as she did wouldn't do.

Bathing quickly, she reached for the soap and lathered it into her hair, the scent of lilies blooming in the steam-filled room. Then she pulled herself from the milky water and groped about for a towel, finally discovering her own clothes. They'd been washed, scrubbed and folded, her linen shirt soft against her skin. But she couldn't find her vest. Cahra scanned the room as she had earlier.

That's when she spied a ribboned parcel on the console table by the door. With a card.

Safe travels.

Cahra stiffened. She'd watched Thierre, as Terryl, scrawl enough notes in his carriage to recognise his handwriting. But 'Safe travels'? She frowned, turning her gaze to the box, then slipped the velvety ribbon from it and opened the lid, refusing to draw breath.

She should have. 'By the Seers!'

It was her vest, or it had been. Because whoever had transformed it had not only replaced the worn leather strips and stitching, but also added metal plates shielding the torso, sealed and supported by a layer of supple leather closest to the skin. Chain mail curved from below the bust to her waist, so she'd be protected without her range of motion suffering.

Cahra gaped in awe as she beheld her new breastplate.

And there was more, she discovered, lifting a pair of leather riding trousers aloft, unfolding like a concertina from seat, to knee, to ankle. There was also a new coat with fur hood and trim, longer than her own and better suited to the changeable weather she'd experienced on the road, plus a new shirt, underwear, socks, even brand-new boots.

Ordinarily, the thought of a stranger choosing her underthings would have embarrassed her, but Cahra was too shocked to register it. All of this, each garment more splendid than the last, all from Thierre, a gift for her 'safe travels'. He'd made this happen, for her.

But, Cahra thought, could she accept it?

In Kolyath, she would never have contemplated accepting a gift from a high-born. Nothing was ever free, and men like that expected things in return. But this was Thierre, he wasn't like those nobles. So what was this – amends? One final gesture after she'd run from his kiss? Or was this his grand farewell?

And if she accepted his gift, what would it mean?

Cahra stared at her old clothes, sighing. Her boots, holed before she'd left Kolyath; trousers, shirt and coat the same, especially after that first fight; her socks and underwear, many times over. Even her vest had seen better days. But Thierre's garments? They were unworn, untorn, sturdy and steadfast. Practical for the journey ahead.

Did he want her to stay, or go?

But what could she do here in Luminaux? Adopt Quillon as her new Lumsden and try to go back to the way things were? Too much had happened. What bothered her the most was she didn't know why – why the Sigil of the Seers, why her? Why any of it?

Wyldaern had said Cahra would learn her fate. And she wanted to meet the Oracle. She had to know the truth of what was happening.

If Cahra stayed in Luminaux, she'd only be staying for Thierre. And for what, to watch him marry someone else? No. The choice was him, or herself.

At least if I choose myself, I'll never be betrayed.

She was a survivor. One that would accept new garments for her journey ahead. And maybe something to remember Thierre by.

Cahra squared her shoulders, staring at the box.

She dressed in every single item, then towelled and combed her hair, letting it fall in wet waves past her shoulders. Standing in front of the mirror, Cahra stared at her reflection. She looked *strong*. Wild and free in her new leathers, the trousers snug around her waist, her refashioned blacksmithing vest hugging her curves. Finally, a proper woman's breastplate! Cahra raised her eyes to her face, for once not hidden by soot or sweat. Her irises popped green against the copper of her freshly washed hair, the bones of her cheeks and splash of freckles so clear without her mask of low-born grime.

Inhaling, Cahra straightened. And offered the person in the mirror a tentative smile.

A self-assured young woman beamed back at her.

Cahra swallowed, awed to find that for once, she actually felt… pretty.

She took one last look in the mirror. Then strode to the bed, stuffed her old things into her satchel and glanced around the guest room, at everything spun in blue and gold. Luminaux had given Cahra her first taste of luxury. But such things weren't meant for her.

There were other things, important things, and she would learn their secrets. Today. All she needed to do was get through breakfast.

And say goodbye to Thierre.

CHAPTER 27

Thierre stood, hands laced behind his back, as he and Raiden waited for Cahra and Wyldaern on the palace steps, his mind a whirlpool of uncertainty. He was concerned his father would change his mind about the women leaving, but Sylvie had somehow reasoned with the King. For that, he was grateful to his sister. Mostly.

Because there was a piece of Thierre that could not believe that it had come to this, a pang of despair that rioted in his chest as the fact echoed: he and Cahra could never be.

Squinting against the sun that glinted off the marble courtyard, Thierre scanned the castle city and Hael'stromia's black peak beyond. Despite his restless thoughts, he struggled to find the right wording that might sway Cahra from leaving. He had lain awake all night, deliberating over how to extricate himself from his wretched engagement to Delicia, but with no evidence of her unfaithfulness, Thierre was at a loss. And if Cahra was to leave Luminaux, all that he could do was precisely what he had done: approached her at breakfast to ask if she and Wyldaern would accept Queran, Siarl and Piet as their own kingdom-appointed detail. That, and pay his personal tailor to do everything in her power to fortify Cahra's garments – even if that meant enlisting Luminaux's blacksmith and leatherworker and paying them to labour all night long to make it happen. It had been worth it.

In the dining hall, Cahra almost looked to be a different woman. She seemed to stand taller, straighter, her lean muscles perfectly filling the fighting leathers, measured based on Cahra's clothing. Her transformation had been breathtaking, and even Sylvie had stared. Thierre was glad that Raiden and Piet had trained with her, before everything had got so complicated. With the reinforcement of her vest and armoured trousers bolstered by thick, tough leather for key joints and striking points, now Cahra could be a warrior, if she chose.

He eyed Delicia and his mother, their vanity drawing them from the steps to the shade. Their presence complicated the already daunting task of saying farewell to Cahra.

Thierre exhaled, feeling restless, while Raiden was predictably still as stone. He never understood how his friend suffered the standing and waiting that was so much a part of his Captain's duties. He supposed it was the years of Commander Tyne looming over Raiden with a baton at the ready. That no doubt helped, he thought.

Before he could say as much, Cahra and Wyldaern exited the palace.

Their goodbye was a short affair, his family and Tyne bidding Cahra and the Seer farewell with stately courtesy. Delicia, who delighted in wielding her noble status like a bladed weapon, was obviously thrilled to see Cahra go.

Then all too suddenly, it was Thierre's turn.

Wyldaern simply thanked him and walked on, leaving him alone with Cahra. All thoughts fled his head, and he swallowed.

Her first words shattered his stupor. 'Thank you, for the clothes. They're beautiful,' Cahra said softly. There was no harshness to her words, and no explanation for her retreat after they had kissed last night. But she did not seem to be angry. It was a start, he thought.

A start, as all signs pointed to the end.

'You are most welcome,' Thierre found himself saying. There was still so much that he wanted to tell her, only without the prying eyes and ears. But would any of it matter?

Cahra was leaving.

Because what could he offer her, really? This woman, who deserved everything, who deserved true happiness. Thierre knew: if he chose her over Delicia, Luminaux's court would never accept it, not in a thousand years. Sylvie had said it; Cahra was a foreign commoner. Their pairing was unacceptable, to everyone. Everyone, except him.

Thierre and Raiden had developed strategies to infiltrate hostile sister kingdoms, had spied and schemed and stolen information to report back to Luminaux. They had ventured into the keeps of Atriposte's Kolyath and Decimus' Ozumbre – some of the most dangerous places in the tri-kingdom realm – yet for all his clever strategising…

…he was powerless to stop her from walking away.

'Cahra.' Thierre ventured a look into her earthy eyes. 'I wish…'

I wish to the Oracles that you and I had more time.

'Me too,' Cahra whispered, and her smile hit him with the full force of the sun's heat, right between his stinging eyes. Then she halted.

He managed a nod, fighting back tears. But as he did, she caught his hand. As he had touched hers in the light of a cave on his way home, after they had thwarted death, together.

Was that when I fell for her, this blacksmith from Kolyath?

It was too much. But Thierre was trained in courtly etiquette, in masks, so he squeezed her hand and returned that smile. Then he stepped away, her hand slipping from his.

Her farewell was nothing but the look of sadness in her eyes, as she took one step then another, farther and farther away from him until she was vanishing over the crest of the hill that would lead her from his life forever.

She wished to leave. He had to let her go. So, Thierre did nothing.

When Cahra's silhouette was gone, Thierre turned on his heel and left, ignoring his mother's calls and his sister's sympathetic gaze. He simply had to get away, from everyone.

–

Alone in his chambers, Thierre grappled with his restless thoughts. He had done what was expected of him. He had let Cahra go. Yet he loathed the knowledge that something could happen and he would not be there, because he had been ordered to stay. It was not right.

Thierre rose, his urge to move overpowering the ingrained stoicism of his upbringing. Pacing back and forth, he tried to place the source of his agitation, for it was more than Cahra leaving Luminaux. It was the expectations placed upon him as the kingdom's Crown Prince, and what they meant for any future Queen. The never-ending threat of spies or assassination attempts in a realm that was at war. Even more than that, it was how he and his family had been forced to cope, with repression and masks and guards, guards everywhere, his only friends those now charged with defending his life. Thierre had never wanted this life, this loneliness, for anyone, certainly not for Cahra, not even for Delicia. So, he had resigned himself to letting his feelings dwell beneath the surface. It was his shameful secret: that his life was a glorious cage, while Cahra's was a life of freedom. He wanted her to live it.

But now, he felt strange, frenzied even, and his chest pained him. It was not her kiss, or even the idea that he might wring some confession from her as to her feelings for him. Cahra and Wyldaern faced real dangers from Luminaux's enemies, yet he was languishing, useless, in his chambers.

Thierre eyed Cahra's longsword, the one that she had crafted for him in Kolyath, brought to his rooms on the previous eve. Its pommel twinkled under the candelabra's flames. Cahra had not hesitated to warn him of the danger in Kolyath, Thierre thought.

And he could not stand idly by and let her face such threats, he realised with clarity, when he could do something more than letting his guards handle it. Her burdens were not his, that much was true. However, if he was not with her and something happened…

He would not endure it.

So, though he had scarcely returned and not yet unpacked, Thierre prepared to leave his kingdom once again.

–

Thierre was almost ready when there was a sharp rap at the entrance to his quarters, the door flying open. Only one man knew him well enough to be so bold.

'Thierre,' Raiden warned, marching in.

'I cannot permit Cahra and Wyldaern to go into the Wilds alone,' Thierre told him. 'Not with our enemies uniting at our backs.'

'You haven't,' Raiden argued. 'You sent your three best guards to protect them. If you can't trust your own people, you may as well not have them.'

'It's not about trust! It is about an unholy alliance that we have no intelligence on, no figures, no logistics—'

'Exactly why you cannot even think of doing what I *know* you're thinking of doing. The risks are uncharted.'

Thierre switched tactics. 'And what if Cahra has more to do with the prophecy than we thought? Wyldaern never told us her reason for taking Cahra to meet the Oracle. What if there is more to her actions than we know? Unless, I – *we* – accompany them.'

Raiden was yet to reply, which was a good sign. They both knew how the King and Commander Tyne desired every advantage regarding the prophecy. Resisting a grin, he opened his mouth, but Raiden cut in, cursing, 'Damn it, Thierre! Then we leave now. We order three companies and—'

'No, our time is past. If you and I do not leave now, we will not reach them before they exit the gatehouse, and I do not know where Wyldaern is taking Cahra.'

Raiden looked ready to throw something. '*Fine*. But any of our people we pass on the way through will escort us.'

Thierre nodded. 'Agreed.' He placed a hand on his friend's arm. 'Pack with haste and meet back here in five minutes.'

-

Costumed as Lord Terryl and keen to find Cahra, Thierre messengered a scribbled note to Sylvie, who would be furious, both at him and the second-hand blast she was sure to receive from their father once he learned of his son's defiance. But as time ticked by without Raiden appearing, a creeping fear gnawed at Thierre. Something was wrong.

With a glance to Cahra's longsword, Thierre buckled it to his belt, hoisted his pack and set off for Raiden's rooms.

Thierre rounded a corner, and instantly ducked back. Perhaps his note had made its way to Sylvie too quickly, for Commander Tyne had accosted Raiden outside his quarters. The Captain spotted him, his face weathering a storm of emotions as Thierre watched Raiden struggle with whether to halt his plan altogether. Finally, Raiden threw up his hands in what looked like intense agitation, until Thierre glimpsed the signal to go forward. His old friend had come through for him in the end. Thierre nodded his thanks to Raiden and spun to make his getaway, appraising the exits.

There was a servants' passage beneath the palace that came out by the second-last turn before leaving the kingdom proper. With any luck, he would catch Cahra and the others there. Thierre drew his hood and hastened along the dim torch-lit path, tossing a 'Hail King Royce' to anyone who gave him a second look. He prayed Raiden had managed to convince Tyne not to launch a full-scale mission to apprehend him.

After what felt like an agonising stretch of time, the dimness of the tunnel gave way to light at its far end. He charged it, adjusting his cowl as he slowed to enter the flow of traffic, sweeping for anyone he knew.

For the briefest of moments, Thierre's heart sunk as he failed to spot Cahra and Wyldaern, or Piet, Siarl and Queran. But… *There!* Before the gate, the ermine fur-lined hood that he had been so adamant about.

Cahra.

Thierre moved towards her, trying to hurry without drawing attention. Approaching the gate, he pulled a map from his pocket and pretended to consult it, noting his father's own Royal Guards, who looked set to halt him, when a voice rang out:

'Guards!' The helmed men stood quickly at attention as a fellow officer approached. 'The Captain requests advanced support at the sky terrace, immediately!'

Thierre exhaled. It was one of his and Raiden's coded phrases, created on the off chance that one day Raiden might need to aid Thierre in escaping the kingdom, if overrun. The guards suitably distracted, Thierre folded his map and replaced it in his pocket, resuming his search for the black and white fur hood.

At last, Thierre neared the gatehouse, the kingdom's final checkpoint, and its jet gate. He watched as Cahra and the others proceeded forward, Piet speaking with the guards, the man's imposing bulk unmistakable. Thierre knew that they would be enquiring about the group's return and he strained to listen. What would Cahra's response be?

Her reply floated to him on the breeze: 'We'll see.' Despite the thoughts tumbling around inside his head, it warmed him to hear the possibility in her voice, even now.

He knew the ranking guard on duty, so, as he had done so many times before, Thierre moved for the checkpoint. The guard offered him a dutiful nod, before stepping aside to let the Prince pass. Then, moving through the black gate, Thierre quickened between the trees to reach Cahra, his focus solely on her and making sure that she was safe.

Thierre didn't see the weapon coming down behind him until it was too late.

CHAPTER 28

The lush, towering trees of the evergreen Wilds were silent, like Cahra, as Wyldaern led the way to the Oracle. In the time of old Hael'stromia, three roads forked from Luminaux: to the west, the road that retraced their steps to Kolyath; to the south-west, the road to the capital; and to the south, a third route that once led to Ozumbre. That road was destroyed centuries ago, Piet had said, as Cahra eyed it from outside Luminaux's black gate, the cobbles ripped up and hurled to the wind, the ancient path overgrown. Like so many people in their realm, the road had retreated into the anonymity of the Wilds.

Safety and security in hiding. Cahra understood all too well, yearning for both as her uneasy legs carried her into the unknown.

Piet had asked if she or Wyldaern wanted to ride the palomino mare saddled with everyone's bags, but both preferred to walk; the Seer, because she was used to it, and Cahra because, without the distraction of forcing one boot in front of the other, she feared she might do something stupid. Like go running back to Luminaux.

What is Thierre doing right now?

She tried to leave the thought behind her.

Instead, she gently patted the tan mare's powder-white mane. Cahra had a feeling the horse was more than just a pack-mule for the journey; should they be attacked, the palomino would be the fastest way for them to flee. Ahead, she watched Wyldaern and Piet chat quietly, Queran roaming somewhere at the rear of their party. Siarl had slipped into the underbrush shortly after they'd set out, her impressive silver daggers unsheathed, her long braids swept into a high knot atop her head. Cahra wondered why Queran hadn't left and taken to the trees, as he so often did to leverage his marksmanship. Unless it was on purpose, she considered – to lull any who might ambush them into thinking she and Wyldaern's guards were as they seemed, no one lurking as a countermeasure beyond the pastel blooms speckling the forest floor.

No wonder Thierre thought so highly of his Royal Guards.

Yet the idea of more trouble… Wyldaern turned to laugh at something Piet had said, the Seer seemingly unfazed, and Cahra envied the way the woman had about her, that ever-present calm. No matter what was going on around her, Wyldaern always appeared unperturbed.

Cahra, however, was only growing more anxious as the hours passed. Their path was getting dimmer the deeper they waded into the Wilds. Colder, too, and she shivered, buttoning her new coat, the chill in the air unnervingly like Kolyath's.

Was it just the cold that had her shaking?

The Seer must have noticed the apprehension on her face, Wyldaern explaining to her, 'The cave systems we are nearing are beneath mountains, hence the cooler turn of weather.' She nodded to Cahra's outfit. 'The fur lining of your coat is fortuitous.'

The clothing Thierre had gifted Cahra was fortuitous indeed. It was so comfortable, from the premium-grain leather of her skin-hugging vest and trousers, to her coat and boots. She just hoped she wouldn't regret wearing in new shoes for the first time on a day-long hike. Maybe she should have taken Piet up on riding the horse.

It didn't matter, because soon Wyldaern was pointing a slender arm towards the rocky tor that dipped and then ascended into staggering peaks, their icy ridges dark and dizzying.

Staring intently at the precipitous terrain, there was a lightness, a peacefulness to the Seer's face that Cahra had only caught in glimpses before. Piet left the horse grazing in a small clearing a short distance away, stripping it of its saddle to disguise it as a wild mountain mare, as Siarl emerged from the wilderness to join Queran.

'We have reached the caves,' Wyldaern told them. She pushed through tangled thickets and layer upon layer of viny overhang to reveal a portal into blackness that, in spite of her eye for detail, Cahra somehow hadn't noticed. Placing the saddle inside the cave, Piet then Wyldaern ventured into the dark. Cahra rolled her shoulders, willing herself to tap into that old state of resting alertness she'd once worn like a second skin. She wasn't surprised to see Siarl and Queran armed and battle-ready, Siarl swapping one of her long blades for the shorter, throwing kind, her bowman companion aiming an arrow back at the cave's entrance. Ahead of the group, Piet lit a fiery torch.

'It's cold as Kolyath in here,' Cahra muttered as she walked. She could feel her nerves morphing from mild tension in her neck and shoulders into something else as the cave path began to climb, the dark all-encompassing.

'You seem to carry little affection for the kingdom.' Wyldaern's voice drifted to her.

Cahra snorted loudly. 'There's not much joy to be found in that Hael-forsaken place. There's a reason I left, you know.'

'The kingdom was not always like that,' Wyldaern said softly.

'That's not been my experience.' She folded her arms, continuing on.

'Cahra,' Wyldaern said, slowing to fall into step beside her in the narrow tunnel. 'Consider why you call the man the "Steward". Atriposte is not Kolyath's rightful monarch. He simply minds a place, the kingdom's keeper in the absence of its ruler,' the Seer said.

'I suppose,' Cahra admitted. Only Atriposte wasn't some figurehead. He'd been in power her whole life. Stories of blue-blooded high-borns didn't matter in places like Kolyath. Not when power could be stolen and used to suppress an entire people. 'Why is that?'

Wyldaern stared straight ahead. 'The royal family was assassinated, centuries ago. Atriposte's forebears seized their chance then.'

Cahra watched as Piet's torch cast fingers of spindly flame into the darkness, feeling something like trepidation materialise with them. She swallowed, trying to find a way to abate the growing disquiet inside her. She opted for distraction.

'I can't believe it takes you so long to get to the Oracle,' Cahra said.

'It is a journey,' she confessed. 'A pilgrimage that I endeavour to make once a month, if I can. The rest of the time, I wander, practicing what She has taught me and calling on the Wildspeople and any villages that I find, should they require aid.'

The Seer's answer reminded Cahra of Thierre. She swallowed the lump in her throat and asked, 'What kind of aid?'

Wyldaern's gaze grew thoughtful in the flickering torchlight. 'Whatever people need. Helping their healers with herbs and elixirs, scrying for guidance on sowing and harvesting. Sometimes, tending the fields is help enough,' she said warmly, her voice light and lyrical.

'But not the weather?' Cahra joked, fighting to steady her nerves.

'Alas, no,' she said with a hint of amusement. 'That, I cannot control.'

'Shame,' Cahra said glibly with a shrug. She would've liked more than a torch in this freezing cave. Rubbing her arms, she asked, 'And you've been coming here for how long?'

The Seer tilted her head, thinking. 'Almost a decade now, I suppose.'

She squinted at Wyldaern in the dark. When they'd met, the Seer hadn't seemed that much older than Cahra. Maybe she'd been wrong.

Or maybe, the Oracle had helped Wyldaern when the woman was younger, just like Lumsden had helped her, she thought.

Spying a pinprick of light at the end of the tunnel, it should have filled her with relief. But all Cahra suddenly felt was a nameless dread.

'What is the Oracle like?'

'She is the last of the three Oracles in existence,' Wyldaern explained. 'The lessons She has taught, the knowledge She has shared… I would never have known such otherwise. She will enlighten you, too.' Wyldaern smiled. 'Would you like to meet Her?'

Slowly, Cahra nodded, and strode on until the dot of light became a gateway into a new world.

The cave tunnel opened into a long meadow, walled on all sides by sawtooth cliffs. Turning in a slow circle, she had the crazed notion they were nestled in a lopped peak of one of the ice-capped mountains she'd seen outside the caves. At the end of a pebbled walkway through wild dandelions, creeping juniper and the fierce magenta blooms of fireweed, Cahra could just make out a high-roofed cottage, wooden panels basking in the late afternoon light.

One moment, she'd been inside the cave's winding maze. The next, she found herself in a rustic garden in full bloom. It should have taken them hours to walk to such a place.

'It is a veiling,' Wyldaern explained to her. 'The ancient Oracles did not just "see" things.'

Cahra frowned, wondering what other magicks awaited them. Thierre's people stopped, cautiously raising their weapons.

'Please, there is no need,' Wyldaern said, beckoning Cahra toward the winding path.

Exhaling uneasily, Cahra and the others followed.

They passed through a central ring-shaped garden brimming with verdant ferns, then crossed a bridge, the sound of running water echoing against the grounds' rock-faced walls. The Oracle's dwelling grew as the group neared, a small cabin with a thatched roof, lived in yet sturdy, soft pillows of smoke puffing from the chimney to the cyan sky.

And then they were standing at the Oracle's front door. The last of her conduit kind, the banished, the 'heretics'. Hael'stromia's ancient Seers. Cahra's body went rigid.

Wyldaern didn't knock. She stood, Cahra beside her, at the lacewood door and waited. Thierre's people exchanged glances, Siarl looking uncomfortable as she shifted, hands itching for the comfort of her blades. Not a minute later, the door opened. A middle-aged woman appeared before the group, peering out at them.

Cahra clamped her mouth shut. She hadn't known what to expect, but she definitely hadn't expected the Oracle to *not* be a crone.

The woman couldn't have been much over five feet tall. Even Cahra rose above her, despite being of average height herself. The Oracle's garments, like her mountain dwelling, were humble, homespun and not the faded black of Wyldaern's robes but something more like what Cahra would have seen walking the Traders' Quadrant in Kolyath or even Luminaux – modest, functional peasant-wear. Yet one thing stood out as striking to Cahra, besides the woman's dark complexion and tight curls.

It was her eyes: a prismatic shade of lavender, like amethyst, that made Cahra blink.

She'd seen that crystalline colour before.

The Oracle's gaze locked onto Cahra and she somehow wondered if the woman had heard her 'crone' thought. Did All-seeing mean mind-reading?

But the Oracle just turned to Wyldaern, a smile breezing across her wizened features. She surveyed their company, holding the front door open. 'I am Thelaema. Tea?'

It was then Cahra remembered where she'd seen amethyst in someone's eyes before, and saw it again as Wyldaern passed her, the Seer's irises edged in the same hue.

Cahra joined Siarl, Piet and Queran in a shared look as they crossed the threshold and trailed Wyldaern into the Oracle's home, shutting the mottled door behind them.

Scanning left to right in the deceptively spacious cottage, Cahra wandered into a curious pocket of the house. Instead of walls, this room was made almost entirely of windows, the curved glass panes doming high overhead, like she was standing in a giant bubble. It had a generous view of the scenic gardens and could have been a sitting room, except for the peculiar items Thelaema had left on display: an obsidian mirror; an etched bowl of brass, filled with water; and an immense crystal ball. Cahra bent over, peering suspiciously as though she might glimpse a miniature of herself inside it.

Piet motioned to Siarl and Queran, already inspecting the house for access points other than the one they'd entered through.

'So many windows,' Queran murmured.

'Do you not find my home sufficiently secure, Queran Head-splitter?' Thelaema spoke without looking at him, arranging six bone-white teacups around a large teapot on an occasion table between two large sofas.

Queran's eyebrows were a fox-red line. '*Arrowhead*-splitter,' he corrected, adding, 'Madam Oracle.'

'Ah, but arrowheads were not your first victims, were they, son of war?'

Piet turned at the remark, Wyldaern placing a hand between the blond warrior and Thelaema.

'Be still, Piet, kin of Klaas, Luminaux's Gavel of Justice. I could level such truths at any, nay, all of your Prince's merry band. Or any of the tri-kingdom armies.' The Oracle's gaze was fierce despite its pastel tint. 'Besides, you are not why we are gathered.' She looked at Cahra. 'But you are safe. A perk, if you will, from the days and ways of old.'

Piet stationed himself outside the room with the curved windows, Siarl peeling off to patrol the house. Queran trailed after her, frowning, an arrow slack in his hand.

'The ways of old?' Cahra repeated. Thelaema gingerly lowered herself into her seat, a rickety chair at the head of the walnut table, and nodded.

Cahra sat on the sofa by the door, Wyldaern opposite, pouring them cups of herbal tea. It made her think of Queen Avenais in Luminaux.

'I don't understand,' Cahra told the Oracle. 'Luminaux welcomed Wyldaern and nature magick, and herbs aren't forbidden like in Kolyath. Why are you living all the way out here?' She glanced between the Seers.

Thelaema pinned her with a look. 'As I believe that you know, once trust is broken, it is toilsome to repair in full. Seers may have lost the kingdoms' trust, but so did they ours. And so we have remained, as recluses in our Wilds. However,' the Oracle said, 'that is not your true question.' Thelaema leaned into a sun-bleached cushion and sighed, a grateful smile forming on her lips. She opened her eyes, peering at Cahra, seeking something. 'And you are Cahra. You took great pains to come here, and I am thankful. For while I am fond of visits from my favoured pupil,' she said, patting Wyldaern's hand, the Seer handing the woman a teacup, 'it is you and I that were to meet.' Thelaema straightened, as if anticipating Cahra's question. 'I am High Oraculine Thelaema, last of the Order of Descry, the Seers of Hael'stromia and Keepers of the Reliquus.'

Cahra latched onto what she knew. 'The Reliquus. You mean Hael?'

Thelaema smiled. 'As Keepers of the Reliquus, we three Oracles were charged with being responsible for Hael'stromia's, indeed the realm's, most valued gift. We were wardens of the Netherworld's supreme achievement. The power of creation and destruction. The—'

'The weapon,' Cahra breathed.

Thelaema's pale eyes flashed. 'Yes.' She paused. 'Your questions are many, as they should be,' the Oracle said, reaching out to Cahra, who jumped at the unexpected contact. 'However, the answers…' Thelaema and Wyldaern exchanged a look, as if speaking silently. 'The information will be new to you, what it means. I know that there will be consequences. What I can tell you is that we are here. The Descry, as ever, serve Hael'stromia.'

Cahra's brow creased. 'What do you mean?'

'Cahra.' Thelaema commanded her attention kindly. 'You were orphaned as an infant. How do you know your name?'

'I don't know.' Her earliest memories were of living as a beggar on the streets. 'Maybe I named myself.' She shrugged, leaning back.

Thelaema studied her. 'And you can recall no earlier?'

She lowered her head, hair falling in a shroud around her. What was there to recall? She'd been a child of death and destitution. 'No.'

Thelaema nodded. 'So, you do not remember your life in the Wilds?'

Cahra looked up. She wasn't of Kolyath?

'Your birthplace,' Thelaema began, 'was a village between Kolyath and Luminaux. Closer to Luminaux, as they were more tolerant, of the special, the magickally minded.'

'Wait.' Cahra shook her head, trying to get her bearings. 'Are you saying I'm some kind of Seer from Luminaux?'

'No, child,' Thelaema chortled, then grew serious. 'However, the reason that your family was in hiding in the Wilds—'

Her *family?*

'—is that your kin necessitated concealment. For centuries, your family lived peacefully, without incident, outside Kolyath.' Thelaema stilled, the air pressing upon Cahra. 'Once your parents, friends and village were destroyed, the decision was made: to secrete you within your ancestral lands. So, you were placed in Kolyath, close to Seer sympathisers, to monitor you and ensure that you did not fall into the wrong hands.'

Somewhere around the mention of her family, her parents, she shut her eyes. With everything that followed, she didn't dare open them again. But at 'the wrong hands'...

Her palms were clammy, shaking on her leather knee guards.

'But I did fall into the wrong hands,' Cahra said, fighting to keep her voice steady as the hurt, the anger, flooded her body. She stood, even as her legs threatened to give way, taking a step backwards, then another, retreating from Thelaema's ridiculous words, until she was bracing herself against the Oracle's shelf of curiosities.

Wyldaern stood, but Thelaema raised a hand as Cahra went on.

'I was a child, living in the wreckage of a tyrant's reign,' she said, her voice strangled, heart hammering. Cahra could feel the pins, the needles in her arms and chest. Stabbing her. 'Some weeks, I didn't eat, drink, for days on end – none of us did, the homeless kids. And when I did manage to scavenge any food, it was rotting on the streets. I was sentenced to years in the Steward's dungeons, all from stealing to survive, and it was only because of Lumsden that I didn't—' The thought of the old man was too much. Cahra inhaled, snarling. 'Before Lumsden saved me from it all. And you're telling me this was someone's decision? On purpose? To sentence a kid to such cruelty, even after the death of my parents and village, my greatest sin being I was too young to remember it? What kind of person would *do* that?' The hilt of an athame was in her hand now; she must have picked it from the Oracle's shelf. 'Tell me who gave the word, and I *WILL* kill them!'

Silence. There was fear in Wyldaern's eyes.

Thelaema raised her amethyst orbs to Cahra. 'It was I.'

Cahra stumbled, nearly falling – then whirled on Wyldaern, the dagger still in hand. 'I *trusted* you! Why did you bring me here?'

Wyldaern raised her palms in a stricken plea. 'Cahra—'

'And you,' Cahra choked out, fury blazing in her eyes as she held Thelaema's gaze. 'You cast me into this nightmare without a second thought. To live in poverty, and for what? You don't even know me! *WHY?!*' She screamed the word, Siarl, Piet and Queran charging from all corners of the house. Thierre's guards stood, bewildered, weapons drawn as they searched for the source of Cahra's turmoil.

Then Thelaema stood and tranquillity swept the room, the tension that had been there, electrifyingly hot, seeming to suffocate and die. Cahra panted in the sudden hush of stillness.

'Kolyath is the reason,' the Oracle proclaimed. 'Your destiny was written in Hael'stromia. Cahra, you are more than you know. *You* are the rightful heir to the sister kingdom of Kolyath. And your true name is Princess Cahraelia.'

Cahra blinked, dumbfounded. Then, as Thelaema's words sank in, it was like someone flipped a switch and her shock gave way to a tidal swell of laughter. She doubled over, howls escaping her in uncontrollable waves.

Princess! It was completely, utterly ludicrous.

Wyldaern's eyes pleaded with Thelaema. The Oracle's face was an impasse. *A mask.*

Cahra remembered Hael's words. It seemed it wasn't just the tri-kingdoms who were seasoned players.

'You were no longer safe,' Thelaema tried to explain.

Cahra laughed even harder, an edge of mania racking her gasps. Her stomach ached as she doubled over the sofa, wheezing. 'Safe? When have I ever been *safe?*'

'In Kolyath, as an urchin, you were hidden in plain sight. There you would see, learn. Experience Atriposte's rule and grow to hate it, to defy it. So that when the time was right…' Thelaema broke off as Cahra's laughter turned to salty tears. 'You would be ready to fight. And so that, one day, you would meet the Oracle. And I would give you this,' Thelaema said. She opened a wooden chest on the table and picked up a metal object.

Cahra could barely comprehend anything by now, but she recognised the black swirls and spikes of Haellium, engineered to wind around a central mechanism, an indentation at its elaborate eye. The ornate device was roughly the size of Cahra's palm.

'This is the Key,' Thelaema said quietly as she pushed the dark relic towards Cahra. 'The Key to Hael'stromia, and all that it entails.'

'*For when the Seers reappear, when the Key has been bestowed, when the mark walks the path to enter the Nether in life, then shall Hael rise again,*' Wyldaern murmured.

'We the Seers, Oracle and apprentice, are here. The kin of the hammer holds the Key. The journey to Hael'stromia is all that remains, where the Reliquus may be freed after 399 years of awaiting the prophecy's fulfilment. Only the weapon's blood master, the Scion, can activate the Key and access the capital. Your time approaches, Cahraelia of Kolyath.'

Cahra just stared. At the Key, at Thelaema, and at her supposed friend, Wyldaern.

'Why.' Her voice was alien to her own ears. She could feel the old numbness pushing back, like it used to, as a child. In a world she'd cruelly been tossed into.

'Because it seems, Cahraelia, that you were fated to call upon the Seers to complete our final task. It was your sword, was it not, that signified the first of the omens?'

'How?' Cahra mumbled.

Thelaema smiled tightly. 'You are the last of Kolyath's bloodline, a sister kingdom of old that Hael'stromia held sovereignty over. Our sigil would have been present at your birth,' the Oracle said, as if that explained anything at all.

Cahra stared into empty space. 'I don't even know how old I am.'

'You are eighteen years old,' Thelaema said gently. 'Your birthday was the day that you gave Prince Thierre the sword. The day that you both fled Kolyath.'

A sob escaped Cahra's lips, as she whispered, 'How can you possibly know that?'

Thelaema gazed into Cahra's eyes then, the woman's glistening with regret. 'I saw. Because I am the conduit, the final theomancer.' She exhaled. 'And my duty here is done.'

Finally, Cahra looked, truly looked, at the Oracle's strangely coloured eyes, and saw: Thelaema wasn't of middle years. She was as ancient as the Oracles of old.

Because she *was one*, Cahra realised, jaw dropping, and she knew it to be the truth. Thelaema was the last Oracle to exist, to meet the Scion and bestow the Key, as told by the prophecy she'd helped divine. Like Hael, she'd survived for longer than anyone deserved. And that life had required strength and resilience honed from years of seeing, knowing. Waiting. All this time, for Cahra.

Her eyes flashed to Thelaema's. It was as if the thought had been sown, then grown in her own mind. The Oracle nodded.

Then Thelaema put a hand to her head, Wyldaern immediately at the woman's side.

'Are you all right?' The Seer asked her mentor.

'Yes, yes,' Thelaema said, batting her apprentice away. She turned to Cahra. 'Please, do not blame Wyldaern for the glimpses she saw without knowing your entire story. The All-seeing works in more onerous ways than mysterious ones, I am afraid.'

Cahra glanced at the contraption – the Key – that rested on Thelaema's low table. She had no idea how to make sense of any of this mess.

Thelaema paused, sensing her agitation. 'Cahra. There is more to learn.'

'What more could there be?' she managed, voice strained.

Wyldaern replied, 'Why your village was attacked. Why a Steward sits on your throne. What must occur now that you have the Key.' She glanced to the Oracle.

As if in answer, Thelaema pushed it closer. 'Take it. It is yours.'

She longed to yell she didn't want it, to pick it up and hurl it through the room's glossy windows, shattering the glass. But she didn't. She could feel the metal calling to her, urging her to take the Key from the table. Cahra looked at it uneasily, ready to recoil her fingers that crept towards the occult oddity, yet she didn't stop them. Instead, staring intently, she cupped it in her hands, tracing a finger over the dip at the Key's centre.

Suddenly, the world spun and darkness encroached, dragging Cahra under.

CHAPTER 29

She was falling.

Plummeting through the air, Cahra's breath was ripped away. Her blood raged like wildfire in her veins, bile shooting from her stomach to scald her throat. She tried to breathe, tried to scream, but could do nothing as the floor of Hael's tomb converged at lightning speed. Refusing to let the looming tiles be the last thing she ever saw, Cahra closed her eyes.

In an instant, Hael was there, as he always was now, her protector.

Her only shield.

He caught her, his powerful legs braced against the stones, arms wrapping Cahra in an embrace. At the feel of his sturdiness, her head against the broadness of his chest – at the realisation she'd stopped falling, she sank into his grasp, her breaths heaving, the smell of burning in the air. She had survived without shattering her back or skull, thank the—

Seers. Cahra froze, her thoughts derailed.

Hael stared in the direction of the presumed ceiling for a time, then gazed at Cahra. The abreption of their last vision had held; he was still lovely. His midnight hair cascaded in wild, sleek spikes that edged past his shoulders, his cheekbones sharp enough to draw blood as his lips peeled back into a feral snarl, wolfish fangs glinting in the blackness. Cahra tried to focus on his ethereal beauty, rather than what had just happened.

But Hael was having none of it, asking, '*What in the name of Tenebrius occurred?*' The fires of his eyes were blazing black, which she'd begun to guess was related to his emotions. He hadn't let go of her. If anything, he was clutching her even tighter, an immovable fortress.

She bit her cheek. The last thing she wanted was to talk, but what was the alternative? Sit and bear the icy tiles as they bit into her palms, staring into the endless dark, and let the cold numb the pain threatening to dash her against her insides, her blood and guts and bones? Looking into the ever-burning eyes of the only one who knew what it was like to feel this alone, she took a shallow breath.

'I know, about my family. About Kolyath.' She swallowed. 'Who I am.'

Hael's flames guttered, the blackness receding ever so slightly to a wine-red, and in their softened glow, she saw the quiet compassion etched across his face. The sorrow.

Suddenly, the dam Cahra had been pushing so hard to uphold burst irreparably free. Not because of her bloodline, or even Kolyath's varied cruelties. It was that she'd had a life. Parents, people who loved her. Something she'd never had the courage to imagine for herself, the scrawny girl skulking in filthy alleyways, weeks-old dirt staining her face as she watched for Kolyath's guards so bigger, older kids could brawl over mould-mottled bread.

She'd had a mother and a father, and someone had killed them, all because of the prophecy's burden Cahra now bore. Because of her.

Hot tears stormed her face and she cried, big wracking sobs that left her wretched. Hael froze, unsure of what to do. Finally, he set her down, and Cahra gripped him, the only anchor she had now. The only person she could trust.

Tentatively, he held her. Then slowly, he seemed to remember human comforts, embracing her gently, his flames reduced to embers.

As Cahra wept for a life she never knew.

–

'Did you know?' Cahra asked him, closing her eyes. She'd finally stopped crying and they were sitting on the floor against the altar, Cahra atop Hael's robe, her knees hugged to her chest as she leaned into his strength. His shoulder felt so natural against her cheek.

'*Of your kin?*' He looked at her, palms resting on the knees of his crossed legs.

'My parents,' she said, wiping her face, the darkness of the tomb welcome for once. 'My line.'

His gaze was soft, unflinching. '*Of your bloodline, yes. The Scion is always born of a sister kingdom line. Kolyath is an opportunity,*' he told her, if gruffly. Then Hael paused. '*However, I did not know of your kin's fate. I am sorry, Cahra.*'

She nodded, then sighed. 'I think you mean Cahraelia,' she muttered.

'*Your true moniker,*' he mused. '*You do not approve?*'

Cahra made a face. 'It sounds like the name of a dainty flower.'

Hael's lips curled as he rumbled a laugh. The sound was mellifluent, like deep, warm chimes.

'*It is your truth,*' Hael said. '*Just as you, Scion, are my own. We should address why you were sent to me today.*' Cahra nodded, then straightened. '*The second omen is significant, as much for you as I. The first omen – the Sigil of the Seers – awoke me from my slumber. Before you, er, arrived,*' he gestured to her fall from the sky, '*I sensed the Key's beacon flare upon your touch. The second omen has now come to pass.*'

Her anxiety caught her by surprise. 'What happens next?'

Hael frowned. '*The Oracle did not impart this knowledge?*'

Cahra shook her head. 'There was no time. I touched the Key and it transported me. Well, "transported" is maybe not the best word.' She scowled. 'But no, the Oracle did not.' Cahra had a feeling Thelaema was the kind of person to not impart a lot of things.

'*I see. Well, I must now impart something to you. After which, the second omen requires a rite that we must perform, together.*' Hael's expression hardened, the lightness of his laughter moments ago gone. He stood, but he was fidgeting.

'It can't be that bad,' Cahra said. Could it?

Hael was silent, his lips pursed.

Well, that wasn't an answer. Cahra got up, twisting her body to sit on top of Hael's black altar. If he was going to tell her something bad, she wasn't waiting on the ground for it. She leaned forward, legs hanging over the edge, and resisted the urge to hurry him up.

They were eye level, and for all his poise, he seemed taken aback by her direct gaze.

'*The Scion, and in this case, the prophecy's omen-bringer, is always of Kolyath, Luminaux or Ozumbre's royal bloodlines,*' Hael said, '*as Hael'stromia is sovereign to all. The Key…*' Pausing in his stalking, he faced her. '*Do you know its function?*'

Cahra rolled her head from side to side and grimaced, bones cricking as she tried to loosen her taut muscles.

'Thelaema said all that was left of the omens was for me to come to Hael'stromia and free you. She didn't say what the Key opened.' Cahra looked around them, rubbing her neck. 'I'm guessing this room's door?'

Hael's smile was tense. '*That is not all. The Key unlocks this chamber – my shrine – yet it is also used to access the palatial temple, as well as each of the capital's gates.*'

'Oh.' Cahra frowned. 'Right. So if the Scion, the omen-bringer, is a royal, and that Scion is me, and I have the Key, and that frees you here…' She looked up at him, frowning. 'I still don't understand.'

This time, Hael's smile was unencumbered, his fangs flashing in the murky light. '*This is what I must impart to you, Cahra – Cahraelia.*' He bent his knee to sink before her. '*I may curse the Oracle for not revealing your true mantle, however, given the nature of what you have learned today, I appreciate her hesitation.*' Hael looked at her with such intensity that Cahra found the bile was roiling in her once again, and she gripped the edge of his stone altar. '*Only a blood heir to one of the kingdoms may dare hold sway over the Hael'stromian realm. It is the duty of the Scion, aided by the Reliquus. The Key breaks the seal on the magicks that constrain me and my powers. Once the seal is broken, the capital may rise to her feet.*'

Cahra nodded, tallying everything he'd told her, the picture forming.

She whispered, fearful as she spoke the words, 'So where does that leave me?'

Hael rose so swiftly she gasped. A shadow flitted across his face, inches from hers, as he pressed his lips together. Then his expression softened.

'*As Empress of Hael'stromia, and Master of the Reliquus. Me.*' He bowed reverently. '*I am yours to command.*'

Cahra recoiled. 'You can't be serious,' she stammered. 'Being told I'm a Princess is enough fun for one day, thanks.' Except Hael didn't joke. She leapt from the altar, bare feet hitting the tiles with a slap. 'There's no way! What business do I have being *your* master?' She gaped, incredulous. 'I mean, you're a magickal warrior. I can't even fight with a sword.' Cahra was circling him now, the urge to move, to do something, anything, searing inside her. 'Hael, I can't be an *Empress!* I'm not like Thierre, I'm not a real royal, I haven't been trained! I don't, I *can't*—'

Thierre, she thought helplessly. This was made for someone like him, not her, someone trained in courtly, well, everything.

Someone had made a horrible mistake.

'*Cahra.*' Hael wisely reverted to her name. '*It is your truth. Only the Scion can communicate with me, prior to ascending. Here, we are between the veil and void. The capital's magicks draw you and I, our astral essences, together as Scion and Reliquus. The Oracles themselves could not reach us here.*'

Cahra put her hands to her temples, rubbing at them. Her head pounded.

'This is ridiculous.' Their astral essences? As in, their *souls?* She leaned against the altar, the stone a stark support. 'How can it be me? There are a dozen other high-borns for the job – what about King Royce of Luminaux? Even the Steward knows more about ruling than I do.' Cahra winced, voice straining as she said, 'Hael, you have to help me, this can't be right!'

He moved for her, saying, '*I will, I swear it. However, I can assure you that it is right, in every sense. You are the Scion.*' He paused. '*And you, too, are of high birth, Cahra.*'

She sagged back against the altar. She hadn't even thought of that.

'*Would it help you to hear of the final omen?*'

Sure, what was more prophetic madness? 'Okay,' she said numbly.

'*As I have told you, there is a rite. The Key has bound us, and the third omen awaits. You will need to journey to Hael'stromia and use the Key to unseal the temple and this room. However, this final stage will be fraught with danger as the tri-kingdoms may not abide by you and what has been ordained. And presently, I cannot protect you.*' His body tensed as if the idea was unbearable. '*There is a temporary resolution, however: a period of time where, due to our tether, my powers may be conferred upon you for a short while.*'

'Really?' Cahra sat up, intrigued. 'What kind of powers? Will I be able to turn to smoke and fly around too?'

'*Not quite,*' Hael replied with a glimmer of humour. '*However, you shall be gifted my strength, speed, stamina, agility, perhaps some residual combat instincts.*' That last one was well-developed in her already, at least. '*They shall fade, little by little.*'

'Okay,' Cahra said, trying not to sound disappointed about the flying. 'And the rite?'

'*It is as before,*' Hael said. '*The price is your suffering. Only, for this omen's rite, there is, ahem, an exchange.*' A muscle in Hael's jaw twitched and Cahra narrowed her eyes. It was the first time he'd raised her suspicion.

'What kind of exchange?'

A pause. '*My negative emotions, for yours.*'

'Oh,' Cahra said. 'So I would receive your – feelings. And they would, what, fuel me with your powers?' He gave her the slightest nod. 'You've done this before?'

'*Yes.*'

'Is it painful, like last time?'

'*More for me than you.*' The truth. Then what was the problem?

Cahra folded her arms. 'Hael, I don't know how this has worked with other Scions, but I need honesty. And you look worried.'

Was that embarrassment in Hael's eyes? His flames were threshing like a cat's tail. '*Honesty. Of course.*' He paused. '*I merely wish to prepare you for what you will receive.*' Hael hesitated, adding, '*My suffering, that is.*'

His discomfort made more sense now. Embarrassment about her feelings hadn't even occurred to Cahra last time. She wondered if it should have. Just what happened on the receiving end of this abreption? *I guess I'm going to find out.*

Cahra met his gaze, determination filling her. 'I'm ready.'

'*Cahraelia of Kolyath,*' Hael stated, gazing at her intently. '*Do you accept your birthright as Scion, and Empress of Hael'stromia?*'

She hadn't anticipated that. Cahra felt frozen for a minute, the familiar urge to run clawing at her chest, the instinct nurtured by a childhood spent living in fear and uncertainty. But that fear clashed with something else: the desire for knowledge. A week on the run and where had it gotten her? And this wasn't like running from Kolyath's guards as a child, tearing down alleyways and over rooftops. She didn't want to call it destiny, like Thelaema. But no matter how her instincts screamed at her to flee, Cahra found herself looking to Hael. If she could free him from Hael'stromia, for the first time, she'd have real choices in her life.

She'd have power, the power to forge her own path and figure out what everything meant on her terms. She would never be anyone's pawn again.

Not to mention she'd have Hael's magicks on her side. At Thelaema's, Cahra had wanted to shatter the windows in that glass ball of a room. Here with him, she could see the possibilities.

Cahra squared her shoulders. 'Okay. I mean, yes,' she said.

'*Very well.*' Hael moved to their space on the tiled ground and sat cross-legged again. Cahra followed and sat opposite, willing her leathers to heat her, her anxiety rising in short, shallow breaths. Still robeless, even the distraction of Hael's sculpted chest wasn't enough. She stared at the muted crack of light in the doors sealing his tomb, then shut her eyes tight.

'*Cahra.*' The soft, rasping sound of Hael's voice had her squinting one eye open. '*There is nothing to fear. You have done this before. All will be well.*' He took her hands then, lifting them gently so she and Hael were palm to palm, his satiny skin warm, soothing even. '*As before, close your eyes. Inhale. Slowly, deeply. Then exhale.*'

She sucked a breath in and relaxed, Hael's words hypnotic as they vibrated on the air. Then, pressure, in her hand. Was he squeezing it? No, she realised, it was that slicing pain, the pull of the abreption through her palm, though not anywhere near as agonising as last time.

She exhaled through her teeth, still not getting how this worked.

All of a sudden, Cahra's keen senses noticed something new. A heat, a tingling, in her left palm. If the sting in her right hand was pain, the pull in her left was – what, pleasure? She shivered, the sensation certainly reminiscent of the handful of times she'd—

Wait, from his suffering?! The thought hit her like a brick, and she could feel herself resisting the idea. But the more she did, the more it seemed to block the flow between them. She tried to breathe into it, to let it go, but...

Cahra couldn't help herself. She opened her eyes and looked into Hael's, his fiery, supernatural eyes that had ensnared Cahra since the first moment that she'd laid eyes on him. She watched as his dark flames undulated, like they were dancing beneath the moonless sky, her breaths mirroring their gentle ebb and flow.

And she *saw*.

A series of images, flashing as raw emotions flowed between them.

Hael – young, human Hael – training with a great-hammer, bare feet fast and fluid, in the sunlit throne room at the apex of Hael'stromia's pyramid. *Happy. Free.*

Then Hael, chained to his tomb's altar, writhing and screaming in excruciating pain as magicks from the blackness of the earth, the Netherworld, purged him of his life.

Cowed, caged. An abomination.

Cahra saw as Hael spilled his first blood as the realm's weapon, his powers blistering, as he was ordered to slay an Emperor's rival for a consort, knowing that it would destabilise one of the sister kingdoms.

She saw as Hael disintegrated into smoke to enter one foe via the air and explode him from the inside out, blood and gore spattering the Wilds as the enemy ran for his life.

She saw as Hael stared down an army marching outside the gates to Hael'stromia, then rained black fire upon the thousand-strong host, their death wails expiring on the wind.

She saw as Hael was forced to endure, to submit, time and time again, to the whims of petty, egocentric rulers of the realm, men who didn't care for their people or their lands, only for themselves and what they could gain. As it had been for 600 years before the fall.

This was the legacy of the Reliquus, Hael'stromia's 'ultimate weapon'.

And he *hated* it, she thought, shock gripping her as the realisation took hold.

The countless Scions Hael had witnessed rise and fall, bloom and wither, an endless succession of human overlords. It had almost broken him. Until the death of the last, the Emperor before Cahra, also hailing from Kolyath. All because Hael hadn't been there to protect the man. And then Hael'stromia had fallen.

That was when Hael had finally surrendered to the darkness, lying dormant as he waited for the prophecy. For her. With the anguished hope that somehow, this time, his next Master might be different.

She couldn't breathe. *I should've said no! Because this birthright—*

Then, abruptly, the onslaught ended, leaving Cahra with the same disconcerting sense of peace she'd felt the first time they had performed the abreption. She shook her head, trying to feel more present in her body, although her eyes were open, fixated as they were on Hael. The way he returned her gaze made it clear he felt the same sense of peace, which calmed her. He'd been through so much, she thought.

Too much.

Cahra leaned forward, grasping his hands as she looked into his fiery, boundless eyes. 'Hael, I will never, ever be like those men, I promise you.'

His mouth fell open in surprise. '*How—*'

'You were right. This time *will* be different, okay?' She didn't want to be a reminder of his pain, but he had to know her heart. If nothing else, they could both hold onto that truth. 'I swear it.' Cahra stared into his eyes, not breaking his black gaze.

'*I believe you.*' Hael's words were quiet, barely a push of air from his lips. '*I saw your suffering, last we met. You are different from the other Scions, Cahra.*' It took a moment, but he softened as they sat on his robe in his chamber, the temple's shrine, bound by the dust and demise of centuries past.

Cahra breathed out, relieved. 'Good.' Returning his smile, she squeezed his hands. 'We will find a way through all of this. Together.'

And I will find a way, she vowed, not letting go of Hael. A man, no matter what Wyldaern said about his otherworldliness.

I will find a way to free you. And not just from this tomb.

CHAPTER 30

Her eyes still closed, Cahra awoke to a strangeness in her own body. It wasn't the bed; every bed had felt different since Kolyath. This was something else. She could feel, smell, the fresh linen of the sheets, coarse against her calloused fingertips as she grazed the flax fibres interweaving to form the fabric.

Hael, she could *count* those threads.

And she knew things. Like that Thelaema had just hobbled down the hallway and into the glass ball of a room at the other end of the house. Cahra heard the Oracle's lopsided gait, the creaking groan of the wicker chair as she sat.

Wyldaern's approach, however, was lighter, although just as distinctive, the Seer's robe swishing against her sandals as she glided down the hall.

Cahra had *never* had hearing this good before, and hers was excellent. Was this all part of Hael's powers, the ones she'd received from their rite?

She sat up as Wyldaern turned the doorknob, its strangled squeak louder than it should have been. The Seer froze when she realised Cahra was awake.

'Oh!' Wyldaern said quickly, 'I didn't—'

'Wyldaern.' Cahra figured they may as well talk, while the abreption strained to hold and her emotions weren't all-consuming. She gestured for the woman to come in.

The Seer hesitated by the door, fiddling nervously, before stepping inside to shut it.

'Cahra,' she began, leaning heavily against the wood, 'I am sorry.'

'I know,' Cahra said quietly.

'Please, let me finish. If I had known the true scope of what Thelaema was to disclose, I would have revealed that which I did know. No one should be expected to bear what you learned today all at once.'

Her shoulders slumping, Wyldaern moved for the seat beside Cahra. 'I am so sorry for your loss, and what you had to endure.'

Cahra could feel a crack in the veneer of her abreption's perfect peace. 'You don't agree with your Oracle's methods?'

'I would have done things differently,' Wyldaern admitted.

Cahra said nothing. 'You can answer my questions now, can't you?' The Seer nodded. 'The vision that led you to me. It was because I'm the Scion, not just a Kolyath Princess?'

There was guilt in Wyldaern's eyes. 'So, the Reliquus revealed all to you. Good.' She fingered her Seer's pendant. 'Yes. Thelaema shared it, so that I may bring you here to learn your fate as the realm's Empress.'

Cahra's mood darkened at the word, but she let it be. That, she would address with the Oracle directly.

'And the 'tell none'? It was because of the white light?' Frowning, she murmured, 'Like the crack of light outside Hael's tomb.'

Again, Wyldaern nodded. 'If I had required any evidence that you were the Scion, that vision was it. We saw what lies beyond the void's eternal darkness. It was a confirmation.' The Seer fidgeted with the bell-like cuff of her sleeve. 'When I told you to "tell none", that was because you travelled with others and I knew not how Luminaux's royals – how Thierre – would react if he, they, knew your true role. I was trying to protect you.'

Cahra didn't doubt Wyldaern's words. But the trust between them…

'I thought we were friends,' she whispered. Another, bigger crack in her abreption. Piece by piece, her sense of contentment was slipping from her.

Wyldaern clutched Cahra's hand. 'We are,' the Seer said adamantly, looking pained. 'I did not want this, to upset you after you had already suffered so greatly, all in the name of some long-awaited, fateful obligation. Yet, it is as Thelaema said. I did not see all the facts. Had I told you one thing, and left out core facets that, with such context, would later have been perceived as untruth, would that have been more, or less, helpful to you?'

It was fair. But Cahra couldn't help feeling tired of the secrets, the omissions, after everything that had happened with Thierre.

Unlike Thierre, however, Wyldaern had warned her, told her there were things she couldn't say but that the Oracle would. That at least put the Seer above the Prince.

Was this her life now? Judging who was least false, instead of most trustworthy? She remembered what she thought after finding Thierre's gift.

If I choose myself, I'll never be betrayed.

'I need air,' she said, tossing off the bedcovers.

'Cahra.' Wyldaern's face was drawn, the Seer sitting wearily in her small armchair. 'Please do not go far. We are safe on these grounds, but...' Wyldaern's peridot eyes fell. 'Cahra, I truly am sorry.'

Something in Cahra softened. Then she turned and walked away.

–

Throwing the front door open, Cahra exhaled a lungful of air, breath misting, and stepped from the Oracle's mountain cabin into the midst of the chill starry night, late as it was. She remembered her vision. And thanks to Hael and their abreption, her pain and anger didn't overwhelm her. She didn't suffer. But she felt disappointed, in so many people she shouldn't. And while she still felt disconnected from it all emotionally, rational in a way she rarely was, and she saw what the Oracle had tried to do, and why... Cahra would never have subjected a child to her poverty-stricken upbringing in Kolyath.

Yet Thelaema had got what she wanted. Cahra was a survivor, the trait scribed into her very blood. She'd never be a courtly high-born; where others used artfulness for gain, her talents were brute force, resilience, weaponry. Now she had the most deadly weapon of all.

And his powers were coursing through her.

Cahra could feel everything Hael had spoken of – his stamina, speed, strength, agility. She'd moved from the cottage to the central garden in what felt like a few quick strides. Even senses like her sight, she thought, peering at the purple clusters of night blooms that bordered the Oracle's long garden. Under nothing but pure starlight, details leapt out at her: the snowy sprig that housed the flowers' pollen, dotted and ridged like a minuscule tree trunk. She could hear the squalls and wingbeats of owls she couldn't see and taste the icy winds of faraway rain on her tongue, which she couldn't begin to fathom, for there were no clouds in the late-night sky. Cahra spun in circles, delighting in the exquisite sensations.

Is this what it's like to be Hael?

She heard Thelaema's footsteps before the Oracle had reached her own front door, despite Cahra being half-way down the grounds. But she didn't turn. Instead, she sat on a bench overlooking the garden's pond, bright orange fish darting and swirling beneath a sky mirrored in their pristine waters. Cahra stared at the small ripples the fish made, their fins rocking and rowing to churn the glassy surface.

'Did you conclude the second omen's rite?' Thelaema was puffing. It wasn't exactly a short stroll to where she was.

Cahra turned to face the Oracle. 'You mean the one you didn't tell me about, forcing Hael to enlighten me instead, along with his other grand revelation?' Glaring at the woman, she felt another shard of anger seep back from someplace. 'Your *Empress* says yes.'

Thelaema was indifferent in the face of Cahra's scorn. 'I would have informed you, had he not. Your actions necessitated an interlude.'

'*My* actions?' Cahra stormed. 'You doomed me to a life of suffering!'

Thelaema's eyes were as cold as the night air. 'Ozumbre doomed your parents, not I. Your village was razed. You were not safe there.'

Cahra twitched, desperate to hold onto the abreption's simple ease, her self-control.

'And I was in Kolyath? Why not bring me here, to this spelled, magickal safe haven, where you've apparently dwelled for centuries?' she shot back.

'Because I am no proxy for that which you required: a hard education.'

'The hardest,' Cahra said, grinding her teeth. 'It's a good thing I didn't end up here, with you, if it meant becoming such a heartless crone.'

Thelaema's flinch at her words would have been imperceptible, if Cahra had been without Hael's preternatural sight.

'You will learn, Cahraelia of Kolyath, that difficult decisions care not for your emotions, only for the end's results,' the Oracle muttered.

'My name is *Cahra*.' She was on her feet now, squaring her shoulders as she hurled: 'And what are your emotions telling you about this particular result?' The abreption, and the peace she'd felt with Hael, was completely gone.

And something else was burning in its place…

'That the vision instructing my actions did not allude to a capricious adolescent!' Thelaema snapped back, then froze, staring at Cahra. Right into her eyes.

Cahra looked down, catching a glimpse of her reflection in the pond, waves of heat rippling in the air above her curled fingers.

Her eyes were *glowing*.

She gasped, hands flying to her face. 'What's happening?'

'It is the omen's rite,' Thelaema warned her. 'Your tether with the Reliquus runs taut. You will reap the powers that he has granted you, which shall fade before your next vision. That is, until you free the weapon in Hael'stromia.'

'And when Hael's out?' Cahra said, still staring at the water.

'The restraint on his dark magicks shall cease and he and the capital will be restored. Once that happens, you shall have no need for such augments of your own. You will be under the protection of the Reliquus, as well as Hael'stromia proper.'

She turned from Thelaema to the stars. The moon was new and absent from the sky, but Cahra could just make out its position, the darkness where it would have shone silver. She shook her head in irritated silence.

'A vision is why you sent me to Kolyath?'

Thelaema sighed, lowering herself to the metalwork bench next to Cahra. 'Why else? I am not so cruel, despite what you may think of me.' The woman's next words were sombre. 'I considered bringing you here. Yet, when the Seer who saved you brought you to my care... I saw what must be done.' Her voice dropped to a whisper, words heavy with emotion.

Cahra stared at her. 'You never thought to just *not* do what your vision told you?'

Thelaema's pastel eyes flashed. 'As a High Oracle of the Order of Descry? No.'

Cahra rubbed her face with the heels of her palms, knowing she couldn't reason with the woman. But before they could argue some more, Thelaema spoke, not looking at her.

'I cannot take back my actions, nor would I. However...' Something like remorse contorted the Oracle's wizened face. 'I can apologise for their results. For your pain.'

It was all Cahra had ever wanted to hear, an acknowledgement of her suffering. Now she had it from the person who'd changed her trajectory, however, it didn't feel enough. But after living with Lumsden, Cahra knew it was the best she'd ever get from someone of Thelaema's years and prickly disposition.

Cahra blew out a breath and asked her, 'What happens now?'

The Oracle was a conduit to magicks Cahra would never understand. But the woman also knew what came next, for the third omen and beyond.

Thelaema huffed a rueful laugh, no doubt marking Cahra's failure to absolve her. 'Now, it is time for your various questions.' The Oracle craned her neck, eyeing the heavens. 'You are here now, Cahra of Kolyath. I can tell you everything.'

So Thelaema did.

She told of how Hael'stromia's Order of Descry was exiled 399 years ago, when the Oracles failed to foresee the Emperor's assassination, then broke their neutrality by coming to the aid of his Kolyath royal family – all while Hael was trapped inside the falling capital. According to Thelaema, Emperor Brulian of Kolyath was slain by an Ozumbre assassin, his Queen Inana bundling their baby, Cahra's ancestor, and rushing from Kolyath into the Wilds, aided by a court Seer. By the time Thelaema found them, she and her High Oracle counterparts had predicted the loss then resurrection of the capital in present times. She knew that without Hael, Ozumbre would not stop, so Inana was ordered into hiding. Never to return.

Cahra's sharp intake of breath at Thelaema's story caught half-way to her chest. *Maybe it was why Thelaema hesitated with me as a baby.* Her throat tightened. Ozumbre had outmatched the Seers before, and it had cost the realm its Emperor.

With its bloodline presumed dead, Kolyath could not forgive the Seers for their kingdom's calamitous loss, and banished them, Ozumbre supporting the stance on nature worship and magicks before their involvement in the assassination was known. So the Seers were cast out, scattered to the Wilds like Inana and her child, doomed to roam a realm that didn't want them. Until it would deem them and their prophecy useful once again.

In the interim, Kolyath's nobles appointed a custodian, a line of Stewards growing in lieu of any royals. Unfortunately, with this act, a new wave of cruelty swept the kingdom, culminating in Steward Atriposte.

Thelaema sat, her back rigid as she hunched, hand gripping the bench's iron armrest. 'I was near Kolyath when Brulian was killed.' She exhaled, the sigh of a woman who'd borne the brunt of 400 years of blame and internalised it. 'To this day, I do not know why the Nether failed me, failed our Order, or why Hael could not escape.' She looked up, away. 'Why he did not come.'

Cahra was silent. After what she'd seen in their abreption, she knew Hael. He'd move not just mountains, but entire oceans, to protect any Scion in his charge.

Something had gone horribly, horribly wrong.

'Brulian and Inana,' Thelaema said, 'were honourable rulers. Kolyath has not seen their like in an age. Yet Brulian's undoing was failing to recognise and confront his rivals, and not deploying the Reliquus when he and Inana frequented Kolyath.' Thelaema sagged. 'And without Hael, they were not strong enough to defend the kingdom against Ozumbre's forces. Brulian and his kingdom, your kingdom, paid for that ruinous mistake.'

She gazed as if through Cahra then, through her skin and bones and on to something else inside her, the way Lumsden used to. For the first time, Cahra felt somewhere within her crack an eye open and stare straight back.

'Your task will not be easy. There is much to overcome, and not just from the current warmongering rulers and their sundry forces. Even once Hael'stromia has arisen, you will still face adversity, hard choices that will challenge you on a personal level.' The woman paused, looking at Cahra. 'You and Hael—'

Thelaema frowned, and something ratcheted up inside Cahra in palpable warning, moments before every candle in the Oracle's house flared an alarming shade of crimson, the red haze sweeping like a forest fire through the chalet.

As Thelaema said, 'Someone is here.'

'What in Hael?' Cahra grabbed Thelaema's arm as the Oracle whirled, Piet, Siarl and Queran charging from the house, Wyldaern at their heels.

'The danger is not here,' Thelaema told Cahra. 'It is...' Her face went blank as the Oracle's second sight withdrew between the veil and void. 'It is the caves,' she whispered, eyes on Wyldaern before nodding to Thierre's guards. 'Their Captain Raiden followed us. He and his accompanying Royal Guards were ambushed.' Thelaema cursed under her breath.

'What?' Cahra repeated, the muscles in her body tense, every instinct primed to fight.

The Oracle's pale gaze flashed to hers. 'All tri-kingdoms are present.'

Cahra closed her eyes. *Thierre?*

'The Prince is not with the Captain,' Thelaema said quietly, reading her thoughts as the others arrived.

'Good.' Cahra updated Raiden's trio as Thelaema made for the house, Wyldaern by her side, the Seers speaking frantically.

'We must aid the Captain,' Piet argued. The stern look on Siarl's face said she agreed, while Queran withdrew two arrows from his quiver. 'We cannot leave him at the mercy of Kolyath and Ozumbre's armed forces.'

'I wouldn't expect you to.' Cahra watched Thelaema from outside the glass sphere of the Oracle's round room, a speck of motion in the distance. What was she doing?

'Then we must go,' Piet insisted, broad shoulders turning with purpose.

'Piet, wait,' Cahra said, as the group looked to leave. 'Wait for Thelaema to get back. If Raiden's been ambushed, we need to know how, and how many there are, as well as where in the caves Raiden and his guards are fighting.'

'She's right,' Siarl said. 'The tunnels were pitch black. An ambush would be easy, not to mention traps. We need to avoid whatever waylaid the Captain.' Her dark brows furrowed.

'Agreed,' Queran told them. 'But therein lies the problem. If we move with a torch, they'll sight us from a league away. Unless they're in the midst of combat, which might help.'

Cahra looked up at the invisible moon again, still able to mark its location in the sky. 'I may have a solution for that,' she said, as Thelaema and Wyldaern rejoined them.

'Where is the Captain?' Piet immediately asked the Oracle.

'Too far from the entrance to flee, too close for us to feel overtly comfortable.' Thelaema glanced to Wyldaern. 'I cannot be discovered.'

'I will not let that happen,' Wyldaern vowed, mouth set in a firm line.

Siarl interjected. 'The sooner we reach the Captain, the less you have to worry. How many enemies? How did they ambush him? Do traps await?'

'They breached a collapsed tunnel.' Thelaema leaned heavily against her apprentice. 'Your Captain's men are outnumbered three to one.'

'Traps?' Queran pressed, red eyebrows taut. The Oracle shook her head, looking as if she was standing by sheer force of stubbornness alone.

'We shall lead them from here,' Piet told the Seers. He looked to Cahra.

She felt fastened to the ground. *I thought I'd have more time—*

'I know,' Thelaema murmured to her.

'Go,' Cahra told Piet. 'I won't be long.' She couldn't stymie her nerves as she waved Thierre's detail away. Piet nodded, the group leaving to descend on the caves.

When they'd gone, she turned to Thelaema. 'You know what I'm going to ask you.'

'Yes,' the Oracle said quietly. Wyldaern retreated, giving them privacy.

Cahra couldn't breathe as she strained to speak the words:

'How… how did they die?'

Thelaema didn't answer right away.

'Your mother and father knew the risks; their responsibility, once you were born and named Kolyath's heir. By then, your kin had been in hiding for centuries.' The Oracle paused to clear her throat. 'And yet there were always threats, tragedies. Death. No matter where Brulian and Inana's descendants went, it was as though someone, somewhere, always knew. Your family became nomads, ever on the move to stay beyond the reach of their enemies.'

Thelaema's eyes fell, the slightest tremor in her voice as she carried on.

'With the union of your parents, however, and after so long without incident, they decided that it was time to settle with those they trusted – to establish a real life, with you.' The woman wavered. 'But Ozumbre found you, and struck one final time.'

In that moment, standing in the dark of night, the thought pierced her like an arrow: Cahra didn't want to know. She didn't want to touch, didn't want to mar, any inkling she'd ever had about her parents. The fantasy, that maybe they'd been happy.

That maybe things hadn't ended with their blood.

But there was no time to turn back now. Hands trembling at her sides, Cahra asked, 'What happened?'

Thelaema exhaled, a single, long, unbroken breath, her small frame shrinking as she prepared herself. Her voice grew quiet as a grave.

'It was day. You were sleeping within the house, tucked away in a corner. Whenever I scried with my crystal ball to see you, I was perpetually confounded by the volume of noise that you could sleep through,' she said, her wooden chuckle huffing into a near-sob. 'Your village was nestled, hidden in a glen deep in the Wilds… Your parents were outside. Then, a band of Ozumbre cutthroats came.' Thelaema swallowed, her eyes wet. 'You were the sole survivor.'

Cahra was frozen, her blood like mortar setting, hardening into stone beneath her skin.

They died, they all died, while I… slept?

But she'd never slept well in her life. Not once, she thought, as the numbness rose, pins needling her, from her distant soles to the tips of her fingers. She was standing, but it felt like her limbs were slipping farther from her every second. Her entire body started shaking. It wouldn't stop.

Thelaema's eyes drifted over Cahra, voice soft yet firm as the woman murmured, trying to anchor her back, 'Cahra, you must hear me. Your mother and father adored you, and you are so like them, you know: your mother was an artist, and she loved to paint and draw. And your father,' she said, a grief to match Cahra's in her eyes, 'he was the village carpenter, making furniture for your mother to paint. Hammering, the warmth of working with wood and crafting artworks with his hands, filled him with such joy. Something you have in common.'

Tears spilled down Cahra's cheeks at the mention of her father wielding a hammer.

Just like her.

'They knew, from the moment they held you in their arms, what their duty was. They would lay down their lives a thousand times over, to see you safe, happy and secure. In the end, that was precisely what they did.'

Cahra's voice cracked. 'But why?'

Thelaema struggled to her feet, facing Cahra, then gently took her hand.

'Because they loved you.'

At those words, something inside her broke beyond repair. Silent tears giving way to heaving wails, she crumpled to the ground, her legs buckling under the weight of her grief and emotions that rampaged like the sea; a storm inside her veins, each wave pulling her under. Salt water – her tears were the salt of Kolyath's coastline, her mother and father's legacy, Brulian and Inana's, their kingdom's. A sea people, stripped of everything, the ocean lost to them after Hael'stromia's fall, when the walls outside each kingdom went up forever. Cahra's body shook, feverish, as she sobbed, her pain too consuming to escape.

She wanted to cry, to stay bawling, writhing, screaming, on the grass forever. To mourn the family she had never known, all because of one kingdom's greed and hatred. But she couldn't. Raiden – Piet, Siarl, Queran – they needed her, and they needed her now. For the sake of her companions, those still alive, she needed to get up. To help them.

She was *not* going to let another band of cutthroats from Ozumbre, or Kolyath, win.

Cahra grasped two fistfuls of grass and heaved unsteadily to her feet, Hael's reflexes already kicking in to keep her upright. Stable. Too bad she felt nothing of the sort.

Seeing her rise to her feet, Thelaema and Wyldaern neared.

'Cahra,' the Oracle broached, tone shifting into urgency. 'There is something else.' Her jaw was tight. 'When Hael'stromia fell and the Oracles' magicks ceased to flow freely, we Seers could no longer rely on our single, unified prescience. I was no longer All-seeing; the Netherworld still powers my visions, my divination, but I do not know all as I once did.' Uncertainly, she continued, 'I have wondered, since the day you and I met, whether one of my fellows survived exile, survived the centuries, as I have. I have wondered whether someone has been watching, waiting and knowing where to strike so that your kingdom's bloodline remained dormant. What if,' Thelaema said, raising her eyes to Cahra's, 'whoever was watching has found you?'

Wiping her eyes, Cahra's mouth fell open. 'What? But who?'

Thelaema put a hand on her arm, eyes shining. 'You must go. Please understand, we needed you to be strong enough to face what lies ahead.'

'And what is that?'

Thelaema, who'd procured something in the shadows, handed it to her. 'Bloodshed,' the Oracle told her, as Cahra gazed in perfect astonishment at the great-hammer in her hands. It was sublime, even in the black of night, the handle hewed from ebony, with glittering gems of black diamond, ruby, sapphire and grey musgravite, depicting the capital and its kingdoms. Peering at the great-hammer, Cahra had the gnawing suspicion it was forged using the metal of Hael'stromia's black gates. *Haellium.*

'All hail the kingdom of Kolyath's kin of the hammer, heir to the royal bloodline, Princess Cahraelia. A Princess, now an Empress.' Thelaema and Wyldaern bowed in unison.

Cahra watched as the magickal haze of Thelaema's mountain cabin deepened to a red as dark as blood, knowing her time was up.

'Thank you,' she told them, turning for the caves. Then paused, whispering finally, 'My parents. My village. What were their names?'

'Palben and Kyreen,' Thelaema said softly. 'Of the village of Kolbyrg.'

My mother's name was Kyreen. The agony of that knowledge seared into her, until Cahra's body felt alight with flame. Looking down, the water reflected her glowing eyes. Slowly, she raised her head to the Seers.

And heard Thelaema speaking into her mind: *Fear not. You have Hael's powers now.* Her last words echoed as Cahra sprinted for the caves.

Put them to good use.

CHAPTER 31

This time, striding into the caves, Cahra went first. Piet, Siarl and Queran tried not to gawk as the amber glow of Cahra's eyes faded to the dimness of a faraway star.

'What happened to you?' The question popped from Queran's mouth, seemingly before the archer could stop it.

Cahra tossed over her shoulder, 'Depends, how much do you know?' She could feel Piet eyeballing the hammer Thelaema had gifted her.

'You're Kolyath's heir,' Piet murmured. 'Kin of the hammer.'

Siarl admitted, 'And, well, the rest.' She bowed, adding, 'Empress.'

Cahra nodded, unsure if they could see the gesture in the dark. She cleared her throat.

'A few things have changed,' she said, Queran chuckling behind her. She supposed her eyes *were* glowing. Luminaux's fighters followed as Cahra set a brisk pace.

Queran asked, 'So, you're our torch now?'

Cahra almost laughed herself. 'Apparently,' she said, as they stole furtively through the extensive tunnels. 'And our guide. It turns out I can see in the dark.'

One of the unexpected perks of being bound to Hael'stromia's weapon.

She could see every nook and chink in the striated walls of the cave system, the limestone of its floor smooth as marble, barring the occasional chunks of rock.

But she couldn't think about what gems she might find in these ancient caves. Her focus was finding Raiden and his guards. Alive, she prayed.

They'd been plunging through the darkness for what felt like over an hour when Cahra's ears twigged to something up ahead.

'We're close,' she whispered.

Queran raised his bow, arrow nocked. 'You can hear them?'

Cahra nodded, guessing he couldn't. 'It's muffled. Wait, that was metal. Weapons. They're fighting.' She exhaled. 'That's a good sign, right? Fighting, not silence?'

Piet's voice intoned from behind, 'Let us hope so.' Dual flashes of silver told Cahra that Siarl and her daggers were ready.

They charged.

Within a minute, Cahra, Piet, Siarl and Queran were upon the scene of the battle.

Before the second omen's rite, it would have been impossible for Cahra to make out much. Hastily tossed torches cast flickers across the grappling soldiers, the glints and clangs of swords disorienting in the dark, echoing caves. But now with Hael's enhanced senses…

Cahra watched as Piet struck first, swinging his hammer into a Kolyath soldier's ribs with a devastating crack, the enemy flying sideways into the wall. Siarl hurled one of her throwing daggers past Piet and into the eye of a soldier ahead, swooping to thrust then yank the bloody knife from the man's skull before springing into action, every inch the warrior silently doling out death. Between them, Piet and Siarl cleared a path forward as Queran's arrowheads sailed to impale his targets one by one, Kolyath and Ozumbre's forces falling to the Prince of Luminaux's elite Royal Guards.

Cahra spotted Raiden at the same time as Piet, who started battling his way towards his Captain, the sound of metal meeting metal everywhere around them as weapons clashed. Eyes darting between the fighting men, Cahra turned the great-hammer in her hands, until her gaze chanced upon a uniform she didn't recognise.

But she knew that pin.

Ozumbre.

Something snapped inside her at the thought, into place or out of it, she couldn't tell. The forces of Ozumbre, standing right before her…

She'd fantasised about destroying Atriposte's stranglehold over Kolyath for years. But Ozumbre was the kingdom that had caused it all.

They murdered my parents. My village. THEY'RE the ones who did this.

Everything she'd suffered – not just this night, but every miserable day of her life – every wrong, every hurt she'd limped through. It was

Ozumbre's fault. Now, here they were. Cahra glanced down to see the great-hammer glinting in her hands.

Justice was finally within her grasp.

She didn't have time to dwell on the emotions that drowned her in that moment: pain, the blistering rage that overrode her fear. She raised her hammer, eyes narrowed, snarling as she remembered Thelaema's words.

That she'd been raised to be strong. And that she had Hael's powers.

Put them to good use.

'Enough,' Cahra uttered in a voice so harsh, so unfamiliar, that she didn't recognise it. It should have scared her. But tearing forward, she grabbed the plate shoulder of an Ozumbre soldier and yanked him back so hard he crashed into one of his comrades. Before he could right himself, her hammer found its mark, colliding with the soldier's breastplate to buckle the armour completely. The man's comrade bellowed and, seized by a giddy surge of raw, wild power, Cahra didn't hesitate as she blocked the man's sword with her hammer's head before heaving the blade back at him to gore his own neck. Arcing her weapon in an overhead strike, she sealed the soldier's fate, dust shuddering from the cave ceiling on impact.

A single word rose like a bubble from her darkest depths.

Destroy.

Cahra didn't stop.

There was no time to wipe the carnage from her weapon as someone else attacked. Even in the din and dark, she could sense the enemies at her back and she dived then rolled as the cut of a blade missed her by a thread. Laughing, Cahra spun, swinging her hammer to hook the swordsman's ankle and send him sprawling to his back. She vaulted atop the soldier, and seeing he was from Ozumbre, dropped her hammer and began pummelling the man into the ground with her blacksmith's fists, bearing down again and again, the sickening crunch of his nose just one of countless blows to succumb to her unforgiving pain and rage.

Destroy!

Her body thrummed with exhilaration, the Nether-magicks writhing.

Cahra didn't stop.

For the first time in her life, she felt *powerful*, darkness shooting to spiderweb across her body, through her veins, electrifying her being.

Like Thelaema's cabin, her vision was a haze of red and she was vaguely aware of her eyes glowing, her fists still smashing into the soldier's skull with a primal energy. By the time the crack of bones had turned to squelches, dust kicking up at the brute impact, Cahra was a breathless mess.

As was the blood-soaked body pinned beneath her.

'Cahra!' Wyldaern shouted.

With effort, Cahra glanced up at the Seer's voice, and it was then that she realised the fighting had died around her. Their support had turned the battle. She stared back down at the Ozumbre soldier, slack and unrecognisable; a black, barbarous fire burning somewhere deep beneath her surface, a place she hadn't even known existed. Until now.

'Please,' Wyldaern begged her, nearing step by cautious step. 'This is not you, Cahra. It is the Reliquus' powers. They are consuming you.' The Seer attempted to reason with her, but there was a waver in Wyldaern's gentle voice.

How would you know? After all that I have endured, everything that I have learned? How would you know anything about me, anything at all?!

Throwing her hands over her ears, Cahra recoiled at the voice screeching in her head. But it was right, she thought, shaking. Wyldaern didn't truly know what she was capable of, that she had come so close to killing Atriposte that night, in the dungeons all those years ago. And that she'd only been a child.

A child acting out of self-defence, she argued numbly.

The voice roared, *This time, you have a choice. Take your vengeance!*

Eyes shut, she furiously shook her head. *Vengeance IS a choice! This was all a choice!*

'No, no, no!' she cried out, voice louder every time, ricocheting roughly through the caves. All she'd needed was to knock the soldier out. Instead, she'd beaten the man to a bloody pulp, with such deadly, terrifying ease. Was he even breathing? The blood on her hands…

By the Seers. Nausea roiled from Cahra's stomach to crest in the back of her throat and she dry-retched as her thoughts spiralled, off their axis and into the noxious realisation that Hael's magicks had caused this violence. *Her* violence.

'Cahra?' Wyldaern called softly, faltering as her name hung in the air.

She hurled herself backwards, scrambling off the Ozumbre soldier, breaths ragged, as she thought frantically: *What is happening to me?!*

It all took place in an instant.

Locking eyes with Wyldaern, pleading for help, Cahra was panic-stricken as the soldier at her feet wrenched a dagger from his belt to stab her. Yet she could feel it happening, even though she was staring at Wyldaern; could sense it as if watching the two events unfold in concert. Cahra saw Wyldaern's lips tear open as the Seer made to scream her name. But before she could make a sound, Cahra had hefted one foot, booted the knife from the soldier, then lifted her other boot – leaping into a kick—

'*Cahra, NO!*' Thelaema's voice thundered, the caves trembling.

And though Cahra shouldn't have been able to, her instincts were responsive enough that she halted in mid-air, landing effortlessly, two boots in perfect silence.

The silence of death.

Because Thelaema had sent the soldier flying with a *look*. And the result was as though Cahra had kicked the man after all – kicked him with the full force of her strength and Hael's unholy powers. Thelaema's magick had obliterated the man's chest. And blown a gaping hole in the dripstone wall of the caves.

Cahra may have nearly killed the man, but she'd been possessed by Hael's magicks – the Nether's bloodlust. But the Oracle…

Cahra swallowed.

Thelaema cut that man down like it was nothing.

Her eyes floated to Wyldaern's as the weight of Thelaema's actions struck them both. The young women stared at one another, dust flaking from the ceiling like fresh snow.

Paralysed by her horror, sinking further into herself with each breath, Cahra stood – until finally Raiden rushed to her, glanced past, looking for someone, then went rigid.

'Cahra,' Raiden managed to choke out, shaking her. '*Where is Thierre?*'

CHAPTER 32

Cahra's heart was attempting to leap from her chest in the eerily torchlit tunnels. Catching Raiden's wild grey eyes, she stumbled over her words.

'Thierre's not with you?'

Raiden shook his head before admitting, 'He wanted to go with you, to the Oracle. Stupidly, I agreed. But Commander Tyne discovered us and we got separated. I assumed he'd made it to you and the others, but...' Raiden looked up as Piet, Siarl and Queran approached, all reflecting the look on their Captain's face.

Panic. The Prince of Luminaux was missing.

Cahra dared a glance at Wyldaern, the Seer still staring blankly at the soldier, the one Thelaema had slain.

All because Cahra had lost control of Hael's powers, and nearly killed someone.

Turning from Wyldaern, Cahra tried to swallow the quaver in her voice as she asked, 'So what do we do?'

'Return to the palace,' Raiden said. 'Notify the King and Commander.'

A shuffling sounded, Thelaema coming slowly into view.

'High Oracle,' Wyldaern cautioned, 'some of these soldiers are merely unconscious. It is not safe—'

'Bah,' Thelaema said, dismissing her concern. 'I have seen it.'

Was that all she saw? The Oracle had told her apprentice she couldn't be discovered. So why did she intervene? *Did Thelaema see me, bludgeoning that soldier—*

Raiden, realising whose presence he now graced, spun to the Oracle. 'And Prince Thierre? Please, where is he, High Oracle? Is he close?'

Thelaema's amethyst orbs flickered to Cahra. 'The Prince, I cannot see.'

Her warning echoed. *What if whoever was watching has found you?*

Cahra stood, still feeling Hael's magick in her body, and thought.

'What if...' Setting her jaw, Cahra said, 'What if I left for Hael'stromia, right now? The last omen is for me to go free Hael. If I could, we'd have the weapon to find Thierre.' She glanced at the Oracle.

Of all the people she'd thought would object, she hadn't expected Raiden to be first. 'While I appreciate your offer, it's too dangerous. We don't know where he is and, besides, the sheer number of Kolyath and Ozumbre military camps between here and the capital – it would be a death trap. Our best course is to return to Luminaux.'

'But I have the weapon's powers now,' Cahra argued, her voice rising in frustration. 'It'll take a day to get back to Luminaux. In a day, I could make it inside the capital and—'

'I concur with the Captain.' Thelaema interrupted. 'Despite the powers you possess, you are assuming too much, Cahra. A mindful response is required, not a rash one.'

Cahra's anger flared. 'What if it's too late by then?'

Raiden's iron eyes hardened at Cahra's words. 'We all want to find Thierre, but we can't risk everything just because you say so.'

Cahra clenched her fists, the power of Hael's dark magick surging through her veins. She spun to Thelaema. 'Isn't that the point of being an Empress?'

Raiden exclaimed, 'I'm sorry, *what*?'

'Meet Your Imperial Majesty,' Thelaema said with an exasperated sigh.

'I'll explain later,' Cahra told Raiden, then stepped towards the Oracle. 'It's not just a hunch, this is our *chance*—'

'And if you fail? Then what happens to Thierre?' Raiden demanded.

Cahra was about to retaliate when she felt a firm hand on her shoulder, silencing her.

'I understand your fear, both of you,' Thelaema said calmly. 'But the Captain is right. We must pause and think strategically. Your temporary magicks, potent as they are, do not grant the certainty of victory.'

But you *could*, Cahra thought to the woman. *You're an Oracle, surely you could see—*

Thelaema locked eyes with Cahra. 'I am telling you. It would be folly.' She held Cahra's gaze long enough for her to understand. Hael's powers wouldn't be sufficient.

Cahra's mind still whirred. *Did I expend too much of them in the fight?*

Tension lingered, heavy in the air.

Cahra shook her head. 'Strategy or not, every second we delay is one Thierre may not have. If he's missing, we need to assume it's bad.'

Raiden, his face still simmering with anger, seemed to listen. Finally, he spoke again. 'We can discuss this further at the palace. We need to gather as much information as we can before making any big decisions.'

His words weren't a comfort, but she swallowed her protests. For now.

Piet clasped Raiden's arm, 'Sir, time is against us, and these caves have been compromised. Getting behind Luminaux's walls is wise, especially if we have no leads on the Prince.' One of the enemy soldiers began to moan.

'Oh, we'll have one,' Raiden gritted out, signalling to Siarl, who nodded and left, twirling one of her long daggers. *Interrogation time.* Raiden turned to Cahra and the Seers. 'Get to Luminaux,' he told them. 'Our squads will ride with you. Siarl and I will follow.'

Wyldaern's brow furrowed. 'You were ambushed,' she warned him. 'Is it safe?'

'For you?' Raiden glanced at the wounded soldiers littering the ground. 'It seems so,' he said, gesturing to Cahra and the Oracle.

Wyldaern nodded, looking to Cahra, who saw it again: the doubt. Her and Thelaema's actions had disturbed Wyldaern. 'There is much that you have missed, Captain.'

'Indeed,' Raiden said. 'Catch me up when we next meet.'

Cahra turned from him and Wyldaern, resisting the pain of her friend's fright, towards Thelaema. 'What do you need from the house?'

'I have all that I need,' was the Oracle's reply as she handed Cahra a black pouch. The Key.

Taking it, Cahra exhaled and lifted her great-hammer. 'Then we go.'

–

The palomino mare snuffled, tossing its head as it finally eased into a wearied walk. They'd ridden hard through the cold night, cutting the time it had taken to reach Thelaema's mountain home by half, and were now on Luminaux's lands again. Thelaema sat behind her, gripping Cahra's waist lightly, Wyldaern riding with Piet. Following them, she tried not to stare at her Seer friend. Or look too hard at her own bloodied knuckles.

Had Wyldaern's mentor done this before, bypassing incapacitation for outright death? Cahra repressed a shudder, afraid to think on it further with Thelaema at her back.

So far, the Oracle had been determined not to speak of what happened, or why she'd deterred Cahra from going to Hael'stromia.

'How can you not find Thierre?' Cahra muttered to her. 'You're supposed to be the Oracle, All-seeing and all that.'

Thelaema's tone was curt. 'I told you. After the capital's fall, that privilege was lost. However…' She paused, deliberating. 'I have a theory.'

Cahra noted the bedded posies emerging by the roadside. The kingdom was close by. 'Tell me.'

'There have been times such as this, when my foresight has failed me. If another powerful Seer survived, as I did, what if they are the reason? What if, as the Seers were once unified in our sight, our physical separation from the capital's magicks now blocks us from one another?'

Cahra frowned, hands on the reins. 'Is that how it works?'

She felt Thelaema shrug. 'It is likely. Who knows?'

Cahra snorted. 'I would've thought you.'

Thelaema tensed behind her. 'I did not create the All-seeing: it is born of the Nether. My role is simply to interpret it.'

Meanwhile, Cahra's mind was whirring. 'So you think a Seer is blocking you and your visions of Thierre. On purpose?' Thelaema was silent. 'Think back,' Cahra pressed her, 'to the times your powers failed. What is the link?' Minutes passed as Thelaema brooded.

Cahra did too, saying aloud, 'It doesn't work like this with you and Wyldaern, does it? I mean, you're not blocked from her, right?'

'No,' Thelaema said slowly, 'I am not.'

'Then maybe we're asking the wrong questions. Maybe it's not the "what" of this.'

Who has the power to rival an Oracle's?

The realisation hit Cahra hard. She was no stranger to others' cruel self-interest. But had the woman ever considered her and Cahra's worlds colliding: a Hael'stromian Oracle, gone rogue? After all, what other being might survive Thelaema?

The woman's voice was the rolling promise of thunder on the horizon as she marked Cahra's words. 'Not what,' Thelaema repeated darkly. 'But *who*.'

PART THREE

'When the mark walks the path to enter the Nether in life'

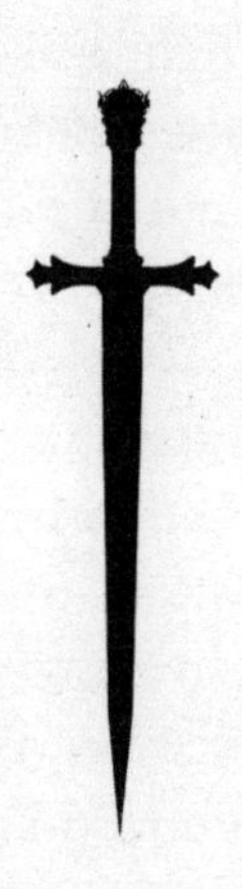

CHAPTER 33

In Luminaux, Cahra watched the King and Queen rush out the palace doors onto its steps, looking like they'd been roused from fitful sleep. Day was breaking, pale light leaking from the eastern skies, the kingdom's mountain peaks curled defensively around the castle city. Cahra and the others hadn't rested either, her exhaustion weighing heavy as a high-born quilt as she dismounted, offering an arm to Thelaema.

But before she'd taken two steps, a shrill voice rang out across the courtyard. Delicia, skirts bunched in her hands, dashed to them.

'Where is Raiden? What news of Thierre?' Then Delicia spied Cahra, her lemon-jade eyes narrowing. '*You!*' the woman cried, thrusting a decorated fingernail at her. Cahra stood, taken aback by the woman's distress. 'Where is Thierre? I know that you know something! What is between you and my fiancé, you bucolic little—'

Wyldaern opened her mouth, Delicia shushing her with a manic hiss.

'*Lady Delicia.*' Thelaema stepped between the women, the warning unmistakable. 'You will not utter another syllable to the Scion, or by the All-seeing, I shall have you thrown in a dungeon cell for the next twenty-four hours. Do you heed me?'

Delicia spluttered incoherently. 'And who, by the Oracles, are you?'

'I *am* the Oracle, girl,' Thelaema said, amethyst eyes positively blazing. Then she tromped off towards the King and Queen.

Wyldaern just smiled at Delicia and withdrew.

But Cahra saw in the noblewoman what she saw inside herself. The feeling she was numbing in order to keep moving forwards. *Fear.*

So she said nothing, holding the woman's hateful gaze, before trailing Thelaema inside Luminaux's palace.

Back in the den of war, Cahra's name for the room was apt. Thelaema announced herself and recounted their story, evidently no stranger to royals. At first, Luminaux's King, Queen, General and Commander were stunned. But as news of Thierre's predicament sank in, King Royce's leash on his fury and fear for his only son slipped its restraints. Then Raiden and Siarl returned from their interrogation in the caves, the warrior woman's face smeared with blood. Somehow, Cahra didn't think it was her own.

'What in Hael happened?' King Royce bellowed at the Captain.

He winced before replying, 'I aided Thierre in disobeying your decree.'

'And who are you, to harbour such designs?' The King snarled, spittle flying, the blame for Thierre's plight all over his face. As it had been on Delicia's.

Cahra felt like screaming, not at the King or Raiden, or even at Delicia, but at herself. If only she'd stayed here, Thierre would be safe. She leapt to her feet, desperate to move.

'Compose yourself,' Thelaema counselled King Royce as she nursed her teacup, but Cahra suspected the sentiment was for her as the Oracle flung a charged glance her way.

Queen Avenais placed her hand upon the King's. 'There is no fault here, dearest. Thierre is wilful and has been since he was a boy.'

'Oh, there is *fault*,' the King seethed, navy eyes like churning tides as he locked them squarely on Raiden. 'You are my son's protector, not his friend. You are his protector, and you have failed him in your duty. Just as you have failed your King.'

Raiden flinched like he'd been slapped, eyes dropping to the floor.

Cahra started, 'Now, wait just a second—'

But King Royce flashed her a look that would have silenced a noble twice her size. 'Enough.'

She ceased her pacing at the room's rear, looking down at King Royce at the head of his fancy wartime table, questioning, 'You'd silence me?'

To her shock, he swallowed then shook his head. The acknowledgment was slight, but it was there.

Cahra had just rebuked a King of the sister kingdoms. To his *face*.

She sat, trying to stop her body shaking, and went on. 'Something obviously happened to Thierre either before – in which case, you've got a problem – or after he passed through the gatehouse at the entrance to the kingdom.' Cahra turned to Tyne. 'So which is it?'

The Commander's lip curled. 'After. One of the guards on rotation knew that Thierre was approved to enter and exit the gate, so the Prince used the man to slip through.'

Cahra nodded at Raiden and Siarl. 'What did you learn in the caves?'

But Raiden seemed not to have heard her, his crestfallen eyes trained on the floor.

Siarl responded in lieu of her Captain. 'That Kolyath and Ozumbre have our Prince.' Her deep brown eyes creased, pained by the words.

Thierre's parents stiffened, their worst fears confirmed. Queen Avenais gripped her husband's hand, her lashes dampening with tears.

But Raiden lifted his head to Tyne. 'It's worse.'

King Royce looked positively murderous. 'How could it possibly be worse?'

'The longsword is gone. I believe Thierre took it.'

By the Seers…

Cahra knew what anyone with knowledge of the prophecy would think upon seeing that sword. She closed her eyes, remembering Jarett's ugly threats to Lumsden:

'If you do not hand over that brat, I will make short work of you… Who was this weapon commissioned for?!'

And the fear in the little master blacksmith, not for himself, but for her. Cahra's stomach twisted, like it was caught in a clamp back in the smithy.

Then something else occurred to her. Raiden was right, it was so much worse.

'Raiden,' Cahra said, 'Thierre has been to Ozumbre before, hasn't he?'

'Yes,' Raiden conceded. 'He has.'

'And did he use the same identity as in Kolyath?'

Raiden breathed his next word. 'No.'

Commander Tyne caught on. 'So,' the man began through gritted teeth, 'if Thierre's in joint custody of our enemies with the sword, at best they'll think he's the omen-bringer. And at worst…' He rubbed his furrowed face with both hands. 'He's a tri-kingdom spy.'

Though she knew the room had fallen silent, Cahra couldn't hear anything over the rush of blood in her ears.

Sylvie, who'd secreted herself in a corner, arms folded across her silver breastplate, pushed off from the shelves she was leaning against and strode for the room's strategy table.

'Thierre was taken outside our walls. That's no small job. If it were me, I'd send my finest.' The General glowered at the map as if she might terrify its pieces into talking. 'That means Kolyath's Commander Sullian, or Ozumbre's Commander Diabolus, and their elite units.' Sylvie began cross-checking reports with the map's red and grey figures. 'I will find them,' she growled, brows as ferocious as her father's.

A pause, before Wyldaern finally ventured, 'And yet, Thierre is not the omen-bringer.' She exchanged a glance with Thierre's sister, then looked to Thelaema.

Commander Tyne exhaled. 'Exactly. Therein lies the problem.' He eyed King Royce. 'If they interrogate him, he won't have the answers they're looking for.'

'Not about the prophecy.' The King's words, like his eyes, were hollow.

If they interrogate him. They mean if they torture him. The bottom fell from Cahra's stomach. And she was falling with it.

Raiden stared at his Commander, asking quietly, 'Will he endure it?'

Thierre could die. The thought spun endlessly in her mind. King Royce had been right. *This is all my fault.*

Thelaema's glare – the Oracle's thought – hit Cahra like a fired arrow. *Hardly.* Thelaema turned her scrutiny back on the royals.

Commander Tyne's face was grim. 'Thierre was trained.'

Something in King Royce shrunk at the word, deflating him. Trained – as in, to withstand torture? Cahra bit the inside of her cheek. *Surely they didn't mean…*

Tyne stood defiant. 'He will endure.'

The dark place inside Cahra surged again and she knew it wouldn't be long until her eyes glowed like a meagre imitation of Hael's.

Would Thierre really be able to withstand torture? Kolyath's Steward had a spymaster, that she knew, but the ruler's twin Commanders were just as accomplished at violent coercion. The idea of a Kolyath soldier – or Ozumbre, given their reputation for butchery – breaking his fingers or pulling his teeth to get Thierre to talk quickly turned her mouth to ash.

'They won't kill him,' Tyne said into the silence. 'Thinking he's the omen-bringer makes him valuable. They'll wait for the Key.'

Cahra reached into her pocket. 'Which will never be bestowed,' she said softly, producing the black velvet pouch.

'You have it?' King Royce leapt to his feet. 'The last omen approaches! Go, girl, to Hael'stromia! Summon the weapon and save my son!'

Cahra glared at Thelaema. *Like I said.*

Wyldaern cut in, frowning. 'And if Cahra is attacked by Kolyath and Ozumbre's allied forces on her way to Hael'stromia?'

Queen Avenais turned in desperation to the Seers. 'Is there nothing that you can do? We have herbs, all the divination herbs that—'

Thelaema laughed mirthlessly. 'We thank you, however, herbs will not aid that which I cannot see, when such things are veiled from even my aged eyes.'

The room descended once more into a heavy silence.

'Unless…' It was Wyldaern. Cahra's body tensed, her heart pounding as she listened. 'You cannot see the Prince, but perhaps I can? Or at least, gain us information, some clue as to where they may have taken him. By focusing my sight outside the gate…'

Cahra said slowly to Thelaema, 'You said your visions aren't blocked with Wyldaern. Maybe she's not hampered by whoever is blocking yours?'

Considering, the Oracle nodded to her apprentice. 'Do so,' she said.

Wyldaern sat back quickly, cross-legged, in her armchair, and shut her eyes. The royals leaned forward as the Oracle sipped her tea. Then Wyldaern frowned.

King Royce, voice hoarse, said, 'What is it?'

Wyldaern gave a slight shake of her head, her words floating to them as if from far away. 'That is just it. Nothing,' she said, then jerked. Sylvie started, stepping closer.

Raiden did the same. 'Look for any signs of a disturbance, anything out of place, if you can. You may see something we couldn't.'

'The air, the *blood*—' Wyldaern's eyes were open now, but it was like she couldn't see the people gathered around her.

'Blood?' Queen Avenais's gaze was fraught with alarm as she gripped her husband.

'We found blood on the ground a ways from the gatehouse,' Raiden said quietly. 'Not much, but enough.'

They all watched as Wyldaern spasmed, violently this time, then returned to the room, her peridot eyes lucid.

'What did you see?' King Royce cried, beating Thelaema to the question.

'A struggle,' Wyldaern said, dabbing the sleeve of her robe to her damp forehead. 'And a man. A soldier of Kolyath, I believe, by the pin. Tall, lean. Protruding brown eyes,' Wyldaern recalled. 'He and others ambushed Thierre not long into his journey.'

Cahra halted mid-step as something inside her burst into livid flame. The shards of emotion she'd been piecing back together since her and Hael's abreption converged at once: there was no fear, no sadness, no guilt floundering inside Cahra any more.

There was only Hael's Netherworldly darkness.

'*Jarett*,' Cahra snarled, his name spewing from her with such force it shook the room. The Commander and his sadistic Kingdom Guards were always a part of her night terrors, haunting the recesses of her memories. Thierre wasn't the only one who'd been taken prisoner.

Cahra exhaled, the air crackling as fire burned within her core.

And from her eyes.

Queen Avenais gasped, her own eyes, her mouth, wide with terror.

'Cahra,' Thelaema warned, reaching for her arm then flinching and hissing as her skin scalded Thelaema's fingers. Wyldaern rushed for her teacher. 'I survive yet,' the Oracle muttered. Picking up a napkin from the sideboard, Wyldaern placed it in a teacup of cool water and pressed it to Thelaema's inflamed hand.

Cahra blinked, staring at her arm. She'd burnt Thelaema without even trying. But before she could dwell on it, Sylvie's voice cracked like a whip.

'What in *Hael* is Commander Jarett doing outside Kolyath? That's Sullian's arena.' Sylvie's fists were clenched so hard Cahra thought the woman might break her own knuckles.

'Finishing what he started,' Cahra said, her speech guttural. 'And addressing his failure to capture Thierre and I in the first place.' No one said what she was thinking.

That Jarett had made up for that now.

All eyes were on her as Thelaema said, 'Peace, Cahra. We will locate them.'

Cahra could barely acknowledge the Oracle without feeling as if her own restraints weren't slipping but galloping away. All she wanted to do was destroy, *everything*.

But as the room filled with palpable tension, she felt a troubling pang of guilt. Shame. *I nearly slaughtered a man in that cave.* She sighed. *I've done enough damage for one day.*

Thelaema's gaze slid to Cahra once again and the Oracle said into her mind: *The Reliquus is the Scion's guardian. His Nether-powers exist to protect you. You only did what Hael would have, had he been with you.*

Cahra glared at Thelaema. *Is that supposed to make it okay?*

The Oracle's amethyst eyes cooled. *It was an enemy soldier, in self-defence.*

At first, but not by the end. And that's not the point! Am I so beyond punishment now? So important that my life ranks above all others? She remembered with sudden clarity Thierre telling Raiden he couldn't keep putting the Prince's life above everybody else's.

'I cannot be responsible for any more d—' Any more deaths. Finally, she understood. To Thierre, his future wasn't worth risking other people. Not if it meant their lives were forfeit.

Cahra had nearly beaten a man to death, all because of Hael's Nether-powers and her own supposed fate. She scowled at Thelaema.

Wyldaern picked up on the flurried exchange of looks between Cahra and the Oracle, surely sensing a disagreement brewing. But the Seer relaxed as Sylvie handed Wyldaern a cup of tea from the Queen's platter.

King Royce's shoulders slumped. 'Will they demand a ransom?'

Commander Tyne had moved to stand alongside his General and the tabletop map. 'It's likely.'

'What could we possibly ransom?' Queen Avenais, who'd been muted in her tears, finally succumbed to sobbing into her husband's shoulder. The King pulled his wife into a tight embrace as she said, 'Royce, however do we get him back?' She dabbed at her eyes.

'Thierre only wanted to keep the kingdom safe. It is why he dreamt up those assignments, to aid us, to see a future without war. He just wanted…'

'To help,' Cahra finished, feeling empty. *There is value in helping others.* That's what Thierre had said to her.

While she, on the other hand, had spent her whole life running, hiding, from so much. Loneliness, sadness. Happiness.

Love.

And her hidden wish.

To be acknowledged, for her life, her suffering. As Thelaema had, with her apology. To be seen, finally. To matter, to someone. To be more than just a lowly beggar, for once.

Now, as the Scion, as Empress, she would have those things.

But before all that, Thierre had been there. And despite how things had ended, that honour would always be his. He had seen her, and while he had lied about his own truths, he had not shied away from her own. He had helped her, and she valued that.

An idea started to take shape in Cahra's mind.

Meanwhile, King Royce had fixed his stare on Commander Tyne, who vehemently shook his head as the King replied to his wife, 'There is but one thing more valuable than a Luminaux Prince.' Royce stood quietly. 'A King.' Queen Avenais burst into tears anew. 'Tyne. Offer them a trade.'

Cahra stepped from the back of the room, Thelaema's sharp gaze slicing into hers.

There is value in helping others.

Thelaema's spitfire words pierced Cahra's mind: *Do NOT even finish that thought.*

But Cahra knew. When Hael had told her of the unimaginable, the inconceivable – that she was an Empress – her first thought had been Thierre. That it should have been him, that he would have known exactly what to do. That he'd spent his life training to be King and knew what all of this required. One day, Thierre would rule Luminaux, and that role was something he'd been groomed for since birth. Not Cahra; she wasn't a leader, not even close. Regardless of the Key or the capital or the weapon, *Thierre* was the smart choice, whereas she didn't have a clue. Until now, that is, she thought.

She didn't need training to know her next words were the right ones.

'You're wrong,' Cahra told King Royce. 'There's something even more valuable.' She looked around Luminaux's den of war, knowing once she spoke the words out loud, she could never take them back again.

Good. Maybe if I do this, I can save a life, instead of destroying one.

And that life would be Thierre's.

Thelaema, like Tyne, shook her head, the Oracle's eyes shooting daggers: *Cahraelia – Cahra! DON'T!*

A sense of resolution washed over her. Cahra turned to King Royce, her voice steady. *This is how I help.* With newfound determination, she locked eyes with Thierre's father.

Taking a deep breath, Cahra said, 'An Empress trumps a King.'

CHAPTER 34

Cahra stood in the wake of her decision, bracing for the inevitable backlash.

Sure enough, Thelaema's composure shattered on impact. 'That is, with certainty, the most ridiculous sentence that anyone has ever uttered. You *cannot* be serious!'

'Can't I?' Cahra challenged her, looking around Luminaux's den of war.

Wyldaern met her with empathy. 'I grasp your motivations, truly I do.'

The numbness that had been Cahra's saviour all these years, that had kept her standing at the thought of Thierre being tortured, finally threatened to buckle beneath her emotions. Cahra gritted her teeth at the pain that needled her body.

'Yet it is precisely as you said,' Wyldaern went on. 'An Empress trumps a King and a Prince. Your safety must come before Thierre's.' Her friend's tone was pleading.

'Why?' Cahra fired the question at the Seers. 'Because you say so? Because it's my "destiny"? Because I have no choice? Let me tell you about choice,' Cahra argued fiercely. 'I have never had a choice in my life. And now you're telling me I'm finally in a position to make a choice that really counts – except I can't? What good is this stupid birthright then?' She spun to Sylvie. 'What would Thierre do if our roles were reversed?'

Luminaux's General stood, the waves of her black hair stark against her blue finery. Sylvie's eyes – Thierre's eyes – cut to her father's.

'He would volunteer himself. And if you said no, he'd simply break free of the palace.'

Despite everything, Raiden chuckled sadly.

Cahra faced him, then Sylvie. 'Exactly.' She turned to Thelaema, warning her, 'This is not up for discussion.'

Thelaema's amethyst eyes hardened into violet chips of ice. '*If* we were to suffer this idiotic half-notion,' she snapped, 'what precisely is your plan? Apart from giving yourself over to the rulers inciting the deaths of your realmsmen at every turn?'

Cahra exhaled. It was a good question.

Commander Tyne spoke. 'The two rulers have always desired Hael'stromia's weapon first and foremost,' he said slowly. 'It's the primary reason for the war.' He looked at Cahra. 'In the event of an exchange for Thierre, I find it hard to believe they'd kill you.'

Not straight away, she thought. Thelaema didn't have to say a word into her mind. Cahra could feel the Oracle's eyes on her, and the ferocious glare said everything.

Tyne continued on. 'They'll need you to get inside the capital, to access the weapon.'

'But if they try that with Thierre, he'll be discovered as a fraud.' Cahra steeled herself. 'Which is why I have to go. Even if he plays along, that act can't last forever.'

She inhaled deeply, trying to get a sense of Hael's powers. Would what was left be enough for her next move?

'And then?' Thelaema demanded. 'When the Reliquus is freed?'

You mean, when Atriposte and Decimus have no use for me any more? Cahra smiled. *With any luck, Hael will escape from his tomb and rip their heads off.*

Thelaema's irate reply was unintelligible as she threw her hands up and stalked out, shaking her head and cursing as she left.

Wyldaern slid Cahra a glance, before going after her. 'High Oracle!'

With the Seers, her main dissenters, out of the room, Cahra sunk into a leather chair. The same one she'd perched on her first time in this room, she realised.

'You would really do this for us? For him?' Queen Avenais sat, legs drawn to her, the skirts of her brocade gown enveloping the woman like a fine blanket as she hugged her knees. She looked less like a Queen and more like a forlorn little girl. 'Why?'

Sylvie and Raiden were both watching Cahra.

'It's as your General said, Highness. The Prince would do the same.' She'd been so angry with Thierre, but it was the man he was. Thierre's talent *was* people, and bravery. Cahra's talent had been shirking both.

If it came down to who should survive out of the two of them, Thierre had done far more for the realm than she had. Even if he'd had a lifetime to do so.

A lifetime he'll continue to have, she swore. King Royce was surveying her, and the determination in her bearing. Finally, he nodded.

Tears filled Queen Avenais' eyes. 'Luminaux will be ever in your debt.'

Cahra nodded blankly in return, no words left. Thierre had got her out of Kolyath. Now it was her turn to free him from it. Even if it sent her back into its clutches.

And the Steward's.

Gemstones. Her fingers tightened on the arms of her chair. *Hematite, tourmaline, jet. Hardest, blackest jet…* Her breaths quickened, each one feeling harder, faster than the last.

The door to the room creaked open then, as Wyldaern returned, Thelaema in tow. Cahra's eyes were closed as she thought to the Oracle, *I refuse to argue with you any more. I've made my decision and I intend to act upon it.*

Soon. No matter how much it terrified her.

'And how will you get word to Kolyath and Ozumbre of your proposal with the haste we need?' Thelaema asked the question aloud so Luminaux's royals could hear.

To Cahra's surprise, Wyldaern was the one who answered. 'You could, with a vision?' The Seer turned to face Thelaema. 'A message to Steward Atriposte and King Decimus.'

King Royce's haggard face brightened. 'Is such a thing possible?' Maybe he'd been doing the same as Cahra and no doubt Raiden, weighing how long Thierre had been gone with how long the Prince might have left.

Whatever the people in this room were going to do, they'd better hurry.

Thelaema looked as if she might renounce her apprentice, her gaze an amethyst abyss. But she grated out, 'It is. And the terms?'

'Thierre, for myself and the Key.' *Unhurt,* Cahra thought at the Oracle. She prayed it wasn't too late to demand such a thing.

It is. Thelaema's words clanged through her, slamming into Cahra with full force. She felt the air go out of her. *I shall amend to 'unmaimed'.*

They'd hurt him. Hael's powers trembled at Cahra's fingertips, wrath within her reach.

'And an armistice for the exchange,' Sylvie instructed.

'Perhaps we should take a walk?' Wyldaern whispered to Cahra.

'*Please* do,' Thelaema muttered darkly, turning away to face the royals.

Cahra glared at Thelaema, Hael's fire rising to writhe inside her. *They hurt Thierre.* She knew it was unfair, but she was angry: at the Oracle and the woman's fickle visions, the Nether-magicks that powered the Seers.

Yes, Thelaema had been right: Raiden was in the caves and Thierre was kidnapped. But how did the Oracle know for certain that Cahra going to Hael'stromia was folly, exactly? The woman said her visions flickered on and off. What if Cahra's plan to free Hael could have saved Thierre from getting hurt? But to Thelaema, the only thing of consequence was Cahra.

The absurd notion of her life outweighing someone else's made Cahra feel sick, and the way Thelaema charged so blindly in that direction, as if nothing else mattered…

It wasn't right. None of this was, she thought with an ugly shudder.

'Commander, General. Assemble the kingdom's forces, with troops ready to march on my orders. High Oracle, can you help locate our enemies?' King Royce's words faded as Cahra fought to control her spiralling emotions.

Wyldaern touched her shoulder and Cahra nodded, the two leaving Thelaema and the Luminaux royals to orchestrate war.

Outside in the hall, Cahra let her Seer friend lead her along, the hand-crafted columns flanking their path adorned with mountains and ivy beneath the vaulted ceiling. But she couldn't think of whites and greens.

Not when all she could think of was blue goldstone.

Cahra inhaled. When she loosed the breath from her lips, it was steaming.

She looked at Wyldaern. 'I need to *hit* something,' she said.

CHAPTER 35

Thierre knew that it was bad.

He didn't need the shackles crushing his wrists – or the cuts to his face, his neck, the stab wounds to his chest and stomach, his life's blood oozing to the stonework floor, even the bolted, padlocked door with a horde of guards lusting to finish the blades' work – to know that his predicament had plummeted to new levels.

Instead, a glance from Thierre's good eye – the one not bloated shut – at the people assembled before him was all it took.

To know that he was not long for this life.

Thierre coughed, a gob of blood expelling from his split lips, as his flesh wrung yet another shiver from him. He lowered his too-groggy head, blood pulsing, pooling at his feet.

Yet Thierre had trained to withstand such things. So, despite his body begging him to surrender to, at the very least, unconsciousness, he held on.

And listened. His sister kingdom rulers did not disappoint.

'What says he?' Steward Atriposte turned his back on Thierre, the ruler's heavy cloak dyed Kolyath's infamous blood-red.

'Little,' Commander Jarett reported, cold fury in his eyes at Thierre's resistance. Lamentably, Thierre recognised the spark behind that look. What it meant for him.

More torture. The man lived for the pleasure of his violence.

Stupendous. Thierre sighed, a hacking cough following.

King Decimus of Ozumbre spoke next, eyes on Thierre. 'How long will this take?' Ozumbre was a volcanic land with a dry, oppressive heat, and the ruler was dressed for such, his sleeveless jerkin diverging from Atriposte's calculated finery as King Decimus crossed his arms over his battle-worn vest, his greyish skin visible. The people of Ozumbre had lived for so long under the shadow of their fiery peak that they mirrored their environment, reminiscent of the ash that rained from the volcanic sky.

'If your Commander is not up to such an important task, esteemed Steward, then might I suggest Ozumbre's royal spymaster?' Decimus' teal gaze flickered with amusement. 'Or your own Commander Sullian?'

Thierre could not suppress his tremble. Ozumbre's spymaster was well-known for hacking limbs from his interrogation subjects. He tried to swallow. If the sadist was permitted, the next time Thierre's father received him would be piece by blood-soaked piece.

Commander Jarett bared his teeth. 'Sullian is not required.'

'Are you so sure of that, brother?' Light footfalls sounded behind Thierre.

By the Oracles, he thought. *How many of the fiends are here?*

He watched, helpless, as Atriposte's Commanders, Jarett of the Steward's guards and Sullian of his army, glared at one another. Sullian laughed bitterly, his scarred face full of scorn for his brother.

Decimus' eyes lit up, the King of Ozumbre delighting in the spectacle of Kolyath's Commanders and their vitriol. Thierre supposed the man knew something of sibling discord, given Decimus's own brother, his twin Diabolus, was Commander of Ozumbre's own army. And the only enemy kingdom senior official missing from this cell.

Jarett turned his spiteful gaze from Sullian's mocking to the Ozumbre King. 'Speaking of brothers, sister kingdom sire – where, pray, is yours?'

'Doing as I was,' Sullian interrupted, one hand at his back as he waved another at whatever was beyond the room's door. 'Readying the forces, a task I shall return to shortly.' He bowed before his Steward. 'But first, I proffer a gift.'

Readying their forces for what?

A blue twinkle caught his eye, then another, and Thierre latched onto it, that hue, and the memories that glided back. Cahra's longsword. The mere sight of it warmed him.

Or was that the fever of sepsis setting in?

He laughed at the futility of his situation, of dying at the most leisurely of paces – and now, of course, the omen-bringer's sword. At least the blade might help keep him alive; that, and him never having crossed paths with King Decimus face to face before, so the room knew him as Lord Terryl and not an iota more. Yet even that cover may not save him for long.

Jarett's gaze snapped to Thierre and his muted laughter. He marched over, unsheathing a dagger and pointing its tip at Thierre.

'Something to say, merchant lord?'

Commander Sullian picked up Cahra's sword, touching his finger to the pommel's Sigil of the Seers. The man smirked as he casually held the blade, its sharpened point angled nonchalantly at his brother. Jarett snarled at Sullian.

'A lord?' a frayed voice pondered, reverberating, from the shadows. 'A lord...'

Oracles, who now? Not Diabolus. Thierre squinted in the dim light.

'A lord.' The off-white cloak of a figure emerged and all Thierre could make out under its hood were two lavender orbs. 'No.' It raised an arm. 'The lord is a fabrication.'

Oh, HAEL.

In a heartbeat, Jarett's cold anger boiled into a torrid rage. He advanced, intending to slash Thierre's throat, roaring, '*In His Excellency's kingdom?*'

Only Sullian had the sense to hold Jarett back. 'Then what is fact, Oracle?'

The white figure withdrew its hood, the man beneath it tutting as he said, 'Now, now. It is rude not to introduce yourself, Prince Thierre of Luminaux.'

CHAPTER 36

'Again!'

Cahra ground her teeth, two hands gripping the great-hammer poised above her head. With careful footwork, she let it fall, the metal block carving a low arc behind her as she hefted on the upswing to raise it overhead again.

'Again!' Piet shouted, in time with her heaving breaths. She'd asked for this, for training drills to channel her anger and fear, hammer in hand, like she would've in Kolyath. Before anyone else got hurt.

The Ozumbre soldier in the caves flashed back to her, the man's pulverised armour, his organs – his ribs, his heart – spilling out from the magick Thelaema had unleashed. Cahra shook the stiffness from her shoulders, as if to oust the self-loathing now battling the numbness in her mind, flailing desperately to save her from her feelings. From herself and what she'd almost done. Cahra gritted her teeth and swung.

Again!

She couldn't rest, couldn't face the idea of being alone with her thoughts now that she'd volunteered her life for Thierre's.

Forfeited it. That's what Thelaema had muttered into her mind as she and Wyldaern left the den of war. She knew the Oracle was angry, as angry with Cahra as the woman was with her own pupil. But even Wyldaern understood that Cahra being Empress didn't make Thierre's life expendable, and she was thankful for that support.

She might trust the Oracle, but Thelaema had made enough choices on her behalf. This time, she would decide the danger she'd be walking into.

And that danger was the two most violent rulers in the realm.

Before she could rattle through a fresh list of gemstones to distract her, Cahra heard footsteps outside Luminaux's training arena.

It was Thelaema, accompanied by Raiden. Piet must have sensed the tension rippling between Cahra and the Oracle, for the warrior dipped his head and withdrew. Cahra lifted the ebony handle of her hammer and twirled it as Raiden and Thelaema neared, the great-hammer's gems dancing weakly in the overcast light of morning.

'Any news?' Cahra didn't look at Thelaema.

'I have contacted the rulers of Kolyath and Ozumbre,' she replied.

Cahra tried and failed to swallow. 'And?'

'As per your terms, an exchange has been negotiated.'

Cahra exhaled. *Unmaimed*, she reminded Thelaema.

Unmaimed, the Oracle confirmed.

The thought still sent a pulse of outrage through Cahra, but it seemed it was the best they were going to get.

She forced a breath down. 'What do I need to do?'

Raiden glanced at Thelaema, then spoke. 'The King of Luminaux has decreed it: our Royal Army marches for Hael'stromia tonight. Commander Tyne and General Sylvanir are strategising as we speak, while our host moves for the exchange point. Today, you may rest, then we depart the kingdom at nightfall. The trade will take place at the capital.'

So this is it, Cahra thought. She was finally going to Hael'stromia. *To Hael.*

Cahra nodded. 'How far is it?'

Raiden cleared his throat, taking in her sombre tone. 'A night of riding.'

She nodded numbly again. 'Okay.'

There was a strained pause, before Raiden stepped up to face her. His eyes were soft.

'What you're doing is incredibly brave,' the Captain said, placing a hand on her shoulder.

What you are doing is incredibly stupid, Thelaema muttered into Cahra's mind.

Ignoring her, Cahra tried to smile but couldn't. 'So long as it works.'

It was Raiden's turn to nod. 'We ride together. Now, I must prepare the Royal Guards, but if you need me, send word. I will be there,' he told her, and Cahra understood. She had Raiden's trust and his support, now.

He turned to go, leaving Cahra alone with the Oracle.

A wave of Thelaema's hand, and the door to the yard slammed behind the Captain.

'Have you completely lost your mind?' Thelaema ground out, each word cracking like a whip.

'You're just mad you're not making all the decisions,' Cahra shot back.

'Thierre is a Prince! Even if something befalls him, Luminaux still claims a King and a Princess. Their kingdom's stability shall remain. Whereas *you*,' Thelaema chastised her, 'are irreplaceable. You are the last of Kolyath and you have no successor!'

'So what?' Cahra threw up her hands, sick of the Oracle's uncompromising attitude. What did any of this matter when Hael'stromia was still an inhospitable smudge on a map? 'What exactly happens if I die, Thelaema? Won't the prophecy just roll around again, with some other Scion at the helm next time? Maybe even someone from Luminaux?'

'I do not know! Yet I will tell you what I do,' Thelaema warned, advancing on Cahra. 'The vision that I was granted before I lost connection to the All-seeing predicted everything that has come to pass. Every single thing. No matter how you wish to be rid of this, *you*, Cahraelia, and all that you bring, even if you despise it, are what I saw!'

'I told you, it's *Cahra!*' she yelled. 'And if what I bring is such a damn gift, then you should have no problem with how I use it!' Why was the woman so bent on controlling her?

'Foolish girl, do you not see? You could die at your idiotic exchange!'

'Somehow, I think you would've seen that,' Cahra retorted.

'And if this is all a ploy? If Atriposte and Decimus refuse to exchange Prince Thierre, to keep him – and *you* – in line, in order to secure the weapon for themselves?'

Cahra took a deep breath. They wouldn't... Would they? 'Like I said—'

Thelaema exploded, the full weight of the Oracle's Nether-magicks sizzling with the smoky purple of her gaze. 'This is not altruism. It is not even your ill-defined feelings for the Prince of Luminaux, which a non-Seer could see, clear as daybreak,' she said, Cahra flushing. 'This is you martyring yourself because you are *petrified* to entertain the thought that you might deserve this destiny, your own rule – instead endorsing Thierre: the pretty Prince and an easy choice for unsaddling your duties.' Cahra froze as Thelaema added, 'When, precisely, are you planning to stop running from your responsibilities?'

Cahra could feel the remnants of Hael's powers flare through her, their stinging heat, as she flung the words, 'How *dare* you! Whose fault is it that I might doubt myself, or any of my so-called gifts, compared to someone who's been born and raised as a *Prince*, trained and ready to rule at a moment's notice? You are despicable—'

Thelaema sighed as she muttered, 'As useful as communing with the desert sands.' She fixed her gaze on Cahra. 'Will you hearken to anything I say, or is divulging who I believe to be blocking my sight just as futile?'

Cahra was about ready to loop her hands around the Oracle's wrinkled neck, but she managed to contain the impulse.

'What? Who?'

Thelaema exhaled again. 'Grauwynn, High Oracularus of the Order of Descry.'

'I thought you were the last of the Oracles,' Cahra said slowly, thinking back to their ride to Luminaux.

'As did I.' Thelaema's face was grim. 'And yet, I believe my deduction to be truth. When I shared your proposal with Atriposte and Decimus, minutes passed before King Royce received a message in kind. Only another Oracle, a spiritual leader, might command that level of connection to the All-seeing, tenuous as the Seers' is since Hael'stromia was lost to us.' She looked troubled.

Cahra asked, 'You never sensed anyone other than yourself might have survived?'

Apparently, her guess was right. 'Not in the four centuries since the capital's fall,' Thelaema told her.

'And no ordinary Seer could have learned to share their thoughts with others?' Cahra frowned, trying to understand. Hael's connection to the Netherworld was mystery enough, never mind the Seers and the All-Seeing. Or how it had granted Thelaema such long life.

Thelaema shook her head. 'No. It is beyond us now, beyond our diluted source.'

'But this source, the capital's magick, it kept you alive and kept them alive too. Why? And why did this Oracularus not make contact earlier? Why only now?'

'All valid questions.' The Oracle pursed her lips. 'I have been unable to perceive him. Perhaps he also experienced this.' Thelaema's eyes flickered to Cahra. 'Regardless, what is troubling is not "why now".

It is that he speaks from the side of those who side against us. Against you.'

And if Grauwynn, a High Oracle, has powers like Thelaema's?

Troubling isn't the word for it. 'Does he know I have the Key?'

'I omitted its mention,' Thelaema told her. 'Given that I bestowed it, that may block Grauwynn's grasp of the omen's passing. However, as old Hael'stromia's High Oracularus, I would not count on that safeguarding us for long. He will learn of it, one way or another.'

Despite everything the Oracle had said, Cahra felt like she was back where she started.

Echoing the same question as earlier, she said, 'So what do I need to do? What *can* we do?' Her throat felt as arid as the capital's black sands she would encounter for the first time. *First, and maybe last.*

Thelaema's gaze met Cahra's. 'You know what you can do. Seek out the Reliquus. Replenish his powers. Enter Hael'stromia with something other than naiveté in your arsenal.'

Cahra cut her a glare, then turned from Thelaema. The thought had occurred to her, somewhere in the dark alleyways of her mind. The memory of what she'd almost done to that soldier in the caves, what could happen if she gave in to Hael's black rage. But if she went to Hael now and told him of her plan, asking for more power, she knew exactly how he'd react. Giving herself to her enemies to save Thierre? It flew in the face of Hael's duty as her shield; he'd never forgive it. Which was why she'd not called on him. He'd be absolutely enraged, and afraid for her. Not without good reason.

So no, she wouldn't make contact with Hael. At least, not yet. She'd need to shut him out for as long as possible. It was the only way she'd be able to keep the promise she'd made, to help Thierre.

Cahra gave her great-hammer a practice swing, the Haellium as dark as the crisis that was brewing outside the capital.

She turned back to Thelaema, still thinking of that soldier in the caves.

'You gave me this in lieu of the weapon. I'm enough before I put Hael'stromia's own to good use,' Cahra told her.

But the look in the Oracle's eyes said what Cahra was thinking.

Enough – for now.

–

Cahra barely slept that day. Rest came in dreamless, surface bursts, leaving her tired and threaded with tension, but resolved. When she did manage to eat, the bread and cheese tasted like sawdust, each forced bite churning in her stomach. Then the call to move out boomed through Luminaux's dining room, scattering soldiers whose boots thundered like a war drum in time with her pounding heart.

Outside, they mounted their horses and galloped for the gate.

Raiden was beside her now, Sylvie on Cahra's other side. Their stony gazes forward, guards flanked her path to Thierre's exchange. The Seers followed, Thelaema and Wyldaern shielded by a ring of Luminaux's Royal Guards in the darkness.

Good. One less thing to worry about, she thought. There was more than enough between Thierre and everything else that could go wrong as it was.

Raiden's eyes lingered on Cahra, his own worry carving lines into the Captain's face. He'd asked if she was all right as they ran for the horses, but 'all right' felt too distant an idea, swallowed as she was by the dread consuming her.

All right? I'm honestly not sure it matters any more.

She'd made her choice in not seeking Hael. Now she had to live with it.

If, by the end of this, she was alive at all.

They'd ridden through the forest bordering Luminaux's kingdom during the night, Cahra's only comfort the sky alight with icy stars. In Kolyath, a night sky without cloud cover was so rare it was considered auspicious. But Cahra was sick of providential omens by now, spending the time staring at those stars and watching their magnification, and Hael's magicks, dwindle into nothingness, the stars dulling to tiny white dots.

When they did, there was a part of her that cursed her human eyes.

But the quick forward march of Luminaux's Royal Army dispelled her errant thoughts, the rhythmic crunch of endless boots on rocks and leaves keeping her grounded. At one point, she turned, peering behind her at their infantry and support units like Queran's fellow archers, followed by the rear guard that defended them from ambush. The army's unit columns filed all the way back to the last village and beyond, a broad formation of thousands spilling down the black-bricked road to Hael'stromia, Luminaux's vanguard leading them onward.

After the forest came the grasslands, and beyond them, the sparse flats leading to the capital's black sands, where Kolyath and Ozumbre awaited. And Thierre.

By Sylvie's calculations, they would reach their destination soon.

Cahra gripped the horn of her saddle, taking a deep breath as tendrils of apprehension slowly uncoiled, slithering through her veins. The overwhelming urge to whip the reins and bolt from impending danger was almost unbearable, but Cahra refused to run. She'd made a promise to Thierre's parents. She would see it through.

Dawn was close to breaking. Luminaux's mightiest legion marched behind their General, set to converge with the others as the majority of the kingdom's forces swarmed on Hael'stromia. All that was left was to continue on their route to the capital's north-east gate, one of three access points to Hael'stromia, a gate facing the road to each sister tri-kingdom. It had been a stipulation from the rulers of Kolyath and Ozumbre that the trade must take place outside Luminaux's capital gate, likely to humble King Royce. Outnumbered, he would be forced to witness his failure to win the war for the weapon.

But Cahra didn't care for men's bruised egos. Her concern was Thierre.

She heard the trot of hooves and tossed a glance over her shoulder to see Thelaema. Beyond the Oracle, royal blue and gold flags and tabards stretched as far as the eye could see, with seemingly infinite armed soldiers, all marching for their Prince. Cahra lowered her eyes, the Wilds darker and dustier with each hoofbeat. The air still held a chill, but not like before. She watched the specks of sand eddying with the rising breeze.

Cahra gazed out at the changing landscape. She'd never seen so much open space – Kolyath's slums and Traders' Quadrant were so small and cramped in contrast. But out here, the realm seemed to stretch on forever, and with it, the most bittersweet feeling of freedom swelled alongside a sharp pang in her chest.

'It is not too late to call off this histrionic decision,' Thelaema said.

Cahra didn't look at her. 'I thought you said decisions don't care for my emotions, only results?' This one would save Thierre. She exhaled, trying not to let the woman's earlier words get the best of her fraying nerves.

When are you planning to stop running from your responsibilities?

She waited for Thelaema to launch into yet another tirade. But instead the Oracle said, 'The cost is too high if the result is you dead on Hael'stromia's sands.'

'At least if I'm dead, they won't get Hael. "*When the mark walks the path to enter the Nether in life*"? The "in life" kind of gave it away.'

'Not so foolish, after all, then,' Thelaema said, voice softening.

Cahra shrugged. 'Maybe.'

Or maybe not, she thought, remembering the other thing Thelaema had said to her.

What you are doing is incredibly stupid.

Maybe the Oracle was right. That thought, like the gasp that stole from Cahra's lips, snared her as Hael'stromia's jet-black pyramid rose into view, beneath a handful of clouds; like they were carved from heavenly marble, ready to plummet and crush everyone there.

And before the pyramid, an army, their numbers seemingly impossible, dwarfing any force Cahra had dreamt existed in the world.

CHAPTER 37

Cahra stared at the foreboding black gate and shattered walls of the capital of Hael'stromia, grains of sand whipping her face as a sharp gust of wind swept across the arid plain. Despite the open air, it felt thick, stale – heavy. When she swallowed, her throat dry with desert dust, she immediately choked. The air tasted of dead things.

A tidal wave of fear threatened to submerge her, but she clung to hope, to thoughts of Hael, locked somewhere within the inky silhouette of the black tri-cornered pyramid that loomed against dawn's warming blush.

She'd already seen what Hael had called the palatial temple, the capital's pyramid, from the elevation of Luminaux's palace. Back in Kolyath or Luminaux, Cahra had thought each kingdom's 'gate to Hael', with its Haellium spikes and bars, was sinister enough. But now, peering at Hael'stromia's defences – the sky-high metal palings curved around its dark sands, bolstering each gate – and beyond, the bulwarks crumbling and toppling in places, shattered against diehard metal bars… This bleak city was her birthright?

The capital's grim desolation laid bare, Cahra's breath hitched, locked inside her chest. As if sensing it the only safe haven.

But nowhere here would be safe soon.

Kolyath and Ozumbre's armies were fanned like wicked wings between Cahra and the capital, flooding the vast plain before her. The enemy masses racked back as far as she could squint, and she sighed with irritation. Hael's Nether-magicks that gifted enhanced vision had faded, leaving her feeling all but useless. Hearing the sound of armour shifting uneasily behind her, she wondered how Luminaux's forces were faring. She no longer had Hael's powers, but the eerie absence of sound from the capital's side of the battlefield made her stomach flip in anticipation.

Meanwhile, Sylvie's polished detachment was in place as she surveyed the horde by the gate, Luminaux's Royal Army General signalling behind the golden shield of her buckler to Commander Tyne and her Colonels standing by.

Cahra sat rigidly in her saddle, remembering Thierre's description of Hael'stromia as he'd sat beside her in the traders' tavern in Kolyath. It felt like another time, another life, as she gulped down breath after torrid breath, panic clawing its way from her belly. Her eyes flashed from the pyramid to Kolyath and Ozumbre's armies gathered against them.

Against her, just as Thelaema had said.

Cahra swallowed, nausea rising with her dread.

She looked to the Oracle now, Piet and Siarl moving to escort the Seers to the safety of Luminaux's rearward ranks. *This may be our last chance to talk.* And while she fought against herself not to ask the question…

'Thelaema,' Cahra called, before Raiden's squad took her away. *What have you seen?*

The Oracle turned, her face in shadow, before asking, 'Are you certain you wish to know?'

Cahra nodded. 'Tell me.' *Will we succeed?*

It is possible, Thelaema said into her mind. *However, sacrifices must be made. And you must be prepared to accept them. No matter how much they pain you.*

Cahra felt her mouth go dry, remembering the Steward's speeches in Kolyath that spoke of sacrifice, austerity. Sacrifice was never things, but people. *Who?*

Thelaema smiled faintly.

But it was the first time she hadn't answered one of Cahra's questions.

Fear sparked in Cahra's chest, jolting through her. *There must be hope?*

There is. The amethyst of Thelaema's eyes shimmered. *The hope is you, child.*

Surprise stole Cahra's breath at the woman's words.

Then King Royce, seated on his dapple-grey stallion, nudged the steed forward.

'High Oracle,' Piet appealed with urgency, muscles tensed.

Thelaema bowed to Cahra, turning away – then whirled back, eyes flaring violet. *Grauwynn!* The woman's voice was a roar in Cahra's head.

Her own eyes widened. 'He's here?'

Thelaema nodded sharply, her amethyst eyes keen enough to kill. 'Cahra… Tread carefully.' The Oracle's final words to her, as Piet drew the woman into his kingdom's throng of troops. Cahra watched her go and turned, jostling on her horse to see where she had spotted the rogue Oracle.

'Where is the Steward?' Cahra asked in frustration, her gaze now on Thierre's family. The royals were strung like decorations before Kolyath and Ozumbre, but the kingdoms' own rulers were nowhere to be found. Royce and Sylvie were too exposed on those front lines, they could be picked off by a long-range archer—

'Hold, Cahra,' Raiden told her. 'King's orders.' He was counting under his breath. She watched as his eyes flickered across the formations of enemy troops.

Queen Avenais had stayed in Luminaux; if anything went wrong, at least one royal from Luminaux would live to see the day's end. Cahra's horse, the palomino from her journey to Thelaema, snuffled and stamped as if agreeing.

Then Raiden swore, interrupting Cahra's thoughts.

Cahra's gaze locked on him, her body instantly on edge. 'What?'

The Captain exhaled. 'Their forces tally 20,000 combined.'

She forced her next words with a croak. 'Luminaux's?'

Raiden's face was firm but pale. 'Less than half.'

She nodded, shoulders slumping. Sylvie had warned them. But she knew her choice if it came down to her as Empress versus someone like Thierre. She'd already made it.

Thierre was the priority.

'Cahra,' Raiden began, as Kolyath and Ozumbre's soldiers shifted, branching from the rear, something – someone – proceeding towards the enemy front lines.

The absent rulers.

Cahra bared her teeth in a silent snarl as she spied Steward Atriposte for one of only a handful of times in her life, the tyrant of Kolyath in battle regalia, seated atop a snow-white mount. Beside him, twin grey faces gazed at Luminaux's army with interest. *Decimus and Diabolus.* Who was who was anybody's guess though, garbed as they were in identical fighting leathers. A tactic to avoid assassination? Cahra frowned, searching.

Where was he?

Raiden had been thinking the same thing. 'I don't see Thierre.'

Kolyath and Ozumbre's rulers halted several soldiers back from the front lines. Contempt flooded Cahra. They didn't even have the spine to approach Luminaux directly, hiding instead behind their army's pikes, their mounted infantry, their bows and arrows.

King Royce stilled, his face an inveterate mask, his fortitude rallying his soldiers. Raiden's face shone with pride as the King's voice rung out, echoing to bridge the expanse.

'We are here to exchange, as agreed, Lord Terryl of Luminaux for Cahra of Kolyath.' The King of Luminaux marked his adversaries with narrowed navy eyes. 'Where is he?'

A yellow glimmer caught Cahra's eye through a gap in the Wilds that lay beside them. The sun was finally rising.

Moments passed, then Atriposte's voice boomed, 'Ah, yes, of course, the *Lord Terryl*. As agreed, we shall deliver him to you.'

Cahra had seen the hoarfrost anger surface in King Royce before, but not like this. 'Here. *Now*,' Thierre's father commanded in a barely contained snarl.

'As you wish,' Atriposte said, unruffled. 'Simply hand over the girl,' he crooned. Trotting from behind him, Commander Jarett leaned forward on his horse, searching for her.

She was wrong, there was no safe haven. Panic gripped her as she stared at the Steward, recalling how matter-of-factly he'd told her she would die after she stabbed him. Breathing suddenly felt like an impossible task.

Raiden grabbed her reins. 'No,' he told her.

'I have to,' she told him, voice shaking. 'It's Thierre.'

'I know that,' he replied roughly. 'But there has to be another way. I can't let you hand yourself over to those monsters.'

'There *is* no other way,' Cahra argued, her words edged with fear. 'We both know it. And if you slept like I did yesterday – which I didn't – you'd know it's this, or he's dead.' She looked at Raiden, eyes pleading, before gripping his hand and freeing her reins from it. 'He's the priority.'

Raiden stared back at her. 'Thierre *is* my priority. But—' The Captain exhaled deeply. 'But it doesn't mean that you don't matter. You have our people's support.'

Cahra smiled, and it was genuine. 'And I'm so thankful, for all of you, really I am.' She turned her gaze on Kolyath's Steward. 'But I have a deal to uphold. And he and I have unfinished kingdom business.' She took one breath, then another, glad to still be on the horse, not trusting her quaking legs to carry her.

The more she thought about the current plan, the more fear began to rip through her. Because with a night of riding to occupy her thoughts, well, she'd made her own plan.

One: make the trade, open Hael's tomb and let him deal with Kolyath and Ozumbre.

Or, if the trade goes awry, two: beg Hael to replenish her powers, and deal with Kolyath and Ozumbre herself. Both options were risky, and she wouldn't know which she'd be looking at until the trade was done.

But what if Thelaema's right, what if I die? What if I don't make it to Hael in time, and Luminaux's army, all of these people, are killed, because of me—

Damn it! Why did Thelaema always have to be right? Because if something happened, and Cahra needed to fight, Hael's powers were gone. And Atriposte was waiting.

She could see the determination in the faces of Sylvie and Tyne's soldiers. They were ready to die for their kingdom, for their Prince. But would their valour be enough?

Her eyes locked on Hael'stromia's gate once more. The price of failure was too high. She needed insurance. And she knew that Hael could give it to her.

Sliding a trembling hand from the reins, she brushed against the bump of Lumsden's little gold dagger as she slipped her hand into her trouser pocket, gently closing her eyes. Cahra summoned every ounce of her own bravery, willing her breathing to slow.

Please, please work. Then her fingers brushed the Key and she braced herself against the impending void, ready to confront the darkness as it rushed her.

But this time, Cahra didn't fall.

CHAPTER 38

'*Cahra.*'

Hael stood, still as time in his shrine, then moved for Cahra so quickly, all she saw was a burst of black. And suddenly he was towering before her, the inverted triangles of his flaming eyes scrutinising her every inch, as if seeking out injury.

'*How do you fare?*'

'I'm fine,' Cahra said softly, his gaze burning into her. 'Are you?'

Could he sense her trepidation? She'd courted death before, but never like this. Staring into Hael's flames, she felt a knot tighten in the middle of her chest.

'*I could not call to you. I found it… troubling.*' Hael tilted his head and paused. '*That is not why you have come.*'

'No,' she confessed, swallowing. Cahra had never lived an ordinary life, but she wondered if this would ever feel normal, with Hael. Or if her insides would stop feeling like they were staging an uprising of their own, never mind Kolyath and Ozumbre's. She inhaled. 'I'm outside Luminaux's gate to Hael'stromia and—'

'*I know,*' Hael said. '*I can sense you.*'

'You can?' she asked, bewildered.

He nodded once, the hard planes of his face softening. '*You are on the cusp of the capital's sands, my abode. The gates, the Key – a formality. Yet the closer you came today, the more I could feel you, your presence.*'

'Oh,' Cahra said in a small voice. 'Do you know why I'm here?'

'*The tri-kingdoms have convened.*' Hael's flaming eyes, which had brightened to a bold ruby, darkened again. '*Why?*'

'Kolyath and Ozumbre captured a Luminaux royal and are blocking that gate to Hael'stromia. I proposed a trade—' She broke off as Hael's eyes blazed a bottomless black, the guttural sound that ripped from him cleaving the darkness.

His tomb shuddered.

'A trade,' she rushed, 'so they would take me to the pyramid and I could free you.' She smiled, trying to project an air of confidence.

For a moment, Hael said nothing. Then Cahra wrinkled her nose, the air thickening, itching her nostrils, as she inhaled its acrid scent. *The smell of burning*. Glancing down, she watched smoke rise above the age-old dust.

'*An exchange, with the two most callous kingdoms in the modern era?*' Hael rasped, desperation in his voice. '*Cahra, you are in mortal danger!*'

She shut her eyes, exhaustion weighing her to the ground. 'I know. It's risky.' Opening them, she saw Hael was watching her with barely checked alarm. 'It'll be okay. Once you're out, everything will be okay. But we need to do the abreption now.'

'*A safeguard,*' he said, comprehending. The idea seemed to placate him.

She nodded. 'I couldn't let them keep the Prince. At least this way, once you're out, you can do your Scion-champion thing.'

At her words, Hael rose in stature, then paused. '*The Prince?*' There was something to his tone, a coldness. The smoke that was pooling at her feet began to eddy faster, like a whirlpool gaining strength. She was barefoot in their vision again, she realised.

'Yes,' Cahra said, rubbing one foot with the toes of the other. The floor was freezing. 'The one who helped me escape Kolyath. I couldn't let him suffer in my stead, not when what they want is the Scion and the Key.'

'*Precisely why I am perturbed,*' Hael argued. '*For if it is you who suffers…*'

'I won't,' she smiled faintly. 'Because you'll be free, to find me.'

They gazed at one another. Finally, Hael nodded, but he looked as if he wanted to strangle someone, and slowly. Before she knew what she was doing, Cahra grabbed his hand.

'It will be okay,' she said again, her tone soothing. The haze-filled air was pricking her lungs, but she didn't let him go. She could feel the agitation amassing in her body, the buildup of red-hot energy that flashed between her nerves and limbs, sensing for any and all threats, because she knew the reality she faced. The realm's three kingdoms' rulers were out there. Steward Atriposte was out there. And Hael was right, this plan of hers had put her in danger, all to save Thierre. But when she looked into Hael's eyes, she felt like she understood him. His last Scion had died and the capital had fallen. Hael feared for her life.

After what she'd seen the last time they performed the abreption, she knew he wouldn't handle losing another Scion well. And if she lost him? Cahra refused to consider it.

But standing around wouldn't get them anywhere. Wrenching her eyes from his face, Cahra cleared her throat, praying the iciness of her feet would draw the heat from her cheeks. It was so damn cold in here!

'Hael, where are my boots?' she complained, shivering.

He laughed, the sound so joyous that for an instant, she could forget about everything brewing outside the city's black gate.

'What is it?'

Lips still twitching with mirth, Hael lifted his arms. '*May I?*'

Confused, she nodded. He swept her from her feet to sit her lightly on the edge of the black stone altar. Then touched the sole of her right foot, tilting it towards her.

'*See,*' Hael whispered, the flames of his eyes soaring.

When the mark walks the path to enter the Nether in life…

Cahra gasped as she peered at what looked to be a tattooed Sigil of the Seers, the dark symbol's eye within a downward-pointing triangle within a circle staring back at her from the ball of her foot. Below it, more new symbols appeared inked upon her skin.

'I don't know these,' she frowned, pointing.

'*The sacred mark. The third omen is upon us.*' Hael inspected the sole of her foot, tracing the outline. '*The first crest is that of the Seers, as you know. The second is your own: the House of the Scion, sovereign to this realm, scribed in the old tongue.*'

'I have my own crest?' Cahra's voice barely rose above a whisper as she gazed at the Sigil of the Seers and the symbols that formed her Imperial insignia. The first was a rectangle, open at the bottom like it housed a little doorway; the second, a flaming red phoenix atop a blackened crown. Together, the three characters made a pyramid in the centre of her sole.

'*Yes, and you shall need it to access this room, my shrine.*' Hael's face grew serious. '*This is the final time we will meet under these circumstances, between the veil and void. When you next see me, it will be once you unseal these doors. In order to do so, you require three things: the Key, your life – and a scarcity of boots.*' Hael attempted an affable smile, but she saw the worry clouding his features. She gave his fingers a playful squeeze.

'I need to be barefoot? Thelaema didn't tell me that. How unlike her,' Cahra joked, trying to lighten the mood. Hael just nodded absently.

She quietened, wanting to stay but knowing she had to go. Who knew how long she had been gone already? But she needed to ask Hael one final question.

'When you're free, will you carry out my instructions, no matter what?'

She took a deep breath. *No matter if I die?*

In the murkiness of his tomb, Hael vowed, '*I will.*' His words were rough, raw, with the same harshness she'd heard in her own voice in Thelaema's mountain caves. The power, the Nether-magick, of the realm's weapon. Silver lightning forked above their heads.

Cahra could almost feel his power coursing through her. She pulled her gaze from the slivers of electricity splaying above them.

'*It is time,*' Hael told her, Cahra nodding and raising her palms to meet his, as before, ignoring the stinging fear of pain she knew would rack her body. His Nether-powers would be her only defence now.

And with that, their abreption began.

-

A minute passed between Cahra's vision with Hael and her return to the earthly plane. In that time, her horse had moved to the midpoint in between Luminaux's army and that of Kolyath and Ozumbre, then halted, waiting.

When Cahra finally cracked her eyes open, her body thrumming with Nether-power as sandy winds tossed her hair, she didn't need to search. She found the Prince instantly.

Thierre.

Steward Atriposte signalled to someone and Thierre was shoved forward, hands bound before him, still bleeding as he staggered towards his family. Towards Cahra.

He's alive.

Cahra descended from the palomino mare.

Eyes narrowed, Hael's black rage rising, Cahra's gaze locked onto Thierre as she scanned, counting body parts and isolating where he was bloody, limping, and what his injuries might be. Overall, his wounds seemed to be non-fatal and she sighed with relief. Thierre was closing the distance between them, not without effort, but still.

Cahra approached, boots silent on the black sands. She just needed to talk to Thierre, to make sure he was really okay, before she gave herself up to Kolyath.

To the Steward, and what she'd been terrified of all these years.

Cahra and Hael had performed the abreption, but the refuge of its peace strained, the panic crowding in, too fast, engulfing her as Cahra's stomach lurched with thoughts of how the Steward might finally put her to death.

Gritting her teeth, she tried to reason with herself. She couldn't afford to lose her grip.

Think! Gemstones. Black diamond, ruby, sapphire, grey musgravite…

Cahra didn't let herself look at the Steward's face.

Instead, she just ran for Thierre.

'Cahra,' he whispered hoarsely, half-falling against her, clutching weakly at her arms. 'I am fine,' he told her, lungs heaving. 'I am fine.'

He was standing, but up close, Thierre looked anything but fine.

'What did they do?' Cahra's words came out like gravel, the thirst for vengeance boiling.

'Cahra,' he repeated, shaking his head groggily, as if realising something was wrong. 'What are you doing? You can't.' Thierre pulled back to look at her. One of his eyes was beaten shut, the other glassy, unfocused. 'You can't—' His blue goldstone eyes…

I can. I have to.

'It'll be okay,' she told him, looking away.

'No,' he said, shaking his head again, wincing. He gripped her shoulders. 'You cannot go.' And stiffened as his one good eye realised Raiden and his Royal Guards were approaching to secure his safety. 'No! NO!' Thierre yelled, reaching for Cahra as she backed away, hands raised, towards the enemy.

'I'm sorry,' she told him as she retreated, Thierre collapsing onto Raiden's shoulders. The Captain stared, grief-stricken, at his Prince, then turned and saluted Cahra, his fist held staunchly over his heart.

Thierre's legs gave way, plunging to the desert sands as he screamed at his saviours. Raiden, Piet, Siarl and Queran attempted to haul him back behind their kingdom's lines.

'*Cahra!*' Thierre bellowed, struggling and failing to fight his own Royal Guards under their combined strength.

Cahra was shaken but couldn't do anything except continue along her current path. The rulers kept their word. They'd set Thierre free.

Now it was up to her. All she had to do was what every beggar in Kolyath did.

Survive.

But it's not simply about surviving, is it?

Cahra's head snapped up. That *voice*, from the caves.

She watched, heart aching, as Thierre was dragged behind the safety of his sister. Sylvie nodded to Cahra, the General's mask slipping as she glowered, lips twisting in a snarl, in the direction of Kolyath and Ozumbre. The direction Cahra was still moving in.

The voice continued. *If survival was your goal, you would've run.*

Cahra tensed. The whole reason she'd made this decision to trade herself for Thierre was because all she'd ever done was run. That had been her answer to everything.

Deep down, you do not want to. You never did.

Cahra's steps slowed, but she didn't stop. She thought defiantly, *So?*

So, you know what must be done. It's perhaps as Thelaema told you.

She didn't respond. Because she remembered what the Oracle had said:

'You have Hael's powers… Put them to good use.'

Will you? After all that they have done, will you let this Steward get away with it? There was a pause. *Or will you simply wait for another child to die?*

Then Cahra spotted Ellian, the beggar boy from Kolyath with the aquamarine eyes, clad in crude armour on Kolyath's front lines. He was small compared to the gaunt men that suffered alongside him. In fact, there were several of them, kids conscripted to be soldiers in a war they'd never had a choice over. Something loosed itself in her, in her throat, her chest.

This time, the Netherworldly voice was her *own*.

It's time to stop running from your responsibilities.

It's not just about living, Cahra realised with clarity. It's not even about Thierre.

It's this. The nightmarish realm they all inhabited.

Kolyath's Steward. Ozumbre's King. Their bloodthirsty Commanders.

It's THEM. Cahra could feel it then, the burning in her eyes. For the first time, the thought crossed her mind. Could she take them down… All of them?

Could she fight Kolyath and Ozumbre's armies with Hael's powers, and win?

Her eyes flashed again to the boy Ellian, appearing to recognise her as she stared. Confusion filled his young face. But he wasn't who she needed to worry about.

She turned her black gaze on the Steward of Kolyath, Atriposte smiling back at her.

This time when Cahra ran, she ran towards the enemy.

CHAPTER 39

Cahra heard the sounds before she saw them – pikes being lowered, bows being pulled tight – as she sprinted towards Hael'stromia's gate. To Steward Atriposte, and King Decimus, and Kolyath and Ozumbre's allied force of 20,000 men. All while Hael's black fury roared within, a Netherworldly force as ferocious and relentless as the Reliquus himself.

Somewhere inside, Cahra knew she should be frightened and she was. But it was hard to find, to feel fear's hesitation, its paralysis, when her overriding sense was of her arms and legs pumping, lungs heaving, as she snaked across the rapidly blackening sands. Even the motion blur of soldiers as she charged didn't give her pause; the enemy's pikemen and archers interspersed with defensive cavalry that wouldn't hesitate to strike her down. Or would they? It was the gamble Cahra was bargaining on, so that she might level the battlefield just a little. That she might give Luminaux's army some kind of fighting chance. Hearten their soldiers. Give them hope. She laughed in spite of herself, recalling Thelaema's words:

The hope is you, child.

So Cahra kept running into danger. Danger would meet her head-on.

She ducked and weaved, zigzagging as arrows began to fall from the dawning sky. Had Atriposte deemed her expendable now, or was this a calculated move? Did he know what powers she possessed, however temporarily? She scanned for Grauwynn.

More importantly, how was she able to strategise while being shot at? Cahra grunted as she dive-rolled out of the way of a storm of arrows.

No, that wasn't the most important thing, she thought firmly. That question was how she was dodging a hail of arrows in the first place when she was the only person on the plain. How exactly she knew how to break Kolyath and Ozumbre's fortified lines without dying. Because unlike Hael, Cahra wasn't immortal. But for this, it didn't matter.

She'd reached the enemy's front.

And, imbued with Hael's powers, she would make them pay.

Destroy.

The voice from the caves. It was here. And it was *hungry* for violence.

The enemy archers hesitated, their gaze fixed on Cahra's glowing eyes, a supernatural war-bringer on the sandy battlefield.

Cahra didn't, levering her great-hammer from across her back and swooping to sail into an airborne somersault. She landed among their pikemen, her hammer's head slamming into the ground with a resonant boom that sent a shockwave through the enemy's front line, rattling armour and weaponry. Soldiers stumbled as Cahra spun, dancing with unbridled power and grace as she and her hammer arced in circles, its head deflecting arrows mid-flight back into Kolyath and Ozumbre's scattering ranks. Around her, everything was chaos, but Cahra moved through it like an unnatural force, her body at one with the fire in her soul.

The iron tang of blood rose in the air.

Kolyath's Commander Sullian bellowed at his archers to keep firing.

She'd done it. She'd broken their line, but that hadn't been the goal.

Marking Steward Atriposte at last, Cahra freed a hand to point to him, her heart a drum marching in time with the rhythm of her hammer's song.

The Steward. He was her goal.

Destroy!

She charged, great-hammer spinning, her body and weapon a symphony of vengeance, her path ahead clear. The Steward would fall.

Cahra swung her hammer with Netherworld strength, vaulting into the air to tackle Steward Atriposte, his mouth ajar as she ripped him from his snowy horse.

His arrogance had no place in the face of her unworldly power.

Rising to her feet, Cahra seized him by the throat, dangling Atriposte in the air as she gradually clamped the vice of her grip shut until his breath faltered, his life force failing, squandered as the man flailed within her deathly grasp. Her lips contorted into a sinister grin.

DESTROY!

The Nether's siren song called, and its melody was mesmerising.

But before she could choose death, an elderly voice choked out her name.

'Cahra!'

She knew that voice. Had heard it every day for years. Every morning, as the old man attempted to rouse her from deepest sleep, and every night, as he wished her pleasant dreams, knowing how much her nightmares haunted her; as well as on and off all day, each day, with every word of encouragement, of praise, for her growth as a burgeoning smith in a kingdom that hated low-borns having a smidgeon of pride, of worth.

Lumsden.

The sight of him, here, alive and on the battlefield, sent her reeling to another time. Their first meeting in Kolyath's dungeons…

–

Cahra had stabbed Atriposte, ruler of the Kingdom of Kolyath, in the neck, and fled.

But not before grabbing the man's dungeon keys. Careening to the end of the room, she flung herself at the gate to the stairwell, shoving key after key into the stubborn lock. PLEASE! *It was no use. The Steward's wrath-filled stomps were approaching.*

I missed the killing spot, *she thought. It was little comfort as the Steward wrenched her shoulder back, hurling her small frame against the freezing ground. A strangled cry escaped her as her ribs cracked against the floor's stones, her eyes watering as she looked at the man. The anger in his eyes, however, vanished as quickly as it came.*

'That was foolish,' the Steward murmured, regaining his composure. 'Your sentence was lenient; six years for petty larceny. Such a trifle, compared with the attempted murder of a sovereign of the realm.' His amber eyes bored into her, flat and unfeeling, as he pressed a pocket square to his bloody neck. 'That is high treason. The penalty is death.'

The air froze in Cahra's lungs. But before the Steward could bellow for his guards, her sharp hearing sensed hushed footsteps – a moment before the handle of a weapon struck the back of Atriposte's head, and his eyes rolled up as he crumpled to the floor.

She looked up, speechless, as an old man appeared, holding a blacksmith's hammer. He extended a wrinkled hand. The beggar's credo rattled through her: Hael won't help us.

But another low-born might.

–

Lumsden. Kolyath's master blacksmith, her mentor. He was here.

Cahra turned, time slowing to something she couldn't comprehend.

Lumsden is here, she thought, and her heart swelled as the old man smiled at her, his eyes of smoky quartz and amethyst shining. The ring of wispy silver hair around his head ruffled in the dead breeze of the desert, his leather apron smudged with coal and pockmarked by singes like it always was, and a wave of comfort, of nostalgia, surged through Cahra. *Lumsden is here and he is okay.*

Then, a split-second later…

He wasn't.

Cahra screamed, the noise louder than anything she'd ever heard, dropping Atriposte to the sands as she leapt for Lumsden, the old man's body collapsing to the earth, his blood spilling, spurting from his chest, Cahra only dimly noting the blood dribbling from her own ears at her Netherworldly scream.

Lumsden.

She couldn't connect the words inside her, couldn't think them, but she knew.

He was dead.

The realisation punched the air from Cahra's lungs and she bent over the old man, horror-stricken and grappling for him as she fought to breathe, her eyes burning with tears as the light in his went out, his body still. Slowly, she raised her head to the one responsible.

Commander Jarett was standing over her, wiping Lumsden's blood from a rapier. The Haellium rapier she'd forged for the Steward.

'Before you have any further notions of grandeur,' Jarett said scornfully, 'I would pause to consider who else you may care for in your kingdom, girl smith.' Another, smaller struggling figure was brought to Lumsden's feet.

Cahra couldn't look away from the blood, Lumsden's blood, soaking the black sands.

But she had to.

Because Ellian, the boy she'd told to go find Lumsden for a job, was next. And behind him, every child soldier, every young apprentice, every trader from her Quadrant in Kolyath.

'And should they not be adequately motivating, perhaps let us add a few new friends.' At Jarett's words, the other Commander, Sullian, signalled and his longbow archers drew, trained on Thierre and his family, just as she'd feared.

Cahra snarled, the ground beneath her kneeling body quaking. She'd been able to dodge Kolyath and Ozumbre's bowmen, but—

Would she be quick enough to outrun a dozen arrows aimed at Luminaux's royals? She remembered Thelaema's words. *Sacrifices must be made.*

Cahra didn't know and it was maddening. But she couldn't risk them to find out. Not Luminaux's royals, Ellian, Kolyath's people or anybody else.

A guttural howl rumbled inside her, threatening to break loose as she dug her fingers into the sand, biting her lip so hard she tasted blood, as she watched Jarett's guards circle the group of smallest soldiers. Kolyath's child soldiers.

Ellian. *Sacrifices must be made.*

'No,' she said, shaking her head. '*No.*' They wouldn't – they *couldn't*—

Then a voice, an elder man she did not know, echoed in her mind:

My girl, the Steward Atriposte has no qualms about killing every person here, every man, woman and child in his kingdom of Kolyath, to ensure that you understand: the punishment for defying the Steward is death. Not just yours, but your people's.

Cahra heard rasping laughter in her head. *To think that you aspired to save that child, only for the boy to grace this very battlefield.*

Her head snapped up. Cahra knew enough of Thelaema's gifts to guess the speaker: Grauwynn, the other High Oracle. He was here, somewhere, in all of this.

And he knew about her helping Ellian. An icy sweat engulfed her body.

What else did he know about her?

You will yield, blacksmith. Or this time, it shall not simply be a purging of the council, it will be Kolyath's reckoning. And the fault will be yours.

He was bluffing, they both were. Atriposte would never surrender his army, Kolyath was obsessed with winning the weapon because of him! This whole *war* was so that Atriposte could control the weapon—

Cahra's breaths were starting to feel dangerously out of control.

Atriposte wanted Hael. Just Hael.

Why do you think your Steward allied with Ozumbre? Decimus and Diabolus leapt at the chance to slay their share of Kolyath soldiers.

No. Cahra shook her head. Atriposte wouldn't…

As if sensing her question, King Decimus of Ozumbre turned his teal eyes on Cahra, the man's irises like gleaming labradorite. But just like the cracked gemstone, when she looked at Ozumbre's ruler, all she saw was something broken, brutal. Something malevolent. He was *worse* than Atriposte, she realised. And Hael's powers sensed it.

The King of Ozumbre would not hesitate to destroy the kingdom of Kolyath – not just Ellian, but everyone from every Quadrant in the land. Decimus and his twin would leave no survivors. A chill slithered down Cahra's spine at the thought.

The Steward had her and he knew it.

It was over. She had lost.

In the minutes Grauwynn had distracted her, Atriposte arose, dusted himself off and drew another weapon. Cahra glanced blankly at the dagger with the mottled blade.

It was one of Lumsden's.

I have lost the battle, but not the war. Not yet. Cahra forced herself to think the words. But the despair, the rancour in her felt otherwise, rattling the ribs of her lungs like a cage. Like a cell. Her eyes lowered to the blood-soaked sands.

That's Lumsden's too. On the sand. On her hands.

She closed her eyes. Grief burned behind her eyelids.

So, back to option one. There was no other choice.

Atriposte pointed the tip of his blade at Cahra. 'Kneel,' he commanded her, the word laced with cruelty, an undertone to match the vicious sneer that crawled across his face.

And then the Steward paused.

Her wide eyes flashed to the male High Oracle. Did Grauwynn know?

Did Atriposte recognise her at last?

Fighting her thirst for vengeance, for Lumsden, before Steward Atriposte took his own, Cahra bent and placed her head and hands to the matte sands, prostrating herself.

I will take them to the Reliquus. Because it's like I said to Thelaema:

With any luck, Hael will escape from his tomb and rip their heads off.

When Cahra was finally permitted to rise from the coarse ground, she smiled. Then Jarett's Kingdom Guards grabbed her arms, hauling her roughly to her feet and through a crowd of soldiers to Hael'stromia's gnarled gate.

Atriposte jerked his chin at the bars. 'The Key.'

Jarett's own sword was at the ready as Cahra slowly fished the Key from her pocket, Kolyath's guards shoving her up against the gate.

She exhaled through gritted teeth, imagining Hael skewering them all.

The Key snug in her palm, Cahra pushed the inscribed eye of the black relic to the strange warding mechanism of the lock before her. As a smith, she knew a little about how keys and locks worked, but where *this* Key's pin was – or if it had one – she had no idea. The only sense she could make of it was its etched centre, the eye, which was most likely to be where the Key would fit, she decided. So that's what she inserted into the lock.

Gears whirred and clanked, the noise reverberating in her head, amplified by Hael's elevated hearing. She yanked the key free and stepped back, watching as the gate swung not inwards, but inched into the air, the dire spikes that penetrated the sands yielding to gradual extraction. Cahra stared as the spikes at the gate's base – a man's height by the time they'd lifted – continued to rise higher and higher into the air, the gate finally risking a gap big enough for someone to slip through. After four centuries, Hael'stromia was open.

'At last...' There was reverence in Atriposte's voice as his amber eyes beheld it, taking his first steps into the fallen capital, King Decimus of Ozumbre at his heels.

Jarett snatched the Key and pointed his sword at Cahra, gesturing to the faraway black pyramid. 'Walk.'

Cahra glared at the order but complied.

If I had just killed Jarett first... She couldn't finish the sentence.

I could kill him right now, Cahra thought as she stalked towards the palatial temple. Hael's speed, his strength, still flowed inside her. She could easily knock Jarett from his feet, wrench the sword from his hands and sever the man's head, then hurl it at the Steward, because he would be next. After everything those high-born tyrants had done to everyone in Kolyath, Lumsden would be avenged. And so would she.

But to do that, she'd be sacrificing the very people she was trying to keep safe. Kolyath and Ozumbre's forces still numbered 20,000, which was more than she'd seen Hael fight in that vision during the second abreption. She may have some of his powers, but she was no ultimate weapon. She sighed. For now, she let Jarett command her.

It was the only thing she could do, the only thing she could hold onto. Until she got to Hael. You may have won the battle, she thought darkly at Atriposte, Jarett, Decimus.

But Hael and I will be the ones to steal your war.

Moments later, as Cahra was taken away, a horn sounded, and Commander Diabolus ordered Kolyath and Ozumbre to attack.

CHAPTER 40

Cahra crept quietly through Hael'stromia, her senses, her body, primed as though she was awaiting an ambush. The all-encompassing silence jangled her nerves.

Once a flourishing city, Hael'stromia was now a wasteland. Atriposte and his men edged past another ancient relic of a building, a palpable heaviness to the air. Not surprising, given the years of nothingness here, she thought. But no plants, no weeds? And no animals, not even the momentary flap of wings. As if an invisible shield hovered low over the city, keeping it from the reaches of the outside realm. Because apart from the capital's buildings – like nothing she had ever seen, the black limestone structures as vast as Luminaux's palace, projecting both power and indestructibility – the only evidence of bygone life were the chaotically strewn logs that had long since petrified into stone.

What had the city been like, before all had been lost? She couldn't imagine a time where the kingdoms of Kolyath, Luminaux and Ozumbre weren't trying to kill each other. There'd been too much bloodshed as it was, she thought, swallowing back all thoughts of Lumsden and the tears, the grief, that threatened to spill from her like so much blood.

Lumsden's blood. Cahra inhaled a shuddering breath.

'Keep moving!' One of Steward Atriposte's guards manhandled Cahra forward and she bit down on the inside of her cheek to keep from turning and snapping the rat's neck, though she could feel Hael's powers fading. The evil rulers had left their horses by the gate, and she would have laughed at their caution except she too recalled the stories of raiders looking to break in and rob Hael'stromia of its treasure, only to die freakishly, gruesomely... Or so the tales were peddled, rumours to stoke the fires of each kingdom's obsession with it. But now that Cahra was here, walking the sands of the abandoned capital, she couldn't help but sense it too: the latent warning. It was wise to tread softly in this place.

The stench of death was unmistakable.

However, there was one figure who walked without fear, although she couldn't see the person's face. But she knew those robes, even if the colour differed, the man's white not Wyldaern's time-worn black. It had to be Grauwynn, Thelaema's Oracle counterpart.

Which meant her options had shrunk. If Grauwynn was with them, he'd be able to communicate anything she did, any stepping out of line, to the guards who held Ellian and the others hostage, as well as to Kolyath and Ozumbre's armies. Their archers.

One wrong move, and the boy, her people and Luminaux's royals would all die.

So she had to be smart and suffocate the urge to fight. Wait until she found Hael. Cahra ground a heel into the soft black sand that carpeted the capital, pushing her raw anger down and into her boots, the sensation chafing at her.

They continued in the direction of the capital's palatial temple by way of a maze of snaking streets, past more imposing buildings. She squinted, trying to guess their purposes: barracks, treasury, archives? Each was splendid in its own right; one with slate-grey basalt that glistened in the weakened sun, the next carved of black marble with silvery streaks and adorned with soaring columns, a mosaic of inky rosettes and gargoyles with asp-like heads. Cahra glanced at the epigraph above the entrance, its ancient symbols a mystery—

And froze, staring at those marks. She knew one symbol, as she'd seen it on her foot. Hael had said it was the character for 'house'.

Then Cahra turned, suddenly realising the dark building had a twin, but its opposite: a neighbour of shimmering white, the veneer iridescent. The only white building she'd seen.

She put a hand to her chest, a hollowness welling inside the longer she stared at it.

Two opposing houses, she thought, frowning.

But why?

Jarett prodded Cahra forward with his sword, the tip piercing through her leathers.

She hissed, rolling a shoulder as the sting of the blade throbbed at her back, knowing he'd drawn blood.

Finally, Cahra and her captors entered the approach avenue to the colossal pyramid, the long road flanked on each side by a row of what looked to be dark altars like those in Hael's tomb. That itself was enough to give her pause, let alone the two obelisks inscribed from top to bottom with more ancient symbols. But none of those things were what held people's attention in a stranglehold, she realised. That honour was all Hael's, the monumental statue erected before the obelisks gazing down at them all, his likeness uncanny. Whoever had carved such a grand statue had even attempted to emulate Hael's eyes. *Were they fire opals?* Kolyath and Ozumbre's rulers stared. This warning was significantly less latent.

Fingers snapped in front of her and Cahra bared her teeth at Jarett, as Atriposte waved a hand at the double doors beyond the statue. The Kingdom Guards closest to Cahra angled their weapons at her; too many weapons. A sigh burned deep in her lungs.

Atriposte's gaze cut to her. 'Open it,' he barked.

Cahra stepped carefully to the pyramid, the pylons of the gateway set into its stones. Jet curlicues of sand twisted, grains suspended in the air, as if reaching for who lay inside, and she gasped. Waiting for someone to give her the Key, she held out a shaky hand.

Jarett slapped the relic down and Cahra hissed at the Commander.

She did as before, pressing the eye of the Key to the lock. The same clattering and clanking sounded, the doors to the palatial temple heaving open, sand and dust whorling. Blackness awaited them.

As did Hael. He was in the pyramid, somewhere, the thought giving Cahra comfort. Moments later, torches passed between Kolyath and Ozumbre's guards and she was shoved head-first inside.

Beyond the entrance was a cavernous hall with towering pillars that led to tunnels, passageways that proceeded both upwards and downwards to where Cahra could sense Hael, deep below the surface, in what she could only assume were the catacombs.

'Which direction?' Jarett's frog-like eyes glared at her as the path before them forked.

King Decimus spoke. 'We should part ways to search.' Cahra saw it in the Ozumbre King's eyes: he wanted the weapon just as much as Atriposte.

'As you wish,' Atriposte said airily. 'The girl blacksmith, being a Kolyath subject, will remain in the custody of my guards.'

Cahra resisted the urge to swallow, catching a flicker of mirth on the Steward's lips. She could only guess what he had planned.

Hael isn't far. Now that she was inside the pyramid, she understood what he'd meant about sensing her. She could feel their tether, like a hand tugging her along, into the temple and towards Hael's tomb, the temperature dropping as they descended. *He isn't far.*

But she wasn't going to tell the Steward that.

Decimus nodded to Atriposte, Grauwynn accompanying the King as he departed. Cahra watched them go. So it was Ozumbre that had the High Oracle's support? Interesting. And if Grauwynn was gone, then—

'I may still command the Oracle, if that, perchance, is what you are contemplating.' Atriposte flicked his wrist at her, as if dismissing such a tedious exchange. 'Do remember your fellow low-borns, will you not?' The Steward turned, shifting under his Kolyath battle regalia.

Incensed didn't begin to cover how Cahra felt, but she managed to control the impulse to strangle him yet again. Instead, she eyed Atriposte's regal armour.

'Ill-fitting, is it?' Then, smirking, she led them in the direction of Hael's tomb, her eyes lighting the dark.

–

As cautiously as she moved, Cahra couldn't stop the motes of dust that stirred from the triangular tiles of the similarly arched passages. Whoever had constructed this building had gone to great lengths to preserve its style. Every feature, every flourish, was an incorporation of the shapes she'd used the night she'd designed the pommel insert of Thierre's longsword: triangles, circles and eyes – eyes everywhere.

Not to mention her crest, the near-rectangle signifying 'house', and black crown with a red phoenix, both of which now graced the sole of her right foot, and adorned each room, etched into the pillars and reliefs.

Cahra kept moving, every tread of her boots leading her down, down into the underbelly of the pyramid, each step bringing her closer to Hael. She counted the minutes until she could release him from his tomb. Their next step would be ridding Kolyath of its Steward and Commanders, even Ozumbre's King, if necessary. Then Grauwynn…

'Now where?' Jarett's voice rankled her, and she scowled at the man.

They'd arrived at a T-shaped split, each passage looking equally daunting despite the flicker of torches around her.

If she could just split Jarett's Kingdom Guards, then—

Pressure amassed in Cahra's temples and she fought to stay upright at the vision Grauwynn was sending her: Ellian, vulnerable, an axe poised above the boy's hand.

Indulge me. What good is an apprentice without fingers?

No. Cahra clamped her own hands over her mouth, stifling a sob.

Be mindful of your next course of action, blacksmith. Grauwynn's voice paused, letting the words sink in. *This is your final warning.*

Trembling, Cahra took a step to the left, her words echoing over and over in her mind, as she wrestled her panic to stay calm. *Hael isn't far now.*

– –

Cahra's limbs were growing heavy, Hael's gifts waning with each step. After no food or water, the hours without rest began to eat away at her strength. She'd missed her chance, she thought, and now there was no way she'd stop Atriposte or Jarett alone. She needed Hael.

Thankfully, it looked as though she'd found him.

Descending through the pyramid, down ramp upon ramp, they finally neared the conclusion of a twisting passage. And at its end…

Twin hulking doors, forged from the same eerie metal of the gates, towered before her, vanishing into the blackness above. Cahra raised her head, sweat beading along her hairline after the gruelling trek, her face and leathers streaked with the dust of centuries past.

She touched one of the door's handles, the coiled ring icy against her skin, and stilled. Slowly, Cahra brought an ear, then an eye, to where the doors met, not knowing what she'd find but feebly hoping all the same. She listened. Waited. And felt – a breeze.

There's a crack between the doors, like in my visions of Hael's tomb.

Stomach leaping to her chest, she hurriedly pulled back, an eye on that slender crack. A sliver of red flickered in the minuscule gap.

Cahra cried out, throwing both hands against the enormous doors, the flush of relief overwhelming her, as she realised finally – *finally* – she had made it. She was here, this was Hael's tomb. And she was moments away from freeing him. Her plan had worked!

Joy swelled inside her and she turned, unable to hide the elation on her face.

A sudden sharpness stole Cahra's breath, a blade piercing her flesh without warning. She blinked and staggered back in surprise, a searing-hot blaze of pain contorting her face as Atriposte pulled his rapier free. The world tilted on its axis, her vision blurring as her wound threatened to topple her.

'You idiot.' Cahra panted, gripping her abdomen with both hands, as if that would stymie the blood pouring from her stomach; the Steward had managed to stab her below the mail of her plate vest. 'I must walk the path to enter the Nether *alive*.' She croaked the words through gritted teeth and stumbled back against the doors to Hael's tomb.

The Steward pressed the Key into her bloody hand and rammed it into the lock-like seal nestled in the metalwork of the doors. The mechanics of gears began whirring.

'Oh, I am keenly aware,' Atriposte replied. 'Carry on, then. I shall wait right here.' He glanced at his pocket watch. 'You may wish to hurry along, though. With that injury – well, you shall not have very long.' The Steward squared his shoulders, patiently waiting to claim the weapon himself.

Could it happen? If Cahra died, could another ruler control Hael?

Groaning, she sunk to the tiles, straining to unbuckle her belt so she could strap it around her mid-section. The doors were unsealing slowly, too slowly, and she didn't know if Hael could do anything for her now, but at least he would finally be free.

There was only one thing left to do.

Cahra bent awkwardly where she was bleeding to prise off her boots and socks, fumbling as the puddle of blood grew beneath her. Raising her head, she looked at Atriposte.

The Steward, the ruler of Kolyath.

Last time, she'd had a shiv in her hand, and she'd failed. Cahra wouldn't fail again. 'You don't recognise me, do you?'

The Steward's amber eyes regarded her with amusement. 'That I do, girl blacksmith.' He looked her up and down with disdain. 'Jarett always said you were a bitter thorn.'

Shockingly, the man's words didn't touch her.

'No, you really don't,' she murmured. 'I always wondered how, why. The hair, the dirt, maybe? I guess it doesn't matter any more. We're here now.' Cahra writhed, grimacing. It wasn't hard to use the pain of her wound to colour her features, her movements. She shifted the placement of her hands, as though she sought better pressure. 'And I will remind you of exactly who I am.'

She coughed, shivering. The man was right. She didn't have long at all.

Cahra let one hand tumble limply beside her, on the opposite side of her breastplate, where Thierre's people had reinforced her old smithing vest and added stitching for pockets. Or rather, for concealed weapons. She would miss Thierre, his people of Luminaux.

But she wouldn't miss the Steward. Not this time.

Cahra thumbed Lumsden's gold dagger from its sheath, the handle's metalwork and raised details pressed against her clammy skin. She prayed that the old man had found peace.

That she might find it too.

Guide me, Hael…

Cahra exhaled and, in one fluid movement, raised her hand and threw, the dagger slicing through the air, a streak of gold in the dark. Time seemed to slow as the blade spun, and she watched it, her heart gradually flagging as the blade plunged into Atriposte's throat with a sickening thud, the shock clear in his wide, disbelieving eyes.

'My name is Cahra. I am the girl who tried to kill you in the dungeons ten years ago for being the monster you are. For sending children to war. For low-borns dying on your streets while your court laughed, drinking wine and eating cakes. For torturing and killing your own, in public, all for fun.' She sighed, the air in her lungs feeling thinner, emptier, and watched Atriposte's blood flee him in a scarlet torrent, his Kingdom Guards rooted to the ground as they stood uncertain, weapons half-raised. Should they fight or flee?

Their indecision spurred her on. 'I never died. But I've watched plenty of others die. Because of *you*.' She clambered to sit up, her agony and exhaustion fighting for dominance. Her vision was getting hazier and, in the quiet, she heard footsteps in the distance.

King Decimus was coming, his Royal Guards with him.

It had to be now. *Now!* A voice, Cahra's own voice inside her, cried.

With her last ounce of Hael's powers, she *pushed*, rushing Atriposte to grab the handle of Lumsden's dagger, feeling a jolt of savage satisfaction as she plunged the knife in to the hilt.

Recalling Atriposte's words to her child self.

'*The penalty is death*,' Cahra echoed back to him, her last dregs of energy spent, her eyes burning. Not with Hael's Nether-magicks, but from a decade of uncried tears.

Then she wheezed, locking eyes with Jarett, the whites of his own bulging with fear.

'You're next,' she whispered to him. *For Lumsden*.

The words had barely left her lips when a wave of dizziness struck so hard it sent her sprawling sideways to the unforgiving ground.

The footsteps had arrived.

'What trickery is this?' King Decimus said, glaring between her and Atriposte's body. Grauwynn followed, something silver flashing in his hand before vanishing, like the smirk on the High Oracle's wrinkled face. Precious moments passed.

Had Grauwynn seen where to arrive, after the Steward had been slain?

Decimus sighed. 'Well, since the killing has begun.' He unsheathed his sword, advancing on Kolyath's Commander.

'Sister kingdom sire…' Jarett backed a step, eyes whipping to the Steward's guards. 'What are you doing? Seize him!'

'Alliances run counter to my disposition,' Decimus said, swinging his bastard sword. 'Blood oaths, however…' The Ozumbre King smiled, then signalled to his own men.

Kolyath and Ozumbre's guards brandished their weapons at each other.

Cahra tried and failed to lift her head from the floor. She felt so cold—

How long would it take Hael to get free? Could he even break free if she had no physical hope of walking the path that would allow her to somehow enter his shrine alive?

'We had an agreement!' Jarett cried, sword clattering as he blocked Decimus' cut.

The King's grin was sharp as an assassin's blade as he looked at the Steward's corpse. 'It has since expired.' Then, in a graceful arc, he slashed Jarett's throat.

The Commander fell.

Cahra glanced around, her vision clouding, narrowing, her desperation growing, when she noticed her puddle of blood, a well of it running beneath the double doors to Hael's tomb. She squinted as that pool slowly began to drain.

As the final turn of cogs on gears sounded and the great doors of the weapon's shrine slowly cracked to yawn apart.

As the seething silence was broken by a cavernous growl from the depths of the room Cahra had unlocked.

'What is that?' Decimus snapped, whirling on Grauwynn.

'Didn't tell?' Cahra tried to laugh. Blood spattered onto her leathers. 'Bad Oracle.' Her eyes rolled to the King of Ozumbre. 'Meet... the weapon...'

Only then did she see Grauwynn's face, the High Oracle looking upon her with a cold disdain that jarred so much against Thelaema's warmth.

You will die, and Hael will return to me, Grauwynn's voice boomed into her mind.

Then the Oracularus vanished – one second there, the next, gone as if he never had been, the only evidence a blinding, fading light.

A tempest of ash and smoke burst from between Hael's shrine doors, lashing through the gap in a black tornado of cosmic particles before materialising at Cahra's feet to absorb the ghastly sight of her dying body on the floor. The Reliquus rose to face King Decimus and his speechless assembly of enemy guards.

Then he *roared*, the passage quaking with the wrath of a vengeful god.

Hael gathered Cahra into his arms and stood her on two feet at his room's entrance, before retreating with her into the darkness.

Hael. The thought burbled up from somewhere, hopeful, grateful. But she couldn't feel his arms around her any more, she realised.

And she wasn't in Hael's shrine.

She could see Lumsden's smiling face, lined with years of untold stories, before her. Lumsden, the old man who'd taken her in and saved her from a short life and a quick death at the hands of the Steward and his dungeons. Lumsden, who'd taught her how to craft a sword, then any other weapon, giving her the freedom to explore her gifts. Lumsden, who'd tried to teach her to control her emotions, so she'd be equipped to live in Kolyath's unjust kingdom. Lumsden, who fed the Quadrant's strays. Lumsden, who forged belt buckles, sewing needles, kitchen knives, for people who had nothing, and never asked for more. Lumsden, Kolyath's master blacksmith. A good, kind man. A father figure to her.

He was dead. Gone. It should have undone her.

And yet.

All her life, Cahra had feared the dark, because it had been her cell. But as she floated, after all her time with Hael in the darkness of his shrine, Cahra understood.

She could let it go, if she wanted. And she did want to, to surrender and pass beyond the veil and into death's void, as Lumsden had.

Except…

She knew that voice. That sweet, unearthly voice, rising with unfettered panic.

'*Cahra!*'

She wasn't ready to let go of him, that voice that kept her tethered. She'd never be ready to say goodbye.

So Cahra held on, clinging to Hael. His darkness would bring her home.

PART FOUR

'Then shall Hael rise again'

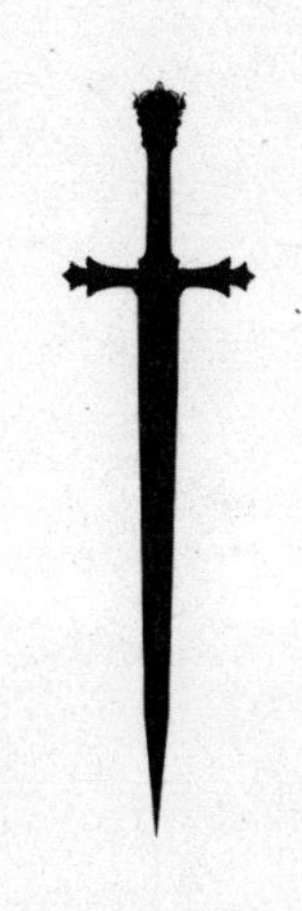

CHAPTER 41

Through a haze of pain and anguish, Thierre watched his people battle fiercely on all sides. His father had dismounted his horse, arming sword and shield glinting under the early morning's rays, Commander Tyne, the King's previous Captain of the Royal Guards, expertly defending him. To their right, Thierre's sister was a brutal, whirling blade, the General letting a foe's cut trap her sword before arcing her buckler behind the man's head and knocking him to the ground, then goring him, off and swinging to deflect the next attack. Those attacks kept on coming, Hael'stromia's sands lightening from their black to the earthy brown of the Wilds with each blood-spattered step Luminaux conceded.

Thierre's people, fighting, bleeding. Dying. Helpless amidst the battle's carnage, he could only bear witness to their struggle.

Through a cough wracked with pain, he dragged an abandoned shield over his head, barely protecting himself from another volley of arrows raining from the forces at the gate. How long could Luminaux hold out against the might of not one, but two skilled armies? Thierre grimaced, hastening to wipe the copper taste of blood from his mouth.

'Thierre!' Raiden's wild cry pierced the air, the Captain's gaze darting frantically in search of his Prince – finally spotting the battered body that was Thierre's current state. Thierre's own Captain had not drifted far, but it was clearly enough to leave Raiden and his guards feeling anxious. With a weak gesture, Thierre signalled to Raiden that he was alive and well. In truth, his condition was in grim contrast to that reassurance.

Cahra. She had exchanged places with Thierre and gone in his stead to face Atriposte, alone. And his father, Luminaux's King – and Tyne, Raiden, Sylvie, the Seers, all of them – had let it happen. Thierre had no energy to be enraged, but he fumed, anger teeming inside as he recalled the look on Cahra's face as she departed, the fatalistic surety in her features. That this, her sacrifice, was required of her. It made him want to scream.

He had. But all his people had done was drag him away.

Thierre's despair was enough to push him face down into the dirt and keep him there. He clenched his teeth, the crushing pain in his mangled body throbbing with every pulse of his blood. And yet…

Grauwynn. He knew the High Oracle's name, now, for all the good that it did. If only there was time for Thierre to prise something of relevance from his fuddled memory. Torture did so little to motivate lucid recall.

Did he see Grauwynn during his painful stumble towards his father? He could not say.

Exhausted and motionless, Thierre's attention was drawn to the momentary lull, the absence of arrows rattling against his shield, and he turned in time to mark the reason why. Commander Diabolus, the head of Ozumbre's Royal Army and King Decimus' twin brother, had entered the battlefield and was strolling arrogantly toward them, sword raised.

Towards his father, Thierre realised. Towards the King of Luminaux.

Thierre strained to stand, to haul himself to his feet, but he struggled under the weight of his heavy shield. It tumbled from his grasp as he groaned, reeling, then tripped and fell onto a pile of butchered bodies. His kingdom's soldiers.

Finding the handle of the shield again, he looped his hand beneath it and pulled, hard. After days without food and water, with more wounds than he could count, Thierre was spent. Defeat welled in him, blurring his only seeing eye with tears.

I cannot help Father.

I cannot help. Not him, nor Cahra. I cannot help anyone.

One more volley and he was done for, Thierre knew, sprawled on the ground, exposed. He only hoped that Ozumbre would not rain death upon their own Commander. But he also knew better than to assume anything with them.

So, Thierre resigned himself to where he had fallen, like Hael'stromia before him, and waited for his Royal Guards as his single working eye drooped closed. In the cold grip of guilt and helplessness, a part of him questioned whether he deserved to live.

But when shaking hands roused him, it was not Raiden's face that swam into view.

Wyldaern. 'Thierre,' the Seer said, her voice frantic. 'I cannot find Thelaema!'

He raised his head. And that was when Thierre saw his father.

CHAPTER 42

'*Cahra!*'

Fear permeated Hael's voice, a panic Cahra had never heard in him before. Her head lolled as she strained to look up at him, breaths shallow.

'Hael.' Cahra's vision dimmed again, but she struggled to sit up from the floor.

'No,' he said, cradling her head as he stroked her hair. 'You must rest.'

'I must *live*,' Cahra retorted, wincing as she peeled her hand from her stomach, her fingers slick with blood. She looked into Hael's eyes – his real, flaming eyes before her, as his steadfast, warrior's arms held her tight. Had she done it? Was he finally free?

'You will.' Slowly, Hael lifted the chain mail below her breastplate.

She gasped at the pain. Atriposte had thrust his sword under the metal links to stab her, then Ozumbre's King had claimed her revenge, and Lumsden's, by killing Commander Jarett. But there was a problem. Cahra knew what stomach wounds did. How they ended.

By the tight look to Hael's face, so did he. 'Healing. *Now*,' was all he ground out.

Cahra tried to reach for him, but her hand, too heavy, fell away.

Hael's lips hardened into a pinched line. 'Cahra. *Cahra!*'

She felt so sleepy… It was like she could hear his voice, but he was drifting from her as the cold shock paralysed her limbs. The last thing she saw before her eyes fluttered closed was Hael dissolving into smoke. And that sound…

Roaring. No, she thought. *Wailing*. Hael was hurting—

Agony wracked Cahra as her stomach wound scorched, burning like glowing coals, before a hot and cold sensation crept from her toes to the tips of her fingers. She was slipping, sinking somewhere lightless. Water… *Water?*

She was floating. On a gently lapping river of night.

Am I dead? Or just unconscious?

Either way, she should have her wits. Cahra tried to focus, but in this vision-like place, overwhelming exhaustion accompanied her thoughts.

So nearly dead then. Now what? She tried to move, to roll from her back, to swim, but her body wasn't having it. Frustrated, she exhaled, trying to think. *Hael?*

She waited, but no answer came from him.

Cahra was alone.

She wasn't sure what to do as she waited for – what? For Hael's magick to work, while she floated down a dreamscape river? Cahra glanced to one side, flinching as she saw the river was on fire, black flames licking at the riverbank.

Where were these mystical waters taking her? Why was she here? *Where* was here? *What was happening?*

Right now, Cahra knew Hael would be doing everything in his powers to save her life. The question was, what was *she* doing?

No.

The voice came to her from nowhere, and even in Cahra's weakened, weightless state, she jumped, spluttering in the unearthly fire-water.

The question is: what do you want?

Cahra's thoughts stilled, if only briefly. It was a question she'd never dared to think, never dared to ask herself. Such pondering was for spoilt high-borns, not the likes of her.

But then, she technically wasn't a low-born any more. She sighed.

Still running, I take it?

Cahra's face darkened. Okay, yes, she'd avoided the question, she thought, scowling. She didn't know how to answer, given she'd gone from poor and expendable, to the realm's Imperial sovereign in a heart-beat when she'd become the Scion. Duty came first now, right?

It was just like she'd said in Luminaux. She'd never had a choice in her life before. Now someone was asking what she wanted?

Then it occurred to her. *And who are you?*

Still running. The voice lilted with amusement. She'd never heard the voice before, that she knew, so it wasn't Grauwynn or Thelaema. This was someone – *something* – new.

Cahra swallowed. *Fine.* She squinted her eyes shut, forcing herself to concentrate. *Want, want... What do I want?*

To stop running from my responsibilities, she thought.

The voice chuckled. *That is the Oraculine talking, her projection of your duties.*

Ugh. Cahra rolled her eyes. *Peace in the realm?*

This time, the voice laughed outright. *Clever. But no.*

Cahra was starting to get annoyed. *Seers, what then?* She racked her brain to come up with something big, something vital. What had she missed out on, in her life?

What had disappointed her, broken her, as a child? Stunted her in its painful absence? What had Thierre and his family, who seemed so close, experienced that she hadn't?

There was only one thing. One thing she would regret never pursuing, if she died now. One thing she'd wanted to hold on for. And had, for a few minutes, before here.

Eyelids still closed, she breathed, summoning the only word, the only image she could think of as Hael's face took shape in her mind's eye. A single word escaped from Cahra's lips.

'Love,' she whispered.

A dark figure rose before Cahra in the rippling water, and bowed.

'*Then your journey on the River Tenebri is at its end,*' the figure said, aloud this time. '*Do give my regards to Andruit, won't you?*'

–

As Cahra finally began to awaken, she felt it: the slowing blood of her gored stomach, congealing at the site of her injury. Her skin and tissue, each strand threading and weaving itself back together, the pain dulling to a distant thrum to disappear just like her sword wound, as if no puncture had ever existed. Lifting her head, she was stunned to find she could move, sit up, maybe even stand, feeling stronger than expected. Hauling herself gingerly to her feet, Cahra looked around in silent disbelief.

And trembled as her hopeful eyes met Hael's.

Swirling like a benevolent windstorm, he'd transformed from his smoky cloud into himself again. But gone was his tattered Seers' robe, replaced by a black floor-length coat, collared and narrow at the waist, with hems that fractured into flame-like slits. From his hair, inky, velveteen and shining as fiercely as his firelit eyes, to the dewy moonstone of his bare feet as his coat grazed the tiles, Hael was a vision. His wine-coloured eyes, softly blazing, beheld Cahra. She could only do the same.

'Do not fear,' Hael told her. 'This room, this shrine, is our hallowed domain. As of now, none can enter except you and I.'

She just nodded. Hael's voice had changed, maybe with the corporeality of his form. The wraithlike tenor wasn't as pronounced, which made sense, given he'd been behind the veil in their visions. But she surprised herself by finding she missed his Netherworldly tone.

All traces of softness left Hael's face, seemingly at the look on hers. 'Are you hurt?' He fell to his knees, hoisting the mail below her breastplate to peer at the site of her wound, invisible to her eyes. Hael's gaze bore into hers, cheekbones sharp with unreleased breath.

'No,' she said, unable to help the broad smile that broke across her face. 'The opposite.'

Something loosened in Hael's features. His fires, a moment ago raging, alight with alarm and dread, had banked, rolling softly like the waves of that mysterious black river. His grip on her relaxed, affirmation of her presence, her survival. That she was here, with him. That she was okay.

Hael rose to his feet then, his expression hardening as his gaze swept to the tunnels, pale lips curling back to reveal his brilliant fangs, so white in the darkness.

'They will pay, each and every one of them, for hurting you,' he said, his voice low and lethal.

He turned to leave and, instinctively, she reached for him.

And felt…

An electrifying surge of heat, like standing one step too close to a white-hot forge, its embers radiant and crackling with molten energy. The sensation was potent – a bolt, a jolt – a spark that ignited something deep in her core, setting her soul ablaze. In that singular, defining moment, she felt a sensation more intense, more profound, than she ever had.

It felt like…

Being undeniably, exhilaratingly *alive*.

Cahra and Hael stood, staring at one another in the darkness.

Hael's face was too blank, too carefully composed as he whispered to her, 'I must go.'

'Wait,' Cahra pleaded, lost for words. 'I…'

She looked at Hael, and the realisation began to crystallise inside her mind, clear and brilliant as a rare diamond.

Why she ran from Thierre. Because no matter how much she thought she'd desired the Prince, it would have been a huge mistake. And it would have cost both of them, deep down. She knew they could never be, even if she was a royal now. She'd said goodbye to Thierre not for her sake, but to spare him future heartbreak.

Because while she did care for the Prince, her own heart yearned for someone else.

Thierre wasn't who she wished to be with.

The answer was staring straight at her, in the form of a man with fire for eyes, patient and hopeful as he waited for her to speak.

'Hael,' she said, exhaling his name like a wish.

Slowly, gently, Cahra took his hand.

CHAPTER 43

Thelaema retched, her body yielding what little food had touched her stomach to the sands. It had been an age since she had attempted teleportation. And yet there was no time to waste, because she felt it: her connection to the All-seeing flowing from a trickle to a torrent, as the dam that had curtailed the source of her Oraculine's magicks evaporated at last.

In the garden below the Reliquus' statue, seedlings emerged from the blackened dirt, clear signs of life to indicate that Cahra had succeeded. Hael was free.

However, with her High Oracle's powers came the insight that she was not alone. There was one other. And theirs was a reunion four centuries in the making.

Thelaema braced herself and inhaled, the capital's desert air parching her lungs before she pushed off against the obelisk outside Hael'stromia's pyramid, the palatial temple open. She looked to the row of empty pedestals that bordered the approach avenue, knowing Hael's hounds would soon arrive.

But the Reliquus was not her purpose here, Thelaema reminded herself.

Finally, as she had seen he would, her High Oracle counterpart descended the steps, their home as Oraculine and Oracularus of the Order of Descry, 399 years before. Fleetingly, Thelaema wondered if Grauwynn had been granted the same vision from the All-seeing that had led her to him now. If he had some sort of plan.

She supposed it did not matter. They had both lived long enough.

Before she left the battle, the Nether had bestowed upon her crucial information: the person behind Hael'stromia's fall. It was veiled, though she had not known it at the time. Veiled by her very counterpart. Her partner. Veiled by Grauwynn, from her.

He was the orchestrator of it all. But his motivations remained a mystery.

She would learn the reason for his heresy.

Grauwynn noted her at last, pausing. Thelaema stepped from behind the obelisk and directly into his path, in the centre of the forsaken road to their former temple.

'Grauwynn.' A greeting, and a warning.

'Thelaema,' he said softly.

She could garner nothing from his impenetrable face, his voice as neutral as the taupe pallor of his skin, as he stood towering above her on those steps. They stared at one another with the same periwinkle eyes. The colour of the Seers.

'Is that surprise?' Thelaema pondered. 'Or stoicism? I never could tell.'

'Nothing shall surprise us shortly,' Grauwynn replied, lowering the hood of his robe. It was not their garb, that of the Order of Descry, their robes black as these hallowed sands. This was something different, light instead of dark, however shabby. Thelaema squinted at it. The fact that it was shabby, worn, was odd. Which god did it belong to? How long had he worn it?

Was this why they had been blocked from one another's foresight?

'I suppose. In which case, cease your dallying and peddle whatever lies you must.' Formidable words. She would not dull them.

It was simple to disguise her peering at his attire with peering at her fellow Oracle. Was there nothing left of her former consort? The idea of him renouncing their beliefs…

Grauwynn chuckled. 'How I have missed you,' he confessed, a hint of something like remorse betraying his gaze, his wrinkled face echoing the sentiment. 'Your shrewd mind.' Then he switched tack, pressing against the gatehouse to her thoughts.

Shall we continue in the old ways?

Thelaema shoved back, prepared but still surprised he should attempt it.

'Four centuries, no word, and you wish to communicate in the old ways?' Thelaema's words were acid, burning on her tongue, as she said, 'Why do you ally with Atriposte and Decimus? They do not respect our ways, our prophecy, nor the All-seeing's chosen Scion. The one that *I* have been shaping, safeguarding, all while you have been—'

Thelaema halted, full of scorn. 'Astray,' she finished, waving her hand at his wayward off-white robe.

'Have you spoken your fill?' Grauwynn straightened, pinning her with a stare that once upon a time might have given her pause. No longer.

She retorted, 'Of course not!'

'Then in the time we have left before the All-seeing recommences from the source, would you prefer your sweet lies, or the truth?'

'What manner of question is that?' She moved to march on him, and it happened, the gentle, urgent tug of her Oracle's intuition. In her mind, she saw a flash of silver – then red. She knew that red, those vermillion flames.

By the Nether, what has he done?

Thelaema bore no sign of her thoughts. Yet Grauwynn was right. Soon, the All-seeing would return the Oracles to their state of oneness, their unity of mind. Once that happened, she and Grauwynn would be able to divine each other's every move. She had to strike. Now.

Thelaema took a step forward. 'If I asked for truth, would you offer it?'

Grauwynn stood, robe stark against the black steps of the temple. 'Would you listen?'

Thelaema chanced another step. 'I would.'

If only to know, before she killed him. Aptly, Grauwynn failed to see her thoughts.

'All that we had prophesied has transpired,' he said, hands clasped in his robe's cuffs. 'The Reliquus has arisen. All that is left is the capital's rejuvenation.' Like hers, his gaze had fallen to the garden at the base of Hael's statue.

Thelaema waited. 'And?'

'Once again, your shrewd mind,' Grauwynn repeated, laughing and cocking his head. 'And, my Oraculine, when it has, I shall conclude what I began. The Nether-magicks of the Reliquus will finally be conferred.'

'To whom?' Thelaema asked slowly.

Grauwynn, the male spiritual leader of their Order, smiled. 'Why, to myself, of course.'

Thelaema stilled. 'And the Reliquus?'

'Andruit? The boy has lived far longer than any mortal,' Grauwynn said dismissively. 'He shall return to the dust from whence he came.'

'His immortal existence is but a consequence of the Netherworld magicks that we, the Order of Descry, augmented him with,' Thelaema argued. 'A course of action that I warned against more than once. Now you wish to strip the Reliquus of his blessing – worse, his life? You have not the power to do it nor the permission.' Tenebrius would never stand for it, she thought. Hael, or Andruit as he had been when alive, was Tenebrius' chosen vessel.

Even Grauwynn would not court angering the God of the Netherworld.

'Oh, but therein lies the beauty,' Grauwynn said. 'For I indeed possess the power.' The Oracularus revealed a shining dagger. *The flash of silver.*

Thelaema froze. It was the blood-blade with the falcon handle from Hael's ritual that had reanimated him and created the Reliquus. Such an idol, on the day of Hael's resurrection, could be enough to end him. And Cahra would be next, she thought. *A capital coup.*

Grauwynn continued. 'Hael'stromia's defences cast our Order out, after I tried and failed to draw the darkness from the Nether, and all while the Reliquus failed in his duty of protecting his Kolyath Emperor charge. I have had four centuries to discern my mistake.' Raising the dagger, he went on, 'It is this: I should have killed Hael first. Then, perhaps, our Xan would never have detected me. And never had to die in vain.'

Thelaema's heart faltered, and she stumbled as she cried out, 'You killed Xan?'

Xan, as Oraculant, was more than their fellow High Oracle. Xan completed the triad as the crux of the Order of Descry, the great harmoniser between Thelaema and Grauwynn's temperaments, maintaining an equilibrium so that no single Oracle exerted control.

Their beloved Xan had died during the fall of Hael'stromia, a wound that had never truly healed for her. Grauwynn's confession ripped it open, hanging in the air like a ghost.

She rapidly blinked away the tears, her breaths shaking as she grieved. *I should have killed Grauwynn!* But at least, with her passing and his, the realm could usher in a new Oraculine, Oraculant and Oracularus. Starting with Wyldaern.

A new era of the Order of Descry, she thought weakly. A better one.

'Such a course of action I cannot allow,' she whispered, the weight of her sorrow grounding her as she prepared to do battle. 'You know this.' Thelaema lifted her eyes to his. 'Why, then, did you not simply kill me?'

Grauwynn's gaze cleared just a little, to the warm violet that had enamoured her younger self, as he murmured with finality, 'I so wished to hear your voice.'

With a sigh of regret, he pointed the dagger at Thelaema and unleashed a sizzling bolt of black fire.

CHAPTER 44

Hael had been the Reliquus for a thousand years, deathless for fifty-fold longer than his human life span. In that time, he had watched as the realm's Scions, Emperors, rose and fell, sovereigns of political – and personal – fate and failings. Not once had Hael entertained the comical notion that a being such as he might chance upon the phenomenon known as 'love', that his Masters either chased with unflagging ardour or decried. Such bonds eluded Hael, even in his mortal life.

But now?

Impossible, implausible, utterly illogical.

Yet as Hael struggled to reconcile it, he sensed the truth within his ancient heart. And in that moment, as Cahra gazed with such life into his open eyes of fire, he knew just what he felt for her, and he could never tell her. Because she was his Master.

Cahra had freed Hael from his tomb, only for him to ensnare himself anew.

He stilled, visualising the ebb and flow of Nether-magicks cycling through his body. He needed to calm himself, lest his eyes betray him. Gratefully, there was violence to be had, and nothing soothed him like the song of war.

He smiled, the mask in place. 'I must attend the sacrilegious wretches in your temple.'

Cahra put a hand to his cheek – and for a mere moment, he melted against her touch. She closed her eyes, resting her head against him.

'Be careful,' was all she whispered.

'It is they who should possess a care.' Hael paused. 'Please, stay here. The powers that you accessed are no more,' he told her, torn between leaving and staying by her side.

Cahra made the choice for him as she nodded, stepping back. Hael's cue to show her, have her see him as he really was. Not the weapon, but a monster.

Hael smothered his flames as a low rumbling swelled and he changed, splintering, his very essence descending into smoke and ash, a jet windstorm that choked the sparing air of his shrine room and its dim passages as he speared for the doors to explode them open, rocking them from their hinges as the metal showered down.

His battle cry echoed through the temple, a defiant proclamation of the Reliquus reborn, trumpeting his desire for vengeance.

–

It had been an age since the screams of worthy victims had graced Hael's immortal ears, and he smirked as Kolyath and Ozumbre's soldiers clamoured to flee the pyramid.

Flee *him*.

From his shrine, while speaking with Cahra, Hael had tracked the forces' deafening stampede and deduced precisely which level, which wing, which hall to materialise amidst in order to inflict the most chaos upon the enemy's ranks. So, he spirited into the dark and dust, reappearing in the dead centre of those stricken, traitorous men.

And he would raze them to the Netherworld-forsaken ground.

After 399 years in captivity, Cahra's adverse emotions were not enough to satiate him. He needed more, and the first thirteen mattered most. But unlike with her, this process would scarcely be so peaceful. After what the tri-kingdoms had done to Cahra, Hael would ensure a like for like. Namely, their suffering as punishment, for hers.

For he was free at last, dark magicks sparking at his fingertips, with centuries of bloodlust to slake. It was a simple task of flitting from foe to quailing foe, draining soldiers of their suffering then stealing onto the next. Mere moments after his arrival, the innermost men had fallen to the floor, the abreption leaving them as lifeless husks, each death feeding and strengthening his fires within. His enemies leapt back, their faces stained with horror, just as Hael was stained with the blood of their comrades.

Arms outstretched, Hael loomed above them all, sighing softly, as the negativity of his victims surged within him, activating every dormant aspect of his infernal existence.

As the hewed features of his humanoid face descended into chaos.

As he curled his fingers before him, the squat nails he'd borne for centuries extending, sharpening into his gnarled talons once more.

As both eye sockets caught fire with the celestial heat of a thousand suns, fangs growing to protrude like jagged sabres from his elongated jaw.

As a monstrous, blood-curdling howl erupted from his mouth and the lick of undiluted power Hael had sensed in Cahra, which had triggered his transformation, ended with the full restoration of his Nether-powers – and the second of his forms.

He spoke. 'Know me as Hael. Reliquus of the Order of Descry, and Vassal Champion to the Scion, Empress Cahraelia of Hael'stromia.' He lowered his chin to the ground, relaxing into readiness for an easy victory. 'It is my pleasure to deliver you to my lord Tenebrius… *And from this life.*' Hael snarled into the darkness, the temple's foundations trembling.

Thus, it began.

Kolyath and Ozumbre's soldiers near him froze, making them effortless prey as he lopped heads from torsos with his bare palms, gore spattering the walls of the black temple. Following this, most took flight, the unbridled panic sending contingents both scurrying towards the surface and back into the bowels of his abode. One, two, three senior officers drew their swords to face him, courageous yet futile. He swooped to slash one man's throat, swirling flawlessly to impale another's chest – blood spraying from the mangled heart – before turning on the final enemy Captain. Hael's grin widened as he kicked a broadsword from the man's grasp, caught it by the blade and crunched it between his Reliquus teeth, the metal snapping under the tensile strength of his jaws. His opponent's eyes bulged with fear. The reek of urine followed.

Hael advanced, soundless despite his hulking frame.

'Your kingdoms assailed my Master, your rightful Empress to the realm.' He paused. 'There will be no mercy.' Words lashing with savagery, Hael disintegrated into his dread ash and smoke, life and death's own matter – a product of the sunken fires of his true abode – and charged the airways of his opponent, shooting for the lungs and erupting to detonate the soldier from the inside out. Chunks of mortal meat rained in the darkness.

He had cleared one level of the temple.

Then Hael flew, lethal and limitless, for those fool enough to near his Master.

CHAPTER 45

Dressed in a stolen Kolyath army tabard, her dark brown hair tucked beneath a large helmet, Wyldaern followed the path laid out by her vision, slipping through the enemy's front lines all the way to Hael'stromia's gate. She moved quietly inside.

Now, she raced down the capital's streets, guided by her pendant's subtle divination. She prayed her vision would lead her to Thelaema and the reason the High Oraculine had disappeared in the midst of the battle.

Wyldaern dashed around a corner only to stop short, a sob escaping her before she had the chance, the sense, to silence it.

The avenue to the pyramid lay in ruins, chunks from the majestic stone pedestals scattered like a broken puzzle, as though they had exploded. Two sky-high obelisks, looming behind an imposing statue, also bore the marks of the cataclysm. And at the far end of it all, Wyldaern spotted two figures.

The familiar form of her mentor stood in contrast with the bloody scene, as Thelaema drove a dagger into the chest of the stranger, the body sagging, folding under the weight of her High Oraculine's blow.

Wyldaern dashed closer, each step bringing her within earshot of their final words.

'No one will follow in your sinful footsteps,' Thelaema murmured.

The dying man managed a grim smile, lips paling, wheezing with the words, 'Yet, I have already chosen my disciple.' His last breath escaped him in a moan.

Thelaema sighed heavily, face etched with exhaustion, as though she might do the same.

Frozen in disbelief, Wyldaern looked on as Thelaema wrenched the dagger free and sent it soaring into the air, silver glinting in the scant light. An incantation on her lips, the blade halted mid-flight, spinning leisurely as it hovered. Then it began to glow white-hot, transforming, dissolving into a cloud of fine ash. Thelaema sank to her knees.

With a sudden gust of wind, the remnants of the weapon were swept away, lost to the endless expanse of Hael'stromia's blackened ground.

Then Wyldaern was scrambling, robe collecting sand as she pulled Thelaema to her. The torso and hem of the Oracle's dress was ripped, bloody.

'I survive yet,' the Oraculine grumbled. This time, Wyldaern knew it to be bravado. The wound to Thelaema's chest was too great; Wyldaern could hear the sucking sound of air through punctured lungs. The woman was powerful, long-lived, but she was no Reliquus.

'It will be all right, child.' Thelaema patted her hand, coughing. 'It is the way of life. And I have endured for longer than I should have, to fulfil my omen's role. Now, it is time to bless a new Oraculine of the Order of Descry.' At Wyldaern's shock, her teacher shushed her. 'You have trained for this, Wyldaern, just as Thierre was trained to become King.'

Wyldaern fought to recall her decade of studies, saying shakily, 'What must I do?'

Thelaema gazed up at her, a deep smile gracing the High Oracle's wizened features. She seemed to grow older by the moment, lavender eyes paler, more translucent, as she said, 'Take my hand, my dear.'

Wyldaern gripped both hands, not wanting to let go, but she could feel the weakness in Thelaema's grasp as the woman held her hands in kind.

'See,' Thelaema whispered, so little breath left in that word.

Wyldaern's eyes stung. *No*, she thought futilely. *No. You cannot go.*

And still, I must. Thelaema's voice in her mind was comforting, but that did nothing to dull the ache of what Wyldaern knew would come.

I am not ready, not for this. It was true. But she also knew her thoughts were selfish, if only because she would miss her mentor dearly.

Well, that is a comfort. She heard Thelaema's soft laughter. *Now then, there is much for us to do, and very little time in which to do it. When the honour was bestowed upon me and I was initiated as you will be, I had the Order's brothers and sisters for guidance. I expect that this will be the hardest part for you. But the Reliquus is well-versed in our ways, our rites. He may resist, but he is loyal. Trustworthy. However, I must tell you.*

Thelaema paused. *The Scion and the Reliquus. They cannot be permitted to entangle.*

She struggled to understand. Entangle? She could not possibly mean—

They cannot be. A liaison between a Scion and the Reliquus, should it end poorly, places the future of the Hael'stromian realm in jeopardy. She is your Empress, and he is her fate-sworn servant, her Vassal Champion, forged to kill and protect her then outlive her, as Hael has done for a millennium to secure our domain. Cahraelia is his Master. They cannot be.

Wyldaern was astounded. *This is your concern?*

It is. Swear that you shall not permit such an entanglement, under your remit as the new Oraculine of the Order of Descry.

Wyldaern was not convinced her remit was Cahra's intimate affairs, but she also knew Thelaema's life force was dwindling. She swallowed.

I swear it. Now, the initiation of which you spoke. What must I do?

She could sense Thelaema's smile, but it was fading. *Nothing, dear. It is I who must confer my magicks, my learnings, to you.*

Then Thelaema took Wyldaern's head in her hands.

See…

And Wyldaern's mind expanded, exponentially…

Somewhere, she heard Thelaema's last words, as both their thoughts and memories swirled and Wyldaern absorbed Thelaema's own. Every facet of the Oracle's knowledge.

Aid Cahra and the Reliquus in the capital. When you are able, return to the cabin. You will find all that you desire there. You will always be my favoured pupil, dear Wyldaern. And our Order's hope for the new era. Farewell.

When Wyldaern opened her eyes, Thelaema, like the elder robed man, was gone. Grauwynn, the old Oracularus, Wyldaern now knew. The initiation had worked.

As the lone surviving Oracle, Wyldaern had Thelaema's memories, her knowledge.

Fortuitous, as she saw Hael in her mind's eye, materialising with Cahra.

Wyldaern turned, Hael's spell slicing a hole in the dimensional fabric between their mortal plane and the Nether's veil. The Reliquus, shrinking from one of his infernal forms into something more humanoid, studied Wyldaern as she quietly returned his fiery gaze.

Cahra bent over, looking pale, as though the teleportation might make her retch.

'Well met, Seer. I am Hael, Reliquus to Empress Cahra and your Order of Descry.' His voice was like the wind that howled to rattle dying leaves from autumn trees.

Wyldaern had been told about the appearance of the Reliquus, but Thelaema's words were insufficient for what loomed before her – his spiked hair and milky skin, and by the blessed All-seeing, those fires! She knew he had no eyes, for they had perished with his human body during the ritual that made him the weapon; but how did those flames burn so? Inverted, blazing down but so as not to scorch his cheeks? It was a Nether-born mystery.

And so, Wyldaern endeavoured not to stare as the Reliquus – *Hael*, she corrected – stepped from Cahra's side and bowed to Wyldaern, palms pressed together.

'It is I who should be bowing to you, Hael, for you have secured our Empress.' Wyldaern did so, curtseying deeply, for she was thankful.

'The duty of the Reliquus,' Hael told her, as if his actions necessitated explanation. Yet his features were soft, humble, as he inclined his head to her, regarding Wyldaern in such a way that she had the distinct feeling he knew what had befallen her. 'Such duties persist.' His gaze flickered to Cahra. 'Battle is waging outside the capital. If Kolyath and Ozumbre fail to capitulate, I must douse the flames of war.'

Cahra asked, 'And how do you plan on doing that?'

Straightening to tower over his Master, Hael turned in the direction of the gate that faced Luminaux's forces, now the battleground for its faraway kingdom. 'With my own.' Hael made to leave.

'What?' Cahra grabbed his arm. 'You can't go out there alone! Raiden said they have 20,000 men, and even with Luminaux behind you, you're just one.'

Not one, and not a man, Wyldaern mused. *Where are you going, Hael?*

Hael's eyes flashed to her. *I have located Ozumbre's King. Cahra nearly died at the hand of the Steward and that wretch. My powers may have healed her, yet the affront cannot be permitted. The capital's justice must prevail.* His fires sizzled black.

Wyldaern's mouth fell open. Telepathy? How in the known realm… She had never managed it before, only Thelaema possessed that power—

The power of the Order's spiritual leaders.

Hael offered her a smile, speaking aloud. 'Please keep Cahra safe.'

Cahra huffed. 'You really think she can protect me better than you can, or myself?'

Amusement kindled in Hael's eyes as he beheld his Master.

Was Thelaema correct about the two of them?

'I shall return to you,' Hael said softly to Cahra, before looking askance to Wyldaern. 'Besides, she is the new High Oracle.' With that, Hael's form dissolved into ash and smoke, vanishing behind the veil, to re-emerge and wreak havoc on Kolyath and Ozumbre's soldiers, no doubt. Wyldaern could not blame him.

Meanwhile, Cahra blinked at her, stunned. 'Wait, you're the *what*?!'

CHAPTER 46

Spiriting through the veil, Hael transported himself to the capital's Luminaux gate, his infernal sight on Decimus of Ozumbre as the King absconded for his army. Now that Hael was both liberated and magickally revitalised, his Nether-insight granted the occasional detail, such as the name of the Ozumbre army's leader and twin, Commander Diabolus, who was battling mid-field with King Royce of Luminaux. It was to his wretch of a brother that the King of Ozumbre now scurried.

Hael smiled darkly. The illusion of safety always helped his Reliquus cause and the exquisite abreption that inevitably followed.

So, he did not rush, instead drawing himself to his full height as he calmly traversed the sable sands between himself and Kolyath and Ozumbre's men stationed by the gate.

His sands. His gate. It had been 399 years since the realm had witnessed Hael's might, the might of the monstrosity the Seers had brought to life with their dark spells.

It was time to remind the sister kingdoms why Hael was designated 'the ultimate weapon'.

The fact that he would be avenging Cahra's suffering? Another boon.

Hael had left no Kolyath or Ozumbre soldiers alive within the temple, and his focus was solely on the enemy, numerous as Cahra had warned him. Yet her disquiet was borne of what she had seen during their second abreption: a bygone victory against Ozumbre in the first twenty-five years of Hael's existence as a Scion champion. Then, he had been but on the precipice of his true powers and still discovering them. Now, as he stood beneath the gate, the Haellium a metal infused with his blood... now, was different. He may have been resting for nearly four centuries, but he was a thousand-year-old immortal warrior fuelled by dark magicks and the Nether-plane beyond the veil and void. The powers of creation. And of his destruction.

Hael would educate these mortals in precisely what that meant.

None had noticed him, fixed as they were on the conflict before them to the north-east. How lamentably human, Hael thought, to heed only the obvious danger and nought beyond it, as he cast his own spirit spell: the scridon that let him 'turn to smoke and fly around', to quote Cahra's amusing depiction. He did appreciate such magicks, Hael admitted, summoning the Nether to slit a hole in the veil between planes. Smoke billowed from it as he materialised on the killing grounds, venting a blast wave that floored the fighting around him.

'*Decimus!*' Hael bellowed with the full force of his occult voice, the fires of the Nether roaring, crackling in his words. Ozumbre's King narrowed his teal eyes from the midst of his forces. 'Surrender.' Hael drew out the final word. 'Now.'

To his merit, Decimus strode forward, the King's voice clear as he laboured to yell across the mess of battle lines. 'So, you are the ultimate weapon! Well, I must admit, I was expecting a rather elaborate sword.' Decimus gestured. 'Would you not prefer to join us?'

'Join us?' Kolyath's Commander Sullian stepped from Decimus, questioning him. Then Sullian glowered at Hael. 'When will you heretic Seers learn? *We do not need you.*'

'Your Steward needed me,' Hael enlightened Sullian. 'It was his plan, in fact, to wrest control and utilise my powers to slaughter you all. Though I see that Atriposte did not speak so plainly with his future victims,' he mused, smirking.

Oh, how the All-seeing was favouring him, this day.

'Debate is immaterial. My order remains. Surrender.' Hael paused, telling Decimus, 'You will not live to regret the alternative.'

From where he stood, Hael sensed King Decimus' doubt, if only for a split-moment. Then Ozumbre's ruler laughed.

'Be on your guard, weapon.' Turning from him, the King raised his sword and signalled for Commander Sullian to continue.

Despite his protracted life, Hael had never been a creature of patience. He extended his own arm and unfurled his fingers towards Decimus.

Smiling.

The gasps of Kolyath's army carried on the wind, as the King of Ozumbre's blade was whisked into the air – and evaporated into smoke, tendrils curling to the sky.

King Decimus stared at Hael, at length grasping his fatal plight.

Hael's smile widened, revealing his predatory fangs.

Then he blew a whispered breath, knowing his words would reach Decimus' ears only.

'*I warned you.*'

Standing at the forefront of where Kolyath and Ozumbre's forces converged, Hael raised his arms, the sand-streaked soil of the lands between the capital and the Wilds cracking, sundering to reveal the crust below the surface of the sands and the red-hot fires of its depths.

His depths. His core. The fires of his destruction.

Hael stretched for the sun, commanding rock by molten rock, semi-liquid magma spewing above Kolyath and Ozumbre's armies, their lines shattered by the makeshift plates on which they now crouched, cowering. Soldiers watched open-mouthed as lava shot past then rained back upon them in a hiss and sizzle of screaming, human flesh.

He had vowed it, for Cahra. *To the Netherworld-forsaken ground.*

Then Hael scridoned to Decimus, pressing a honed talon to the Ozumbre King's neck. Unnecessary, as Hael could destroy Decimus even if he was in another kingdom, but mortals tended to respond with more gravity to such threats. The sharp intake of the man's breath was sweet satisfaction. Behind the curve of his nail, he felt Decimus swallow.

Before he exacted the realm's justice, Hael deigned to speak. 'One final note, King.' His claws outstretched, he grazed Decimus' throat. 'When you do reach the River Tenebri, please say hello to Atriposte and Jarett, from your Empress.' Hael's flames blackened as he thrust his talons into the King's neck and hoisted the man's body like a limp rag doll.

It was then that Hael began to feel the air, the will, go out of Ozumbre's armed forces. 'Your King is no more. Yield.'

Yet the army's officers, scattered across the remnants of the kingdom's lines, charged.

Hael sighed inwardly.

So be it.

He flicked his hand, palls of coal-black smoke exploding either side of him as the baying of his Nether-hounds echoed through the strand. It had been centuries since Hael had called upon his shadow jackals, and he bowed to the skeletal beasts, nodding.

For his hounds would be ever so hungry.

Then Hael turned, slashing the head of Ozumbre's dead King from his shoulders, and left his Nether-hounds to hunt.

'As the realm shall learn, I possess a long memory. I will right my former wrongs,' Hael murmured, advancing on the highest-ranking official left in Kolyath's army.

Commander Sullian scrambled across the jet sands.

I will avenge you, Emperor Brulian. For Cahra and all who came before her.

It was time to set about ridding Kolyath of its villainy, once and for all.

Time for the leviathan of Hael's third and final form.

But before Hael could trigger his darkest transformation, he sensed something.

Hael! Wyldaern's voice cried, desperate and wavering, as if unsure of her new powers.

He shot into the air in a flurry of ash and smoke, searching the battlefield.

An agonised howl, raw and rageful, sounded from Luminaux's end of the plain – and he felt a tremor within the dirge of life expiring. *The fires of destruction. Of ruling life, lost.*

Hael, not having met Luminaux's Prince, nonetheless somehow knew the man's voice. And despite the young man's feelings for Cahra, woe swelled in Hael's chest as he watched Prince Thierre rip King Royce from the grip of the sword that gored him, the two of them sagging to the ground. Thierre raised his head, vengeance in his eyes.

The King of Luminaux was dead.

Above him stood the King of Ozumbre's twin, Diabolus, sword dripping with blood.

CHAPTER 47

Cahra and Wyldaern raced back through Hael'stromia's raised gate and onto the battlefield. Its sands were cracked, the crevices filled with rapidly cooling molten rock and the smell of liquid ore and charred meat saturated the air. The bodies of Kolyath and Ozumbre soldiers were broken, flung and laid to waste – hundreds dead – the splintered plain eerily silent, except for the sound of someone weeping. Cahra kept running, past Kolyath's army and to—

A devastating sight met her eyes. Thierre was kneeling on the ground, with his father, King Royce of Luminaux, dead in his arms.

And standing before them was Hael, one arm raised as his Nether-magicks suspended Commander Diabolus of Ozumbre high in mid-air. The Reliquus extended his other arm and wind lashed at the battle-ground, the clouds darkening, the heavens looking ready to rip open. A monstrous pack of skeletal dog-like creatures, positioned defensively around Hael, howled.

'No soul will harm a sister kingdom's ruler and live to tell of the deed,' he boomed, his eyes walls of jet flame. 'Not while I defend the capital.'

The tri-kingdom armies stared, frozen in awe and horror, as Hael flicked his wrist and unleashed a fireball, striking Diabolus true, the Commander's body bursting into flames. The inferno writhed, a swirling firestorm climbing to the sky with a deafening roar that sent a sweltering shockwave across the land, the force knocking Cahra and Wyldaern from their feet. Around them, the ground trembled, as though the very realm was quaking with sheer terror.

Then as quickly as it had come, the storm ceased, the sky clearing as clouds scattered to the corners of the realm. Only singed ashes drifted to the sands.

Ozumbre's army Commander was no more.

Wyldaern's eyes widened as she stilled to witness Hael's merciless precision. 'The Reliquus. He really is…' Her voice was a whisper.

…the ultimate weapon. Cahra swallowed.

How had she ever thought she could control Hael's magicks?

Death inhabited his every step as Hael prowled away. But then his gaze found Cahra and Hael's fires sparked back to life, his features softening. He pointed.

Cahra followed his line of sight until she settled on the subject of his attention, Kolyath's army Commander Sullian, kneeling, blood-spattered, on the ground.

She spun to Hael. He simply raised his face to the morning sun, basking in its glow.

He'd left Kolyath's Commander alive, for her.

Cahra stalked to Sullian and stood, scrutinising the Steward's military Commander, apprehended and glowering at her. She'd been so afraid of Kolyath's soldiers catching her and her friends as they journeyed through the Wilds. Looking at the leader of Kolyath's army, she felt sad and angry for those like Ellian dragged into this endless war.

'It was never Atriposte, or Jarett, or even you,' she said to Sullian. 'It was all of you, Kolyath's high-borns, who never gave a damn who lived or died outside the castle keep.' Cahra stilled to find her hand was itching for Lumsden's gold dagger again. She exhaled, grinding her teeth as she shook free of the impulse, then let her arm fall by her side.

A tiny tendril of her abreption's old peace unwound inside her.

Sullian opened his thin, high-born mouth to insult her with some disparaging remark. Cahra shook her head at him.

'No,' she said. 'No more.' She turned her back on the man. 'Hael,' she asked, 'does Hael'stromia have a dungeon?'

'Three,' Hael replied. He angled his chin from the sun's warm rays and surveyed her. 'Is that truly what you want?'

Cahra looked out at Kolyath and Ozumbre's forces, rudderless and powerless against the arrival of the ultimate weapon. She gazed up at Hael.

'For now.' Then she remembered her own dungeon escape. 'The securest one we've got,' she told him quickly.

Hael nodded. Then, dropping into a deep bow, he moved faster than her eyes could follow to render Sullian unconscious, before descending into the Nether's smoke with the former Commander of her kingdom's forces.

But before he did, she caught the look in Sullian's eyes… The entitlement. The rage. Cahra knew it well.

Just as she knew the old ways in Kolyath, the Steward's ways, wouldn't go quietly. There would be a period of adjustment, and she would need to meet it head-on.

She sighed. There was a lot to do, it seemed.

In Hael's brief absence, Cahra looked to Thierre. The Prince was clearly lost to grief. Her gaze shifted to Raiden, to Sylvie, both wounded but standing.

'So, that's the weapon?' The General arched a sleek brow. 'If your Reliquus can't end the war between the sister kingdoms, I dare not think who or what will.'

'The fighting does seem to have stopped,' Cahra admitted, pausing before telling her, 'I am sorry for your loss.' She glanced at Thierre, the Prince unmoving, unhearing.

Sylvie's blue eyes misted. 'Thank you for your words. And for securing my brother.' She wiped her face, sighing. 'What is expected of the kingdoms now?'

Hael returned from wherever the dungeons were – and with Cahra's great-hammer – moving to tower behind her. With a solemn grace, he held the magnificent weapon out. The air seemed to thrum with otherworldly energy as he presented Cahra with her Haellium hammer.

'Surrender,' Hael said, a remnant of the Nether's rattle in his voice. 'As I instructed them.' Drily, he added, 'Twice.'

Cahra resisted the urge to raise a brow. So he had attempted diplomacy? Maybe she and Hael *were* changing, she thought.

She hissed to him, 'What do I do now?'

He looked upon her calmly. 'Permit me,' Hael said. She nodded and he straightened, rising above the tallest soldiers as Cahra noticed for the first time his monumental height. From their visions, she'd assumed he was only tall compared to her.

'*Sister kingdoms of the realm!*' Hael began, launching his voice across the battlefield. 'I am Hael, the Reliquus – the weapon of prophecy – and Vassal Champion to the Scion. The prophecy has now come to pass, and the capital will open to you in but a short time… However, only if you surrender.' He paused, indicating Cahra. 'And pledge your fealty.'

Cahra froze, panicked. *Now?!* She didn't exactly look the part of an Empress with her dishevelled leathers, marred in her own blood.

She turned to Wyldaern and saw the Oracle was watching Sylvie and Raiden sadly. They were waiting for Thierre to say something.

Cahra's heart ached for Thierre, reeling from the magnitude of King Royce's death. She wondered if Sylvie and Raiden waited for nothing. But just when she thought reaching the Prince was a lost cause, he laid his father down gently. Then he spoke.

'Luminaux recognises the sovereignty of Cahra of Kolyath as Empress to the realm, Hael'stromia and the three sister kingdoms.' Thierre thrust his longsword into the ground, the sword Cahra had forged for him. The sword that had started it all.

'So says King Thierre of Luminaux. *All hail!*' His words rang in Luminaux's ranks, Tyne, Sylvie, Raiden and their people all clasping their fists to their chests.

'*ALL HAIL!*'

The call reverberated as Cahra stood, frozen, taken aback by Thierre's endorsement. How was the man standing, speaking so steadily with such royal poise, when his body was bruised and bloody and broken, and his father was lying dead at his feet? She blinked, unable to comprehend it.

And thought, how could she possibly compare to a ruler like Thierre?

This was why she had exchanged herself for him. Because no matter their history, their differences, Thierre was a leader and the King his people needed even when their hearts were burdened with such grief.

Maybe she could learn something from the Prince, now King.

'You have Luminaux's support,' Raiden said softly.

Cahra exhaled, remembering their conversation before the battle.

'The question is, does Cahra have theirs?' Sylvie stared at the remaining sister kingdoms.

'She will,' Hael said. It was hard to miss the warning in those words. He faced them. 'Kolyath, Ozumbre. Do you accept the terms of your surrender, and pledge your allegiance to your prophecy's Scion, the Omen-bringer, and your new supreme sovereign of the realm – Empress Cahraelia of Kolyath, now of Hael'stromia?'

Ugh, that name again. Cahra tried not to wince.

But she couldn't hold onto the thought, not when the ringing in her ears, the buzzing in her head was blotting everything else out.

Empress. She was *Empress* of the realm. How had she gotten here? And, worse still, how would she live up to everything that title meant? A ruler, a leader, when in her head, she was still the same poor smith from Kolyath. How could she possibly be responsible for an entire realm, and its three kingdoms containing more people than she could count?

Suddenly, an ocean of faces gazed at her: Kolyath's soldiers, Ellian and the other children, the traders and apprentices of Kolyath, the aged veterans past their warring prime. Her view widened to Ozumbre's army, Cahra watching their faces cloud with suspicion and fear. Both kingdoms knew only tyrants for rulers, who wielded their sovereignty with cruelty and death. Who was she to ask anything of these people? They had no love for self-imposed rulers.

Cahra's mind raced as an idea began to take shape.

Glancing at Hael, she stepped forward. Three pairs of the shadowy hounds he had summoned moved with her, their muscular forms slipping through the space between people like spectres. The hounds' flaming eyes scanned the crowd as vigilantly as Hael did, before they sat on their skeletal haunches, still as death.

'People of the tri-kingdom realm,' she took a deep breath, trying to project her voice. 'I am Cahra, from the kingdom of Kolyath, so some of you may know me. But that is not all you know, and it is our shared plight.' Cahra frowned, struggling to think of what to say, as she fought her shaking voice and body. Hael's affirming nod breathed courage into her.

Cahra steeled herself, continuing on. 'The problem is that this realm knows only the evil of rulers, a Steward and a King, and their Commanders, their courts, who don't care how you, me, or anyone else barely scrapes a life together in this blasted realm. All we *know*,' Cahra cried, thumping her chest, 'is the opposite of what they have in their high-born castles. Poverty, hunger, sickness, danger. Death. Always death,' she told them, letting herself feel the air inflate her lungs, give her strength. 'No one should ever have to live like that. Like I did. Like so many of us do in the kingdoms of this realm.

'But maybe we don't have to any more. You've seen Hael, the "ultimate weapon".' Cahra watched as his flames shifted. 'Yet he is more than that. And he is here to *help* us, to help me, in figuring out what the kingdoms really need. Because it's not another token ruler, that's for sure.' She gazed at Hael, his mesmerising eyes, and looked out at the crowd. 'So if you do wish to pledge your allegiance to me, fine. But if you don't, that's fine too. All I ask is: give me some time to find us common ground.'

Give me time to learn what I can do to help. Cahra thought of Thierre.

Maybe she wouldn't end up making such a bad leader, after all.

Cahra waited, heart pounding in the stillness. No matter what, she had made her stand. And gazing into Hael's ember-glow eyes, Cahra knew that she was not alone.

In the aftershock of her words, silence stretched across the plain, the air thick with the weight of expectation as soldiers stood, motionless as Hael's statue in the capital.

Just when it felt the world itself had stopped, her hammer sparked to life in her hand, seeming to pulse with the emotions flooding her: mad, buoyant hope; but also trust in herself and the people around her. The great-hammer began to glow, the light becoming a brilliant flare that reflected her inner strength, her inner fire.

And from this resplendent light, a creature erupted into the sky.

'A phoenix,' Hael whispered, his voice barely audible as he watched the creature soar. 'Cahra, your crest – it is a blessing!'

The phoenix, incandescent in its fiery brilliance, spread its wings and shot above Cahra to soar across the bloodied battlefield, a majestic symbol of hope amongst the carnage. Its trail of flames blazed red against the perfect azure of the now-cloudless sky and awe filled her every breath as it swooped, unleashing an ethereal cry that echoed over the capital's jet sands. Finally, in a dazzling display, it dived, disintegrating into a shower of sparks at her feet.

The palpable silence that had enveloped Hael'stromia was at once shattered by the collective gasp of all three armies. If Cahra's words hadn't reached them, the phoenix did, the symbol of rebirth searing itself into the memories of all present. As the last vestiges of the flaming bird faded, she locked eyes with Hael.

A gratified smile tugged at the corners of the Reliquus' lilac lips.

It was hard to know who was in charge of Kolyath's army, with Commander Sullian in custody, but after a flurry of discussion, a group of men parted and a grizzled, high-ranking officer stepped forward.

'I am Marl,' the man said to Cahra. 'We accept the weapon's terms. And your own.' He clutched his fist, holding his sword to his broad chest.

Cahra withheld a sob, knees buckling, but Hael was there, catching her before she fell. She had never expected acceptance from Kolyath; the cruel kingdom Atriposte had built had always felt irreparable and like it would last forever. But the Steward was gone. And the idea that her kingdom could finally be free, be something more…

She nodded to Marl, a heartfelt lump thick in her throat. 'Thank you.'

Then Cahra glanced to Ozumbre.

Unlike Kolyath's, their army was silent. Finally, a Captain stepped up.

'While we appreciate the sentiment in your words, we would welcome further dialogue before committing to a course of action,' the high-born answered her. 'As you said. To find common ground.'

'That's fair,' Cahra told him. 'What is your name?'

'Captain – Lord – Swithan,' the man said.

Cahra gave a nod. 'Then I look forward to speaking further, Swithan.'

The noble's face hardened, but he simply nodded as, behind Cahra, Hael loomed, his unearthly eyes a deterrent against any argument.

'It is settled. The Empress shall send word in the coming months, when the capital is ready to host the sister kingdoms of Kolyath, Luminaux and Ozumbre in a united celebration. All peoples will be invited, including those of the neutral lands, the Wilds,' Hael continued. An all-kingdom event was unheard of, and a ripple of excitement stirred.

But would old hostilities?

'Peace will be a prerequisite,' Hael said, before Cahra could voice the issue to him. He turned slowly, facing each kingdom. 'Now, return to your lands. We shall call upon you once the capital is ready. We bid you all farewell.' Hael's eyes caught Cahra's as he paused, then dropped to one knee. 'ALL HAIL CAHRAELIA, EMPRESS OF HAEL'STROMIA!'

Hael's depthless voice resounded across the battlefield, and Cahra's mouth fell open. Luminaux and Kolyath's people followed, kneeling.

One by one, heads bowed, spreading like a never-ending wave that broke across the land.

'Hael—'

Hael murmured, in a voice so quiet it seemed to find its way directly into her ear, 'They must accept you, in this new era.'

'I guess…' Cahra said, then cleared her throat as she realised he, Wyldaern, Thierre, Sylvie, Raiden, Tyne – *everyone* – was still bowing to her. 'Rise, please,' she begged them. The scene was unbelievable.

Her whole life was unbelievable now.

And it would never, ever be normal again.

Thierre, watching, interrupted her thoughts. 'Then it truly has all come to pass?' Voice wavering, he masked it with one of his courtly smiles.

'I suppose it has,' Cahra said softly. She didn't want to ask him if he'd be all right when she knew he'd be going back to chaos. The King's funeral; a new Luminaux monarch; everything with Delicia, how ever that would turn out. Thierre would face a challenging time. 'Whatever happens back at home, know that you've got friends here,' she said, her voice low. 'I'm here if you need someone to talk to, okay?'

Though her words were meant to comfort him, she thought maybe she'd said the wrong thing as something tightened in his face.

Thierre nodded. 'Friends,' he murmured.

Cahra saw Sylvie gaze across Luminaux's forces, many of whom were injured and being attended by war physicians like Merali.

'Your soldiers fought well today,' she told the General, feeling the same responsibility when she looked at Kolyath's army. She placed a hand on Sylvie's plated shoulder.

'We did. At heavy cost,' the General replied, casting a glance to the banner where Luminaux's healers worked tirelessly. 'Morale is difficult in times like these, but we'll hold. We always do.' Sylvie's eyes flickered to Cahra. 'We won today. It's enough.'

Cahra clasped the woman's arm. 'Yes, we did.'

Thierre looked to Sylvie, Raiden, Tyne, his guards and people. His family and friends. 'It is time. We depart for Luminaux.' The new King's blue goldstone eyes shone with sorrow. 'Farewell, Empress… Glory be.' Thierre bowed again to Cahra, his people following.

'Keep in touch,' Cahra said to Sylvie. Glancing at her brother, the General nodded. Then took one look at Wyldaern and swept the Seer tightly into her arms.

Cahra's brows shot up in surprise. She hadn't realised they'd become friends.

'As will I,' Raiden told Cahra, smiling. She hugged the Captain.

'Take care of him,' Cahra said. She had a feeling it wouldn't be easy.

'I promise,' he said, Raiden's smile fading as quickly as it had come.

Piet, Siarl and Queran stepped forward, bowing as one. 'It has been our honour, Empress.'

'And,' the gentle warrior said, 'please do return to train at the palace any time.'

She raised an arm to each of them, the allies she'd made on this most difficult journey. 'Thank you. The honour is mine,' she told them. Then Luminaux's army moved out.

Cahra watched as Thierre's people gathered their wounded, mounted their horses and bid her, Wyldaern and Hael farewell. She remained until Thierre turned back to her at last, a smile on his face. But the expression seemed fixed and his blue goldstone eyes were wistful. Then he, Sylvie, Raiden and his people turned to the north-east and trotted away from her, back to Luminaux and their kingdom of light. As they dwindled to tiny dots on the horizon, a sigh escaped Cahra's lips. With their departure, a piece of herself would journey with them, forever bound to Luminaux and her memories of the kingdom.

And the people in it who'd helped change her life.

CHAPTER 48

Once Luminaux's army vanished into the distant Wilds, Cahra surveyed the gate to the capital of Hael'stromia; her capital, it seemed. Opening soon to every kingdom, every person in their long-surviving realm.

What do I do now?

She glanced to Wyldaern. The look on the Seer's face – the Oraculine's face – seemed to be asking the same thing. Wyldaern rubbed her eyes, no longer peridot, but the amethyst of a High Oracle of the Order of Descry.

Cahra reached out gently for Wyldaern's slender arm and asked her, 'Are you all right?'

She knew it was a stupid question, but it was a quiet acknowledgement of their shared pain. Wyldaern had lost Thelaema today, her mentor, as Cahra had lost hers in Lumsden. That loss, they would carry with them. Hael had retrieved Lumsden's body, and though the customary rites awaited, it was a task for another day. When hearts and minds felt steadier.

Wyldaern faced the dark city. 'There is much to do. Much to think on.'

Cahra's gaze flickered beyond the gate to Hael'stromia's sands, barren as they were. She knew gardening would be the least of her problems.

'Yes,' she admitted.

'Then, we begin.' Hael strode to the gate, twirling Cahra's great-hammer in the air. She eyed the vast pack of skeletal Nether-hounds trailing behind him.

'Really? Well, while I appreciate the enthusiasm, how are the three of us supposed to clean up the capital for a party? Including the pyramid's hallways,' Cahra added, shuddering at the idea of carting the dead from the temple; or maybe it was those hounds.

'Perhaps we can request aid from the kingdoms?' Wyldaern suggested.

Hael was silent, a playful tilt to his lips.

'What is it?' Cahra asked him. His inky hair and coat were so striking in the daylight against the luminous skin of his face and chest.

'There is less to be done than you think. Yet there is much for us to discuss,' he said, reaching the gate. He gestured for her to go first.

From the corner of her eye, Cahra noticed Wyldaern watching them, her gaze distant. There was a tightness around her eyes, a stiffness in her stance that had not been there before. Unease gnawed at the edges of Cahra's happiness, a worry she couldn't name.

Brow furrowed, she took a step. 'Okay, but I don't really understand—'

The words died in Cahra's throat as Hael glided from behind her and, together, they crossed the capital's threshold.

And the world around them began to bloom.

With each step Hael took, seedlings sprouted and flowers grew from the desert sands in exotic shades of flaming red and orange, jewel-like blue and purple. The ground pulsated, returning to life, all because of him. She watched the spectacle in awe as Hael kept walking, the habitat reacting to him passing, trees and shrubs shooting from the ground to thrive anew in shimmering shades of black, gold, copper and richest brown.

In minutes, the capital had transformed from a barren wasteland of sand and stone to an idyllic oasis, a sanctuary, the city's black buildings that had lain empty but intact for years erect and proudly polished, resplendent in the sun's embrace. The capital had become a different place. Hael had breathed life into Hael'stromia again.

Looking out over the expanse of her new city, Cahra felt a sort of vertigo, like she'd stepped off a cliff's edge and was free-falling into the unknown. Was this really her life now? She was no Thierre, born and bred for royal rule. She was just Cahra, a girl from Kolyath and a village in the Wilds, who'd somehow found herself carrying the weight of an empire.

A girl who had wielded extraordinary dark magicks, and felt their absence keenly.

She couldn't shake the shadow of longing that coiled itself inside her as she gazed out at the wondrous vista unfolding before her very eyes. For a fleeting moment, Hael's powers had been hers to command, a dark and supreme force that had given her a taste of something she'd never known before: power, not to mention near-invincibility. But now that she was Empress, the prophecy fulfilled, she was expected to just relinquish that strength. Cahra was meant to be grateful, to entrust Hael to protect her in his role as champion. To accept her human vulnerability, her human helplessness.

Except… Cahra was tired of being helpless.

But these were thoughts for another time. There was so much to do, and she had to focus on the path ahead, magick or no magick. Cahra took Hael's hand.

He watched her carefully, as if the flames in his eyes sought the source of her tension. Finally, Hael said softly, 'Is this to your liking?'

Cahra dragged her gaze with effort from the dark paradise awaiting her to settle on the wine-red of Hael's billowing flames.

'It's beautiful,' she breathed in astonishment, in spite of the thoughts that swirled inside her. 'How did you…?'

Hael picked a tiny bud from the prickly shrub at Cahra's feet. Placing it in her cupped hand, he touched it, watching as one by one the petals unfurled, shimmering, opening to reveal a ruby-red rose blossoming in the centre of Cahra's outstretched palm.

Hael retracted his hand and she looked up at him. 'You were right, to say that I was more than simply the weapon. Legend knows me as such, a creature of destruction, yet my Nether-magicks are also born of creation. They are the dual aspects of life,' Hael said. 'This is your seat of power, now, Cahra.' He gestured to the glorious capital around them.

'I can shape it to whatever you may wish.'

She gazed around, taking it all in. 'I love it. Exactly as it stands.'

Love.

She remembered her bizarre conversation with the figure on the River Tenebri. Before, love was a word that had never carried any real meaning for Cahra. She'd never been in love, or been loved that way, not until she left Kolyath. Even her feelings for Thierre had been infatuation more than anything else, she'd come to understand. While he'd been the first to show her attention, affection, maybe even something deeper, it had not meant the Prince was the one for her. It just meant he'd been the first. Not good, not bad, just first.

But first hadn't been enough. Not once she'd realised how little she knew of Thierre, of his whole self when it came to trust and love. Somewhere along the way, she'd known she needed more, from whoever might occupy her heart, if one day at all. Someone who could, would, not just see all of her, but share the same things. Someone who wouldn't keep secrets. Someone Cahra could be herself with, and simply be.

She'd once seen herself as someone who hid and ran. After all, it had been her life. But with Thierre, she'd opened up. She'd dared to step up and trust someone. Now, she craved someone who would bare themselves to her in kind. Someone brave enough to try. Someone she could not only love, but also respect.

Was Hael it?

She stopped looking at the lovely landscape and gazed up at him, smiling. They had time, she thought, to find out.

Then Cahra asked, 'Hael, who is Andruit?'

Hael paused, his face giving away nothing. 'That is a name that I have not heard in a tremendously long time. A name that belongs to a life past, to a human man who once was and, I suppose, in some ways, still is now. A name that belongs to a long, complicated story. However, I will tell you about it, later… if you like.'

Cahra's smile widened. 'I would, very much,' she said. Then she turned to Wyldaern. 'So you and I have new jobs now.'

'We do,' Wyldaern granted, softly.

'I was thinking… maybe we could both learn together?' Cahra blew out a breath. 'Because honestly? I'm going to need all the help I can get.'

'I would appreciate that,' Wyldaern said in earnest. 'Thelaema left so quickly, and her memories – there is a lot of history to sort through.' The Oracle glanced to Hael.

'There is a lot of history I'd like to change,' Cahra replied, frowning. 'Scions to improve on. An Oracularus whose actions cannot be allowed to happen again.'

'Well, I, for one, am certainly not about to misappropriate the Reliquus' magicks, of that you can be assured.' Wyldaern inclined to Cahra. 'You have my oath, I swear it.'

'This time *will* be different. That's what I can swear,' Cahra told her. 'For me, that's no bowing, no curtseying, from either of you. Never from you, and never to me.'

'I…' Wyldaern looked at Hael, as he nodded. 'As you wish,' she said.

'Good.' Cahra paced a few steps. 'And no titles, no—'

Wyldaern laughed, taking her arm. 'As Hael said, there is much for us to discuss.' The Oracle stilled then, staring up at Hael'stromia's pyramid, the palatial temple.

Their new home, the three of them: Empress, Oraculine and Reliquus. Cahra looked at Hael, the immortal weapon, whose life was inexplicably bound to hers; then at Wyldaern, her Seer friend who'd walked alongside her through trials and triumphs alike. Cahra wasn't alone. They would face any challenges as they had today.

Cahra smiled. 'Then let us begin.'

And with that, Cahra, Wyldaern and Hael continued onwards through Hael'stromia to forge a new path, a new era. A new alliance. Together.

EPILOGUE

Hael and Cahra stood, side by side, in the dominating dark.

'You are not required to do this.'

The Empress' two-toned eyes of brown and green slid to his. 'I know.'

Hael nodded. Then he stalked down the murky passage.

He had scridoned them to the entrance of Hael'stromia's most intolerable dungeon. The dungeon masters of old had forged many peculiar keys and locks that only existed in locations of extreme security so as to lower the chances of lock-pickers becoming familiar with any of their inner workings, the door to the hall beyond covered in such mechanisms. Hael nodded to two of his hand-picked Imperial Guards. The men saluted, bearing a ring of what would look to any human like strange keys.

'I'm assuming you've got a reason for not scridoning us inside?' Cahra murmured, spying the nine different types of locks secured to the Haellium dungeon door ahead of them. She patiently waited as a guard worked his way through opening each one.

Hael had hesitated to bring her here, a vision in her brocade gown with its threads of black, red, silver and gold, her hair shining like a copper coin. Especially after he had seen through their abreption what she had endured in one of Kolyath's dungeon cells. Atriposte was lucky that Cahra had already ended his life, for Hael would not have curbed his violence. He was still tempted to journey to the Netherworld and butcher the wretch all over again.

Looking upon his Empress, he smiled grimly. 'An attention-grasping way to arrive.'

'Ah,' she said, brow knit in thought.

Another minute, and they entered, the door swinging closed with a piercing screech. He walked first, Cahra close behind.

'Seal it,' Hael ordered the guard. The heavy door shut, a clamour of locks and keys fastening outside.

Hael raised a hand, sprightly fire sparking to life in his palm as a makeshift torch for Cahra's benefit. His nocturnal vision was impeccable in the dungeon's blackness, though said blackness was deepening the farther they moved into the moist, bracing air. With time, the temperature underground would thaw to an arid desert heat, but until that day, the glacial chill was useful, particularly given their current guest.

The stone path they followed, carved from the bedrock itself, snaked downwards, eventually met by an enormous metal door, his metal, sealed with two locks and several bolts. Cahra stepped up, her head brushing Hael's shoulder, and frowned.

'The guards have the keys,' she murmured, glancing at him.

'They do,' Hael said. 'Fortunately, I have others.' His eyes flickered in her direction. 'You may wish to look away.'

Cahra's frown gave way to confusion. 'Why?'

Hael put two fingers from his unutilised right hand into his mouth and bit down – then tore with his fangs, ripping the tops of them off. Cahra gasped, gripping Hael's elbow as he spat his severed fingers onto the tiles, his own blood dripping from his mouth.

Only half of two of his fingers remained, Hael slipping one, then the other, into the keyways with a definitive twist. Both locks clicked open.

'Hael! By the Seers…' Cahra exclaimed, staring from him to his bloody finger bones, the ancient keys to this wing's locks. She rushed to wrap his fingers in her skirts, squeezing as though to staunch the flow of his rusty ichor. 'Doesn't that *hurt?*'

Something in his chest constricted as he watched her try to help him, unaware that his self-inflicted injury would heal by the morrow.

'It takes much to hurt me,' he said gently. 'But if I did feel the physicality of pain… well, your care would certainly be soothing.'

Only magicks, like that of the night that he had been reborn the Reliquus, gave him cause to reconsider his beliefs about true agony.

Hael watched Cahra's shoulders loosen at the softness of his words.

She eyed him, giving him a look that was undone by the tug of her full, flushed lips into a smile, as she said, 'Locksmith, tomorrow. I'm not having *this*,' she stressed, waving an arm at him bleeding onto her fine gown, 'be a regular occurrence for you.' Cahra shook her head and sighed. 'Honestly! What horrible excuse for an Emperor would let you—'

With his marred hand, he squeezed the two of hers that clasped him, bending to look into Cahra's eyes.

'I heed you,' he conceded, unwittingly staring at her in the dark.

She was so beautiful, he thought, the green of her eyes dancing in his palm's firelight as she gazed back, seemingly forgetting his wound. His neck curved to hers; they were near, so near that he could see, hear, the delicate hummingbird's pulse of her life, below her jaw.

Hael leaned in, at once struck by the overwhelming urge to press his mouth to where his breath ghosted along her skin.

Cahra watched him, chest rising and falling with shallow breaths, and parted her lips to exhale a quavering rush of air. His hand was still bunched in her skirts, he thought absently, their mouths but a whisper apart as he burned to close the space between them.

Then, the realisation of their proximity seemed to strike like the force of his powers and Hael stiffened, nodding at the door.

His voice was hoarse. 'Would you mind? The bolts.' The flames in his other palm rippled. 'I am reluctant to douse your only light source.'

'Of course.' Cahra blinked. Then she hesitated, more worried about his exposed bones than any torch. But she gingerly unwrapped his hand and sprung to unlatch the door's bolts.

In the silence, Hael stood rooted to the ground, wrestling with the untamed yearning to kiss her, to allow Cahra's touch to spiral into what could never be. His fantasy, of a life, a future – without the two of them as Master and Vassal.

Of course, his wish was farcical. Who was Hael without his calling, his Nether-magicks?

And should it bother him, he thought, as she yanked free the final bolt.

Should it bother him that he had no answer… None at all?

Hael's torso tensed as he suppressed the human urge to sigh, then led them onward.

Their moment, like everything in his protracted life, had passed.

He and Cahra entered his blackest dungeon. Indeed, his hand would heal; until then, the blood dribbling down his chin, his jaw, his fingerless hand, would serve as a reminder to the evil caged ahead, of what Hael truly was.

Supreme destruction. Even if it was his own.

'Prepare yourself,' Hael told Cahra, whom he knew had seen worse in her short years. Still, every cell beheld its horrors. This was no exception.

As they accessed the hall, the flames licking Hael's palm burned brighter, lighting his gruesome face and fangs, his footsteps thundering against the walls. He wanted his prisoner to hear, fear, that someone approached. He lowered his chin, the fires of his eyes burning black, knowing how the vision of his looming, gore-soaked figure lit a torch to mortal men's fears.

And, oh – how he would make Kolyath's Commander Sullian *fear* him.

–

When their interrogation was over, Hael and Cahra left, her hand laced through his. All prisoners eventually spilled their secrets to the Reliquus; their secrets, and their blood. Commander Sullian had been no different.

Or so the pair had thought.

–

Sullian was barely clinging to consciousness, head hanging over the metal back of the chair on which he sat, its frigid spikes stabbing into every point of contact with his flesh. Shackled to the torturous iron chair, he knew not how long that heathen monster Hael would incarcerate him here. But he assumed that he was intended to die in this foul-smelling place, this putrid prison of dank rot, the stench of death carried on stagnant air.

With the grievous injuries the weapon had inflicted, and the state of his black cell, Sullian presumed such an end would not take long.

This is where I die. After his life of service beside his Steward, oblivion would be perhaps a respite, the best that he could hope for. If, indeed, that was his destination.

'So be it,' Sullian snarled to the darkness, with what little energy he possessed. He could feel his body withering with each tenuous breath.

He would die, at blessed last. He would be glad of it, he thought.

That is, until he felt... a wind. Rushing, rising, whisking the detritus from the dirt.

With monumental effort, Sullian battled to raise his head, his skull heavy as a stone. A light flared, blazing white in the dungeon's gloom. A portal opened.

And a figure stepped through.

The man was garbed in a robe, off-white like Grauwynn's, the High Oracularus of Descry; pristine and clearly tailored, by the look of the spotless cuffs and hems. He removed his cowl, studying Sullian, who drooped, bathed as he was in his own blood.

A moment later, a brilliant light, pure like the sun, lit in the man's outstretched palm.

Sullian bolted upright, pain searing across his body.

'Who are you?' He spoke slowly, jaw throbbing from where Hael had struck him.

'Commander.' The man in white circled him like prey, not answering his question. 'Your brother, Jarrett. He is dead?'

Sullian ignored the ache inside his chest at the stranger's words. Sullian had hated Jarett in life, hated their rivalry for Atriposte's favour. His admiration.

Yet, he had loved his cretin brother, also. Head sinking, he nodded.

'And Atriposte? The Ozumbre twins, King and Commander?'

'The same,' Sullian rasped, his voice likewise raw from Hael's blows to his throat.

In the light of the man's interior sun, Sullian could see hair of brown, tinged with the russet of desert earth, and discerning slate-grey eyes. The man smiled.

'You are the last, then,' the man mused, quiet pleasure in his voice, as he turned to light the walls of Sullian's decrepit cell.

Sullian supposed he was, but the last of what? A people who had rejected Cahra's rule, this horrid, heretic peasant Empress? And the Seers, their foul magicks – plus the malignant, daemonic magicks of their ultimate weapon, Hael?

If this was the future of the realm, then Sullian wanted no part in it, he bristled.

The man burst into laughter. 'Oh, my dear Commander,' he sighed, then straightened. 'How entertaining you shall be. Well met – I am Nektro. And this is no place for you to die. I offer you an opportunity. Now,' Nektro said, gesturing to the portal shimmering behind him. 'Shall we leave Hael'stromia to its downfall?'

ACKNOWLEDGEMENTS

A Kiss of Hammer and Flame was born 17 years ago, and in that time I've accumulated quite the list of people to thank, but I'll keep it short.

To the ultimate strategist, my agent Sarah Hornsley, who instantly invested in Cahra and Hael (and Thierre, bless him) – THANK YOU! Your fateful email changed my life's trajectory.

To my brilliant editor, Emily Bedford, whose love of romantasy and excitement for this series was obvious from day one, thank you for going all in. You've been a dream to work with.

To my publicist, Kate Shepherd, and everyone at Canelo and DK who worked on my debut (hello, sales teams!), your talent and expertise mean the world. I am forever grateful.

To Nick de la Force, my partner in crime: 5-star husband, would marry again. Your unconditional support during my frantic leap from corporate to writing full-time is what every husband and father should aspire to be, and I love you to the moon and back.

To my sister, Holly Barnes, may the ACOTAR meme ping pong never stop. Thank you for believing in me. Fairy spice rules!

To my best friends, Nicole Wright and Brent Gibson, who knew me before I knew myself, when I was just a baby rebel queuing up ridiculous songs at our local pub for laughs. Ole, ole!

To Ramona von Pusch, my fellow creative extraordinaire, whose career is now accelerating exponentially. To the arts!

Thank you to my Curtis Brown Creative novel-writing alumni, The Write Inn: Andrew Michael Hurley, Danielle Cahill, Rachel Driscoll, Christine Gregory, Pete Hardy, Jodie Marshall, Barbara Pollak and Jade Reilly, for your friendship, critiques and support – especially when I was querying and on sub. Special thanks go to Barb and your RITA-winning romance brain and invaluable notes. The mince pies are on me!

To my Lucy Cavendish Fiction Prize shortlistees: Matilda Battersby, Rosa Chalfen, Jenny Epstein, Sarah Glover and Laura Ward-Smith, I met you all at exactly the right time. Thank you for the laughs, the support and the chaotic sherries!

To Aleesha Csanki, you will always be my fellow nerd girl and archaeology expert for all things Egypt.

To Neil Byrne and Suzy Cantrell, for listening to me rave like a madwoman about my synopsis while you were on holiday in Oz in 2016. And to Neil for being my medieval weapons expert!

To Gayle Catt, my primary school teacher, for encouraging a lifelong love of reading that culminated in this book. Teachers, especially primary teachers, are everything, and you were the best.

To Vicki El-Shamy, my high school teacher, who ignited my love of English literature. You were tough but always fair because you knew I had the potential to do, be, more. Your classes helped me survive high school – and that is no small thing.

To Judith Beveridge, my first creative writing tutor at university, who taught me about writing craft and poetry. Five minutes in your class, and I knew beyond a doubt this was the path for me.

It's definitely not the Oscars, but I can hear the exit music – so my heartfelt thanks also go out to: Kristen de la Force, author Tarquin de la Force, Sophie de la Force, Adam Davies, Marc Barnes, my gorgeous nephews, Lisa Collins, and anyone else I've no doubt forgotten! Many thanks to the #WritingCommunity on social media, especially #BookTok.

And to whoever's still reading this… *Thank you*. I wrote this book as my little goth engine that could, praying that someday, someone might love it like I did. If you're still here, then I am hoping that you did (which is good news for you, as there are two more on the way)!

Finally, to my mother, Marjorie, who never got to read *A Kiss of Hammer and Flame*, but who I hope would be proud of me. I love you, Mum… I did it. x

READ ON FOR A SNEAK PREVIEW OF *A CROWN OF BLOOD AND MAGICK…*

Empress Cahraelia of Hael'stromia leaned forward atop her throne, its matte-black snarl of metal wrought with dire spikes and horns. She clenched her fists, nails carving angry crescent moons into her palms, her breathing shallow as weapons clashed below the dais.

Cahra's weapon, Hael, her immortal champion, moved like smoke amongst the storm of glittering blades, untouchable as he cast his scridon spell to effortlessly flit between opponents. Hael vanished here and reappeared there, wielding a thousand years of martial expertise in combination blocks and strikes too devastatingly perfect to belong to any human man.

Disarming a low parry, Hael paused long enough to cast a teasing glance her way, the flames of his eyes smouldering. She thirstily drank in the shock of hair that fell sawtoothed to his shoulders, dark as raven's feathers, so stark against his glassy moonstone skin. Cahra bit her lip, gaze roaming over the muscular bulk of his chest, the taut lines of his stomach, the forked tails of Hael's coat whipping in his wake – and a heat rippled through her that had nothing to do with the desert air. Hael enjoyed showing off his prowess, for her.

A thrill blazed to life inside her, its flames licking, burning until it felt unbearable. *Veil and void, when can we get out of here?*

Exhaling, Cahra fanned herself and sank into the pile of silken cushions at her back. In the centre of the sunlit chamber, Hael sparred against his hand-selected Imperial Guards, their strikes ringing off the vaulted stones at the apex of Hael'stromia's pyramid, the palatial temple that was now her home. It was mid-morning and her growing court had gathered in the throne room for their weekly show of Hael's Reliquus powers, all kingdoms accounted for.

Except one.

Cahra surveyed the three corners dividing the triangular room, one for each sister kingdom that she oversaw as Empress. Here, the contingents of her emerging Imperial court each staked a space to demonstrate their allegiance, the corners for Kolyath and Luminaux teeming with ambassadors, lords, ladies and esteemed subjects, like representatives of the guilds she'd requested from across the realm.

But Ozumbre's corner remained painfully empty. Cahra sighed, not for the first time.

Hael raised his head to her, one of his fires flickering in question from afar. He must have heard her exhale, she thought, offering him a glimmer of a smile. *I'm fine.*

This time, she sucked in a silent breath, the sweet aroma of lilies buoyed on a breeze into the high windows from the capital below, wedge-like shards of light cutting swathes across the demonstration. Smoothing an imagined wrinkle from her fine charcoal trousers, her fingers lingered on the brocade fabric, the wide legs draping with the grace of a full skirt. Her chest was cinched by a black sculpted breastplate of the same metal as her throne: Haellium, the everlasting ore, and she shifted beneath it. Such measures kept her safe, like Hael did as her protector.

All Cahra had to do was ignore that every time he scridoned off to Kolyath or Luminaux, she felt as keenly mortal as anyone else in this room, Imperial Guards or no.

Human. Helpless. Like when she'd lost Hael's magicks, and nearly died at the battle for Hael'stromia three months ago. Only Hael had saved her life.

Cahra gave her head a slight, firm shake, determined not to let thoughts of the past ruin her morning once again, as Wyldaern so often counselled her as High Oraculine – her Seer friend busy preparing for Hael'stromia's realmwide celebration of unity.

And the coronation that would follow.

Cahra swallowed. The burden of a crown was already bearing down upon her, and it wasn't even on her head yet. But days from now…

How can I possibly hope to usher in an era of peace, when Ozumbre won't attend court? Worse still, what would she do if they did? The kingdom murdered her parents, her family—

Hael angled his chin, studying her. As usual, the room was wholly in his thrall, the acoustics seemingly designed for such spectacles and the audiences they drew, as the crowd's awed murmurs crested like a tidal wave. The din surged, a cacophony that rattled her senses, and Cahra gripped the throne's armrests, resisting the sudden, desperate urge to leave.

When she dragged her gaze from her bone-white knuckles, Hael was still watching.

One of the guards, almost as big as him, lunged from behind and locked both arms around Hael's neck, attempting to wrestle him to the ground. But Hael wasn't playing any more, snapping his arm up then twisting to tip the man off balance, finishing with a palm strike to the solar plexus. The guard went flying in a blur of Hael's inky coat-tails, the exchange over in a heartbeat; Cahra only knew what happened because Hael had taught her that manoeuvre earlier this week. Effective, she had to admit, watching as he offered a kindly arm to the fallen guard.

Hael raised a fist, the demonstration over. Applause erupted as he nodded to Illiam, his deputy and Captain of the Imperial Guards, who took command as Hael moved for Cahra.

'I'm fine,' she insisted in the face of Hael's unrelenting gaze. He said nothing, only nodding as she rose from the thirteen-foot throne. A hush descended like a curtain, people bowing as she walked the plush jet-black carpet, a royal gauntlet, that led her from the room.

As soon as they were out of sight, Hael gently took Cahra's hand and scridoned them away – away from the court, and the realm, everything submitting to the Netherworld between the veil and void: the chaotic, whispering static of pure darkness, all of her worries melting away, until finally, Hael was the only person left. She peered into the beauty of his infernal eyes, and a song rose in her heart as Hael smiled, her safe haven. And her undoing.

The moment they materialised again, their lips met.